THE ROCK CHILD

Forge Books by Win Blevins

Stone Song

The Rock Child

THE ROCK CHILD

WIN BLEVINS

A TOM DOHERTY ASSOCIATES BOOK

NEW YORK

This is a work of fiction. All of the characters and events portrayed in this novel are either fictitious or are used fictitiously.

THE ROCK CHILD

This book is printed on acid-free paper.

A Forge Book
Published by Tom Doherty Associates, Inc.
175 Fifth Avenue
New York, NY 10010

Forge® is a registered trademark of Tom Doherty Associates, Inc.

Design by Bonni Leon

Library of Congress Cataloging-in-Publication Data

Blevins, Winfred.
The rock child / Win Blevins.—1st ed.
p. cm.
"A Tom Doherty Associates book."
ISBN 0-312-86400-0
1. Burton, Richard Francis, Sir, 1821–1890—Journeys—Utah—Fiction. 2. Indians of North America—Utah—Fiction. 3. Tibetan Americans—Utah—Fiction. 4. Washo Indians—Fiction. I. Title.
PS3552.L45R63 1998
813'.54—dc21 97-34388
CIP

First Edition: January 1998

Printed in the United States of America

0 9 8 7 6 5 4 3 2 1

This book is dedicated to three men who bear the spirit of Asie in the world so splendidly that I used them as models:

to Adam Blevins, my older son
to the novelist Max Evans
to Raghunath Pradhan of Kathmandu . . .

also to Dub, age two, squatting on the pavement and smiling snazzily at the camera.

ACKNOWLEDGMENTS

A WRITER RECEIVES many gifts in writing a book—brainstorming, information, company, solace, encouragement, and other essentials—sometimes even a place to live. I continue to be wonder-struck at people's generosity, and deeply grateful.

My first thanks on this book are to Michael, Marilee, Sarah, and Tessa Enright. You gave me great hospitality at a critical time, and helped me rediscover my path. Special thanks to Sarah, a teenager who gave up her phone for me.

Brot Coburn and Didi Thunder, my neighbors in Wilson, Wyoming, opened the door to Nepal to me for the first time, loaning me their house in Kathmandu and answering endless questions. Brot, this book owes much to you.

Multitudes in Nepal were helpful. Raghunath Pradhan accompanied me through the Annapurna region. Marguerita Kluench provided spiritual guidance. The Tibetan and other people of the Annapurna region gave me inspiration.

Linda Svendsen and Kent Madin of Boojum Expeditions, old hands in Kham, loaned me books and answered questions about Sun Moon's home country. Linda and Jennifer Read, another lover of Tibet, read the first draft and made valuable corrections. Adam Blevins and Jenna Caplette read the manuscript and made key suggestions.

These people provided essential information and insight into the mysteries of Tibetan Buddhism—Brot Coburn, Ethan Goldings, Tashi Woser Juchungtsang, Paul LeMay, Wangchuk Meston, and the monks of the Sera Je and Drepung Monasteries.

Kathleen Gear steered me toward Kali, a seminal idea. Dick Wheeler helped me through the complexities of Virginia City. Max McCoy came up with fecund thoughts and pieces of information about Richard Burton. Lenore Carroll came up with marvelous bits of information.

Dr. James Weiss helped with medical verisimilitude. Miriam Biro of the North Lake Tahoe Historical Society went above and beyond the call of duty. Dick James offered expertise on Mormonism. Lyman Wear unknowingly provided one of Asie's pet phrases, "heckahoy." The Reverend Dale Salser helped me with the marriage ceremony of the 1860s. Stan West lent me his wisdom about a key scene.

Leeds and Nyla Davis offered hospitality, comradeship, and knowledge of the Tahoe region; Leeds, thanks for a quarter century of friendship. Teresa Jordan and Hal Cannon gave hospitality and thoughts about Mormonism. Rudi and Lynda Unterthiner loaned me their Idaho cabin as a haven for writing.

It was especially good to get collegial help from other professional writers, who took time and energy from their own projects for my sake: Thanks again to Brot Coburn, Kathleen Gear, Teresa Jordan, Max McCoy, Stan West, and Dick Wheeler.

Thanks to Phil Heron, Tyler Medicine Horse, and my other sweat brothers for companionship in the lodge.

As always, Clyde M. Hall, Shoshone-Bannock, acted as my close counsel in matters about Indians. He also discovered the splendid mandala in beadwork that graces the cover of the hardback edition of this book. Aho, my friend.

Jenna Caplette walked through the unexplored country of Asie and Sun Moon's adventures with me, brainstorming all the way. Jenna, part of your spirit is in this book. Thank you.

A journey is a person in itself; no two are alike.

And all plans, safeguards, policing, and coercion are fruitless.

We find after years of struggle that we do not take a trip;

a trip takes us.

—JOHN STEINBECK

Oh, isn't life a terrible thing, thank God?

—POLLY GARTER,
in Dylan Thomas's
Under Milk Wood

THE ROCK CHILD

The Legend of the
ROCK CHILD

BEFORE THE MEMORIES of the grandfathers of the oldest men, the people came to where the rivers from the great lake and the small lake flow together, a good place to hunt. Looking about for a spot to dry their meat, they saw a great rock, as high as three men and with steep sides and a flat top. There they put the meat, safe from pilferage, as they thought.

Only after a big flock of crows stole the meat did they see their error.

Now they feared a hungry winter.

So with their drums, their dancing feet, and their singing voices they asked the spirits for aid. The Spirit of the Wind sent a great storm. As they drummed and danced and sang, thunder rolled and lightning crashed.

When the storm cleared, the great boulder had given birth to a small boulder, resting on its top. Amazed, the people climbed up to see the wonder. Then they were more amazed: The Rock Child swayed at the slightest touch—even a child could rock it, even a faint wind.

And the people understood. If birds came again to steal the meat, the Rock Child would sway and frighten them off. And they gave thanks to the Spirit of the Wind for this miracle.

INTRO

Sweet gizzards, I can't bear it.

The news came by mail yesterday, for a letter with bad news will find its way to even a far place like this. She is dead. First him, last autumn, and now her, on as fine a day as man ever saw, sunny and a sky higher than heaven and the lake the color and feel of a thousand thousand sapphires, the wind a kiss, and all the Earth my friend. I sit on the shore and gaze out over the sapphires and feel the sunlight and the gentle breeze and listen to the gentle lapping of the waves and say to myself, *She is dead.*

They are both dead. I can barely even write the words. They are both dead.

Last night I went straight for the eighty-eight keys of my balm of Gilead. I plunked that piano, picked that banjo, beat that drum. Sent those blue feelings right up into the sky. The glory feelings, too, and today I did have glory feelings sometimes, and scared feelings, bad scared and lonesome. Sing those feelings out to the grasses and the trees, I said to myself, let the birds wing them up, let the clouds and the running waters bear them out farther and farther into the world. Make those feelings more the world's song, and less mine all alone.

It doesn't work. All last night and all day today, play and play, make up new tunes, not sleeping once, make grief into music and let it fly away like sound.

Now the sun is setting behind the mountains, and I know even my music won't take away the lonesome. Also, I have muttered all the cusswords my bringing up permits me. Jehu nimshi. Stars and cornicles. Heckahoy. Bear's ass. Jeehosaphat. Sweet gizzards.

So this one time when making music is not enough, I will set it all down. That's what my son has been urging on me all these years. Tell the story, tell the story.

I will relate the journey we did, me, Sun Moon, and Sir Richard Burton.

In the summer and fall of 1862, during this country's War of the Rebellion, we three traveled together in danger across the Great American Desert, from Salt Lake City to California. And never did three companions play in three more different keys.

Jeehosaphat, it is a tale.

Who were we? Sun Moon was a rare flower—a nun, matter of fact, from the fabled kingdom of Tibet.

As the world knows, Sir Richard was a British soldier, spy, author, explorer, devourer of adventures, and madman.

I was . . . well, I was a half-Indian kid didn't know anything, name of Asie, sounds like Ozzie.

The rest will have to come out as the story goes along.

If you think our journey seems unlikely, it is fact. And life is a flabbergaster, but we'll get to that in a minute.

Heckahoy, I promise you some fun, for this is the kind of story I like, adventure, fitted out with tribulations and triumphs galore—abduction, imprisonment, hairbreadth escapes, near misses, hardship, starvation and thirst, flight, shooting, showdown, you name it. I hope you will see in the end, though, our story is even more a sojourn of the spirit, of three spirits, a fumble through the dark toward light, what light we could find.

I will tell it true. It is fixed in my mind as letters cut in marble. Sun Moon told it to me deep as she knew how, more than once. I have Sir Richard's letters and journals to prompt my memory. I have pondered on everything over the years, and some parts about other people I have just plain figured out. If this is not the truth, it is my truth.

I will tell the tale in my own way, and you will have to bear with me on certain things. My grammar is nothing much, and I have a lifelong habit of making up words, or tweaking them a little in a new direction, the way I make up chords or tweak notes of a melody. My son would like to set it all proper, but I'll tell it in my fashion, and ask him only for companionship in my time of grief.

You may want to know if my story has a moral. Stories are supposed to have morals, they say. This is a truly flabbergasting story—a British uppity, a Buddhist nun, and a scalawag half-breed on a great journey together. Maybe it needs a moral more than most. I am not coy, but believe in telling things right out, so here it is.

Sun Moon and I used to talk about what life is. She said it is an endless series of circles—years, months, and days all circles, each life a circle making one full turn and circling back to come round again in many incarnations, and she saw a wholeness in the circles. That's the way Buddhists see things.

An old Indian taught me another way. When you're born, he said, the spirit of a rabbit comes ahead of you and takes off running. It runs some particular path on the earth, a path you can never see. But whatever path it runs, you'll follow that. The rabbit might stop and go, might twist and turn crazy-like, might double back on itself, jaunt off at queer angles, and every way make no sense. Anyhow, you must follow it, even if you try not to. It's your path.

Both tellings were right, but the way I see it, life is something more. It is tip to toe a flabbergastonia. Sorry, one of my made-up words. The meaning will come clear to you by the end of my story. It is a grand flabbergastonia, a jimmy-joomy flabbergastonia.

PART ONE

WE FALL IN TOGETHER

CHAPTER ONE

First off, Sun Moon and me each came close to dying, stars and cornicles, and got sprung back to life. Seems like a good place to start. Me first.

I was in the yard of Boss John Aldrich's General Mercantile loading up the wagon, and he was as impatient with me as usual.

"Asie, get a move on!"

"Yes indeedy." It pleased me to say it that way, a little pflumphed up, because it would irk him. Then I started whistling. I knew what annoyed Boss John. He'd been annoying me since the day I came to work for him, and the Mormons longer than that.

"You'll be late!"

"Yes indeedy."

I switched to a new tune as I smoothed the breast collar flat and rubbed the mare on the chest, which I believed she liked. Heckahoy, no sense in asking what *late* would be, because Boss John never told customers any special hour, just "tomorrow morn" or "long 'bout noon" or "in the latter half of the day." I never figured out why John Aldrich then acted so determined to rush everybody and everything. I suspected it was because the man had antsy blood, roily bowels, or hot hair. Boss John always hurried. He'd rush the sun even if it shortened his own life, that was just his way. First it kind of tickled me, but not any longer.

I started arranging the load in the wagon. Boss Aldrich never paid no attention to what weight was where. Of course, Boss Aldrich didn't have to drive it out to the Alpha farm today.

"You on Injun time, boy?"

That stopped my whistling. I bit my tongue. I didn't care to be called an Injun, even if I was, and I didn't like the usual Mormon word, Lamanite, any better. My years in the Kingdom of Deseret had taught me that being a Lamanite among the Saints was no privilege. Boss Aldrich didn't agree, of course. "You're lucky to get to be a Saint." But then Boss Aldrich was in too much of a hurry to see some things.

I set the sack of pinto beans next to the flour.

Heckahoy, I thought I'd as soon be an Indian, the way I was born and started growing up. But I really didn't know. Folks said maybe I was Shoshone, but I hadn't been around them enough to know what they were like. Last time someone asked me what tribe I was, I'd answered, "I'm a whistler."

I switched to whistling "Come, Come, Ye Saints." Whether Boss Aldrich liked me whistling or not, he wouldn't have the nerve to shut down the Mormon anthem.

Stars and cornicles, I was a whistler. I could whistle any tune anyone ever heard, high parts and low parts, brassy as a trumpet, piercing as an oboe, soothing as a flute. It was my ambition to whistle a whole band, or at least a calliope, at the same time, drumming with my hands and feet.

This whistling started when the oldest of my adopted brothers, Little Peter, got a tin pipe for Christmas when we were both ten. I never wanted anything so bad in my life, but Little Peter wouldn't share. I took to whistling harmony with him. Before long I could do virtuoso stuff and Little Peter could barely finger the notes. Little Peter quit, and later gave me the pipe. By then it was one of my musical weapons. I had a banjo. I played the piano in the parlor. And I had my whistling. To me music was . . . It felt like a kind of glory.

I even learned to imitate birds with my whistles, except that wasn't exactly whistling. Twice I even got an osprey to converse with me. I kept that part of my music to myself.

"You gonna take them groceries to the Alpha or turn into a band?"

I nodded amiably in Boss John's direction without meeting his eye. I climbed onto the spring wagon, started the mare with a cluck, and launched into "Green Grow the Lilacs."

The time is out of joint. That's the phrase I said to myself sometimes, irritably. At twenty-one I wasn't sure what all it meant, but I felt things weren't right.

This morning, for instance, the moon and the sun were up at the same time. This happened regularly, once or twice a month. Every time I saw the moon in the daylight sky I thought of that phrase: *The time is out of joint.* What exactly did it mean? It was a line the bishop often quoted, from the Bible or *The Book of Mormon.* Well, seemed to me the sun and moon shining at once meant the time was out of joint, or else I couldn't think what would. Even the day and the night mixed up.

The morning was fine after a solid week of rain, I liked that. Sun on my back, mud under my wheels, squishing. I was headed north along Bear River with this wagonload of supplies to the Alpha farm. "Be on time," Boss John kept saying. "You might get stuck, you might be late." *The time is out of joint.* Worry, worry, worry—white people were always worrying about time. *Stars and cornicles,* I told myself, *if I don't watch out, I'll turn white.*

I'd been feeling out of joint for years, maybe ever since I came to the Mormons. Recent-like it was worse. I kept having a feeling right at the bottom of my ribs, in the center, that said something was wrong. Sometimes it gurgled up, sometimes it sank down. Sometimes it was somewhere else, in my head, like out-of-tune music. Usually, though, if I paid attention, a bad feeling was somewhere.

I wished my blood was red, every drop of it. Even if I was half-Indian, I'd lived among white people ever since I could remember. Was it crazy to want to be red? I didn't know.

I wasn't a man to take things apart in my head. To me that was what white people did, especially the bishops in their preachments in the meetinghouse every Sunday morning. I just listened to my insides. What they said was, *Something isn't right.*

The mare was lagging. I flicked the traces against her lazily. She didn't like hauling for Boss John, and neither did I. Alpha farm was several miles ahead on the other side of the Bear River. *Don't be late!*

What do I care?

The time is out of joint.

The symbol of the Mormons for themselves was the beehive. They were busy as bees, it said, creating their divinely revealed utopia, the state of Deseret. This was a great source of pride.

I didn't want to grow up to be a bee.

Wait! Is that music?

I could almost make out a melody.

No, it's the wind.

Yes, the wind. A lane bordered with poplars ran toward a farmhouse to the west. The wind was moving in the poplars, murmuring, making the slender leaves into thousands of bells.

It really does sound like music.

It wouldn't be *that* strange. In a way I heard music in my head all the time. It was part of what made me different from everyone else. But this wasn't the same, this wasn't the music in my head, it was only half music, and it wasn't inside me, it was . . .

Suddenly I felt wild, excited.

It must be a fever.

I came to a turn. Straight north stretched the road to Fort Hall and Eagle Rock. To the east reached a narrower road, rockier, less traveled. I geed the mare around to the right. Something swelled up in me. I almost laughed out loud at myself. *Something,* something like the spirit, I guessed, the spirit that rose under the tent at that gospel meeting I went to in Ogden, something that fiddlers got going whenever they played, *something* . . . Whatever it was, my hands sent it down the traces to the mare, and she whinnied and jumped into a trot.

Fifty yards ahead the road crossed the river on a bare bridge of rough, clackety planks.

The half music came back—whistling, humming, singing, tinkling, beating, but only half-sounding, only half-heard. This time it couldn't be the wind in the poplars, they were far behind.

It was the wind soughing, the wind almost singing.

No, the river, it was the river, swishing, burbling, splashing . . .

The horse's hoofs clattered onto the bridge. The planks banged and rattled and clanked, a din even louder than the hoofs.

It's coming.

In the middle of the bridge I stopped the mare. I looked into the water as it rushed downstream, away from me. It was high, torrential from the rains and the runoff, rushing and roaring and taking up too much space in my head.

The music teased my ears, the music teased my mind.

The waves tossed themselves like white heads. I could imagine their mouths, open and calling, calling out to me, all crying out the same eternal song of . . . *I cannot hear.* The mouths were rushing downstream, turned away from me.

I heard a roar.

I swiveled my head upstream.

A wall swept toward me, a wall of water.

I watched. The wave proceeded toward me, majestic as a monarch. It raised itself, gleaming, curved.

I was transfixed. Through time and timelessness I waited. A word from the tent meeting plunged wildly in my mind: *Baptism.*

The axe of my fate cocked itself over my twenty-one-year-old life, hesitated, and cut downward.

Fury.

I pell-melled into the river.

I was underneath the water in a calamity. Rocks were battering my body, and the river knocked at my mouth and nostrils, hammering to get in. I flailed to preserve my human life.

Then, suddenly, sound saved me from calamity. I heard . . . music, glorious music.

I swam in a spirit of welcoming into the music and into my death and into . . .

Darkness.

CHAPTER TWO

1

I SAID THIS story started with us each, Sun Moon and me, coming close to dying and getting sprung back to life. Her turn was way back the autumn before, the day she came into Hard Rock City, Idaho, against her will. Here it is, the way she told it to me.

Hu-u-u-ung. HER CONSCIOUSNESS sang with this sound. *Hu-u-u-ung.* It was the seed syllable of Akshobhya, the immovable, the unfluctuating, that which cannot be disturbed.

Sun Moon sat with her back straight, her hands resting below her navel, palms upward, right on left, thumbs forming a triangle. Her neck was slightly bent, eyes slightly open. *Hu-u-u-ung.* Though the wagon bumped and the world passed through her field of vision, she kept her mind empty. *Hu-u-u-ung.* She did not yet feel the center of the wheel, that which cannot be disturbed. She breathed. *Hu-u-u-ung.*

"By God and by damn," began Jehu the freighter. The iron band squeezed her throat. It grabbed her there when her bad troubles started, began on the road to Chengdu, in China. An iron band that felt like it was not around her throat but inside it. It came and went unpredictably, and always it squeezed. She was afraid of it, and steeled herself against it, against it.

"By God and by damn," Jehu repeated. The man had a voice like a metal wheel rim on rock. She opened her eyes wide, blinked rapidly, wriggled her trunk. Over the weeks she'd found it was best to bring herself back to the world of impermanence voluntarily, not wait for Jehu to bang her down. Besides, she couldn't concentrate through the clamp of the iron band.

"Best we get you fixed up." He reined the mules to a stop. Sun Moon shook her head, trying to get rid of the clamped feeling. Far below the road she could see Hard Rock City, a village of tents and shacks deep in a twisting canyon. It was as ugly as she expected. She pulled the mantle farther onto her left shoulder. Her nun's clothing was the emblem of her dedication, which no one in this land understood. *If I cannot regain the world of the center of the wheel, this incarnation will be wasted.*

She ordered herself, *Stop!* Since that day near Chengdu, she seemed to have no control of her thoughts and emotions. Or none except to squeeze them till they obeyed. *My gods have abandoned me.* Sometimes she felt so empty she gave in to despair. Then she would demand obedience from her foolish feelings again. Only on this long wagon trip, when she had turned to regular meditation, and started remembering the goddess Mahakala, Paldan Lhamo, protector of women in danger, had she begun to regain a little peace. Unfortunately, as a nun in her twenties, she was stronger in book learning than in the practice of meditation.

Then why be swamped with dread now? This is giving in to fear.

Pictures, smells, and sounds flickered through her mind—the glow of butter lamps, the smell of incense, the endless reverberation of the voices of countless monks and nuns—*om mani padme hu-u-u-ung*—the freedom of a world without lust, jealousy, ignorance, and anger.

She looked sideways at Jehu. His grin was mad brown teeth, his hair was wild and scraggly, his eyes filled with lust for flesh, money, and power. *Why do I let such a creature affect my inner self?* She took a deep breath, let it out. The air was cool and wet, and felt like loss.

She made her eyes follow the dark line of willow bushes along the creek at the bottom of the canyon. She shaped words for them in her own language, not in uncomfortable English. It was the time of when the season arced toward winter. Willows curved sinuously as a serpent down the canyon, painting the undulating colors, tangerine and wine against the dun grasses. Above, pines, firs, and cedars darkened the mid slopes of the mountains with their mysterious greens. Autumn aspens daubed brilliant gold, the color of monks' robes, onto the evergreens. Higher yet the slopes prophesied the coming season—they sang in chaste white of change, winter, death. On the topmost ridges the setting sun painted the snow the pink of meadow blossoms.

She felt a pang. *Home.* Home did not feel like the halls of the convent where she had spent a decade, not even the good times of the celebration of the Lamp-Burning Festival on the twentieth day of the tenth month. The rhododendron color reminded her of the meadows where her family camped in the summer, where the people gathered for the Zharejia each summer. In this cold, mountainous country summer felt remote. On this continent the meadows of the summer camp were as far away as one half of a heart cleaved from the other. *I want my home.*

Her mind flooded with pictures of the last Zharejia, Boiling-Tea-among-the-Flowers Festival, she had gone to with her family. The cluster of white canvas tents with the black or purple stripes on the seams and ruffled borders of green, yellow, and red, appliquéd with the eight auspicious symbols. She saw the curing meats (butchered always by non-Buddhists) and smelled the rich foods like milk and butter from the yaks, sausages, mutton, wheat cakes, and *qingke* wine. She heard the sounds of the several families of relatives gathered together for pleasure after the hard summer's work, the gaiety, the inviting looks of the young people seeking lovers, the happy talk on the embroidered cushions, and the dancing to the jingle of the copper bells. She remembered the people dressed in their best clothes and sporting their gold, silver, jade, and ivory jewelry. Young men played Tibetan flutes, old men made music on their yak-hide zithers, women danced—it was a time of pure joy.

Most of all she remembered the flowers, worlds and worlds of flowers, splotches of yellow, pink, violet, and red in a green carpet stretching from timbered mountain to timbered mountain.

That summer she'd ridden out on horseback with a dozen relatives and friends simply to admire the flowers. A young man had tried to catch her eye, an attractive fellow, actually, and she'd had to suppress her response. Many monks and nuns, when visiting their families, indulged in love—it was not a violation of the vows at that time. But not Sun Moon. She had decided to keep not only chastity but virginity.

She reveled in her mind's eye picture of her country, a mountain country so different from this one. Not dry, harsh, full of spiny cactus. A country lush with grass that fattens the ponies, brimming with water until some meadows became bogs.

Virginity, a woeful choice.

Jehu had taunted her with it. "Yes, this Tarim paid a thousand pieces of gold for you, he bought you, he ordered your abduction, he had you shipped like freight halfway around the world. And next this Tarim, this man who desires you, he intends to throw your virginity to the vultures."

She had spent long hours wondering what sort of man this Tarim could be, to commit such an act. Tarim was an odd name for a Chinaman. He must have a spirit utterly foul.

The men who seized her had permitted her to keep it. The contract, they explained, with lecherous glee. On the great ship, in Gam Saan, San Francisco, her virginity remained to her, and on this trip far into the interior of a continent she knew nothing of. All for the contract Tarim had made. Which contract was to come to fruition tonight. *Hundred-men's-wife.* That was what they called it, or in the English she was learning daily, *a whore.* She had been abducted and shipped across the Pacific Ocean to become what the contract demanded, a whore.

No virgin. Her mind twisted nastily. *Hundred-men's-wife.*

She brought up in her mind a picture of Mahakala, the dark woman of dreams who wore a necklace of human skulls and ate men, so that they might come back as something higher, and as creatures neither male nor female. *Help me, Mother Mahakala.*

"Stick out them hands, Polly. We're gonna make a little show."

Though she still missed many of Jehu's words, she knew his meaning. She held her hands hard at her sides. "Not China Polly," she said. "Sun Moon."

Jehu grinned. "Sure, Sun Moon," he said mockingly. "Now stick them hands out."

She held out her hands and felt the rope bite against her skin. She turned her eyes away from the humiliation of seeing him lash her hands like a slave. In her mind's eye she saw the faces of her mother and father when they were alive, and imagined the look of shame. At home slaves were but half-human. They butchered meat, they were blacksmiths and cobblers.

No China Polly. This was a small victory, but important. She refused to be called China Polly or China Mary. That's what the Inji of this country called all Asian women. Inji was her people's word for Britisher, the only white people they knew.

The battle over her name started the day she entered the country, and it turned into an auspicious event. At customs she had been herded off the ship with scores of Chinese men and women, the men excited, eager to get to the gold fields, the women passive and morose. Sold by their families for gold, or sometimes kidnapped, they were resigning themselves to their fates as hundred-men's-wives.

The customs scene was hubbub and confusion. None of the American agents spoke Chinese, so Chinese men met the ship and helped the newcomers through customs. Their names were recorded, and it was attested (truly or falsely) that they were entering the country voluntarily. For the male immigrants the Chinese were usually family members, and helpful. For the women they were pimps. The women made their marks on the official paper with only the pimps' words for what they were signing.

An old man named Ah Wan met Sun Moon on behalf of Tarim. When the customs agent asked her name, he answered Soon Ming. He explained out of the side of his mouth that he had to give her a Chinese name—she was officially Chinese, not Tibetan. She protested to Ah Wan in Chinese and tried her few words of English on the customs agent, but he didn't understand. "Soon Ming," Ah Wan repeated.

"Sun Moon," the agent said, and began writing.

She recognized the word *sun* and stopped protesting. Her name in her own language was Nima Lhamo, and Nima meant "sun."

Ah Wan didn't know this, but he chuckled at the new name, and told the agent, "That's right, Sun Moon." Thus she entered the United States officially.

Later they were walking to wherever he lived. He had tied her ankles together loosely so she could not run. Not that she had anywhere to run. "Sun Moon," he said later, "*yin yang*, opposites in one. Auspicious."

He had no idea how auspicious.

On the ocean crossing she had felt consumed with hatred, hatred for the men who had abducted her, hatred for whoever her jailers would be in America. It was a terrible conflict: She raged with hatred, but that feeling could not be the path of a nun. Her first goal in the convent had been to master the texts assigned to her. Recently she had starting meditating in hope of ridding of herself of the four afflictive emotions: lust, jealousy, ignorance, and anger. But she had a thought. The Tantras taught that a seeker could come to a quality of mind through its opposite, as Mahakala with her dancing perpetually both created and destroyed the world.

Peace through violence, then, and love through hatred. Though she understood the Tantric path but dimly, she thought it might now be the only way for her.

Her new name seemed to confirm that. Sun Moon, a unity of opposites.

Now Jehu jerked the knots on her legs tight. *No need*—she slapped the words at him silently. On all the long journey from Gam Saan, San Francisco, she had never tried to escape. Why? She spoke almost no English then. She knew nothing of the country. Her skin marked her as Asian. Someone would have turned her over to one of the tongs in a breath. And that would be worse than anything this ruffian might do, and worse than what was intended by the man who bought her, this Tarim.

Jehu knotted her legs. "Be tricky mebbe stand," he said, "wagon move. Lean on seat." *You speak English to me as though to a child, or an idiot.* At least he wouldn't be in her life beyond today.

He climbed on and started the wagon. Unable to protect herself, she fell like a log. *Ouch! My hip!* She rolled against the side of the wagon and sat up. She caught her breath. *I despise you. I hate you. I abhor and loathe you.* She scooted to ease the pain in her hip.

Her heart churned in the currents. She had taken the five vows of a nun, holding especially high the prohibition against killing or other violence. Recently she had devoted herself to seeking freedom from the afflictive emotions through meditation. *Yet I feel violence, terrible violence. It rages in me like storms, it flows like torrents.* She felt like she was choking on it. Whenever she felt the rage, she felt the tight band across her throat, squeezing.

She thought of the other way the Tantras taught, seeking a goal by embracing its opposite. *O Mahakala, take my destructiveness and redeem it, transform it to . . . Violence is peace, Sun is Moon, life is death.*

The wagon bumped into a deep rut, and lurched. She swayed and nearly fell. *All day every day my spirit sways and spins, like a twig on a raging river.* She forced her trunk upright.

The trail changed to an imitation of a road. Strange buildings jutted their faces at her, fancy wooden facades in front of canvas roofs and walls.

"Stand up, Polly. Let 'em see you."

"Not Polly."

Jehu glanced back at her derisively. "I mean Su-u-un Mo-o-on."

Strange men hurled their eyes at her. Sun Moon stared back at them. "Look at the celestial heathen," one cried.

"Ahoy the Chinee!" someone shouted.

"Stand back, boys, she's mine."

"She *everybody's!*"

"Ahoy the whore."

Demons, demons. She saw her body being stripped of flesh, stripped to bones. In imagination the demons drank her blood, ate her flesh, and broke her bones.

I give birth to Mahakala through my brow. She leaps forth, armed with sword and noose, wearing a tiger skin, garlanded with human heads. Her tongue lolls, seeking blood. She decapitates and crushes all the demons. She drinks their blood. Then, intoxicated, she dances and dances and laughs maniacally and dances and dances and laughs.

Since she could not control her anger, she would embrace the forbidden feeling, yes, would give way to volcanoes of hostility, yes, she would seek redemption in horror.

Sun Moon turned her face to the men jeering at her and looked straight into their lust-driven eyes.

Whore! Chinee whore! She understood that word. In Gam Saan, San Francisco, Ah Wan had shown her what happened to the women in the cells—two bits lookee, four bits feelee, six bits doee. "You're lucky you were sold to the interior," he said. She still saw in her mind the hopeless, despairing faces of the Chinese teenagers at the windows of their cells, brittle, lightless lanterns of yellow paper.

She glared at her taunters. *Mahakala, fight for me.* Fear jangled in her limbs. *Sometimes the way past an evil is through it.* A Tantric devotee deliberately embraced the forbidden, deliberately violating all five vows of virtue, in order to discover that the clean and the unclean were one. *Mahakala, guide me.*

Her nerves flashed rages of fear. She would walk the way of unchastity. In imagination the touches of her abductors pummeled her, real as blows. She would be hurled into the pit of the unclean, the abyss of horror.

No! The band around her throat tightened until she gasped for breath, panicky.

Bracing her bound wrists on the side of the wagon, she forced herself up awkwardly. Legs against the board, she held her body erect. She stared at the men. Some lost their nerve and cast their eyes down. Other beamed at her with lechery.

Leering faces flooded her mind, grasping hands, pounding bodies, attacking *lingams*, her violated *yoni*. She quavered. *Am I strong enough to pass through the violence to peace, through the profane to the sacred? Mahakala, Mother and Creatrix, protect me. Give me strength to fight.*

She dared not frame the further question in her mind. *Would I commit the act ultimately forbidden? Would I kill?*

A rage of something—fear? bloodlust?—lightninged up and down her spine. She could not believe that she could follow the Tantras and come to love through murder.

"Well, boys," someone jeered, "who's first?"

Raucous laughter. Her eyes looked at the middle distance, without focusing, and saw none of them. Instead she forced herself to behold a carved image of Mahakala, skulls around her neck, Mahakala the destroyer, Mahakala the devourer of men.

2

TARIM PICKED UP a piece of paper from the bar of polished wood, the bar where men drank the whisky that made them crazy. He handed it to her. It was written in Chinese ideograms. He watched her face as she read it.

She had a noble face, he thought, with high cheekbones, wide-set eyes, and a lovely sheen of bronze skin. He could tell little of her body beneath the nun's robes, but they would come off soon enough. He wanted her. He noticed the desire in himself, almost with amusement. Even at his age he wanted women as fiercely as ever. And of course he would have her.

"Shall I read it to you?" he inquired in his soft, hoarse voice. It had been hoarse for twenty years, a throat injury from a knife.

She snatched it rudely from his fingers and eyed him hard. *So you want to prove you can read.* She studied it.

He observed the changes in her face. The creature felt sorry for herself. Perhaps she thought a hint of an appeal for sympathy, a gesture of the victimized, would affect him. He smiled to himself. *You do not know me. You will never know me.*

Tarim was of a hardy race, the Uighurs. They lived in East Turkestan, the part of China west even of Mongolia, north of India and Tibet. Yet they shared little with Chinese—the Uighurs were Turks by blood and by tongue, Moslems by faith. Living midway on the great trade route from Europe to Asia, they had been acquainted with every conqueror marching east or west, and had found ways to adapt. They became traders, great traders. They spoke all the principal languages of Asia and the Middle East. They knew the Chinese were only one more invader and interloper. The Uighurs, Turks, would outlast them all.

As a youth Tarim traveled far, apprenticed to his father, who traded the gold and jade from the region's mountains. Tarim fell in love with gold. He discovered early that he disliked people, especially his family. So he left home to seek gold by trading in the sables of the vast Siberian forests. He acquired fluency in the Russian language, his fourth tongue, and found his way to the Pacific Coast of that land. He made no friends, established no ties. He learned peoples, customs, and religions, and came to despise them all equally. He gave himself a new name, the name of the great river of his rearing, merely because he liked the sound of it. He took what he wanted, and thought of those who did less as weaklings. He grew rich, and always lusted for more.

No one could tell what kind of man he was. Asians thought him a dark European, Europeans a light Asian, and none could say which was his native tongue, for he never spoke Turkish. People despised him, the Chinese because he was not Chinese, the Russians because he was not Russian, and so on, the way of the world, the stupidity of the world. They knew two facts about him—he was very short, and his face was very misshapen, which gave them final reasons to despise him.

Seeing profits in the hides of sea otters, Tarim bought a ship, hired hands, and crossed the ocean to Russian Alaska. In ten years on one of the islands of the Alaskan peninsula, he built a small empire. Then came disaster. The Russians turned the savages on him, drove him out, and stole his life's work. They were white, they were Christian. He was dark, a heathen, and ugly. What did such a man matter to them?

So at fifty years of age, Tarim came to Alta California, penniless, seeking another fortune in the hills of gold. In the ensuing years, he followed the gold hunters from strike to strike, boomtown to boomtown, and preyed upon them. He collected money. He played with people, and laid down layer upon layer of his contempt for them.

A year and a half ago he gave birth to a very good idea for making money and debasing people in a single act. Chinese whores were popular in the gold camps, popular and hugely profitable. He would have whores—white, red, black, and yellow. Also he wanted something special, a whore who would be the talk of the camp. He wrote to a man he knew in the Chinese city of Chengdu, a man who would do anything. A nun, he said, a Buddhist nun. He offered a thousand dollars in gold, enough money to buy all the man's daughters. He knew that nuns sometimes were not virgins, but the gold seekers saw only what they wanted to see. They would behold the brown robes and see a heathen virgin.

Now, as the woman stood before him studying the piece of paper, Tarim had a rare experience. He felt an emotion. He was amused.

"Read it aloud," he said.

Sun Moon set forth in a clear, steady voice.

" 'I, Sun Moon, a citizen of China, came to Gum Saan, the United States, voluntarily.' "

She eyed him contemptuously. "Lies." She turned back to the paper.

" 'I acknowledge my indebtedness to Tarim for my passage on the ship *Fast Maisy* across the ocean.'

"More lies.

" 'To repay that debt I indenture myself to Tarim to work . . .' " Now she had to control her voice carefully. *Just as I feared. In a legal paper.* ". . . 'as a hundred-men's-wife for five years.' "

Her grandmother had taught her first. *Male-female, good-evil, sacred-profane, Sun-Moon, all are one.*

Nevertheless. She drew herself up. She was tall and slender for a woman of her people, taller than Tarim. She was a Khampa, and had been raised with the pride and haughtiness of those independent nomads and traders. She looked him witheringly in the eye. "No," she said. "Ah Wan told me I would work serving whisky. I will never work as a whore."

"Read," Tarim commanded.

She read the rest silently. Tarim had paid $1,000 for her services for the next five years. *Oh, precious American dollars.* As an indentured servant she would earn no wages. Tarim would provide her room, board, and clothing. For every ten days she was sick, she would serve another month. If she was sick a month, or conceived a child, she would serve another year.

At the bottom was a character that pretended to be her signature. It wasn't—she would never sign her name in Chinese characters but in Tibetan ones. What American would know that, though? What Chinese would know it?

She stared at Tarim and said in a low, even tone, *"Kyakpa sö!"* These were the rudest words she could think of, the same as the phrase she heard the Americans use, "Eat shit!"

Tarim cocked his hand. *He is going to strike me.* Even as a child she had never been struck, yet it was half what she wanted. *Fight me. Now. I will rise as Mahakala and drink your blood.* He was old, sixty at least. *I am more than your match.*

She quailed. *Whatever the Tantras teach, I cannot bear to foul my spirit with murder.*

His hands trembled. *Go ahead, hit me.*

With a visible effort Tarim lowered his hand. Yet his spirit roiled and seethed in the ugly afflictive emotions. She felt contempt for him.

Her mind jangled. She reminded herself numbly, *I have compassion for all sentient beings in the suffering that is earthly life.* That was the teaching of her entire existence. *Yet Mahakala destroys and creates, dancing always, laughing madly. And they are the same, to destroy and create, to love and to kill. Rise in me, Mahakala.*

She felt dizzy. She held on to the bar for support. *Who am I becoming?*

Calmly, with a false courtliness, Tarim gestured to the bar, the lines of bottles, the furnishings. Though it was only a tent with a false wooden front, he'd made the tavern look well outfitted.

"When the barbarians drink too much, they set aside their manners, their lusts become inflamed . . ."

She interrupted him. "I need no explanation of that." She forbade pictures of her drunken abductors to enter her mind. "Whether they're made mad by whisky or opium." The Chinese were fond of opium, but her people had nothing to do with it.

She saw Tarim's nostrils flare a little, and his lip curled. *Fine to be able to read a man's mind by the signs of his body, and to command it by a small insult.*

He turned his back to her, led the way to the back of the building, and opened a narrow door. "A private room," he murmured in a tone implying great good fortune. Beyond his outstretched arm she could see a cubicle with a narrow cot. "Here you will sleep, and here you will serve the barbarians."

She took a deep breath. First came the fear, then the anger. *The warlike spirit of Mahakala is in me.* That spirit intoned, "I have been abducted. A Chinese court would behead my captors. I am not indentured to you or anyone. I demand to go home."

Tarim continued as though he hadn't heard her. "The other drinking establishments have hundred-men's-wives, white and red and black women, and their business exceeds my own. You will be something special." He paused. "You will wear the robes. Always."

He held her eyes, and she saw something even more frightening. His eyes were cold as ice-covered stones. And he was permitting her to see that. He was letting her know.

He gestured for her to enter by the open flap. She stepped through and put her hand on the cot intended for whoring. *Oh, to be alone.*

"Many barbarians actually prefer Chinese flesh."

Her mind sloshed like water in a swaying bucket. *My chastity may be taken from me, but not my spirit.* She fixed him with her eyes. "I am not Chinese, I am Tibetan," she repeated.

He looked back at her hard. No, it wasn't anger in his eyes, it was amusement.

"I will never be a hundred-men's-wife."

Tarim chuckled, and closed the door.

Nowhere to run.

During the journey to Canton, she had been drugged, her spirit defeated. On the ocean during the passage, where could she go? When Yoo Wong threw herself overboard, Sun Moon had felt envious. But she couldn't follow—this precious incarnation as a human being was not to be thrown away; dying prematurely would be ill karma.

In Gam Saan, San Francisco, she remembered Mahakala, the protectress, and began to recover her spirit. She would have risked anything to escape, but Ah Wan kept her bound and got her quickly onto a ship for Oregon. Then she was thrown onto Jehu's wagon with the rest of the freight headed for the interior. The interior of Gum Saan, a country she had barely noticed on maps. Soon she acquired enough English to find out from Jehu she was in the United States, not Mexico. Now she began to feel the Khampa within her, and the warrior. *Thank you, Mahakala.*

After a week Jehu untied her and let her sit on the bench like a human being instead of lying on the floor with the sacks of flour. Why not—where could she go? She was no longer crossing a wide ocean, true enough, but what troubles faced her: Her English was poor. She didn't know where she was. If she escaped, she would be helpless. She knew the end—someone would turn her over to a tong. She remembered the women peering out of the windows of little cells, faces paper masks, brittle on the outside, empty on the inside. No, the way of the warrior was to wait.

Now she calculated. She turned all the way around in her tiny room once, then all the way around the other way. *I will wait. I will learn English, learn the country, learn the people.* She sat on the floor, crossed her legs in the lotus position, consciously straightened her spine, took the first relaxing breath . . .

Suddenly the door flap opened. Tarim came in with rice, a few spoonfuls of vegetables, and tea. *No, no, he won't starve me to death,* she thought appraisingly. *I am a valuable property.*

She looked at him sharply. He grunted something, set the bowl and cup down, and retreated. She reached for the food. Stopped. *What would I not give for some* tsampa *in tea?* It was roasted barley flour. She took thought and placed the bowl back on the floor. She turned her consciousness inward and breathed deeply. She felt the breath come in, felt it go out. *First the spirit,* she thought, *then the body. Then war.*

3

THE CELESTIAL HEATHEN gave a copper with one hand and took silver coins with the other. The coppers were cent pieces, used to copper bets. Porter Rockwell looked around the room at men who reeked of greed and lust. He could taste it, foul as brackish water. Damned Chinee. Celestial? Bear's ass.

Fourteen men, as Rockwell counted them. *Thirteen drunk,* all but himself. All were white, though half of the population of Hard Rock City was yellow. And the sheriff, Conlan, was among them, come to debauch a nun. It confirmed Rockwell's opinion of American lawmen.

A corner of his mouth lifted in a bitter, one-quarter smile, as much as he'd permitted himself in near twenty years, since that day at the Carthage jail when the best friend he ever had was murdered by a mob. The friend was Joseph Smith. Porter Rockwell had been the Prophet's protector, and he failed Joseph that day. He hadn't smiled since, not really.

Drunk or sober didn't matter. He was smarter than most of them either way, quicker of hand, and especially meaner. He'd found that mean made all the difference.

It surely helped in his line of work. Porter Rockwell was an avenger. The Destroying Angel, the gentiles called him. The apostates called him the same. If the powers judged someone a threat to the Church of Jesus Christ of Latter-Day Saints, especially a fallen-away Mormon, one of a group of destroying angels, the Danites, got rid of the trouble. Rockwell was a Danite leader, and his solutions tended to be permanent. If he was an embarrassment to some of his people now that Mormons were better established, he didn't give a damn. If he occasionally got other work, like delivering gold coin to Hard Rock City, Idaho, he was glad.

It was done. He wasn't worried about this Conlan for a moment, or any other lawman. Now he wanted a woman.

Rockwell paid his dollar and took the copper from the heathen's palm. He eyed the Chinee hard. Rockwell knew his impact on people. He was taller than most, well formed, strongly built. His hair hung wild and stringy below his shoulders—Joseph had prophesied that he would always be safe if he did as Samson should have done, leave his hair uncut. His eyes, he knew, looked halfway between cunning and mad. Which, Porter Rockwell sometimes thought, might be the truth.

I could almost gag on the booze and lust. Fourteen men wanting the nun, gambling for the chance to mount her, inflamed by the thought of violating sacredness. Rockwell didn't give a fig for their sacredness.

The room breathed like a panting toad. He didn't like crowds. He didn't like gentiles. Sometimes he didn't even like Saints.

He himself didn't need to pant. His need was colder than that. He was going to win.

Everyone said the woman was beautiful. She'd been on display this afternoon riding through town on the wagon. Everyone had heard—a nun whore coming!—and ninety percent of the town was male.

Rockwell had watched from behind the lined-up mob. He didn't judge her beautiful. She was off-color. Rockwell preferred white and delightsome. She had an air about her that snagged his interest, though, something in her carriage or in her eye—she felt untouchable.

Tonight Rockwell would touch her, and she would never forget it. Once he'd banged into a whore and banged and banged, deliberately, insatiably, not stopping even when she threw up on him. It made him feel powerful.

This whore was floating on opium, the Chinee said, but Rockwell would wake her up. She would make him feel his juices flow.

It was a stiff price, a dollar just to gamble for a chance to top a woman. It would be the first time any man mounted this woman, said the Chinee, but you couldn't trust him—no telling what heathen had been at her on the other side of the world or the long trip here. And Polydamnesians and white men, too, for that matter. Rockwell didn't care. The one she'd never be able to forget was him.

"Ready, everybody ready," called the Chinee. His body poised like a banty rooster, head cocked high, eye bright. Each man perched his copper on his thumb, ready to flip. "Throw your prayers and coppers into the air. When the coppers come down, may the prayers go up." The heathen flipped his queer little noisemaker to a crazy climax. "Now!" Fourteen coins spun high in the air. At the top of the spin the Chinee called heads or tails. Then fourteen coins landed in palms (three drunks dropped theirs but picked them up), fourteen hands slapped them over onto the back of the other arm, and thirteen mouths smiled or frowned.

Cries of joy and agony. The fools were getting very worked up. Not Rockwell. He would win this round and every round by a simple stratagem. He was dexterous with his hands. He could make a coin appear in an empty palm faster than anyone's eye could detect. He could stick an empty hand to your nose and make a playing card pop out. He could juggle seven balls. He could make a knife dance through the air and between your ribs. With either hand he could shoot a hole in a high-spun coin. For Porter Rockwell making a copper appear right side up was child's play, and this was a fool's game.

Actually, it was too bad no one would see him cheating and accuse him of it. Rockwell would enjoy punishing that impertinence, especially in front of Sheriff Conlan.

The heathen whirred his noisemaker. A roar rose with the mounting clamor. The six men who survived the first flip spun their coins into the dingy light. Porter Rockwell concealed a second copper between his fingers and gave a nasty one-quarter smile.

4

In the dreamy world people were moving around her, and the voices made a low, low rumble. She was naked in the dream, maybe—somehow she couldn't open her eyes to see herself or move her hands to touch herself. But the moving, rumbling people were looking at her naked and pointing, leering, and laughing at her. She couldn't make out the dream-world words, but the talk sounded ugly, threatening—the sound the earth would make, she imagined, before a landslide. Her body quivered.

From a distance she heard thunder, low. It was going to rain. She writhed. She was afraid of being naked and cold in the rain. Somehow the rain would be filthy, it would soil her, she had to get out of the rain . . .

A rough hand touched her shoulder.

Trying to awake, she felt a curious floating sensation, like a boat sailing not on water but on mist. *Opium.* She remembered from her time with the bandits . . . *This is what opium feels like.*

Hands under her back and knees. She forced her eyes open and saw the hairy top of a white-man head. She could feel the air on her bare skin, bare all over, every inch. A dozen men's faces leered at her. Her robes lay beneath her body, and every inch of her was exposed to the leers.

I call upon Mahakala.

"Here we go, Polly," said the American. He scooped her up in his arms.

Mahakala, destroyer goddess, eater of men, help me!

She screamed. With all her body and spirit she howled, shrieked, and screeched. She wriggled and fell. She thumped back onto the table where she'd lain. The white man looked at his empty hands. His mouth looked amused, his eyes angry.

Men's voices laughed raucously.

The air felt cold between her legs, and almost hurt her nipples. She covered herself with her hands. *Mahakala, come to my aid.*

"Polly, you don't want to cause trouble." The white man had a bony face, wild eyes, the longest hair she'd ever seen on a man, and those awful eyes. *The eyes of a man with a spirit he has killed, the eyes of a destroyer of self and others.*

Behind him, peering faces, loud laughter. She thought about it.

Naked doesn't matter. She cocked her arm to hit him and felt her wrist grabbed by a cruel hand from behind. Both wrists.

"Now, Polly," a mocking voice said, "this ain't goin' to hurt you none."

Another voice put in, "It might be celestial!"

Men's laughter lashed out.

"Name not Polly," she said calmly. "Sun Moon."

"Polly!" several voices snapped. "China Mary!" boomed others.

Long Hair reached out and pinched a nipple between thumb and forefinger.

She squirmed with pain. "No!" she yelled. She tried to slap him, but her hand was held firm.

"Polly don't like us," said a voice with mocking melody.

Long Hair looked her in the eye. She could feel his angry spirit now. Her attempt to slap him had been foolish, silly, childish, unworthy of the strength of Mahakala. Cold air and cold eyes caressed her *yoni.* He stretched a hand between her legs.

Goddess destroyer! She kneed Long Hair hard in the face.

He snapped upward, holding his head.

Drinker of blood! She kicked him in the nose, and his blood gushed.

Hands ripped her backward, some on her head, some on her shoulders and hips. One smashed her right breast. Another groped at her crotch. *Destroyer of worlds!* She kicked free of that hand, but was pinned on the table.

She spat at Long Hair's face. Then she saw his eyes. Fear flickered in her like lightning.

"Stop! Now! Stop!" It was Tarim's voice, yelling in English.

She watched Long Hair's eyes, the color of dirty ice. His dagger danced into the space between their faces. It oozed as the blood oozed down his face. It weaved back and forth like the head of a snake, bewitching. Her mind reached for the name of her goddess-protectress but could not find it.

For a moment the world stood outside of Time. As she watched the tip, the dagger struck, somehow swiftly and slowly at once.

The left side of her face burst into agony. The pain bubbled and boiled and spewed. She threw her hands to her face to hold her left eye in its socket.

Flashes of redness. The pain and heat, like falling into a volcano. The rushing darkness. *I will be blind.*

CHAPTER THREE

1

Porter Rockwell raised his Arkansas toothpick to eye level and regarded the blade, the cleanness of the shiny edge. With a finger he checked the stickiness of the blood.

Tarim trembled, watching him hulk over the unconscious woman's body. *Her face will be ruined. No man will want her.*

Rockwell examined his coat and shirt. Bloody. *Will he kill her for the sake of his clothes?*

Tarim found it too much to bear. He knew who the barbarian was, the bodyguard of the king of the Mormons in Salt Lake City, a killer. To strike at an enraged killer, giving away more than twelve inches and a hundred pounds, that would accomplish nothing. Especially not in a crowd of white men who would side with him, and the sheriff at hand.

A thousand dollars in go-o-old. We slapped the earth.

Tarim stepped forward with his face under control. "Sir," he said, "Rockwell, the whore belongs to me." He gyrated his arms. Playing from weakness nearly drove him mad. *I must have the whore.*

A thousand dollars coming back at the highest price a Chinese whore ever got, no two bits, four bits, six bits, lookee, feelee, doee. Accumulating at a hundred dollars a week. He figured that he would get his entire investment back five times over *each year.*

Not now. Tarim's heart pounded. He felt gold coins slipping from his fingers.

"The whore is mine," he repeated. Though his knees quaked, he forced himself to sound reasonable. He stepped forward between the barbarian and the whore, took off his American frock coat, and covered her nakedness with it. He looked at the crowd defiantly. His hand itched for a dagger, but he knew better.

Then he saw the eyes of the white men. *Mad,* he thought. *They stare at her* yoni *and hardly see her terrible wound. In their eyes Asians are not people.*

He dared look at Porter Rockwell. The barbarian shifted his stare from his blade to Tarim. He yearned to strike before the big man even sensed danger. He quivered.

"Give me a rag," said Rockwell.

Tarim gestured to the barkeep, and out came the one used to wipe tables.

Rockwell held the dagger up and wiped the blood off. He took pains, getting the blood out of the corners of the guard and off the handle. He let the silence grow.

"I will pay for your clothes," Tarim put in. "She did not hurt you."

"Another rag."

Tarim scurried and brought one. Rockwell wiped the blood off his face, mustache, beard, and neck carelessly, like it didn't matter.

"All right, heathen," he said, "the whore is yours. Property, property, almighty property." He grinned madly at the crowd, then fixed Tarim with a terrible glare. "You tell her that if I ever see her again, anywhere, I'll kill her. Got it? Simple. I'll kill her." He gave the watchers a look of grotesque companionship. "And ship the body back to you, of course—she's your property."

The watchers chuckled on cue.

He sheathed the dagger. "You tell her that, heathen."

2

*W*HEN *S*UN *M*OON swam up from the darkness and her consciousness awoke to the world again, the first thing she saw was Tarim, peering at her intently. Though his face changed after she opened her eyes, she was too woozy to see his spirit. He held a teacup to her lips. Gratefully, she sipped. Then she realized it was not the Tibetan tea she grew up on and loved, salted and buttered, but one of those perfumed Chinese brews she disliked.

Tarim spoke brutally. "You acted the fool. The man you kicked was Porter Rockwell, a famous killer, the cruel right hand . . ."

She stopped listening. She knew a man with foul spirit when she saw one. *I kicked him in the nose. I brought blood.* A grim joy pumped in her veins. *I regret only the quaking fear I felt for my own flesh.*

"You are lucky," Tarim went on. "Rockwell's nose was not broken, so he was content to cut your face and disfigure you. The doctor doesn't know about the sight in your eye yet."

You talk about me like I was a prize yak.

"Rockwell announced that if ever he sees you again, he will kill you."

Tarim let the words sit. She studied his face. She had found that she could read people's emotions in their faces easily, and sometimes that told her whether they were telling the truth or lying. Tarim was telling the truth.

"Simple as that—if he just sees you. You mustn't even go out on the street!"

Ah! You want to keep your investment of precious gold close to home, in the closet. Right now your investment is ill. And unattractive.

He looked at her speculatively. "I wonder, disfigured, what use you will be to me."

She felt a burst of elation and a twist of agony. *Am I so ugly now that the white men won't want me for a whore?*

Tarim half smiled and left her.

Am I so ugly the white men won't want me for a whore?

Her eye screamed at her. It raged in its socket. If she opened her eye, the light would stab her and kill her.

She rolled over. She thrashed. She rolled over and thrashed and rolled over and thrashed.

"Here," said Tarim. "The doctor says to give you this for the pain."

She held out her hands into the darkness. They received a cup. She sipped, and recognized the taste of laudanum. She drank.

She felt a hand on her shoulder. Not Tarim's hand, a gentle touch.

"Who are you?"

"The doctor," said a man's voice, soft but firm.

She let the hand stay. It felt good.

"While you slept, I sewed the edges of your skin together."

"My eye," she said.

"Can't tell about that yet. May heal, may not."

"Will I be blind?"

She could feel the hesitation. "Three possibilities. One, it will hurt like hell for a couple of days and heal completely. Two, it will heal and you will be blind, or see nothing but light and shadows. Three, it will get infected and you will die."

The word *die* stabbed her in the heart. *Mahakala, protector of women, help me live.*

"I'll do my best for you," the voice said.

She touched the hand with hers. The oddity of her own gesture thrilled her, and she took her hand away.

"Thank you," she said.

"Drink this," he said.

She drank, and swam back into the world of the opiate.

"*Open your eyes,*" the voice said.

She opened the good eye.

"Both of them."

She quailed. Then she forced it open. The lid felt rusty.

Light. A picture.

A hand covered her good eye.

"You see me," the voice said.

"Yes." And it was no longer just a voice. A man of middle age with a face that showed the bones beneath and a gray mustache. His eyes were deep with the sadness of living in the world, and with compassion.

"You see me clearly."

"Yes."

"The danger to your eye is past," he said. "But there's a new danger. Your face wound is infected."

He touched her hand, and she did not take it away. "I'm sorry. I'll do my best for you. Drink this."

The infection brought her respite. Most of the time she slept. She asked Tarim to leave the door flap to her room open so the southern sun would shaft through onto her legs. Sometimes she meditated. Lying flat on her back was not an ideal position, so she sat up when she could. Either way, her spine was straight, so energy could flow freely. With the return of her meditative practice, she felt her spirit a little stronger. She did not know about her face, or her body, and she barely cared. She could feel that her face was very swollen. If she sat up a few minutes, it got hot, and throbbed. The doctor admitted she might die. Often she fell into the waywardness of despair.

I have lost myself. That was what had happened. Her abductors didn't do that to her, or the men who took her like a carcass to Canton, or those who penned her up in the hold of the ship coming across the great ocean, or Ah Wan, or Jehu. *I did it to myself.* For the spirit is free. Only the human being it inhabits can sully the spirit.

After her abduction she failed to meditate every day, to find her own center, the hub of the wheel, and spend time there. *I did it to myself.*

Odd, how the white men did me a favor. Even your enemy is your teacher.

A scratch at the open door flap. The doctor. Though she had mostly been half-conscious through his ministrations, now she looked forward to the kindness of his voice and touch.

"I'm glad to see you awake," he said. "You're getting stronger, Polly."

"Not call me Polly."

"What do you want me to call you?"

"Sun Moon." Her voice scratched, unaccustomed to speech.

"Sun Moon," repeated the doctor, chuckling.

Yes, she knew. Funny to white men. Daytime star and nighttime star. "Sun Moon," she repeated.

"Sun Moon," the doctor said formally, "I'm Harville Park. Call me Dr. Harville. I hear that your English is fairly good. If you don't understand what I'm saying, stop me."

"Understand."

He touched her eyebrow very lightly. "The cut goes from here, through the upper lid, into the eye, and down the cheek." He touched her just below the cheekbone. "I believe the infection is on the retreat." He forced a smile. "You'll have a piratical scar."

"Piratical?"

"Like a robber." He made a mean face.

If you only knew. Her mind stampeded with pictures of her abductors.

He held up a mirror. "Do you want to see yourself?"

"No." *For the rest of this incarnation I will not think of myself as I was, Dechen Tsering, of Zorgai Convent of the holy land of the Pöba, born Nima Lhamo, named by my parents Sun Goddess. Nor will I see myself as a whore scarred by rapists. I will become a holy warrior, a unity of violence and peace, life and death, Sun and Moon.*

The doctor looked at her inquiringly.

Why are you not telling me what's important? She asked him directly. "I will live?"

"Yes," he said. "I expect so."

"Be strong?"

"Yes."

Her heart spun with fear. *So. Tarim will make me whore soon.* She swallowed hard. "Be whore then."

"I guess so," he said.

She declared softly, "I never be whore. I never be whore."

He looked at her a long moment, then nodded. "I will help you if I can."

Speaking made the cut hurt, and made her face puff until she thought it would burst. Talking was painful. But she wanted to talk to this healer.

"I will tell Tarim your life is in danger. I can protect you for a while."

She looked beyond him at the weak sun low in the sky. The winter was going to be long, but maybe she would survive it. "You help me?"

"What do you want, Polly? . . . Sun Moon?"

"Incense," she said.

Dr. Harville's face quirked. "Incense?"

She nodded.

"All right. The Indians use cedar and sage. I'll get you some."

Then I can conduct my puja.

"Anything else?"

"Speak English good," she said. "Read English." *Because it's a long road home.*

When the doctor was gone, she felt gingerly of her face. Around the cut her flesh warm and tender—she imagined it red. The cut felt rough, jagged, wildly sore. *I am wounded.*

Tarim stood in the doorway, head and eyes immobile, face as petrified as his spirit.

Dr. Harville preempted his speech. "She's not ready. She can keep walking a little, best outside. During the warm part of the day. I'll go with her." Dr. Harville actually rose to confront Tarim now. "But she's not ready to do any work of any kind, and won't be for weeks."

Tarim cocked his head sideways around the doctor and pointed at her. "One month sick, one year more work," he said, waving his hand like a blade.

Sun Moon didn't care what he said. *I won't be here one year, much less five or six.*

Tarim stalked away.

"Thank you," she said. Often she thought she could get up and work. She wanted to. But even a short walk with Dr. Harville tired her out.

As they walked, and any time they were together, she was learning to speak English better and better. Sometimes he also read to her, and helped her puzzle out the sounds of the English alphabet one by one and put them into the strange words.

"You are a good student," he said. "You work hard."

She nodded. *I am becoming a good student of the ways of the warrior-goddess. What would you think if you knew my reason for learning to read?* She looked at him. No, she wouldn't tell him. There was little he could do for her. Unnecessary risk.

Finally Dr. Harville let her help Tarim in the store, finding items for customers, counting their coins, or weighing their dust in payment. She stayed on her feet as long as she could—she was determined to learn about Tarim, his household, his businesses, his customers, both white and yellow. Even red. *I need to learn everything.*

Tarim's tavern was a new business, she found out, but the store had operated for a year. "I am a trader," he said from time to time. The white, black, red, and yellow customers peered at Sun Moon and whispered among themselves.

She learned to weigh things in the American scales. She learned to make change with the unfamiliar coins. She learned to take in gold dust, weigh it, and give credit. Once she dropped a few grains of gold dust between the scale and the jar. Tarim hissed while he swept it up.

She noticed then how carefully he swept the floor of the store and the tavern at night, checking the ordinary dust for flecks of yellow.

From the whispers she found out more. Tarim had arranged the grand opening of his tavern so that Sun Moon would be the main attraction, the deflowering of the virgin nun. She had spoiled his grand opening. She smiled grimly.

Sun Moon watched for chances to walk through the store in the dark, when Tarim was gone. He lived in the store, and kept a Tibetan mastiff on guard besides. But sometimes he disappeared for an hour or two after the tavern closed, and Sun Moon heard that he went to a woman. She made tentative friends with the big dog, named Sonam, which seemed mean and stupid. *I will not be your second Tibetan lackey.*

She began memorizing a list of what she would take when she escaped.

At the first opportunity she also stole a pocketknife from a kitchen drawer and kept it in her clothes every hour of every day, to be ready to fight. She reminded herself to steal a whetstone later, so she could keep it very sharp.

Openly, she roasted barley on the stove and ground it into fine powder. This would be the *torma* she would offer to Mahakala. To perform the ritual she had begged a small shipping box to use as an altar, a place to burn incense, a place for the food for the protector deity, an object for her prayers and chants.

As she made these preparations, she worried. *Will my face repel the white men enough? Or not? It doesn't matter. They will have to kill me before I whore for them.*

One night when Tarim was gone, she lit half a dozen candles and placed them next to the full mirror in the store, the one customers used to look at their new clothes. She averted her eyes until the crucial moment. She drew herself up straight in front of the mirror. She laced her fingers over her eyes. She opened the fingers enough to peer through them, and naturally saw nothing but a face covered with fingers. She watched the candlelight flicker on her fingers and her black hair. Slowly, one by one, she lifted the fingers up, and still saw nothing. Abruptly, like pulling away from a hot stove, she jerked her hands away.

My face is gouged. From her forehead above the left eye, through the eyebrow, through both eyelids, onto the cheek ran the ugly ditch. It was still partly scabbed. The stitches had stretched the skin near the wound tight, and the wound itself was a pucker.

She sank to her knees and burst into tears. She flung her face down into her hands. Then, facedown, away from the mirror, ashamed, she snuffed out the candles one by one. She never knew how long she knelt there in the darkness, weeping. Finally the iron band gripped her throat and cut off the tears.

OTHER NIGHTS, ALONE or not, she laid plans. She knew that Tarim had poured laudanum into her tea that first day. Now she ate or drank nothing she didn't prepare herself. She determined to become useful as a cook, a maid, and a clerk in the store. *Maybe I can become so helpful Tarim will give up on making me a whore.* But she didn't think so. *The virgin nun with the awful scar.* It might have even more appeal.

By day she paid attention to the common talk, trying to figure out the way back to Gam Saan, San Francisco. Hard Rock City was a new mining town, miles off the old wagon road, the Oregon Trail, the way Jehu brought her. That was a hard way to San Francisco, northwest to Oregon and then south by ship. To the southwest, the direct way called the California Trail, stretched terrible deserts. But she heard about a roundabout route, a wagon road southeast to a big city called Salt Lake. There you could get a stagecoach. *Better than a ship to Gam Saan,* she thought. *Cheaper. And safer—you can get off a stagecoach.*

She could always hope, too, that the pursuers would look in the wrong direction, assume she had gone the way she came, toward Oregon. But if they looked in the right direction, that was fine. *I have within me Mahakala, eater of men.*

She stole a copy of the map of Idaho Territory Tarim sold to customers, and another of what was called the Far West, kept them under her thin mattress of ticking, and studied them by candle at night, when Tarim was asleep. As she learned to read the words, *Snake River, Great Salt Lake, Idaho Territory, Oregon Territory, Utah Territory, Nevada Territory,* she pieced together a picture of her journey. Southeast from Hard Rock City, in what they called Idaho Territory. Walk several hundred miles by foot to Salt Lake City. Travel west by coach across vast deserts and then across mountains to the big bay at San Francisco. Then a ship . . . *How will I get a coach? How will I get a ship?* She refused to consider. *As long as she lives, a warrior fights.*

One day the doctor brought the promised cedar. The barley flour was long since ground. She mixed the flour with butter to make *tsampa,* wishing she had old yak butter. She shaped the dough into cones. She burned the cedar, and placed the deity's food before the box. First she prostrated herself in front of the altar three times, then sat in the lotus position. She chanted the long-known words, words she had memorized over years, familiar as furnishings in a beloved room. No longer were they comforting—they made her mind bristle with the sense of danger.

When she had finished, properly, she threw the *torma* to the dog.

She set the altar box at the foot of her cot. Would Tarim recognize an altar? Would he care? To the ignorant eye it was nothing.

Sun Moon knelt before the altar. She did a full prostration, then another, then another, and many more. She sought to find the warrior spirit within her, and to accept it.

3

TARIM LIFTED THE flap and stood in her doorway. She was eating the *tsampa* she had made as a relief from the endless rice. "Come," he said, "I want you to meet the new arrivals."

She had no idea what he meant until they went through the flap into the tavern.

Five women sat at plates of rice.

Whores. How did you manage it? The freighters were having trouble getting through the winter weather. Sometimes the store was short of supplies. But Tarim had managed to get new whores for his tavern shipped in. *Gold. He will do anything for enough gold. Like Americans.*

"Sun Moon," said Tarim, "these are the Twin Treasures, Hansel and Gretel." He touched the twins on the head.

They were white blondes, another woman was fair with flame-red hair, one was black, one an Indian.

Am I to fill out your color scheme?!

"Bridget here is Irish." Sun Moon hadn't been able to figure why people talked like the Irish weren't even white people. This woman was so white she looked powdered, but wasn't.

Tarim put his hand on the shoulder of the black. "This is Martha Washington." He smiled nastily and moved on to the Indian. "And this is Count Your Coups."

Tarim started on, but Gretel stood up and glared until she got his attention. "Tarim, we need more'n rice and vegetables to eat. We need eggs, we need meat." She flipped her plate of rice upside down on the table.

Tarim slapped her. Gretel staggered and fell to her knees. "You will eat the rice off the table now," he said softly.

Gretel got back into her chair. Under his glare she started eating rice with her fingers. Sun Moon noticed that the fingers shook. She stared, caught herself, and averted her eyes.

"You start work at dark," Tarim told them flatly. "I will let the miners know. This afternoon you may rest. You serve whisky, dance with anyone who asks, and do whatever else they want. One dollar. I will watch and the bartender will watch. If you try to cheat me, I will beat you."

Now he turned to Sun Moon and beamed. She steeled herself. "I have a surprise. Sun Moon will join you."

I won't!

"The hell she will."

"She is Buddhist, a nun, and a virgin . . ."

Tarim stopped himself, realizing what Bridget had said.

She repeated it. "The hell she will. I won't work with no China Polly."

Sun Moon stifled a gasp. She studied the woman, astonished, struggling for control of her face.

"Me neither," said Hansel. "That wasn't in the deal."

"Me neither," said Gretel, regaining her courage.

Tarim started hissing, "You will do as I . . ."

"No and hell no," said Bridget. "I won't."

Tarim cocked his arm to hit her, but the black woman jumped up and grabbed his wrist. Tarim and Martha Washington glared at each other. When she let go, he didn't make a move.

Bridget flushed with it now. "I see Martha Washington won't." She looked at Count Your Coups but got no response. "Count Your Coups won't. Us white women sure won't." She flung her napkin onto the table. "You didn't say nothin' about no China Polly, and we won't do it. Shaming, it would be. I won't stoop so low."

Sun Moon reeled. *Not stooping to whore, not stooping to work next to blacks and Indians, but stooping to work with a Chinese.*

Tarim began, "I advanced you . . ."

"I'll give your money back. We ain't broke. That Jehu is somewhere making deliveries. We can ride back out with him." Bridget looked at her sisters in sin triumphantly. "We can ride straight back out the way we come in. And we will." She even included Sun Moon in her look of triumph, like Sun Moon would sympathize.

Sun Moon was quietly struggling for breath.

"I will replace you," said Tarim.

Bridget shrugged. "You think there ain't another bar in the West we can't whore? Even in this town?" She cackled. "We'll give you good competition!"

"You will work here! Tonight!"

"We will, but not her."

Tarim glared at them. "We will discuss this again later."

"Yeah," said Bridget, "*way* later."

Tarim grabbed Sun Moon's forearm and turned to leave. Sun Moon was dizzied by the turn, and her anger, and her relief.

"And we'll have some real food," snapped Gretel.

"Yeah!" said Hansel.

Tarim grunted and pulled Sun Moon away. She followed, half-stumbling.

In the back room, she mustered, "I'm going to be sick." She held her hand at her mouth like she was going to vomit.

Tarim shoved in her the direction of her door flap.

She collapsed onto the bed. Feelings surged over her like waves on the ocean. Anger, relief, shame, each rose in a rhythm, lifted her up, and let her fall into the trough of despair. Tears sprouted on her cheeks.

In a few minutes Tarim's voice came. "You are needed in the store."

"Just a minute," she said.

She struggled for control. The iron band was back around her throat, gripping.

She sat up. The band allowed her to control her face, and she was glad of that.

It hurts.

I need it.

In a few moments she stopped the tears. She wiped her face carefully and composed it. *Not a whore. Not yet.*

When she walked into the store, her body was still numb. Her hands were restless, nervous. Her face was blank, inscrutably pleasant.

CHAPTER FOUR

1

She was standing to the left of the door flap, a short miner's hammer in her hand. She controlled her breathing, staying ready.

Tarim was being childish, really. He was a silent man, and would never give himself away by movements as audible as pacing. But did he think she was not used to his slightest sounds? Did he think she could not read his heart? Since the confrontation with the whores, more and more often he had looked at her appraisingly, as a man does when he thinks of taking a woman. Today he had done it repeatedly. Now the tavern was closed. It was past the hour of midnight, perhaps far past. He hadn't gone to his woman tonight. Sun Moon stood ready.

She flexed her fingers on the handle of the hammer over and over. It was heavy enough to stun, light enough not to fracture. She hoped.

No whore. She had told Dr. Harville. He said to stick up for herself, which was a funny white man way to say it. Dr. Harville was a good man. She prayed for him, and gave thanks for his help.

She kept telling Tarim in Chinese, "No hundred-men's-wife." He smirked at her. The only thing he would understand now was the hammer. She asked Mahakala for strength under her breath. *Destroyer and Creator.*

Her door flap stirred. Tarim had put all the candles out, so she had only faint moonlight through the back door window to see by. But Sun Moon's eyes were accustomed to the dark. She rubbed the steel across her open palm.

A finger eased the flap open an inch.

I shall try not to kill him! Tarim was her protection from the white men, such as it was. They didn't respect her person, but they seemed to respect his property. As long as he owned her, they would not expect to rent or buy her without paying. Besides, she was afraid of the white-man law. Dr. Harville told her the white men hanged people for murder. And they would see this as murder, he added, the rebellion of a servant against her proper master.

No, killing would be stupid. So she told herself. But she wondered whether she was simply afraid to release with abandon the joyously destructive spirit of Mahakala.

We Mahayana Buddhists do not kill.

Mahakala transforms and redeems living beings through killing.

The finger pulled the flap well back. Sun Moon was standing in deep shadow. Tarim was outlined by the faint light. He stuck his head in and peered into the shadowed room. She held her breath and hit him in the temple with the steel, hard.

Tarim staggered.

She grabbed his hair and slammed his head down onto her knee.

Tarim growled and fell backward onto the floor.

She felt her own mouth fill with blood, and her tongue protesting. She had bitten her tongue hard!

She pounced, knees on his stomach, dropping the hammer. In an instant she had the point of the pocketknife pressed against his throat.

"If you try to rape me," she gasped through her own blood, "I will kill you."

Then it came, the urge to kill. It rose to her throat. She choked it back. *The power of Mahakala,* her mind trumpeted. Her hand trembled, and rose higher.

She belched blood onto Tarim's chest. He grunted.

She ripped at the blood with the knife. The clothes sliced open like paper, and she slung them back, sloshing her blood onto Tarim's arms. She slid the knife along his breastbone, letting the point drag nastily. "This time the flesh," she said through slitted lips. She lifted the knife erect and pressed lightly on the skin between the ribs. "Next time the heart!"

She punctuated the last word with a prick of the blade point.

Tarim gasped.

Sun Moon got off. "Stand up," she ordered. He did. "Turn around." He did. She planted her foot on his lower back and sent him flying into the hall. *Mahakala devours men.*

"Next time the heart!" she yelled, and planted her body in the door.

Tarim scurried off.

She felt the bite of vomit in her mouth, and hated it.

SHE KNELT OVER her basin, washing her mouth out. She was weeping.

Suddenly she vomited into the basin.

Control! she told herself. Through an act of will she stopped the heaves. *Tarim must not hear me, must not think me weak.*

She listened for his footfalls and heard nothing. She held no illusions about a man of such dark spirit. He might come back and kill her while she slept. He might fear her and keep his distance.

She tasted it again now, blood and vomit in her mouth, on her tongue, on her teeth.

Lying on her cot, she flexed her fingers and wiggled her body and felt something else, something ugly. In her fingers, her palm, her arm, skin, muscles, and heart ran an itch, a yearning to shed the blood of another. She convulsed. For several minutes she shivered, and occasionally convulsed.

She remembered her lifelong teaching. She had been given this human incarnation to discover and live out compassion for all sentiment beings. For herself, she must learn to rise above the afflictive emotions: lust, jealousy, ignorance, and anger. Tarim was a sentient being, a suffering being, and she should empathize with him.

Her heart cried for blood.

I have lost nearly everything, but I will keep my vow of chastity.

She listened. She noticed that the candles were still out in the building. She heard no noises. Her breath heaved, subsided.

She ran a finger along the knife edge. Tomorrow she would resharpen it.

She looked in her heart. *The pitilessness of Mahakala, goddess of Time.*

She looked at the altar box, and the cedar beside it. She approached on her knees, struck a match, lit the cedar. Pungent smoke wafted to her nostrils. She prostrated herself, intending to pray, and it hit her. *Tumult, tumult.* Emotions raged through her like fever. Sensations and recollections ran up and down her body like invading hands. Memories of her abduction clanged like hunks of metal in her mind.

Much of what happened when she was abducted she could not remember. Her mind refused. Of the following weeks she had only fragments of memories of the odd reality of the lotus state, life as a sour and unreal opium dream. She remembered fearing that the bandit chief was about to violate her terribly. She remembered his ugly laugh, and his tale of the contract that would protect her for the moment. A man in America, he said, had paid well for a virgin, and he had slapped the earth that he would deliver one. Very well. He cackled. "One day a virgin, next day a hundred-men's-wife!"

She shivered with remembered terror. She still did not remember, at all, what she knew had happened during the first attack. The bandits had assailed her family as it traveled to Chengdu. They had killed everyone but her. She had asked to go with her father and brothers to Chengdu to see the formal flower gardens at the monastery. Her mother had gone along to indulge her oldest daughter, a family holiday. So they were all dead. Her mother and father, dead. Her brothers, dead. Her uncles, dead. All dead.

And me. My heart is dead. Cold. Without compassion. Without love.

She rose from full prostration onto her knees. She shook her head, lolled it back and forth. She felt the iron band around her throat. *I cut off my terror with an iron grip, and cut myself off from my heart.*

Suddenly the sound and smell of the convent rose like warm mist in her mind. She saw the butter lamps, smelled the incense, heard the chants.

Life has scalded that away. I can only boil, and boil. Does anger ever transform itself into anything better?

A hundred *lingams* brushed her imagination.

No!

She bolted upright, lightninged. She looked hard at the altar and pictured Mahakala, the skulls, the corpses, the bloody mouth. In her mind she heard the wild, mad, joyous laughter of mayhem.

I will escape, or I will kill.

She waited, in tumult.

Tarim didn't come back that night.

She touched her own neck with her hands. She massaged it. She couldn't ease the clamp of the iron band within, which was killing her. And saving her.

Tarim accepted a bowl of food from her indifferently, as though from a servant. She ate her *tsampa* standing at the stove used for both heating and cooking. His eyes skittered all around the room, everywhere but at her.

He finished and set down the bowl before he broached the subject. She had been dreading this, whatever it was, since he announced this morning that they would eat lunch together.

"You do well in the store," he said in Chinese, as always. "Very well."

She squelched her surprise, and grew more wary. "Thank you." He would be offended by her not adding the honorific Elder Brother, she knew.

"The customers like you. You are learning English very fast."

"Thank you." *I don't mind English. I hate speaking Chinese with you.*

Tarim looked up at her, and she saw a flicker of wild light in his eyes. He deadened it immediately. Something would come now.

"I erred in considering making you a hundred-men's-wife."

Gratitude spurted in her heart like a warm spring. *Careful!*

"Thank you."

"I will get a better return on my investment this way."

Her heart turned cold.

He turned a bitter smile on her and switched to English. "You will be one man's whore. Mine."

She bit her cheeks until she felt the warm blood in her mouth. *I knew it was coming.* Far fewer than one in ten Chinese people in this Land of the Golden Mountain were women. A wife was a treasure. A concubine might be a greater treasure.

She pictured herself being cared for, given fine clothes, pampered.

Her guts churned with revulsion. "No!"

Even uttered quietly, the word burst out, offensive.

Tarim's mouth snarled. He said it in English again, patiently, as though to a child or a deaf old woman. "You will be one man's whore. Mine."

Involuntarily she bunched her robes in her lap and shook her head no, no, no. She shook and shook it. She felt her face as some puppet visage, her mouth pulled open and shut by a string. "No!"

The iron band around her throat tightened. She moved her hand toward the pocketknife. As though against her will her fingers clasped it. She eased it from the folds of her robes and showed it.

Tarim flung up a casual hand.

"If you try to use me," she said, "I *will* kill you."

Tarim spat the words out slowly. "You will move your belongings into my room tomorrow morning. Tonight you have alone." He smirked at her. "For your prayers."

2

In the dark, in the middle of the night, Sun Moon stood up from Tarim's body. *I have done it.* She had poured the laudanum he sold for medicinal purposes liberally into his evening tea, and he had passed out. She had tied his hands and feet ferociously with hemp. She would have until morning, when Tarim would not appear and the whores would investigate. She bent again, licked her finger, and held it at his nostrils. She could feel the breath—he only slept.

She slipped from his room. She wore the loose cotton trousers, shirt, and thigh-length jacket of the Chinese miners, the sort she herself had sewn for them. On her back was a sack with one pot, matches, balls of *tsampa* wrapped in oil paper, and a coat to keep the rain and cold off. It also held her nun's robes. For the first time in more than ten years she was not swathed in her robes. Her head was no longer shaven. Her hair, longer now, was pigtailed like a man's. She would be walking to Salt Lake City not as a Tibetan woman but as a Chinese man.

Will walking the wrong direction fool them? She smiled to herself, and touched the knife handle in her waistband. *If not, I must be ready.*

Then her mind spun. *How fierce am I? How much of the spirit of Mahakala do I have?* She did not permit herself to frame consciously her main fear about this deceptive route. It was toward the Mormons. Porter Rockwell lived among the Mormons. She fingered her scar. *He will know me by this.*

She touched the brim of her felt hat nervously. *Salt Lake is the best way. They'll be looking for a woman, not a man. And they rape women, not men.*

She glided like a shadow to the boards beneath the pile of kindling. Tarim always kept kindling next to the stove, even now that the weather was warming and they didn't always build a morning fire to take the mountain chill off. Not for weeks had Sun Moon figured out that the floor puncheons there came up, and one of Tarim's hiding places was underneath. A quarter moon ago she had opened the hiding place at this hour, and found gold, bags of dust and coin.

Quietly she stacked the kindling in a neat pile to one side. When she had the bags out, she faced her first decision as a thief—dust or coins? With a deep breath she decided on coins. With dust most storekeepers cheated you—Tarim grew his fingernails very long so he would wedge dust in them when he handled it. How much? Earlier she had thought fifty dollars, what a Chinese miner earned in three moons. But . . .

She had to eat. She had to pay for the stagecoach from Salt Lake City to San Francisco, and the passage from there to China. Tarim had complained several times that he had spent a thousand dollars to bring her across the ocean.

The more she took, though, the angrier Tarim would get. The more she took, maybe, the harder the sheriff of Hard Rock City and all the other sheriffs between here and San Francisco would look for her.

Tarim, would you be angry as a demon if I didn't take a penny? Would the law chase a woman of the Middle Kingdom just as hard for two cents as two hundred dollars?

Dr. Harville had told her how it worked. The master charged that the escaped servant was a thief. The law brought the servant back. The master posted bail, took the servant, and dropped the charges.

I will not be coming back.

She wondered if Tarim would tell the white men to kill her if necessary. She thought he would. He loved his pride even more than his money.

She counted ten of the ten-dollar gold pieces into her hand. *I cannot do it.* She put all but one coin back. She replaced the puncheons and stacked the wood as she had found it. *Faith,* she told herself. Stagecoach? Ship? *Faith.*

She walked like a phantom behind the counter of the store and got a sack full of barley and dried meat to go with it. She didn't like the dried meat—jerky, they called it—but it would last. At least she would have *tsampa,* the food of her own people.

She hesitated. Finally she opened the case containing the derringer, what Tarim called the ladies' gun. It had two barrels, two shots. She picked it up, held it, felt of it. The metal was cold. *Sun is Moon. Death is life.*

She put the gun in the waistband of her pants.

She slid to the back door, barely opened it, and looked out the crack. *Maybe this isn't the time.* When would the whores find Tarim? How much of a start would she have?

She shook her head hard. *This is the time. Go!*

A thin arc of silver gleamed in the sky, like the edge of a sword, pure, bright, and terrible.

I am afraid. Tarim said the wagons took a quarter moon to come from Salt Lake City. *It will take me a full moon to walk.*

Would she get lost? Would she starve? Would the sheriff catch her? She was a thief, with that gold coin hidden in her knapsack. Would some white man kill her casually for sport?

She had planned as best she could. She would walk on the wagon road, but only at night. During the day she would hide in the sagebrush, eat, sleep. *Can I really walk all the way to the Salt Lake? So far, so hard.* Though she'd spent her childhood on horses in Tibet, she wouldn't ride—that would look far too suspicious for an Asian.

She breathed the night air in deep. For another long moment she permitted herself to think of home. Tibet. Her convent. Her studies. Her bed. Her peace, her freedom from violence. *All lost, lost forever.*

She stepped into her room for the last time. She had drilled a hole through the altar box and run a leather thong through it. Now she hung the altar around her neck and under her arm, like a monk, wore a reliquary box. In the box was cedar, and a little butter for *torma.* It felt lumpy under her arm, but comforting.

She stepped out into the darkness.

ALL NIGHT SHE walked through the brush, parallel to the trail. Before starting she had quailed at the thought of the darkness, the shrubbery, the animals, the shadows, the uncertain footing. Now, in fact, she felt calm. After her eyes adjusted, the moon lit the way well enough. The sagebrush was easy to walk through, the road in plain view to her left.

Sometimes her shoulders protested against the weight of the pack. Sometimes a patch of giant sagebrush seemed dark and frightening. Sometimes she wondered about small noises out in the brush. But the terrors of the wilderness were less than the terrors of Tarim's household. She breathed in and out. Occasionally it seemed that her chest might relax, her throat open. But not yet. *Not safe yet.*

At dawn she spread her coat behind some rocks, covered herself with her nun's robes, and slept. At midday she ate. For the rest of the day she watched the trail. Some traffic moved northwest toward Hard Rock City, none southeast. That night she walked through the brush again. When she saw no one following her, she decided to keep walking at night, but on the trail.

That was her pattern. Walk all night. At dawn, sleep, exhausted. About noon build a fire, make tea, and eat *tsampa.* Spend the afternoon in meditation, or in prayers to Mahakala. Day by day, it seemed to get easier.

Touching the altar box with one hand while walking helped her keep her mind off what she asked herself. The questions were relentless as her footsteps:

Are they looking for me on the Oregon Road? Or this trail?
Who is after me? Where? Ahead or behind?
What beasts are out there in the dark?
Have I wandered onto the wrong trail?
How many more days? How many more weeks?
Will I starve?

By the time of the three-quarter moon she saw that she would starve. The jerky was gone, the *tsampa* nearly gone. *If I must choose between going hungry and making food offerings to Mahakala, I will go hungry.*

She was well into the part of Idaho Territory dominated by the Mormons, maybe even in what the map called Utah Territory. She knew little about Mormons except that they and the Americans disliked each other. The Mormons called other Americans "gentiles," and the gentiles mockingly called them "saints." No one knew much about how Mormons would treat Chinese people, because Chinese people flocked to mining camps, away from the Mormon city by the Salt Lake.

I know how Porter Rockwell would treat me.

THE SKY WAS beginning to get light—the road rising to a crest ahead of her was beginning to glow. Time to get off the road, time to sleep. She turned uphill through the sagebrush.

At the top she found a flat place between the bushes to spread her coat. Just before she lay down, she saw it far ahead, a settlement. Her mind jumped with excitement. She made tea and ate while she thought it over.

I must buy barley and butter.

It's too risky.

What's riskier than starving?

I'm so afraid.

The first time she woke up she knew. *I will go into that town and buy food.* Sleep more, meditate, eat again, and then go in. *In the late afternoon, if I have to flee, I will be closer to the darkness. Mahakala, lend me your strength.*

"HELP YOU?" SAID the fat woman behind the counter of Coleman's Mercantile.

Sun Moon felt a thrill of fear. The woman's voice sounded suspicious. *Will they arrest me?* The woman hadn't addressed her as "Sir." Was that because the woman saw through her disguise? Or because Asians didn't deserve respect?

She lowered her voice as much as she could. "Barley, please, ten pounds."

The woman nodded curtly.

Sun Moon knew the words from clerking. "And butter."

The woman looked at her queerly. Barley and butter? But she didn't ask that. "How many pounds?"

Sun Moon held up one finger, not wanting to risk her feminine voice again. She held out the sack she stole from Tarim's store to put the barley in. The woman weighed it in the scales.

"Please take your finger off the scale."

"Yes, *Sir!*" said the clerk sarcastically.

Sun Moon almost giggled with pleasure. She avoided looking the woman in the eye, though—she could feel the anger. She wondered whether the woman routinely cheated most customers, or only strangers, or only yellow, red, brown, and black people. Tarim cheated everyone, and his methods were more subtle than pulling at the scale with a finger.

The clerk didn't try it again with the butter.

She paid with her ten-dollar gold piece. When the woman hesitated, Sun Moon said softly, "Five dollars and fourteen bits."

Suddenly she realized she was speaking in a high voice. She lowered it dramatically. "Please."

The clerk looked off into a corner irritably as she handed over the change.

Provisions on her back, Sun Moon went tentatively to the front door. Through the glass she could see intense sunlight outside. For the moment she liked the shadows inside the store, which protected her like the night. *But the woman may challenge me or turn me in at any moment.*

Touching her altar box lightly, she threw the door open and stepped through.

"*A-mo!*" she rasped. Oh no!

She stepped back so fast she almost fell over her own feet.

The sheriff. Sheriff Conlan of Hard Rock City was walking his mount down the middle of the street, leading a pack horse. The droop of his long mustache gave his mouth a cruel look, and his eyes looked slightly amused. He would look amused, she thought, when he hanged people.

Did he see me?

Sun Moon looked around for an escape. All she saw was the clerk glaring at her with suspicion. *No help.*

She looked back outside. Conlan was riding on. Past the livery, past the land office, past the hotel. *Wait.* He turned his horse to the rail in front of the jail, dismounted, and went in.

Did he see me? Her knees shook. She twisted the altar box on its thong.

No Asian people in the street. I am a white yak in a herd of black yaks.

Feeling like she was stepping off a cliff, she opened the door and strode onto the boardwalk. *Mahakala, help me, teach me, protect me.*

No shouts, no steps, no hoofbeats.

She turned into the alley at the side of the mercantile. *Out of sight.*

She walked fast to the end of the alley, followed a rail fence toward the other end of town, looked around to make sure she wasn't seen, climbed over the rails, and ran into the sagebrush.

Then it struck her. *Sheriff Conlan was going the wrong way.* He had been riding through the main street south to north, not north to south. *He's given up. He's going back.*

No, she told herself. *Maybe he's just riding around today, or just coming back a little.* But she didn't think so. He and his horse looked like they'd put in a long day, many miles. *Maybe he's hired someone ahead to look for me.* She had heard of bounty hunters among the Americans. *Did Tarim offer a reward?*

She found a hillock, sat far down in the sagebrush, and watched. She was safer not moving around now anyway. After dark she would use the road and hurry south.

Thunder boomed. She shivered. The mountain behind her was covered dark with clouds. She shivered again. *Good,* she told herself. *I will walk in the storm and they will stay warm and dry inside.*

After perhaps ten minutes Conlan and another man came out of the jail and went into the hotel. After about another hour Conlan got his horse and rode out of town north. *He's headed back to Hard Rock City.*

She took breath in sharply, and the air hurt her lungs.

Do not be deceived. Hunters are tracking you.

CHAPTER FIVE

1

THE WATERS OF the river lapped at me, and I heard myself singing and whistling at once. *Impossible.* I was tickled by the impossibility. As I started to smile, I heard the music rise . . .

I felt my throat frozen, my lips limp, my voice box quiet. Yet my ears swelled with the sound of my own whistling and my own singing. Besides . . .

Now I hear it. My voice was a woman's, or a child's, or an angel's, or all of those at once. It was also trumpets and flutes, a choir of violins, and the cries of birds.

All these sounds were ones I made, except for one single sound, the thump of the drum. It beat underneath, so low you couldn't hardly hear it, yet it was the center of things, like the hearts of all the birds beating as one.

Suddenly my soul was borne up on the voices of the birds. I spread my wings and flew. I glided, I soared, I ringed my way up the sky in great circles. The wind beneath my wings was music, sacred and profane at once, beautiful and ugly and beyond all in its glory.

When I got halfway to the sun, I turned and looked back at the earth. The air was getting cold, the music distant, the light pale and brittle. I wanted the warmth of earth, and the company of creatures. Slowly I floated back toward the planet.

I luxuriated in the symphony of song. It was mine and not mine. Though I did not make the sounds, the skin of my body, the hairs of my head hummed with them. I was making supreme music—beautiful, celestial music. Occasionally I detected words, but the language was unknown to me, beautiful and euphonious but unknown. I knew only that the words were pure as an echoing fountain, and true as the voice of an oracle.

I am singing with the voice of the birds, and of the sky, and of the river.

Somehow I knew that the meaning in the songs was the spirit of the birds, the spirit of flowing air, and the spirit of flowing water. I knew this absolutely, beyond knowing. It was mine as my breath was mine, my lungs, my blood. At the same time it belonged to all creatures, to the river, to the winds, to the divine.

I sang the song, or it sang me, during one moment that was all of
time and all of
eternity.

I drifted . . .

A thought came at me. *This music is only an echo of what I heard under the waters.*

I drifted . . .

I felt a rock-rock-rocking, world-rocking.

Shifting, swaying, stirring, floating . . .

Light creeping in.

Gentling, easing, breathing . . .

Warmth creeping in.

Sun on face.
Breathe in, breathe out. Breathe deep in, breathe deep out.

From the flux into time and space.

Eyeballs moving. Head rolling.

From sky to earth.

From flying to resting.

Resting on the earth again, I lay still. I felt the sand with my back, my arms, my feet, my neck and head. I felt the cold water on my back and the cool air on my front. I knew where I was—lying face-up in maybe an inch of the Bear River. I remembered how the river came for me, the river swept me away, the river took over my spirit and my life.

At this moment I felt as clear as I had ever felt in this mortal existence. I could feel the sand under my back, even the individual grains. I could feel—praise be!—the sun on my face and body. I could feel the hairs of my head waving in the water. I knew the water was cold, and my skin was shriveling. I would want to get up soon, to rise from the waters. It was not time, not yet.

I opened my eyes to the world, the ordinary world. *To every thing there is a season, and a time to every purpose under the heaven.*

I took air into my lungs. I remembered how the waters claimed me. I remembered my longing for air. Then I remembered a light, the whitest light imaginable. I breathed into that holy light and then . . .

Music. Music flowing as infinitely as waters flow, as winds blow. Sometimes it was song, and I did not know the words.

Now I tried to remember the words. *It was a language I did not know.*

My mind sank back. Fetched up on this sand, in this sunlight, in this gently lapping water, in this air, I began to hear the sounds of the ordinary world again, beautiful sounds, the shushing of waters, the soughing of wind, the brushing of leaves. Beautiful music.

2

WARMTH.

Earth, holding me. Earth warming me.

I stirred. I wiggled. My body melted into the warmth.

"Are you all right?"

A voice, not a musical voice, just a plain, ordinary voice. I smiled. It was a woman's, and very peculiar. I smiled bigger. Maybe all the ordinary voices of the world would sound peculiar to me, now and forever.

I opened my eyes. I cast my everyday sight about. I rolled my head. With effort I brought into focus . . .

A Chinawoman's face.

I grinned. *Whoopee! The world has gone mad!* My funny bone was tickled.

Her face was one inch from mine. Right then, seeing her too close to focus on, it started to happen, this feeling.

Strange. I could feel her arms around me, too. School words came to me—"O brave new world."

"Are you all right?"

A Chinawoman holding me. The feeling was getting its engine started.

I forced my mind back to right then. Did I pass through the hard earth and come up on the other side? I had to chuckle at that. Did I bring her back? Or was I in China?

She lowered me gently back to the sand. We looked at each other. She untangled herself and sat back. The feeling was big now.

I sat up. The world swirled right. I propped an arm out. The world swirled left. I laid back on the sand.

"I love you," I said. I thought that over and repeated it. "I love you."

"Are you all right?"

"Never felt better in my life."

"OK," she said in English.

I wished she would hold me again. I couldn't remember the last time a woman held me. Sure, I knew what that feeling was now. I loved her. Oh my but didn't I love her.

SUN MOON LOOKED into his face, transported.

"What's your name?" the red man asked.

Sun Moon hesitated, wild with strangeness. "Are you all right?" she repeated. The man was strange, and she was strange to herself. *I embraced him.* Only to warm him, to be sure. *I put my chest against his and wrapped our legs together. And I felt like our bodies left the ground and hovered in the air together.*

"Are you all right?" Sun Moon didn't know that *she* was all right.

"Sure," he said, lolling his head back. "Never felt better in my life."

Sun Moon regarded him and called upon herself to live in the ordinary world. *Who are you?* A red man, they would call him in America. Yet his skin, his hair, his face reminded her of . . .

Who am I? Her body felt strange to her, changed. She required herself to be normal.

"Where do you come from?"

"I come from the other world, where I saw the spirits."

Sun Moon shuddered.

"Just now," he assured her. "I heard their song. It is the music of the universe. The stars." He spoke casually, with a smile, as of matters serious but also light.

You came from the river, half-drowned, I can see that. Deliberately, she brought her mind and body under control. She saw truth in his face. Now was the time to . . .

"What's funny is, I didn't know the words. I mean, the language. I didn't know what language . . ." He fell silent and smiled, smiled like a Buddha, like he was receiving a great blessing. She watched his face in amazement.

"What race are you?"

He only smiled his Buddha smile.

Yes, an Indian, you will say. But the dress of a white man. And the features of one of my people. You are returning from . . .

"Are you an oracle?" She trembled. It was a reckless question. Yet the look on his face . . . He said he was returning from the land of the spirits. She had seen that look before, on the face of the Oracle in a prophetic trance. Also on the face of an uneducated monk, a primitive lama more Bön-po than Buddhist, in a tiny village. If this red man was an oracle, that might explain why her body felt strange.

"Are you a *pawo?*" A medium of the old religion Bön-po.

Suddenly he began to shake, violently. He turned over onto his belly, pulled himself onto his elbows, then collapsed onto the sand. He shook, shook like a prayer flag in a gale. He moaned.

Are you going to die?

She reached for him, rolled him over. He had no consciousness of her. She checked to see that he had not swallowed his tongue and was not choking on it. She hesitated. She looked at his face. His body had gone limp, and he seemed to be sleeping.

Something precious here. She felt an idea in her body. Then she sat close, stretched out next to him, and wrapped the stranger in the warmth of her arms and legs. Which felt wonderful to her. She had never touched a man so intimately, or held anyone so close, at least not since she was a child.

She felt the rhythmic breathing of his sleep. She felt her own breathing fall into the rhythm of his, and felt her body relax deeply. She almost felt like saying, "I love you."

3

I SPAT IT out. Tea, I supposed, but it tasted strange. I stared at the stain in the dust. Very spicy, very weird.

The woman sat staring at me. "Ginger," she said. "It restores vigor. I have no *yersa gungbu.*"

I rolled over, crawled a couple of steps to the river, sucked water in, and spat it out, like I wanted to do her funny words.

I looked up and down the Bear River. Yes, I was still on Bear River, even if a China Polly was next to me. I drank from the river, took its sweetness into my belly.

I looked up and down Bear River with different eyes. It would never seem the same. This river took me to the edge of the world of death and brought me back. I was still on its banks, but it was not the same place. I was not the same man. I sat up.

The edge of the world of death.

Life looked different to me now.

Death did not seem frightening.

China Polly held a ball of dough toward me. I took it in both hands, felt of it, and held it to my nose. I always loved it when Mrs. Pfeffer baked and I got to eat the dough.

Love. Yes, love, that's what this China Polly and the whole world were reminding me of right now. But I had no idea what sort of love. Might be the usual sort a man feels for a woman. (Those days I'd had no physical experience of that.) Might be the sort you feel for a sister or mother. Might be the spiritual sort the bishops talk about. I couldn't tell. But love was what it was, all right.

She smiled at me and pantomimed eating. I tried the dough, and it was buttery and good.

Deliberately, I didn't look at China Polly. I kept my gaze on the dough and on my own insides. I had a lot to think on. Not just the love but what happened in the river.

The spirits of the water came to get me. They rose like white horses tossing their heads and stampeded over me.

They took me to the bottom of the waters. There all was surpassing strange. I was in no danger. It was a place to . . .

I didn't have the words. The death of the river had felt . . . jimmy-joomy, which is to say wonderful and more than wonderful.

I recognized in myself the urge to name my experience in the fancy words the Mormons used to describe the revelations of Joseph Smith, or their own ecstasies. The words I heard—were the voices speaking in tongues?

Now, I had never taken seriously the Mormons speaking in tongues. Still, I couldn't help wondering. Maybe there *was* some other world, one seen only with an enchanted eye.

I swam in the river like a creature of the waters. I swam through huge times and huge spaces, ages and worlds.

I sipped the tea again. I had a sense that I'd seen and heard magical places and doings I could no longer remember. I looked at the river. The ages and worlds weren't there. I knew I couldn't recapture those sights and sounds by jumping back into the water. But maybe, maybe . . .

This world seemed dull. Next to the river world, very dull.

The tea didn't taste so bad now. I held the warm liquid on my tongue and savored it. *China Polly isn't dull.*

I had heard a new music. I pondered that, a new music. I could whistle any music I heard, but not that stuff.

I swallowed all the tea.

When I fetched up on this bank, I was still hearing the music.

I thought on that.

Where is it now?

Easy-like, I searched my mind for some sounds. I had them, I did remember, sort of. They were far from the same, though. I wondered whether my memory was a little off, or this world was off. The music sounded truly glorious only in the other world.

If I whistle the music aloud, it will come out . . . different. But I didn't want to make the music out loud, not again. China Polly would think I was for the loony bin. I swallowed. I pondered.

"Thank you, China Polly. Thank you very much for helping me."

"NOT POLLY," SHE said. "Sun Moon."

"Sun Moon," he repeated absently. Odd, how gentle and sweet this red man's spirit felt, almost like . . . *Are you a* pawo? Surely a red man in this unenlightened land . . . A *pawo* of the primitive Bön-po, not an oracle of the Mahayana.

Sun Moon felt wildly confused. *Was it right to tell him my name?* One part of her mind screamed, *HE MAY BE ONE OF THE HUNTERS.* Sun Moon had no illusions about what the hunters on her back trail would do.

She took a deep breath, mindfully, and let it out.

Another part of her mind was thrilled. The world was spirit, and spirit was everywhere, but . . . *My gods have abandoned me. Except for Mahakala. And this young man comes bearing spirit, so . . .*

Protect him. Nurture him. Stay with him. Let him nurture me.

"SUN MOON." I chuckled. "What a funny name." I looked at my companion. A youthful face, a beautiful face. Then, somehow for the first time, I noticed the great scar. I looked at her face again, carefully. Pure. Simple. Pretty. And a *big* scar, above and below the eye, like two big dashes.

I looked into the western sky. Now the moon had set, and only the day star held forth in the sky. I thought, *The time is in joint.*

I brought my mind back and regarded Sun Moon. The eye split by the scar looked bright and alert, somehow even brighter than the other eye. I thought, *Sun, moon.* Like the two stars in the daylight sky this morning, two stars that do not belong together, things in conflict yoked together.

I smiled to myself. I'd never seen a Chinawoman close, and sure never imagined looking at one like this.

Something in my heart moved. Opened.

"Sir," said Sun Moon in a soft, high, melodic voice. "You must eat more. Danger. Cold." Sun Moon clasped her elbows with her hands and mimed shivering.

I smiled big. *How did you get here?* I went to another world and brought back a Chinawoman. I chuckled. "Hey, you didn't tell me your name, Mrs. . . ."

MRS.! HE'S SEEN through my disguise. He knows! Sun Moon took off her felt hat, but she resisted throwing it down disgustedly.

She studied the red man. *He knows. But he can't be one of the hunters.*

Sun Moon called on the iron band to hold down the emotion. She wanted to stay near this man. She was a scholar-nun, hoping to become a teacher of Mahayana philosophy at the great lamasery at Zorgai, celebrated for scholarship. Her special interest was the history and development of Mahayana, including its roots in primitive religious thought, such as the Bön religion of her country. Though as a woman she would never have the degree *geshe,* she hoped to make a reputation as a scholar. *And before me is a red man with a gift of spirit! What a discovery!* The student in her trembled. *What is his gift? Prophecy? Healing?* The hairs of her head itched.

Hairs of my head! Her chest clutched. *My hair should be cut short. I am no longer a nun. I am . . .* She didn't know what. *No longer a nun.*

CHAPTER SIX

1

"WE CANNOT GO, Sir, must rest."

I looked into Sun Moon's extra-bright eye. "OK," I said.

If I asked just my body, in fact, I felt OK to travel. But I didn't want to. I wanted to talk to this rare bird of Asia. Or lie back and hear the new music, the songs of the river. Anyway, where would I go? My job was gone, my connection to the Saints was gone, and the wide world stretched before me.

"OK," I repeated.

Sun Moon tugged at my sleeve and motioned with her head. I followed easy. She led me a few yards to a spot in the willows where brown fabric was spread, peculiar cloth. A low fire was burning, a camp made. I looked at Sun Moon hard. *You're hiding and sleeping during the day,* I realized. *Who you running from?*

"Get off wet clothes," said Sun Moon. "Wrap up. Rest."

I waited for Sun Moon to turn her back, then stripped. "How you tell I be woman?" she asked.

I chuckled. That getup was supposed to make me think she was a man? "Everything about you is woman."

I rolled up in her brown cloths. Sun Moon looked at me kinda queer when I did that. Then she turned back and sat leaning against a rock. "I dress like man," she said, "fool many. Even queue hair." She pointed to her pigtail.

If she wanted to know how I knew, I couldn't help her. "You look like all woman to me."

She's also just plain afraid, I said to myself. Once in a while, maybe without her knowing, her left hand touched her scarred eye. Other times it touched her shirt at the waist. I was tempted to say, "Never mind the knife—you won't need it against me."

Bear's ass! All of a sudden I knew something else I'd brought back from the other side. I wasn't afraid. Didn't know if I'd ever be afraid of nothing again. So her knife just made me smile.

Also, I knew things, and I sure knew Sun Moon meant me no harm.

I smiled big to myself. I rolled up in her brown robes and laid back on the sand. But I had no intention of sleeping. I felt alert. I felt like my senses and mind and heart and whatever other organs we use for knowing was wide-open. I needed to ponder. My old life was done for. I had seen something. I'd felt something with my whole being. I had heard music, sacred music. Who had borne it to my ears? The river and the birds. Especially, now I thought about it, the birds that live on the river or by the river, specially the eagle and my friend the fish hawk.

"We cannot go," she had said. I grinned wide as the prairie. Where would I want to go? Working as a clerk in the merc—what could be more far-fetched than that? Preposterous, that'd be the bishop's fancy word for it. I rolled my shoulders and scrunched my back against the sand.

What would I do?

I had no idea. Somehow that tickled me. I smiled at the sky. Wasn't the sky where my music came from?

Then I shivered. I felt tingles of delight and fear at the same time. For the first time in my life I felt free.

Heckahoy, I'd heard about freedom all my days. I'd been taught the American people fought a revolution to break free of the British. I'd been taught the Saints came clear to Deseret to break free of the prejudice and violence of the gentiles. I'd been raised by Mormons to be free of the superstitions of my own people, whoever they were. I'd gotten an education so I could be free of the shackles of old ways of thinking.

Then, all educated up, what did I do with my life? After I was given to the Saints, I went faithfully to the meeting house with the family twice a week, did chores, went to school when I got enough English, worked toward my endowments, and labored in the merc. I was white as could be. Except that the Saints did not treat me as white and delightsome but as a Lamanite, a person whose dark skin showed I'd been cursed. I myself had no memory of being anything but white.

What kind of half-Injun could I be? The ones the Saints knew out in Washo were Shoshones and Diggers. When I first talked to Shoshones, I didn't recognize their language, so that didn't seem right. And Diggers, I found out all sorts of tribes lived out in Washo, and the whites called them all Diggers, no matter who they were related to or what language they talked. So I'd come to a blind alley on that search.

Ever since the Pfeffers told me I was adopted, which sure made me mad at the time, I had not a notion who I was.

The next thought jolted me. I looked soberly at Sun Moon sitting against the rock. In the whole wide world I penned up my mind in this place with these Mormon folks and in their one language, their one way of understanding. Not a whit of it was my own, not by birth, not by belief.

A whirligig feeling dizzied me. I felt lost. I had let go of everything that gave my life shape, so was utterly lost.

I shivered. I thought, *I'm free. For the first time in my life I'm free.*

I chuckled. *Or am I lost?*

I grinned at Sun Moon. The Chinawoman appeared to be far, far away in her mind. Maybe in China. *Maybe I will go to China.*

I felt silent laughter coming up in me like bubbles. I stretched. I was tickled. I felt like whistling. *Free. Lost. Free-lost!*

2

The music rang. It rang from everywhere in the world to everywhere in my mind, which was the world. It was birds and bells, accompanying a single voice. The voice was the purest I'd ever heard, neither male nor female but somehow both at once. It reverberated like a bell in a tower. I heard it less with my ears than with my bones, my body, my entire consciousness. It was exquisite, soul-satisfying, a fountain of sound would go on forever, easy, bubbling over and over, tumbling on itself, forever creating beauty, forever healing.

I STARTED AWAKE. I'd heard myself singing. I had no idea of the words—or even whether the meaning was borne in words—but I'd felt the music ringing out of me.

Sun Moon was watching me. She had the extra alertness of the hunter, or the hunted, I couldn't say which.

So. I'd cut loose with the music. I brought it into this everyday place. I didn't know whether that was good or bad, dangerous or safe, healing or destroying.

I ought not to do it. I want to do it.

I squirmed. I didn't know . . . I didn't know anything yet. I needed to wait. But wait for what? Just wait.

I looked into Sun Moon's extra-bright eye. That eye felt like a dagger now. "You think I'm crazy, don't you?"

"NO," SHE SAID, "not crazy." Sun Moon considered. Her scar was hurting. That meant, she'd learned over the months, she was in danger. Or at a crossroads, danger one way, opportunity the other.

What should she tell this strange man, this piece of flotsam washed up, about what she thought? Crazy, no, except that divine madness was still madness. As for particulars, he would not know what a *pawo* was. Or a dervish—she had seen wandering dervishes in her country, Moslem initiates of ecstasy. This stranger had their look, something in the eyes far, far away, a light no one else could see. Such people could cross to the other side and come back. Some said they escorted souls to the place of the dead. The young man would know nothing of this. He had a gift, and had not begun to plumb it. She knew more about his spirit in some ways than he did.

Of course, she had only book knowledge. Like many scholars, she did not have a gift, she had merely studied it. Nor had she felt the need of it. She liked the simplicity and clarity found in meditation. No mysteries of ecstasy for her. They felt . . . hard, inimical.

"No," she repeated, "you are not mad." She studied him. *What to say?* She was fascinated.

The pain in my scar. With a lurch she corrected herself. *I must think practically. I am not a scholar, not even a nun. I need help.*

She touched her scar where it came out of her eyebrow, where it sometimes hurt. That was comforting somehow. Then she saw. Yes. Wonderful. Yes. She ventured tentatively, "We could help each other."

As she spoke, she had the sensation of stepping onto a floating log. It might take her downriver, or it might turn and dunk her.

"You could help me," she said.

3

SUN MOON'S STORY sucked at my heart. I listened to how she was raised as a nun. A nun! Wearing these queer brown cloths as robes, staying clear of men, and hours and hours of praying and chanting. Then the part she wouldn't say anything about, getting abducted. But Jumping Jesus–quick, she'd been practically enslaved, shipped like a burlap bag to Idaho, and required to play the whore. I felt the drama of the way she risked her life rather than give in to whoring. I suffered her bad cut with her, the swelling, the infection, the slow healing. I wanted to know more about her weeks of lonely, nighttime flight from Tarim. Heroic, that's what her walk was. I knew heroic when I heard it.

She was not Chinese but Tibetan—what did that mean? It was frustrating that she wouldn't spell it out. "I traveled from Kham into China, I was abducted and brought against my will to the United States. That is all I can say." I knew a closed door when I saw one.

The whole story had a queer effect on me. Only an hour ago I had felt—well, knew in that queer way I found in the river—that all this day-in, day-out stuff was foolishness, these struggles to make a buck, having a spat in the family, getting sick or well, whatever—it was all trifling as the ripples the wind makes on a lake. Compared to the eternal music in the depths.

Yet here across three feet of sand was a human being who was suffering in just that struggle. Torn away from her life, getting enslaved, escaping—it felt hard as thirst in the desert. So . . . Yet . . . Sweet gizzards.

I gave up on figuring this out and went straight for the next step. It was mad, but everything was mad. "How do you want me to help you?"

"First," she said, "you must tell me who you are."

I was surprised that she turned it back on me. So. I took a deep breath. I made up my mind to tell the truth, even if she didn't understand it, more of the truth than ever I knew until now. Right off I had the feeling of pushing my boat into the waters of a stream that no one knew where it went. I wondered, *Is this what it feels like to be free-lost?*

"My name is Asie Taylor. Don't know how old I am, maybe twenty-one. Asie, a name from the Shoshone Injuns, in full Sima Untuasie, meaning first son. It sounds like Ozzie in English, but it's spelled different." I spelled the two words for her. "Name means 'first son,' or it's a short version of 'first son.' Don't know if I was born half-Shoshone or half some other Injun folks. Came from somewhere on the trail to Californy. Big stretch, somewhere in there."

I took another deep breath. "When I was a kid, a fur trapper name of Taylor give me to some Mormons headed for Salt Lake City. He lived at Fort Bridger sometimes, with the Shoshone other times. Made his living trapping or guiding folks across the trail to Oregon or California. He was taken sick and dying, couldn't tell them nothing. His woman was dead. Another woman belonging to another mountain man, a Shoshone herself, told them he called me Rock Child, but his woman, who wasn't my real mother, called me Sima Untuasie.

"So when I was about seven, I ended up in Salt Lake. I don't remember nothing of my real father or mother or that way of living.

"The Pfeffer family raised me as one of their own children, and educated me. I owe them a debt, though I didn't always like 'em. They didn't tell me I wasn't theirs until I was twelve. I hated that. So I decided I didn't want to be Earl Pfeffer no more. I threw out their name for me, took my father's last name, and shortened the name my mother called me to Asie. The family didn't cotton to that, but I didn't care.

"To the Mormons I'll always be a Lamanite, a descendant of Laman, son of Lehi, who was cursed with dark skin because of his sullenness. The light-skinned sons of Lehi on this continent were destroyed by the Lamanites. Among the Mormons I'll always be an outsider.

"I worked in the Pfeffer family store in Salt Lake until I was eighteen. Then in the merc in Brigham City. If I worked hard enough, and tithed, and went to stake house regular, I was part of the Mormon community. If I studied and kept the commandments of virtue, charity, and tolerance, and served my fellow man according to the teachings of Christ, I would have received my endowments, and been a good Mormon."

I held back feeling. "Then I might even been allowed to marry a white woman." I felt salt tears in one eye. "I doubt it, though." I made myself look at Sun Moon and smile. "What else do you want to know?"

"You tell what happen today? How you wash up here on river bank?"

I didn't know what to say. It would seem mad to anyone else, how I had come here. I hesitated. I quavered. I shook. Finally I said to myself, *It being a day of madness, I will honor it with one more mad act.*

Slow and hesitant-like, I told Sun Moon what happened that morning: Dissatisfaction with my life, queer feelings of things not being right, thinking time was out of joint. Now and then exhilaration for no reason. Voices in the trees, which turned out to be not in the trees but in the wind, and then turned out to be in the river. The waves calling to me. The flash flood sweeping me off, taking me to the world of waters. There the darkness. And in the darkness the music.

"When I come back to the world, I was singing songs I never heard before in a tongue I didn't know. Still," I told Sun Moon, "without knowing the words, I knew what I sang, or what the birds and the river sang through me." I shrugged. "The spirit of flowing water. Soaring in the sky. I knew, just knew, knew more than knowing. Like you know your breath, your blood, your heartbeat."

I lifted my eyes into hers, and had one clear thought. *Now she will have nothing to do with me.* I felt easy about that, and in a gentle way curious.

He trusts me with the truth. Had he been older, he might not have trusted her. Had he been Chinese, he wouldn't have trusted her. This young man couldn't even say what people he belonged to, yet . . .

So she began to play with her idea. *Maybe, maybe . . .*

She watched him without knowing what she was watching for. Why didn't he break the silence nervously? Most people would. What a curious man.

Her thought was becoming a plan. *My skin is nearly the same color as his. Our hair is the same black.* She turned the idea round and round. She looked at it with her mind and felt of it with fingers and heart, like feeling the 108 beads of her rosary.

He was waiting. He had inner stillness. Maybe he was worth the risk.

"I no know whether you want help me. I not of your family, or even of your race. You take a risk. I offer you in return nothing."

He nodded. She felt a pang of alarm, because she felt her warning might only be a temptation. *I must ask him and get his free consent, truly free. Otherwise, all will come to grief.*

"If I be caught, I probably am return to Hard Rock City as thief. Then Tarim me bail out jail, take home, drop charges, and make me his whore. For rest of my life. Contract say if try escape, serve rest of life."

She looked into his eyes, trying to see. Her scar hurt sharply. She touched it and got a sense of augury. *Danger? Or opportunity?*

"Big fear not be caught. Tarim maybe so angry tell them OK kill me. I think I have no chance with Tarim now."

Asie nodded.

"Maybe kill you, too."

She took her heart in her hands and dived into the sky of hope. "We look Indian, you and me? Man-woman. Maybe you walk with me few days? Man-woman, no suspect. Walk to Salt Lake?" *And protect me from Porter Rockwell.*

JUST WHAT YOU expect on any business day.

I woke up this dawn as an employee at Boss John's mercantile, room, board, and fifty cents a day, a life to the lullaby of boredom. In every direction, to every horizon, stretched deserts of the ordinary.

By noon, if that's the time, a few things have come up. I've heard a concert from the river and the birds, and no everyday birds. A woman from the other side of the world has waltzed into my life, and she's asked me to go traveling with her. She says to Salt Lake. She means San Francisco. And why the hell not to Tibet?

My funny bone was tickled now, seriously tickled.

I studied Sun Moon. No damn idea. She didn't have any idea. So I took consultation with myself.

Sweet gizzards, I couldn't go back to my old life—I lost the whole wagon, all the supplies, and the mare. Now I *had* to go on the lam from Boss John.

Another thing, bigger. Why would I want to go back, now that I heard real music? Nothing wrong with the folks in Brigham City especially. But I felt as much like going to see Seward's Folly and traffic with the Eskimos as go back to life among the Saints.

Talking to myself like that, I sat there. I meant to consult with myself like a reasonable fellow. But a notion came into my head. I thought of the call of the fish hawk, my bird friend. Fish hawks were here this time of year, but gone in the winter. I could make the fish-hawk call. It was a dot-dash kind of call. Starting slow and flat, it built, rising in pitch and in loudness and feverishness, and then it trailed off. I'd gotten fish hawks to answer my call. I've wondered what I was saying in their language. I took thought. Maybe I oughta try to find out. Maybe I should go wherever the fish hawks go in the winter. Wherever that was. West, the bird scientists said.

Or maybe I was just loony. I'd danced a twirl with death, and now everything seemed different. Couldn't say different *how.* But helping a person from the far side of the world seemed as sensible as anything else. Or going to the far side of the world. Way more fun to be free-lost than go back to my old life.

I realized I was looking at Sun Moon blankly.

"We can travel as sister and brother," she added. I wondered how old she was. Her eyes had seen a world of trouble, and showed it. Still, her face . . . I judged her to be similar to me, though I didn't know for sure how old I was. "They look for a Chinese woman alone, not two Indians."

I love you. It felt good, the loving. I still wasn't sure what kind of love it was, but I thought maybe it included more than she'd want. And me, twenty-something and never touched a woman. In Deseret womanhood seemed untouchable unless you were a Saint, and white and delightsome. I looked Sun Moon up and down.

Then I put that thought away. *Yes, we'll go together. Go to Tibet if need be.*

"We must buy right clothes," she went on. "We must look right."

"OK," I said. "Yes." I nodded, kind of to myself. "Heckahoy, yes."

CHAPTER SEVEN

1

In that same summer, 1862, Captain Richard Burton of the British Army, not yet Sir Richard by a quarter century, came to Salt Lake City for the second time. His first journey, in 1860, was for the purpose of seeing one of the four holy cities of the world, which in Sir Richard's view were Mecca and Medina in Arabia (sanctified Moslem places), Lhasa (the holy city of Tibet), and Salt Lake City, the mecca of the Mormons. He told about this journey in his book *City of the Saints.*

The second journey has been a secret from the world, which thought he was in Fernando Po as consul at the time. In fact he was on one of his cloak-and-dagger missions. Of all his roles, soldier, scholar, author, explorer, the one that made him happiest was secret agent.

Here's the way he explained the whole thing to me and Sun Moon.

The British government wished to present a certain matter to Brigham Young for the Prophet's consideration.

Among Her Majesty's countless minions, only one was on terms of credit with the Prophet Brigham Young, none other than Captain Burton. Who, as chance would have it, was bored with his diplomatic work in Fernando Po.

How could he not have been bored? Captain Burton was by profession a soldier, by temperament a spy. He was the master of many guises.

Disguised as an Arab, at the risk of his head, he made the pilgrimage to Mecca, traveling among Arabs. At various times he had passed himself off as a Persian, a Tibetan, an Egyptian, a Hindu, and a Sufi, speaking all these tongues like a native, and master of every custom and nuance. Expert in all matters about India, Persia, Arabia, the Hind, and East Africa, he spoke twenty-nine languages. (When Sir Richard translated the *Kama Sutra* into English, one of his enemies quipped wickedly, twenty-nine languages including pornography.) Most recently, he was an explorer, the discoverer of the source of the Nile. How long could such a man remain in his study writing books? How long spend his evenings making polite conversation with local potentates? How long do without his wife, for Fernando Po was so primitive white women couldn't live there. It was a fever-hole island off the coast of West Africa so uncivilized I haven't found it on a map yet.

So he was dispatched in the spring of 1862 to Salt Lake. The journey was to be secret, he was cautioned. That was the part Sir Richard liked.

This is how Sir Richard told it to us, and the way he wrote it down. When he knew that his mission would never be revealed publicly, he kindly had his journals of the journey copied out for me.

These journals revealed what he didn't tell us at the time. Captain Burton was indeed the finest Orientalist and linguist of his time, and among the finest explorers. But in the army and Her Majesty's government generally, instead of being praised, he'd been belittled. So at forty he was a bitter man, feeding miserably on the fruits of scorn.

Captain Burton noticed that his host got down from the carriage awkwardly, like a man with chronic back pain. It amused him that the Lion of the Lord had the same frailties as other men.

The two of them walked to the top of the knoll, where they could see the entire city laid out to the south. Burton turned to the west. The sun glinted harshly off the Great Salt Lake. He expanded his chest to let the desert air in. His skin welcomed the desert sun. "Very impressive indeed," he said. "Great strides in only two years."

Brigham Young nodded, immune to flattery. Burton decided to leave the man his silence, whether it was rooted in circumspection, superiority, or an aching back. President Young stood facing Temple Square. Here the man had erected the visible form of his hopes for himself, his vast family, and his people, the faithful of the Church of Jesus Christ of Latter-Day Saints. As an indefatigable reader and researcher, Burton well knew what these hopes were, to strive toward perfection, to have themselves sealed to their spouses for time and all eternity, to have their children and progeny sealed to them, creating an eternal family. He was no victim of the biases and foolishness of their enemies, who would say nearly anything to slander the Saints. No, Burton truly knew, from the testimony of the Saints themselves. He had journeyed across a great ocean and crossed a vast continent, twice, to visit Great Salt Lake City.

Burton appraised the man before him. He had appraised many powerful men in his time, men of many cultures and countries, making reports on their strengths and weaknesses to the Honourable East India Company or to his government. Some of them had been madmen, and the world judged Brigham Young a madman. As it judged Richard Burton a madman.

The world was wrong, certainly about the Lion of the Lord. Burton knew President Young's history. The man had taken over from the dead Prophet, Joseph Smith (now *madman* might apply there), in the Saints' hour of darkness beyond darkness. He had mustered in that moment the vision, the courage, and the requisite ability to inspire. He had led the Saints across the state of Iowa and the frozen Mississippi River, then across the Great Plains, and the Rocky Mountains, not knowing where they were headed. He had designated this valley the place of salvation, and somehow had inspired his people to heroic energies. Few of the world's enterprises in creating utopias were so successful as Salt Lake City.

Burton knew the audacity that required, the foresight, the steadiness, the intelligence, most of all the courage.

Brigham Young knew himself and his people, understood his strengths and weaknesses, knew what he wanted, and was implacable in his determination. Burton would have liked to flatter the man, cajole him, even deceive him, but he knew none of those would work. He was going to be reduced to telling the simple truth.

He felt naked.

"What have you come here for, Captain Burton?"

It was said softly, but Burton was not deceived. The Lion of the Lord had just set aside politeness. The man pivoted and fixed him with a gimlet eye. Burton knew better than to take the fragility of the pivot for weakness.

He also knew intuitively how tough the Lion could be. Burton felt a spasm of cold. He was in a country ruled for five hundred miles around by this man. An astute leader, very much so. A man of indomitable will.

A man of huge responsibilities, and determination to meet them by any means necessary. A man followed by thousands of unquestioning adherents. To make an enemy of Brigham Young in Deseret would be dangerous.

Burton took a deep breath. *Nothing ventured, nothing gained,* he told himself. *A man who sticks his neck out before a potentate may get his head cut off,* he also told himself. "Mr. President," he said, "one art I learned in India is *maalis,* the skill of massage for aching muscles." He did not add that his teacher was a courtesan. "I became an adept. Would you let me try?"

Burton got the pleasure of seeing he had truly surprised Brigham Young. The Lion of the Lord regarded him doubtfully. "Saints do not attend doctors. We trust to the healing hands of the anointed."

"I am no physician," answered Burton. He held up his big hands and flexed the fingers. "My gift resides in my hands alone." *He's hurting severely, or he'd have said no instantly.* "I seem to have a particular gift for backs."

Young looked around apprehensively.

Good luck we came without a driver, thought Burton.

Young removed his broadcloth coat. His motions wanted to be decisive, yet were made tentative by pain. "I will not go further," said Young. He turned his back to the gentile, sat on a boulder, and put his hands on his knees.

For some minutes Burton worked in silence. His fingers found the muscles in spasm easily, and gently stretched them out. At last he said, "That's all I can do in one session."

Young arced his back this way and that. He put his coat back on. Burton could see that he was moving more comfortably. Now when the Lion looked at Burton, his eye might have been softer. For the first time in half an hour the hairs on the back of Burton's neck lay down.

Young repeated, "What have you come here for, Captain Burton?"

"My government is concerned with the disturbances caused by the War Between the States," Burton began.

President Young fish-eyed him.

Burton felt himself want to be garrulous, a sign of danger. Nevertheless, he proceeded. "The fighting augurs to go on endlessly, neither party able to gain decisive advantage. That hurts everyone. It disrupts the economies of both countries. It destroys fortunes. It makes the poor into beggars."

"It also hurts the English mill owners, I believe," said President Young. "Disrupts the supply of cotton."

So the Prophet was not going to permit pussyfooting.

"Yes. The war is painful for our country. Should the North win, and in the process destroy the cotton economy of the South, it would be very painful."

President Young looked vaguely amused. Burton understood. A great issue was being decided, the ethical and legal status of slavery. Burton himself despised slavery. And with all hanging in the balance, his government was most concerned about the profit-and-loss ledger. Ah, well, he was a soldier, not a politician.

"It is no secret," put in the Prophet, "that your government is discreetly helping the South."

Burton made a face. He was unaccustomed to such directness in a political matter, or to being pushed toward his own point.

"We wonder whether the Church should not take a position in this matter."

"You may be too late," said Young.

Earlier in the year, the Confederacy had advanced from Texas northward, taking the capital of New Mexico, Santa Fe, and presumably headed for Colorado. But the Union had turned them back.

"We think not," Burton went on. "That was merely the first skirmish. Southern New Mexico, southern Arizona, southern California—all favor the South. And the mines of Colorado are important. If Mr. Lincoln will finance his war with the gold of California, Mr. Davis will have the gold of Colorado."

Young merely regarded Burton in silence. *A good tactic.*

"We believe you might well act."

"Why would we?" asked the Prophet.

"The Saints can have no love for the people of the North, or their government. Not after Jackson County and Nauvoo, not to mention the Utah War." The Mormons had been hounded out of Missouri and Illinois, with the complicity of the state governments. And the United States had sent a punitive military expedition to Utah in 1857.

"A divided country to the east is no disadvantage to us. Why would we not let the two sides weaken each other?"

Now Burton played his second highest card. "Because the South will prove sympathetic to plural marriage." Polygamy was often thought a brother institution to slavery—Brigham Young himself was reported to have called it so. And Burton suspected that in his heart of hearts, Brigham Young was determined most of all to create a safe place for his Saints to live exactly as they wanted, including their marital practices. He would have bet on it. He had advised his government to bet on it.

Now the Prophet turned away, looked over the city, and seemed to ponder. Finally he said, "What aid could we expect from your government?"

Burton smiled to himself and gave the authorized message. "Immediately, we will provide whatever arms the Nauvoo Legion requires. Additionally, if the Legion coordinates an advance on Colorado with forces from Texas, we will assure that it is well supplied." Burton paused to lend his words effect, then laid down his highest card. "Ultimately, I think what is at stake is more important. Her Majesty's government is willing to consider the idea of diplomatic recognition of a new alignment on this continent, including an independent Confederacy and an independent Deseret. Each would govern itself according to the dictates of its own conscience."

Burton held his breath. All hung in the balance now. How much did President Young resent his removal as governor of Utah Territory? How much did he dream of true independence from the United States?

The Prophet turned his fierce gaze on the captain, and Burton wondered whether the President thought him a hypocrite. He had published his abhorrence of slavery widely. On the other hand, he had written rather favorably of polygamy as he had witnessed it in Asia, and approved of it privately. He felt confident Young knew his position.

At last the Lion of the Lord led the way to the carriage, mounted easily, and took the reins. Burton climbed up beside him. "Captain Burton," said Young, "I cannot answer you today about this matter. I must consult with the First Presidency."

Burton doubted that Brigham Young took much advice from anyone.

"Perhaps you would come to me in the morning day after tomorrow."

So you have already made up your mind. Burton thirsted to know the answer, and feared the worst.

"In the meantime I am indebted to you. Perhaps you would like a tour, to see how we have built up our industries, and the Nauvoo Legion. I will arrange a guide."

Young's eyes glinted, and Burton couldn't help smiling. The President had as much as said, "Since you want to spy on our army and fortifications, permit me to show you around."

"Yes, thank you," said Burton.

"Wednesday morning, then? Come prepared. I have a good man to guide you."

2

A *FACTOTUM LED* Burton to the President's office, and Young wasted no time on preliminaries. "Captain Burton," he began, "I must tell you that the First Presidency has decided that the interest of the Latter-Day Saints would not be served by our participating in the war on either side."

Burton nodded. *Ah, well.* He had never had confidence in this mission anyway. "I understand. I will so inform my government." That would be easy, thanks to the new telegraph lines that stretched from Atlantic to Pacific.

"I must ask you to excuse me now. Your arrangements have been made. My man will show you around. He's instructed to let you see whatever you like."

The factotum escorted him out. Burton could not get accustomed to the coarse phrases Americans of the frontier used, like *show you around.* "He's waiting for you," the factotum said. "Odd, you two look alike."

Surely this was impertinence. Burton cocked an imperious eyebrow at the dolt. The factotum's face, he observed with pleasure, turned to watery whey. *Splendid to be able to addle a man with just an eyebrow.*

They turned into an ill-lit hallway. "Not physically alike," he added, mumbling now. "Something in the . . ." The sentence petered out. Burton suppressed a smile.

Outside a rough-looking frontiersman waited, dressed in the outfit Burton had come to associate with army scouts. "Sir Richard Burton," said the factotum, "Porter Rockwell."

Burton suppressed a laugh.

"Sir Richard," said Rockwell, offering his hand, and Burton had to suppress another.

"Pleased to see you again," he said, shaking.

They had met at a stage station on Burton's previous trip, the explorer and the avenger, introduced by the owner.

Burton corrected, "*Captain* Burton."

"*Not* Sir Richard?" asked Rockwell.

Burton decided on a policy of largesse. These Americans, or rather Mormons, were simply unacquainted with the social niceties. "One should be delighted to be so honored, but alas not yet."

"You wanna be Sir Richard, then?"

Burton was at a loss for words. "Naturally, one . . ."

"A man should have what he wants when he wants it. Sir Richard you be to me," said the scout, grinning monstrously.

"It's improper."

"I was borned improper," answered Rockwell. "Sir Richard."

Preposterous, thought Burton. *But utterly American.* He was amused.

Now Burton regarded two fine-looking mounts. "If you're ready," said the big man.

"Of course," said Burton.

Porter Rockwell. Burton almost laughed out loud. He turned to the factotum. "Thank you," he said in dismissal. *Splendid. Brigham Young provides me with a tour of his country guided by a notorious killer. More than notorious.* To Brigham Young's virtues of subtle and discriminating intelligence and powerful will, Burton now added a virtue he wouldn't have guessed, a sense of humor. *At the same time this is an admonition,* Burton realized. *Assigning the head of the Danites as my guide is a warning.*

Rockwell mounted and waited.

Oh, Mr. Rockwell, I know your reputation, the Destroying Angel of the Mormon Church, the most feared man in Utah Territory. Burton had traveled widely in the East, the Middle East, and even to deepest Africa. *Yet I doubt I have had the privilege of beholding a man as purely dangerous as this one.*

He swung into the saddle and drew alongside Rockwell. He was exhilarated.

And that dolt all but said Rockwell and I are alike in spirit! Burton was vastly amused.

"Your call, Sir Richard," Rockwell said. He gave a mirthless smile.

"I understand there is good whisky to be had in Ogden," said Burton.

Rockwell laughed, a rough sound, a child's fantasy of an evil laugh, and touched his heels to his horse.

What similarity was the factotum imagining? Intimidating aspect, I suppose.

The two men rode down the middle of the wide road as though it were theirs not by command or even ownership but by natural law. Burton eyed the other man curiously. They were both in middle age yet bore an aura of physical power. Each was about six feet, strongly built, rugged-looking. Each sat his horse like a saddle-toughened soldier. Each had an air of readiness, capability, self-assurance. Each was graying a bit, though Burton wore his hair as a gentleman and Rockwell as a border ruffian, long and plaited into a braid. They had faces much aged by hard experience, Burton forty-two, Rockwell somewhat older. They had the eyes of soldiers who have seen many battles, many deaths, and much savagery. Both had the courage, Burton would guess, to admit to much that is evil in all men, including themselves.

But doubtless the factotum saw that each of them had a face that by itself could make men quail. Burton had a mad-looking scar on his left cheek, where a Somali spear passed through. He also possessed what was called the Gypsy eye, which focuses on a man severely until he feels his innards are exposed, then refocuses beyond him, on something visible only to the beholder. The Gypsy eye was unnerving.

Rockwell's look was simpler. It was careless violence, a love of mayhem, a look of pure malevolence as fine as Burton had seen even in Asia and Africa.

He chuckled to himself. He imagined the effect of the two of them simply walking into a bar for a drink. The Americans would see two very dangerous coons, as they quaintly put it. Some would go quickly elsewhere, and ease the constriction in their throats with the whisky the Mormons opposed, made illegal, and provided illegally at high prices.

"What would you care to see beyond Ogden?" asked Rockwell civilly. Then he added softly, "Sir Richard."

Burton shot him a glance meant to be withering, but answered only, "I'm at your disposal."

"Bear's ass!" said Rockwell, and gave a mocking sideways grin. Burton was delighted to hear this Mormon expression, which he had already recorded in his notebook. It was an ejaculation of approval. "Bear's ass! So you have come to see the elephant. I will by God show him to you every bit, trunk, legs, and twitching tail." A flick of amused eyes. "Sir Richard."

"To the Queen!" Burton proposed, and lifted his whisky.

"To Deseret!" answered Rockwell, ever the Mormon partisan. He downed his in one toss.

"Wheat!" Rockwell exclaimed.

Burton couldn't second "wheat," but he recognized it. A few nights before he had listed it in his copious notes as a "Mormon neologism for *good.*" To Burton's educated tongue, however, no Western whisky was wheat. The only standard of quality for Western whisky, Burton had heard, was how far a man could walk after he drank it. The shorter the walk, the better the whisky.

Rockwell slugged down the second glass.

During the last two days Burton had satisfied some of his curiosity. They were doing very well, the Mormons. Brigham Young was shrewder and far more determined than the U.S.-appointed governor of the territory, and the vast majority of politicians. With the advantages of the vast distances of the West and the fanatical devotion of his followers, he would outwit the United States in nearly any way he cared to. Burton had no doubt that the Saints would succeed. *People of religious fervor usually do.*

However, he remained befuddled and intrigued by his companion. Was Porter Rockwell a Saint in spirit? Abundant signs said he wasn't. For one thing, Rockwell liked his whisky.

As Rockwell brought another glass to his lips, Burton said, "Do you not agree with 'The Word of Wisdom' then? Are you a free thinker?"

"A man holds truths he cannot live to," said Rockwell. "Yet a square drink will not condemn a man to eternal dying."

Burton noted the language of Joseph Smith on Rockwell's tongue. He also thought one of the drinkers at the next table was showing undue interest in the conversation.

"You're a good chap to lift a glass with," Burton said.

"I'll drink Valley Tan, mint juleps, brandy smashes, whisky skies, gin slings, cocktail sherry, cobblers, rum salads, streaks of lightning, and morning glories," said Rockwell, his eye slyly on the eavesdropper. "I'll imbibe tarantula juice, awerdenty, coffin varnish, rattlesnake juice, or Pass brandy. Some months I exist mostly on bottles, flasks, demijohns, corbozes. . . ." Rockwell seemed to take sudden thought. "Occasionally

I even drink with gentiles." He smiled at Burton. "Like you, Sir Richard." He held the bottle out toward the back of the stranger. "And you, eavesdropper."

The eavesdropper turned his head and regarded them. Then he gave a slow smile and arose, glass in hand. "Believe I will," he said. His companion also rose and extended a glass. Rockwell poured, and the men joined Rockwell and Burton. Names and handshakes were not exchanged. From the look of curiosity on his face, Burton supposed that the gentile knew Rockwell by reputation.

Eve, Burton named the eavesdropper in his mind, because Eve is the source of all human troubles. Gent, he named the other, short for gentile, and because the fellow was not genteel. From their accents both were Southerners. Eve had the look of a gentleman, Gent a ruffian.

"I was asking my companion his view of sin," Burton began.

"The two blasphemies against the Holy Ghost," intoned Rockwell, "which shall not be forgiven in this world or out of it, are shedding innocent blood and adultery. Those who commit these abominations shall be destroyed by the Lord our God."

"You Mormons commit adultery every night," said Gent.

Burton eased his chair back. If the Destroying Angel took a notion to purify Deseret of one gentile, Burton wanted to be able to stand clear.

Rockwell gave him a grin. "You gentiles have hearts filled with lust," he said. "So you imagine we . . ."

Burton smiled to himself. *Is it possible I'm going to hear a rousing debate between a Mormon and a gentile about the system of plural marriage?*

"I am no polygamist," Rockwell told Gent ominously. "I have but one wife." He did not add, a wife I see only now and then.

Burton wondered if Gent or Eve knew danger when he saw it. *I hope neither of them is the sort of idiot who imagines to make his reputation by whipping a notorious bad man.* Without looking at it, he let himself be aware of his knife, an *assegai,* a short sword of the Zulu, which would be very effective in these close quarters.

He tried diplomacy. "I have observed polygamy firsthand in Asia and Africa," said Burton. "I don't believe it will work among us, but it works among them."

"Are you saying, *Sir* Richard, that you think plural marriage is a nigger thing?" Rockwell's gaze was amused and malicious.

Tingle. Burton was surprised and delighted by the pleasure this whiff of danger gave him. *If Rockwell and I fight, one of us will die very quickly.*

"I'm saying it works in many parts of the world." He held Rockwell's eye.

"Hooray," said Gent. "Listen to John Bull stick up for the Mormons." The fellow at least drew Rockwell's venomous gaze away from Burton.

"I merely report what I have observed, which is that it works well among the Muslims." Now he addressed Rockwell. "Are you aware of Mohammed's teachings on the subject?"

Rockwell cocked an eye. He was willing to change moods, be amiable.

" 'If you have only one wife,' says the Prophet, 'she will think herself your equal and take on airs. If two, they will quarrel eternally. If three, one will be nicer than the others, and they will collude against her, making her life miserable. Four, however, is a different story. Four wives will give each other companionship and become a family. It is the ideal number.' "

"And higher numbers?"

"To have more than four is forbidden," said Burton. "So says the Prophet."

Rockwell's eye glinted. "Not our Prophet, Sir Richard, not our Prophet."

"You don't see nothing wrong with them marrying all them wives?" whined Gent.

"Indeed I do. My complaint of womanhood in Salt Lake City is what the sailor says of the sea." He embraced the city with his outspread arms. "Water, water everywhere, nor any drop to drink."

Rockwell chuckled. So did Burton. Rockwell laughed heartily, and Burton joined him.

"Amazing that anyone would defend polygamy," said Eve, "in this day and age."

Amazing that you bait Porter Rockwell! Dressed head to toe in black, his hair loose and wild and hanging to his waist today, Rockwell looked a Destroying Angel right enough, or a devil.

"Abraham was a polygamist," said Rockwell, eyeing Eve.

Eve is detached. Fascinating.

"King David, too. Nor does the Constitution of the United States say anything against it."

"We of the South hold no brief for that document on any account. What would *you* say for polygamy?" Eve said to Rockwell. He spoke in a genteel drawl, Gent in an uncouth mountain twang.

"Our people are virtuous, our cities and villages are clean. Yours are cesspools of sin."

"Such a gracious description," said Eve. He turned to Burton. "What about the cities and villages of your Asia and Africa?"

"Yeah, how does it sit among the niggers?" added Gent.

Burton looked at them with the greatest curiosity. *Perhaps they are simply mad.* He replied, however, judiciously. "We might better ask ourselves how the system of monogamy is working in our countries—adultery rampant, divorce frequent, houses of prostitution everywhere."

"Everywhere but Deseret," put in Rockwell.

"Yes, of course, the utopia of Deseret," said Eve.

"What do you think about niggers, Rockwell?" The ruffian Gent again.

"Yes, it is Mr. Rockwell, isn't it?"

So they do know. Curiouser and curiouser.

"I prefer people white and delightsome," said Rockwell.

Burton eased his chair back. He wanted a clear field of fire. He did not feel afraid, except of a murder charge in a Mormon court.

"No doubt you think God does, too," said Eve. "I agree. So why do you Mormons act like niggers?"

Burton felt the air turn electric. He waited. His hands tingled wildly.

Rockwell jumped up and roared.

Burton went for his *assegai* and leapt forward—*get inside their muzzles.*

Eve and Gent jerked up and retreated, going for their sidearms.

Rockwell raised the entire table in his massive hands and charged.

Eve and Gent fell over chairs and their feet and each other. Rockwell slammed the table down, crushing them to the floor. He leapt into the air and stomped the table with both feet.

It's over. Will he kill them?

Rockwell took a slow step next to Gent and kicked him viciously in the head. Gent's head snapped, and his eyes glazed.

Burton pushed the point of his *assegai* against Eve's throat. He dragged it sideways and watched red ooze out. "If you lie very still," he whispered in Eve's ear, "only a little blood will trickle forth."

"Sir Richard?" Rockwell's voice.

"Let's stop now and stay out of gaol," said Burton. He looked hard at Rockwell's face. *The man's eyes are mad.*

"You boys have plumb wore out your welcome." It was the barman from behind. He was pointing a cut-off, double-barreled shotgun at them.

Burton said gently, "We admit you have command of the situation."

"I want to see your backs going through the door."

Rockwell said, "They started it."

"I saw what happened," said the barman amiably. "You move along. I'll see to it the sheriff holds these two overnight, so you don't get shot in the back."

Rockwell looked at Burton. Invisible assent passed between them.

"We'll have another bottle," said Rockwell. "Ours got spilled."

Without taking his eyes off them, the barman lifted a bottle from under the bar and spun it through the air to Rockwell. "On the house, Mr. Rockwell."

He never lowered the shotgun until the door kicked shut behind them.

"Bloody relief," said Burton.

Rockwell shrugged his shoulders like they were tight. "The relief was teaching 'em their place," he said.

They unhitched the horses. *This is the chance to learn something about him.* "I thought you'd kill them."

Rockwell cackled. "You think I'm tetched?"

The two swung into their saddles. Burton looked at Rockwell. He could see no expression. The sun was setting over the Great Salt Lake to the west. The big man's wild, loose gray hair was set aflame by the sun, his face deeply shadowed. *I'll take the chance.* "We're both tetched, that's certain," he said. "I was wondering if you're murderous. As is your reputation."

Rockwell touched his heels to his horse, rode a dozen trotting steps, and stopped. Burton came up alongside him and halted. Now Rockwell was looking into the sun. Above the black clothes Burton could see the deep lines in the face, and the darkness in the eyes. *Unreadable.* "Brother Joseph says, Sir Richard, that a certain sin shall not be forgiven in this world or the next. To shed innocent blood. I have done that. I have done it more than enough." He whispered the next words. "On behalf of my friend Joseph."

He raked his horse with his spurs and galloped down the street, his long hair twisting in the wind.

Thought Burton, *I am in the company of the devil.* He took thought and smiled. *How instructive.*

CHAPTER EIGHT

1

I STEPPED THROUGH the door, and said "Howdy."

The trader stopped and set down his fiddle. The man was always singing or bowing or picking. He had a standard explanation. "The Welsh are a musical people." That's why we were friends.

"How, Asie," said Owen Lloyd. This was the trader trying to be funny. I'd never heard an actual Indian say "how." Neither had Owen.

I looked around the bull pen to make sure no other whites were around. I'd loitered outside watching for the chance to catch Lloyd alone. *Can I count on you?* Known to the whites here along the Logan River as Owen Lloyd, the trader was known to the Shoshone as Two Owls—"sown by a Welsh father," he liked to say, "in a fertile Shoshone mother." Which was why I came to him now.

"What can I do for you, Asie?" Owen knew that working at a merc, I wouldn't be here to trade. *But I am.*

"Sun Moon," I said.

She eased through the door behind him. Some folks have an airy way of walking. She had a rooted way that I loved, a right-down-into-the-earth way.

Whatever Owen's reaction to an Oriental woman in his bull pen was, he didn't let it show.

"We want to be Indians," I said.

"*You* already are." Owen was the one white person who'd always told me I needed to find out about the nation I came from, the people whose blood I bore.

I tilted my head sideways, indicating Sun Moon. "Both of us. For a truth. If we look like what we are, they'll kill us."

Thoughts and feelings danced in Owen's eyes. He stared at us for a long while, speculating.

"Blankets," I said. "Feathers. Leggin's. Moccasins. Do you have them? Will you help us? We have a little money."

Owen looked hard at Sun Moon's face. *Don't ask,* I urged him in my mind.

Owen stepped to Sun Moon. "A China Polly as a Shoshone," he said. He lifted her queue.

I couldn't help but be reminded, *The first motion of scalping her.*

"Well, two braids instead of one, for a start." He called to the back room, "Noddy, will you come out here?" His wife materialized, like she'd been waiting. We didn't exchange any greeting. Her Shoshone face showed no surprise. "Would you get a calico dress that will fit this . . . lady? And vermilion, and plain moccasins?" Noddy disappeared.

Owen cupped Sun Moon's face in his hands. "The shape of the face is good. Less round and more shaped than a Shoshone, even." He guided her by the shoulders toward the back room. "Go change your clothes, Mrs. Whoever.

"Now you," he said to me. He held up a bolt of blue trade cloth. "What an Injun you are, lad, never wore a breechcloth." He cut a double arm span. "Come behind the counter and get your pants off." He held the cloth doubled against my waist and nodded to himself. "Your cheeks will show, cute little half-moons between leggin's and breechcloth. Never you mind. Don't be pondering your modesty or trying to cover 'em up. An Injun wouldn't."

Owen put his arms on his hips and stared into space. "Guess I can give you a feather off something old of mine." He disappeared into the back room. I stripped off my pants and covered myself with the breechcloth, holding it awkwardly front and back. The first time, one of those things makes you feel like a fool. I could hear Owen whistling. *We are a musical people.*

Owen came back with a hawk feather and some sinew. "You need to put your belt on and hang that cloth over it, front and back." Then he muttered, "Don't even know how to tie a feather in your hair. Can't paint yourself." He fiddled with my hair and whistled while he worked. "We are artists, and artists are masters of illusion," he said. "You need braids, too." He starting humming. "Illusion is lies done artful-like."

"*We have to* try it," said I.

Sun Moon pouted.

I took the pony's reins, led her into the road, and started walking. I didn't look back. I felt determination in my back. After a little bit Sun Moon followed, mincing.

When she caught up, I said, "We can't sneak around by night on the California Trail. We need to travel in the day, like Injuns would. Not always right on the road, but by day."

Sun Moon whimpered.

Lots of times Sun Moon acted like she was older and smarter than me. This tickled my funny bone. I kept hoping she'd figure it, and listen up sometimes.

I pulled gently on the reins. She was a poor pony, but the price was right. Owen said, "Two Indians traveling on foot? Not good. Every rancher along the way would notice, and keep his horses close-herded that night."

"We can't afford no horse." I looked at the pathetic beast. "*No* horse."

"Pay me later."

"May not be coming back," says I.

"In that case, I reckon I could remember the pleasure you give me making music." He pondered. "The pony is a going-away present."

I started to protest, but he waved it off.

"It can carry all your possibles," he said with a chuckle.

True, we had so little even that pony could carry it.

Now I told Sun Moon, "It's only a couple of hours." Meaning until dark. I knew she would want to walk through the dark—the moon was full. Then I'd have to talk her into moving on the road in the open tomorrow afternoon.

"We've got to trust this," I said. I waved the bottom of my breechcloth with one hand. "We're Indians." I waggled my bottom and looked sidelong at Sun Moon. I wondered what she made of that.

She started walking along the road, and I fell in beside here, leading the pony.

We're Indians. Felt good to me. But . . . *Where do I belong? Do I really want to go to Tibet, wherever that is? What music do they have in Tibet?*

Come to think, I wondered what music the Indians out in Washo had. The Indian music I'd heard seemed mysterious and appealing. *But what is my music?*

An answer came. *Birdcalls with the music of the stars.* Which didn't help.

I glanced sideways at Sun Moon again. I hadn't learned to read her face much. She had a way of not letting anyone see. *The monks and nuns where she comes from, do they ever get music from the rivers and the birds?*

I nurtured a secret hope that my people, whoever they were, got music from the rivers and the birds. I didn't dare voice this hope, not even in my own mind.

I wondered, too. *The words I heard in the river. Do my people speak that language?* Maybe I would recognize it when I heard it, and know them.

I walked next to Sun Moon feeling gratified, confident. She was from the other side of the planet. She had come all the way here. *I can go all the way there. Or anywhere. And I will. To find my music again.*

I wiggled my hips, loosened my stride, and walked. No use in thinking too much. I put a bounce into my step and started whistling.

2

Porter Rockwell paid attention to the motion of his horse instead of the John Bull. He surely preferred horses to Englishmen, and liked the air of the evening and the road better than anyone's rattle-tonguing. Rockwell liked horses, particularly this stallion, a blood bay that was his favorite traveler these days. It was the first horse he'd named in twenty years. For good and sufficient reason he called the stallion Blood.

Earlier Sir Richard had rattle-tongued some more on the subject of plural marriage, which he called polygamy, just like a gentile. He was a case. After defending the Mormon way to the two ruffians in the tavern, he turned coat. "In plural marriages, surely," he began in his uppity way, "there is but little of that choice egotism of the heart called love." Rockwell hardly listened to the John Bull's account of how love could blossom among two, but when spread among three or more descended to mere friendship and domestic felicity. Whatever felicity meant. "And thus gloom," Sir Richard concluded. "That gloom which infects the very air of Salt Lake City, and which all Mormons breathe daily."

Rockwell kept himself and Blood on a tight rein. *Stallions like us need a firm hand.*

Out of respect for Brigham, he was behaving himself with restraint toward the John Bull. *Oh my, yes, the very air,* Rockwell wanted to snort loudly, rolling his eyes sardonically. *Why would you think I give a damn about what some foreigner thinks about Saints? The nerve.*

Rockwell quickened Blood's trot just a hair with his knees. At this pace its trot was smooth as a woman's inner thigh. Rockwell didn't know any person he liked as well as Blood. *Why is the John Bull rummaging around in his head when he could be feeling the silkiness of a fine horse? Or noticing the blood-spouting way the sun is going down?*

Blood. Jesus Christ came indeed to wash away the sins of the world, a blood sacrifice. Joseph Smith had come to restore the priesthood of God. Thus he saved the believers, the Saints. *But maybe he saved them and threw me away.* Porter, this man is a burden to us. Porter, that man is a trouble.

Porter Rockwell felt a warm flush of guilt. He knew he'd thrown himself away, and not all in obedience. Not every killing he'd done was for the Church. *They have the comfort of God's face, and I have forever the coldness of His back.* It wasn't Joseph, or Brigham, it was him.

Porter Rockwell's gut ached sharply. He often felt a rat in his guts these days, chewing and chewing. Sooner or later it would kill him.

Now the John Bull was rattling on about the Lamanites, whom he called Indians. "Lo, the poor Indian, reminds me of a Tartar or an Afghan after a summer march. Lo sits his horse like the Abyssinian eunuch, as if born upon and bred to become part of the animal."

To get away from the John Bull's words, Porter Rockwell put his mind on his joining to Blood. Sir Richard went on for a while about "the custom of the Sioux Indians of cutting off, or more generally biting off, the nose tip of an adulterous woman. It does not surprise me—the same is practiced in the Hind."

Whatever the Hind is, and whyever I should give a damn. And whyever a soldier would rattle-tongue about such stuff. Rockwell found it hard to believe Sir Richard was a soldier, and had been for twenty years. In his experience soldiers didn't rattle-tongue, or rattle-brain either.

"I do not believe that the Lo of the Plains can ever become a Christian," the John Bull went on. "He must first be humanized, then civilized, and at last Christianized. I doubt his surviving this operation."

Rockwell had had enough. The John Bull knew nothing about Lamanites—why did he call them Lo?—except what some book told him. Rockwell not only knew Joseph's revelations but knew Lamanites right up close, firsthand. "Let's lope 'em," he said, and kicked Blood to a canter.

In a moment Sir Richard drew alongside. Rockwell didn't allow himself to look sideways. That's how horses turned competitive. Men, too, for that matter. He wondered, *What would it be like to get into a pissing contest with the John Bull? Bear's ass, no contest—I'm better mounted. A fight might be something else. He acts like he's seen some action.*

Porter Rockwell swallowed hard. Not often these days did he eye men and calculate. *No one's seen action like me.* He spat. *That's why it's boring to calculate.*

He didn't let his eyes roam to the right, at the John Bull. Instead he forced his gaze to the left.

The sun was setting beyond the Great Salt Lake. He put his right hand, the one without reins, on Blood's withers, felt the working of the stallion's muscles, the warmth of its flesh. Dark clouds curdled on top of the Hogup Mountains beyond the lake—dry, desert mountains, rock and sand without a tree or a bush. Desert lake, too salty for man or beast to drink. Dry country beyond, where only the mind's eye could see, white sand, alkali, barrenness, a country scorched and seared. *Like my soul.*

The sun squatted on the mountain ridges, and its light still shot the whole scene red—crimson clouds, maroon hillsides, waters of flowing vermilion. He felt his eyes drawn to the parched hillsides, an old and crusty red, like half-dried blood.

He raised his eyes to the clouds, lowered them to the lake. *Be-e-yoo-tiful,* he said mockingly in his mind, the way his first wife would have said it, the mother of his children, the one who had divorced him.

Looks like bloody pus to me, he thought, and snickered.

Then he saw them—dark, vertical lines against the scarlet glare of the lake. *On the road.* People, but he couldn't make out whether two or three, whether or not mounted. And then, like swirls of dust in the wind, they were gone.

3

"GET AWAY FROM me! Get away!" cried Sun Moon.

Asie stood still, staring straight at her, looking mortified.

"Go!" she whimpered.

Soft! They're too close!

"Go!" *You fool!*

"He's not after you, go!" She gasped breath in desperately. "Act like you're hunting for feed."

Asie slouched away unconvincingly. He got into moods where the world didn't seem real. *Not now!*

She crouched behind a giant sagebrush and tried to shrink, to melt into its shadow. Though it seemed to her silly, like the fear of children, she didn't look up. *If I can't see them . . .*

That was the worst of it. *Them.* She heaved breath in and out. *I saw Porter Rockwell, that I'm sure of.* Maybe she couldn't be confident of him from a distance, maybe she couldn't check by seeing his widow's peak, his flaky skin, his hateful, slitty blue eyes. But she could see his spirit, as you see a twisting funnel of wind, a black whirl, a nothingness, yet it would suck everything in and destroy it.

Why two of them? Impossible! She shook her head violently. *True. Two Porter Rockwells.*

By a mammoth act of will she refused her eyes permission to look up. *Two.* Now she even heard two of them, the clops of hoofs of two horses. The men didn't speak. They were looking in silence, their eyes poking through the twilight, searching for her.

The roots of her hair prickled. Her fingernails hurt like they were peppered underneath. Her belly churned. The scar on her face sucked at the bone beneath.

Thus observing herself, Sun Moon reddened with embarrassment. *He might not have seen me, but he will now. My face glows like a lantern.* They *might not have,* she corrected herself.

She wondered where Asie was, how far he had gone to do his grass-hunting-for-the-pony act. She knew he would come back if she got caught, he would sacrifice himself with her. She shrank smaller behind the sagebrush.

She reprimanded herself. *I am fearful. I must call Mahakala to my side. I must become a drinker of blood and an eater of men.*

Her scar hurt—crisis or opportunity? She forbade her hand to rub it. *I will give scars, not receive them.* She reached for the derringer in her waistband. *Drinker of blood and eater of men.* She took it in her hand and let her long, loose sleeve cover it.

Then she realized. *It's not the scar that aches, it's my other side, it's the right, the untouched side.* A-mo! *The side he hasn't cut. Yet.*

"Hallo! You!"

One of the white men—she refused to call them Rockwells—walked his horse through the sagebrush to her left. *Going toward Asie.* She couldn't see or hear the other white man. She could feel his eyes probing for her, insidious fingers.

"What are you about there?" *That white man talks funny.* A few men at the mining camp had spoken in that odd way—John Bulls, the others called them.

Asie answered something she couldn't make out.

The mounted horse clopped a few steps. The saddle creaked. To the right and well behind she saw the head and withers of another horse, a beautiful blood bay. Squatted, she put her head between her legs.

"You alone, then, is it?" said the Brit.

"Just me." Even Sun Moon wouldn't have believed him.

The John Bull rattled off a bunch of words she couldn't understand. Something about tribe, camp, wanting to trade, some such.

She lifted her head. The blood bay stepped forward. Its saddle was empty.

Skitch! A faint sound of sand behind her.

She whirled.

Sun Moon looked up into the face of Porter Rockwell.

Big as bear paws, his hands took her throat. He lifted her higher than his head. She hung limp, like a dead goose hung by the neck.

"Come here." He spoke low and sharp at the same time. "Sir Richard."

She heard the footsteps of the John Bull—Sir Richard?—but she couldn't take her eyes off Porter Rockwell's face. *And another devil.* She quaked.

Asie's footsteps came toward her. "Put her down!" he said. His voice sounded edged but weak.

"Keep your tongue to yourself." It was said casually, softly. Rockwell set her feet on the ground but kept his hands on her throat.

"This here is Sun Moon," said Rockwell. He let Sun Moon down until her feet rested on the ground. "She's a whore. Comes from Hard Rock City."

Moon put her finger inside the trigger guard, gently on the trigger. She had never fired the derringer, or any gun, but she was not afraid.

"Put her down!" Asie said in a cat screech. He came staggering toward them like a falling-down drunk proclaiming his fighting prowess.

Take your eyes off me and I will shoot you in the heart. If the John Bull lets me live long enough, I will touch my lips to your blood.

"Sir Richard, could you take care of that nuisance? I'm busy." Sun Moon's eyes took in the John Bull, and her heart hurt in her chest. *Bearing of a soldier, fiery visage, evil eye. Another Rockwell indeed.*

The John Bull stepped his mount in front of Asie. "Mr. Lo," he said, "I regret being unable to address you by name. I'm drawing this sidearm. Do not make me use it."

Rockwell seemed to like that—one corner of his mouth turned up.

Asie charged. He came screaming like a monster, arms outstretched at Rockwell.

The John Bull jumped his horse sideways. Horse shoulder hit human shoulder. Asie went sprawling, then came up slowly onto one knee.

"If you rise," the John Bull told Asie, "I will shoot you."

Pause. Asie crumpled to the ground. "Rockwell, you were saying."

Sun Moon drew the derringer with a lurch. *I will drink your blood.*

Rockwell slapped her hand. The gun went flying. The man was actually grinning.

"Sure glad we got that settled. Nearly got tired of waiting for you to make your move." He nestled both hands around her throat again, and squeezed a little.

"How is it you know this woman?" asked the John Bull.

"See this scar on her face. I put it there. She deserved it, and more. Turn the other cheek, they say," Rockwell went on, and gave a sinister chuckle. "So I'm gonna match this scar on the other side." He drew her close to his face. "Right here," he said. He stuck his tongue in her eye and ran it down her cheek like her scar. It felt like a slug.

She pretended to vomit and heaved dry. Rockwell nearly dropped her.

"What did she do?" said the John Bull.

Rockwell's eyes turned toward him, slowly, challengingly, as though noting an offense.

"What did she do? She offended me. I promised her I'd kill her, ever I saw her again. So first I'm gonna cut her, then I'm gonna kill her."

Rockwell turned his eyes back to Sun Moon. She saw a queer, sick pleasure squiggle through them.

Mahakala, give my arms strength. She clawed at his eyes.

Rockwell shoved her back. As she fought for balance, he backhanded her hard. Sun Moon found herself facedown with sand on her lips and teeth.

Humiliation surged up Sun Moon's gullet. Now she vomited. Then she raised her face toward Porter Rockwell and smiled in radiant contempt. She called loudly in the Tibetan language, "Help me, Mahakala!" She added in English, "Kill me, or I will kill you."

"OK," said Rockwell. "Deal."

He lifted her off the ground with his powerful arms, and his terrible hands began to squeeze her neck.

"WAIT," SAID THE other man.

She felt the hands ease, and felt Rockwell's trial, his strain to hold back his ferocity, to stop the flow of his lust for blood through his hands. The energy in his fingers slowed. She felt the blackness recede.

"Who are you, Sister?" the John Bull asked in Tibetan.

Sun Moon's head turned in Porter Rockwell's hands. Her mind spun in the opposite direction. *He spoke to me politely in my own tongue, the language of the Pöba.* Her eyes soaked up Sir Richard. *He called me* pomo, *younger sister, politely, properly, in my own language. Miracle.*

Her voice scratched out in her own tongue, "Greetings, *Gyenla,* Elder Brother. I am *Ani* Dechen Tsering." *Ani* was the word for nun, and her religious name meant Long Life of Great Virtue.

"You are a nun?"

"*Ani* Dechen Tsering of the convent at Zorgai." Her own language felt grateful on her tongue.

"You know this man?" The man's accent was pronounced, yet he spoke properly.

"He tried to rape me. I fought. So he gave me this scar by my left eye."

"Why does he want to harm you?"

She felt the energy of violence running through Rockwell's hands on her throat. *At any moment it will snap out as lightning and kill me, and I will fail Mahakala.*

Eyes still down, she swallowed and found the strength to speak. "He tried to rape me. I kicked him in the face. He cut me. He took an oath that if he ever saw me again, he would kill me." *Mahakala, does a warrior think it martial to fight with words?*

A long pause. Then, "Let her go."

For a moment Sun Moon did not understand the words. Suddenly she realized this Sir Richard had switched back to English. Her mind lifted and plummeted in waves and troughs.

"I'm going to kill the bitch," said Rockwell softly.

But so far the violence in your hands is only waiting.

"Let her go. She's a nun."

Rockwell cackled loudly, like a goose honking. "A nun. Good training for a whore." She felt his eyes turn back to her, and closed her own. "Now I'm going to squeeze. Squeeze your neck until you can't breathe, and the pieces of your neck break in my hands, and you kick and flop to get air, and you die."

She brought all her awareness toward his hands and stiffened the muscles in her neck with her whole will. She had no strength left for her arms or legs.

A GUNSHOT.

Hands dropped her.

She crumpled to the ground. She opened her eyes and looked up. Where the physical form of her killer had stood, she half expected to see empty air. But Porter Rockwell inhabited that space still.

"You bastard!"

"Withdraw your sidearm and drop it." From his saddle Sir Richard held a revolver straight at Porter Rockwell's chest.

"Stuff it up your ass."

Sir Richard enunciated slowly now. "Pull your sidearm out of your belt by the grip with thumb and forefinger only. Drop it. On the count of three. Or I will send lead through your lungs and out your back." The two men looked will at each other, and each knew. "One . . . two . . ."

Thump. The pistol rocked slightly on the sand.

Sun Moon sat up and rubbed her neck. She breathed. Air flowed through her neck and into her chest, sweet air.

She turned her head each way, then turned it twice more, testing. Finally she looked around to see where the shot had gone.

A saddled horse lay on the ground, flat, limp. The blood bay, beautiful and dead. Her heart twisted. Blood ran out the side of its head, just below its ear, down its neck, and into the dust.

"That was a fine horse."

"The next one is for you."

"In this country they hang people for stealing horses."

Sir Richard said, "So if I kill you, they can't do worse."

Porter Rockwell's left foot wiggled. She could feel his spirit wanting to leap at Sir Richard. She felt nothing at all from him toward her. She was dropped and forgotten. She rubbed her neck. She glanced toward the derringer on the sand. *Mahakala, grant me his life's blood.*

"Sister, don't try it," admonished Sir Richard.

Rockwell snickered. But he stood motionless in front of the motionless barrel of the gun.

"Start walking."

"Why are you defending a whore?"

"Start walking. She's a nun."

"I'll kill you. All three of you."

"Start walking. We'll keep your saddle and gear."

"I'll scalp you alive. You'll be able to feel the skin peeling back on your skull. I'll scalp her between the legs. I'll cut his . . ."

KA-BOOM! She saw the dirt fly between Rockwell's feet. She saw alarm leap into his face, and slowly recede.

Don't kill him! Her hands ached to touch his blood, to run wet with it. She wanted to hold her arms high and let it run down to her elbows and under her clothes.

She recoiled. *A-a-a-h-h! So that's how it feels to wish to shed another human being's blood. Mahakala, maybe I cannot . . .*

KA-BOOM! Dust spurted and whirled on the wind up into Rockwell's face. "I have three more shots in this revolver, six in the other, and one in the Hawkin. One will suffice, any one."

From the corner of her eye she saw Sir Richard slip his rifle out of its saddle sheath. His revolver never wavered.

Rockwell's feet moved. She felt as though his body went with them reluctantly. One step, another, another, pulling the body like a mule pulls a wagon. "I'll kill all three of you. You last, Burton, so you can watch. You last and slowest."

KA-BOOM!

She saw Rockwell's feet carry his body away, his back to them. "I'll chase you to the ends of the Earth. I'll go sight-seeing in goddamn China."

The three of them waited in silence, first listening to the *skitch* of Rockwell's footsteps on the sand, then watching his back until it disappeared.

Finally Sir Richard said, "Forgive me for this intrusion into your lives. I am Captain Richard Burton. Sister, will you pick up your derringer. Next time learn to use it before you try."

She spotted it beneath a sagebrush, picked it up, stuck it in her waistband.

A moment passed, Burton's eyes switching from Sun Moon to Asie and back. In his eyes she felt the import of the next words. "We'd best get along. He will be a formidable enemy."

PART TWO

WE SEEK REFUGE

CHAPTER NINE

1

Sir Richard was thinking that Rockwell couldn't follow us on foot. But we soon learned not to sell Orrin Porter Rockwell short. That man gave home to a monstrous spirit.

We struck northwest, parallel to the road that ran around the north end of the Great Salt Lake to join up with the California Trail.

Sweet gizzards, hadn't we spun like a top? First Moon and I were bound for Great Salt Lake City, made up to be an Indian and his wife. Now we were spun around but headed west. And we were in the dark, with hardly no possibles—just three or four days' food, and not enough water to last beyond the night.

I pondered it. On the one hand, Sun Moon did walk across this same road from City of Rocks almost to the City of the Saints. If a woman built like a twig could do it alone, surely we men could walk back. On the other hand, Porter Rockwell had only been a bogeyman in her mind then. Now he was stalking us like a mountain cat. We were weak as new lambs.

We stayed off the road, which was just good sense. "Rockwell could follow the road, but he'll have the devil's own time seeing our tracks at night." That was Sir Richard's figuring. Not that he believed for a moment that Rockwell would follow. "On foot? Without water?" he asked.

"No food, no weapons, across the alkali wastes and these dry, spiny mountains? Even I . . ."

The man's singular fault, if you haven't already figured it out, was his smugness. Wasn't he born to means, to culture, to understanding? Wasn't he an Oxford man? Wasn't he author of a bushel of books? Wasn't he British? Pretty much all white people feel something like that. Sometimes, the less excuse, the stronger they feel it. The British, sure to God, have raised it to an art.

We walked and rode and walked and rode, taking turns on the horses and on foot. The land was parched, but the evening was cool. We might have been heading into the devil knows what. Yes, Sir Richard was crazy to go. But maybe he had his reasons. I was crazy to go, and had no reason at all. Except that ever since I near drowned in the river, things had looked different to me. How? Couldn't say.

Within the hour we knew that Rockwell was right behind us, and having a fiendishly good time. He'd stand on ridges in the moonlight, where we couldn't help but see him. Once when he was outlined by the full moon rising behind, he spread his arms. He looked for all the world like a predator, about to launch into the night air, swoop down, and seize us with beak and talons. It gave me the shivers.

He cut loose. "Aw-ooh, aw-ooh, oow-oow, Aw-ooh!"

I can't spell how it sounded. It was the call of the beast. You could imagine it was a wolf crossed with an eagle crossed with a lion, but it was worse than that. It was the cry of the hunter, the call of the killer, and the cackle of the devil. It gave me triple shivers.

"Can you handle a rifle?" Sir Richard asked me.

"I will shoot him," injected Sun Moon, touching that derringer in her waistband. We were all mesmerized by the sight of Rockwell as predator.

Sir Richard had seen all the firearms expertise from Sun Moon he could stand. He held the Hawkin out to me. "Give it a try. It's too long a shot, but he needs the reminder."

I'd shot my foster brother's Hawkin from boyhood—meat for the pot. They're muzzle-heavy. This one was full stock, caplock, seventy-five to the pound. Since the distance must have been four hundred yards, the only thing that was going to get to Rockwell was the sound.

I knelt, used my knee for a rest, pulled the set trigger till it clicked, and squeezed the other. The report was just a piddle in the desert night.

Rockwell never moved. I saw nothing of what sagebrush, powdery alkali, or snake hole the lead may have crashed into. I half expected Rockwell to cut loose with his demonic cackle-cry. In my imagination it echoed off the rimrock and rattled mockingly between my ears.

"Hold on to the rifle," said Sir Richard. "You may need it."

Even now my bones remember that night. Walk, walk, walk. Through a dry wash, heavy underfoot. Up a side hill. Along a prickly ridge. Back into a dry wash. Across an alkali flat, mud sucking at my shoes. Across a sagebrush plain. Walk, walk, walk.

We led the pony and took turns riding Sir Richard's mount. The rider was the lookout. On every rise I'd stop, turn in the saddle, and look for Porter Rockwell. I saw him twice during the night. Each time cold lightning flickered up and down my spine.

The summer land was dry and cracked. So was my tongue. Worried, I kept my mouth away from the canteens all I could. We filled up with water at Bear River in the first hour, but all night we saw not a drop. Not long before dawn we came to the Little Malad River. A thin trickle made its way snaky-like toward the Salt Lake. The water could be drunk. But where would we find water again?

Sir Richard hauled out his own maps. He was a man for papers like you never saw. He carried maps and charts of my own country I'd have never guessed existed. He had a couple of books in his saddlebags. He had pen and paper to make notes on, which he did, morning, noon, and night. Sometimes I wondered if he saw anything on our journey besides blank paper, paper with words all over it, and the words he was always making up in his head. When we dug for water in a dry creek bed, thirsting, did Sir Richard feel thirsty? Or did he only get whatever description of it was a-borning in his mind? Did he taste the life-giving water? Or only his words for it? Which was real to him, the world or the words?

Anyway, maps said the next water was Deep Creek, twenty-five miles on, two days the way most wagons traveled. We knew we could make it—well, sort of knew. We all wondered when we would weaken, and Porter Rockwell would descend on us, singly or together, and perform a quiet act of murder. Would he even scavenge our bodies?

Finally the sky hinted at getting light behind us, just barely hinted. "I sleep," said Sun Moon. She turned and started scrambling up the steep mountainside. We watched. After a little I saw what she was headed for, a crevice. Those were the places she liked to slip into for rest.

The shadowy pockets in the rock stayed cool even in the middle of a summer day. Sir Richard and I followed. We took turns sleeping and standing guard with the rifle all day. We never saw Porter Rockwell. Even he had scarce chance of sneaking up on us there. He'd want to get our weapons before we could use them. He'd want to catch us unawares.

I'm sure he knew where we were. He was watching and waiting and biding his time.

2

Sir Richard shook me. I woke up quick, edgy. He spoke to Sun Moon. He'd let her sleep all day, without a turn at standing watch. He pointed toward the mouth of the canyon.

Out on the flat beyond I saw the road, the cut-off from Great Salt Lake City to the California Trail. Sir Richard handed me his Dolland. In its magnification I saw tents. One light wagon. Horses and mules hobbled. Men staking canvas over gear, some repairing equipment. Some gathering sage, one building a fire, one filling a pot with something to cook. A dozen men, maybe.

"We must go down there." So he'd been watching them set up camp for a while. It was his way to figure things out and then simply announce what we were going to do next.

"We stay alone," said Sun Moon.

Both of us jerked our heads toward her. We hadn't realized she was either awake or feeling feisty.

Annoyance flashed across Sir Richard's face—he wasn't used to being disputed by a woman, or by a heathen, and he didn't hardly care for that. I wondered how his uppitiness would augur for the future, since I was a wog and Sun Moon was both wog and woman. But Sir Richard had other parts to him, too—he was ever unpredictable. Sun Moon was a nun, and that meant something special to him.

"Sister," he said gently, "we are in an untenable position." I guessed what that big word meant. "If Rockwell wants to pull a sneak attack on us, he'll eventually catch us unawares. But he won't have to. He will get a weapon from some one of the groups passing on the trail, whether a stage, a freighter, miners, emigrants, or whatever. He'll steal it if he has to. Then he'll kill us one by one from a distance."

This argument made an impression on Sun Moon, I could see. It sure as hell impressed me—here came that cold lightning flickering up and down my spine again. It made me put my back flat up against a rock. Suddenly all the shadows laid by all the rocks on that mountain seemed longer and darker.

"So what we do with them?" asked Sun Moon. She didn't give a damn if Sir Richard was white, or male, or more'n twice as big as her.

"Come and we'll see so what," he said, half to himself. I could see his intellect at work. As I learned over and over that summer and fall, it was one wadee-doo of an intellect. Then, he spoke all saucy with confidence to Sun Moon, "Yes, come and I'll show you."

I felt a little queasy. It's all well and good to decide you're done with one way of life and ready to start another, like I did. But when you see the wagons and horses ready to leave for unknown places, your stomach wobbles a little.

Where were those wagons going? Washo? California? Who knew?

Where were we going to go?

"*Hallo the camp!*" The light was almost gone, and we didn't know how the guard would treat us.

"White men?" called a voice.

"Friends," boomed Sir Richard, evading the question.

"Come on in."

We walked close to the fire.

"May we join you?" asked Sir Richard. "We're in some distress."

"White men, my ass," said one fellow. "A John Bull and two dirty Injuns."

I wondered why he called us dirty. Sun Moon is the cleanest, neatest person I've known in this lifetime. I hadn't yet learned how white folk's minds work about people of color—they don't view, they pre-view.

"What trouble you got?" The speaker came forward, evidently the leader. He was about thirty, spade-bearded, tall, strong-looking, half-bald.

"We were set upon and robbed," said Sir Richard. The man was quicker with a lie than anyone I ever knew, and juicier.

"Dirty Injuns," said the previous voice in a high whine, like a screechy fiddle. I saw now it belonged to a fat fellow of about forty. His hair was wild, his clothes messed up, his lower pant legs caked with mud. His belly hung in folds big enough for wings. Fat even drooped over his ankles. No one in Utah Territory, I'd bet, could beat him for being dirty.

Sir Richard wisely made no comment on Fat Dirty's supposition that we were Indians. "If we could travel with you for safety," he said.

Half-Bald Leader nodded. "It won't hurt nothing," he said definitely but without any particular friendliness, and lowered himself onto a rock. "Set."

So there it was. We were bound for wherever the Californy Trail and the luck of the draw took us. I hoped it was the Washo diggings, which might be near where I came from.

All three of us moved closer to the fire, though the night was warm without it.

I studied the dozen men. Miners, for sure, though I didn't know enough yet to spot the pans, rockers, shovels, picks, red flannel shirts, and pants of jean or osnaburg as sure signs. They were no different from most others I'd seen heading for the diggings.

Then I noticed that Sun Moon acted like she was hiding behind me. I turned my head to her.

"Hs-s-st!" she whispered, spinning a finger to tell me to turn my head back to the front.

I did, but I murmured, "What's the matter?"

"Miners!" she whispered impatiently.

Then I understood. To her that meant Hard Rock City. Or at least men who thought of "Chinee" women strictly as hundred-men's-wives. What if they wanted to flip her straight onto her back? What if they'd heard about Tarim's reward? Would they want to haul her back for whatever reward Tarim put up? Easier to turn in a Chinee than pan for gold, they'd think, and more fun.

I got Sir Richard's eye and held it warningly.

He nodded in understanding. "Where do you boys hail from?" he asked. He could talk like ordinary folks when he wanted to. He didn't sound like he was pretending, either. He had the knack of talking just like anybody. Even the way he held his body and used his hands changed when he did it. Afterwards I found out from his books that he'd disguised himself as a Hindoo, a Persian, a Tibetan, and other such as that. Which musta been how he got good at it.

Well, the miners, they loosed their tongues. They were ready to talk like a cloud is ready to rain.

"Mostly we been in Californy," said Half-Bald Leader.

"Northern camps," said another.

" 'Bout went broke," put in a third.

"We seed the elephant, though," said Fat Dirty.

Sun Moon slipped from my back to my side. While she talked but little, Sun Moon, she noticed everything.

They went on and on about the diggings. Having been raised a Mormon, I didn't much care for stories of gold. Brigham taught his people that looking for the earth to throw up gold for you is damn foolishness. I picked that up, and keep it still.

Learned a lot sitting at that campfire that night. Learned what happens to white people when the subject is money. They told how there were too many miners for the gold, no matter if it was a bonanza. They told how the big companies with lots of money to buy machinery for digging and hoses for washing could get rich, but a common man couldn't make a living. Two of them told how they got beat out of a good claim. They told how prices ran high, "so high they push your balls up into your stomach," said one. Every two or three minutes, Fat Dirty would pitch in with, "We seed the elephant, though." Which sounded like it made things OK with him.

What I remember mainly is that the talk of gold made these men's faces get red, their teeth show a lot, their eyes gleam like candles with those mirrors behind 'em, and their bodies throw off heat like fire. It's a whoopteedoo of a reaction. Someone ought to study it and explain it. Or put it in tins and heat houses with it. Indian people lived around all that gold and silver in the Washo District for centuries and never gave a hoot about it. Still don't.

Another item I learned: If a man of color keeps his mouth shut, white folks think he's dumb, or ignorant, or the like. I'd never had this experience. I'd lived entirely with white people my whole life and had always been part of the family, so to speak. Mormons treat Indians OK—it's Brigham's policy. Since these white men didn't know me, though, and to them I was only an Injun, they talked in front of me like I was one of the mules. That's handy to know. Fellow could learn a lot of secrets sitting there looking half-human. Matter of fact, over the years I have.

"There any calico in Salt Lake?"

It was Fat Dirty, addressing Sir Richard, who shook his head no. "All the women in Salt Lake are spoken for, and kept close. It's the only city I've ever been where a man can't buy a woman."

Then I knew what "calico" meant. Sun Moon squirmed next to me, and her agitation felt like prickly heat.

Fat Dirty grunted, wiggled his behind, and broke wind loudly. "We're loco," he whined in the direction of Half-Bald Leader.

"We've done talked about this," said the leader. He glanced sideways at Sir Richard. "I'm going to Salt Lake to sell my outfit and catch the stage east. The others are gonna sniff the wind for gold a while longer."

"There are new strikes in Idaho," Sir Richard said.

I took a deep breath, and Sun Moon claw-gripped my wrist.

"We want somep'n *brand*-new," whined Fat Dirty.

Sir Richard nodded wisely, and nodded again. I wanted to ask him, "What the *hell* is going on?"

Then another spoke up. "All gold is fool's gold," said a high, soft old man's voice.

I'd scarce noticed him before. He was skinny, crooked as a twig, and looked frail, except for his long silver hair and beard. This hair was spectacular, so long you could have tied the ends between his legs, and flowing and handsome. He looked like a picture of a wizard I saw in a book.

"Did you ever hear," he began, "about the gang of miners that went to heaven?"

"Yeah, Zach, we done heard it," put in Fat Dirty. "Twenty times."

"When they got to the Pearly Gates," this Zach went on unheeding, "St. Peter told them, 'Sorry, you can't come in—no more room.'

"The head miner took thought and asked, 'Any miners in there?'

" 'Of course!' replied St. Peter.

" 'Ifn I clear some out, can we get in?'

"St. Peter pulled at his beard a moment. 'I guess so,' he answered.

" 'Back in a minute,' said the head miner.

"Ten minutes later out came a passel of men through the Pearly Gates, pushing and jostling to get gone. They charged right on past St. Peter, waving picks and shovels and shouting in excitement, and stampeded straight down to the Other Place. The miners waiting to get in looked at each other, cocked their heads, nodded, and headed right after 'em.

"The head miner come out of the gates and stopped by St. Peter's side. They were looking at the empty spot where his *compañeros* had stood a moment before.

" 'Well,' said St. Peter, 'there's room enough now. But how did you work that?'

"The head miner grinned. 'Spread some tales,' he said. 'Said color was spotted in the River Styx.'

" 'My, my,' said St. Peter. 'Those men will endure hell for a mere rumor of fortune.'

" 'Yep,' said the head miner, nodding sagely and still grinning.

" 'You may go on in,' said St. Peter, and spread one arm wide toward the Gates.

"The head miner shuffled his feet and wagged his head. After a while he said, 'Naw, I guess not.' He shouldered his gear.

" 'Wait!' cried St. Peter. 'You spread those tales yourself. They're false.'

" 'Yep,' said the head miner, 'but you never know.' And started for the place below."

When everyone got ready to spread their blankets, Sun Moon put her face right into Sir Richard's. "These men go Salt Lake. We go other way. You know all time?"

"Yes," he said with aplomb. "I knew which direction they're going."

"Why?" She shook the sleeve of his shirt. "Not safe! Porter Rockwell there, many Mormons, much help for him, much danger for us."

"I have a friend who will protect us, I'm confident," said Sir Richard. He laid his blankets on one side of Sun Moon's and nodded me toward the opposite side.

"What friend?" insisted Sun Moon. She didn't take to putting her welfare in someone else's hands, particularly not a man, and more particularly not a white man.

He turned to her majestically. "His name," he said, "is Brigham Young, known as the Lion of the Lord. We will ask him for sanctuary."

CHAPTER TEN

1

"*PORTER ROCKWELL IS* trying to kill us." Burton watched most carefully for change in Brigham Young's face. He could see none. "To our very faces he took an oath to torture, dismember, and kill us."

I cannot fail now. Burton had waited until the others left the room. It was high-handed, certainly, but he had gotten by with it. He had demanded to see the Lion of the Lord immediately, and then asked his courtiers and ministers to leave. *It worked.* To drive all before you with the wind of your self-certainty, that was in Burton's blood.

Still no change in the great man's expression. For any statesman one key to handling great matters with aplomb, surely, was to be surprised by nothing. The Prophet's eyes ran deliberately over Asie and Sun Moon. Suddenly the two looked unprepossessing to Burton, even disreputable. A leonine eyebrow raised in Burton's direction. He had no idea what it meant.

The story was quickly told. Sun Moon was a Buddhist nun, shanghaied to this country to work as a prostitute. She had been taken in bondage to Hard Rock City, where Porter Rockwell had won at gambling the right to be the first man to mount her. *We are doing well. The Prophet despises both gambling and whoring.* She fought for her honor, and managed to hold off Rockwell momentarily. He cut her, giving her that scar, and promised that if ever he saw her again, he would kill her.

Burton listened to the sound of his own voice in the small office. It made his knees want to wiggle. This story was as strange as anything in *A Thousand and One Nights,* which he himself meant to bring into English as exotica. Yet their lives depended on it. In its defense plausibility could not be advanced, only truth.

The Prophet merely regarded Sun Moon. Sir Richard's ward—for so he perceived her—ran a forefinger along the rut of her scar, perhaps unconsciously. Would the great man have sympathy for a woman at hazard? Or contempt for a woman who refused to bear children? A minion of a heathen religion?

Burton looked at Sun Moon and Asie and felt admiration. His face was open, American. Hers was hard with a half-successful attempt to hide her fear. *Terror,* Burton told himself. *The young woman must have been awash in terror for a year or more.* To them, this adventure was no game, but life and death.

"Is this true, Sister?" asked the Prophet.

"Just so," said Sun Moon firmly.

"Exactly true?" the Prophet pressed. His few words ran with huge energy. Burton had heard that sometimes in cases of adultery Brigham Young suspended a sentence of death in favor of a tongue-lashing. Burton would have hated to receive such a word-whipping.

"*Just* so," Sun Moon answered again.

The Lion of the Lord turned to Burton. "Tell me once more what happened when you and Rockwell chanced on these two on the road."

Burton did. His account was deliberately simple and factual. He felt sure the Prophet would despise any exaggeration or fancifulness.

When the brief tale ended, Brigham Young let the silence sit. He regarded each of the three of them in turn and let the silence grow steadily, as a hot and oppressive desert sun rises to zenith.

Burton found himself jiggling with foolish hopes. *Remember your back pain and think of me as your Androcles.* He glanced sideways at his young companions. *I have brought you into the Lion's den,* he thought. He could feel his own faith wavering. Presidents and potentates did not become great through sentiment. *I have thrown us at this man's mercy.*

Burton sighed. It was true, he admitted to himself, that only desperation had brought him here. Hiding from the leader of the infamous Danites in the sanctuary of Brigham Young—preposterous. Rockwell and the Danites were the instruments of the Church. Mothers probably used Porter Rockwell's name to frighten their children into good behavior.

Burton found himself perspiring. Hope seesawed with despair.

"Please come with me," said President Young.

The Lion of the Lord rose stiffly—Burton noted that his back needed skilled fingers once more—and exited. Down a hall they all went, out into a garden, through flowers to another building.

The Prophet mounted some stairs, opened a door, and left it to his visitors to follow his massive form. Burton gulped. *Are we going into Lion House itself?* Brigham Young's residence was next to his office building.

"Brother Young," said a middle-aged woman. "Brother Young," echoed a young beauty. The two were evidently supervising the preparation of a luncheon.

"Mrs. Twiss," said the Prophet. "Sister Abigail. These are our friends Captain Burton, Sister Sun Moon, and Brother Asie. They will be staying with us a few days, Mrs. Twiss. Whatever rooms you think fitting."

Captain Richard Burton blanched. On four continents he had seldom been so surprised, or so delighted. *I am being invited into the most secret of chambers, into the very harem of Brigham Young.* For the first time in two decades, perhaps, his deeply tanned skin looked pale enough to be English.

The Prophet said, "We will see to your comfort and your safety." Then the great man indulged himself in a small smile. "Even Porter Rockwell," he said, "has no access to my bedrooms."

For a moment the simple kitchen scene spun in Captain Burton's mind, and he felt woozy.

Mrs. Twiss led them up a set of stairs to the second floor. Seething with curiosity, Burton noted a long, handsomely furnished parlor, with a floral Brussels carpet, mahogany tables, a rosewood piano, a melodeon, a woodstove, a velvet sofa, and gilt chairs. Across the long hall were rooms that appeared to be private. *Bedrooms for the wives,* he thought, and his mind spun with questions.

Up more stairs to the third floor, through a long parlor partitioned into receiving areas. Private rooms stretched in each direction, a score or two dozen by Burton's guess. Compared to the second floor, this one was plain and homely.

Mrs. Twiss opened a door to two identical, connected rooms with high, narrow Gothic windows facing the street. *Can this woman be one of his wives?* Burton's mind leapt all around the possibility. Mrs. Twiss was fortyish, plump, amiable, a bundle of motherly cheer—*and I cannot not imagine her inspiring lust in so virile a man as the Prophet.*

"Dinner is at five," she said. "Very promptly at five." He watched the round, matronly bottom of Mrs. Twiss as she bustled out of the room and closed the door behind her.

The three friends looked at each other, safe for the first time in days. Sun Moon sank into a chair.

Suddenly the door scraped open again. Sun Moon jumped up, and Burton saw the eyes of a bolting deer. "Would you care for anything you don't see?"

"A lamp for reading and writing," said Burton.

"Of course."

I will fill pages and pages with scandal and delectation.

He looked at his companions. *I wonder how long we can stay. Safely.*

2

WHILE HIS FRIENDS napped, Richard Burton wrote in his journal:

> *At last Sun Moon has told me more of her story. I think she broke her silence, in part, for the luxury of speaking her own language, and hearing it spoken back. She fingered her scar often as she talked. She does not realize that it makes her not less attractive but much more—the first mark of life on a cloistered existence, a mark of courage in the face of violence. I admire her.*
>
> *She comes from the plains of Kham, far in the northeast of Tibet, of which I know only by report. Though the Tibet I know is high, dry plateaus surrounded by ranges of great mountains, she says her home country is a well-watered highland, lush with grass and wildflowers. Her convent is associated with the monastery at Zorgai, widely known for the tradition of scholarship in literature and philosophy. Zorgai is but a few days travel from the Chengdu, capital of the Chinese province Sichuan.*
>
> *Entering the convent* (ani gompa *or* tsunpo) *as a mere child, she was thus shorn of family. Now she is stripped of all life's*

small accommodations, even a flask of holy water, a rosary of 108 beads, and a prayer cylinder. Surely she also misses the brown robes she keeps hidden.

Though she avoided my inquiry about her abduction (how I long to lure that story from her!), she specified at length her doctrinal instruction, the memorizing and recitation of texts, the rigorous examinations which she stood, her beginning in the discipline of meditation. She stated, though, that her daily meditative practice has been intermittent in the time that has passed since her abduction, and admitted that she is a comparative beginner in the practice. She seems more the intellectual than the contemplative.

A fascinating incongruity then—a nun whose religious strength may not be the state of her consciousness, the supreme awareness of oneness that proceeds from meditation, but her learning, a creature not of spirit but intellect.

Sometimes anger and violence inhabit her eyes—for which none could blame her! Abducted, perhaps raped, enslaved, attacked by an infamous killer, and now hounded by him. In these misadventures has her faith been shaken? Affirmed? Does she abide yet in the dark night of the soul, seeking, seeking, and as yet seeing only darkness?

Her traveling companion, Asie Taylor, might be the Tibetan instead of Sun Moon, with his tawny coloring, round facial structure, and physiognomy. Where she is often closed to the scrutinizing eye, he is open-faced, easy, open in his emotions, an amiable fellow traveler, good-hearted, curious, showing a trusting spirit, bearing hardship cheerfully, like lamas I have known. Thus this irony: Asie has more of the spiritual serenity which is the object of meditation than even the nun. Perhaps his spirit is his strength! Perhaps her intellect is hers! Oh, delicious!

However, he is not quite *at ease. In many postures of body, gestures of arms, and hesitations of speech is the pull of something he seeks, yearns for. That something is churning in Asie Taylor, keeping him from the serenity which is his nature. Yet what goal could surpass serenity? I know not. Neither does Asie Taylor.*

3

Burton put away his pen and slid the notebook into a jacket pocket. Asie was sleeping. Burton listened to his quiet, even, peaceful breathing and felt envious. He was often sleepless—sometimes he barely slept for months on end. Often that was because he was afraid for his life. Such was the fate of a spy among enemies. The last year, though, he had suffered the pangs of hell for another reason—a reason he had in common with far more ordinary men than he—his wife, whose name was Isabel.

He got up, walked to the high, narrow window, and looked out unseeing onto South Temple Street. Burton had known Isabel for a decade, meeting her first in the south of France, where he loved to go, then in Italy, then in England, whose society he at once despised and longed for acceptance in. She was his ideal of feminine beauty, beauty of face, of form, and of soul. He courted her. She responded to his feelings with similar emotion. Praise be to Allah, not just sentiment but passion! He asked her to marry him. Her family were opposed—they were Catholic, his Church of England. (Praise be to Allah, no Britons knew what faith Burton actually embraced!) Though he converted formally to Catholicism, and Isabel accepted his proposal, the family still opposed the marriage.

Then he descended truly into hell. They were engaged, but Isabel refused to set a date for the wedding. She wanted to wait until her mother acceded. Wait and wait. Years now, torturous years. Burton knew Isabel's mother would never abandon her opposition. Meanwhile, he had got to be forty years old. He wanted marriage. He was frustrated.

Richard Burton had copulated and cohabited with many, many women. In the East women were available, sometimes easier to get than clean drinking water. He wanted Isabel. He had not touched her, and would not before the nuptials. He nearly went mad with frustration. When he came to America the first time, he gave her an ultimatum. On his return they would be married with dispatch, or he would break the engagement, and they would never see each other again.

She made her choice. They were married.

His marriage taught Burton what Dante had not imagined—that a man could at the same moment be in paradise and descend to a lower circle of hell.

Isabel in herself was everything he had hoped for, passionate, intelligent, vitally interested in his adventures, enthusiastic about his writing, dedicated to his career.

She demanded fidelity, which was no surprise, but was difficult. He was not a man to keep his passions within. She insisted that he give up cannabis, hashish, laudanum, and other journeys into the lotus state. And she asked that he cease drinking hard liquor, and be content with the solace of wine.

Not unreasonable, he had told himself at first, for he did love her, and not exceedingly difficult, save for three factors:

The first was that he was naturally clandestine, a lover of keeping secrets.

The second was the necessity of keeping his religious life hidden from view of everyone, even his wife. Burton was a Sufi, a member of the passionately mystical Persian sect of Islam. This devotion required certain customs and rites. One demand of Sufism was concealment: No one outside your family must know of your devotion and practices. In Burton's case, his family was forbidden as well. So he turned a false face not only to his enemies but to his countrymen, the family he was born to, and even his wife.

Some of his religious practice he could pass off as mere eccentricity: He never touched food with his left hand. He shaved his body hair, all of it. He never took the name of God in vain, even among his profane fellow officers. He gave alms generously.

Other practices were trickier to hide: He knelt facing Mecca and prayed five times a day. He observed the Feast of Ramadan in the ninth lunar month, meaning that he did not eat during daylight hours and in that month permitted himself no indulgences whatsoever. Making his hajj (pilgrimage) to Mecca was a fine device on his part—he had gone under the guise of a daring episode of espionage for his government.

The third factor was the trickiest: Burton suspected sometimes that he was quite mad, and that he had become a sensualist and libertine to control the madness. So Isabel's fetters upon his indulgences, intended to ensure sanity in their lives, might well loose his demons.

He had promised her that he would abide by these principles of good sense. Then he had gone out to Fernando Po alone, irked at such an ignominious posting. For a year he had written his pages, kept his journal, practiced his religion, dispensed with the easy tasks at the consulate, and followed his regime of sensible behavior.

Then the mission to America. In New Orleans he maintained sobriety, except for the occasional brandy. In St. Louis he had kept it up, except for laudanum. In Salt Lake he had no opportunity to do otherwise. Yet he felt his demons clanking their chains.

It is discipline that keeps a life in order, he told himself.

First pray. Burton washed himself in the basin provided. He got out his compass and calculated the direction of Mecca. He spread a prayer rug on the floor between the beds. He took off his shoes, knelt on the rug facing Mecca, and recited the great favorite of all Muslim prayers, the Sura 1:

> In the name of Allah the merciful, the compassionate. Praise be to Allah, the lord of the worlds, the merciful, the compassionate, the ruler of the judgment day! Thee we serve and Thee we ask for aid. Guide us in the right path, the path of those to whom Thou art gracious; not of those with whom Thou art wroth; nor of those who err.

Now he went to his traveling cases and removed a phial. He held it to the dusky light. Tincture of opium, laudanum. It had the singular advantage of being easily available in America, from every chemist's shop and every army surgeon. Since it was a usual treatment for diarrhea, any traveler would be expected to carry it. Gratifyingly, it contained two of his necessary elixirs, opium and alcohol. *As long as I keep the use under control . . .*

He drank deeply. He went and lay down on his bed. Before he floated away to the land of Xanadu, he pictured Isabel in his mind. He said to her, *You do not understand.*

THE NEXT MORNING the three travelers borrowed an atlas from Brother Young and inspected Asia. Asie was quiet as Burton and Sun Moon showed him Tibet. Burton pointed out the great mountains that define the region topographically, and the great rivers that flow from the Tibetan plateau and become the life blood of the countries below. He traced the Indus and the sacred Ganges, and told of his travels in India, the Hind, and Persia. Asie's eyes, though, were for Kham and the long river route Sun Moon traveled across China. He ran his finger across the vast blue of the Pacific Ocean from China to San Francisco.

The afternoon Burton spent observing the Young household and writing furiously again in his notebook. Journals were his secret treasure, the ore of his books.

As a writer and spy Burton was caught in a contradiction: His life abounded in real incidents and characters he could not publish.

He delighted in jolting British sensibilities with truths they did not want to hear. Whoever had not been offended by his writing about native mistresses, courtesans, prostitutes, boys for hire, and the like, would be scandalized by his eventual translation of the *Kama Sutra.* He had told many other truths his countrymen were unwilling to hear, even going so far as to advocate passionately the idea that females could and should enjoy sex.

Yet these notes about the domestic life of Brigham Young represented his dilemma. This he could not publish. He held up his pen in exasperation. *Damn all.*

Yet Captain Richard Burton had a splendid secret. One day, when he was in the grave beyond everyone's reach, he would tell all. All about the East India Company. All about England's foolish, self-defeating, blind, murderous, and racist ways in India. All about the British Army. All about the Royal Geographic Society, sponsor of many a Briton's journey of exploration. All about his colleagues and competitors in the mapping of Africa. All about the insanity of the African slave trade. And all, certainly, about his host in the City of the Saints, and his two dozen wives.

With the taste of revenge fresh on his tongue, he dipped his pen.

Surely the domestic arrangements of the world's most famous or notorious polygamist are of interest. Brigham Young's principal residence is Lion House, so called from the lion of stone reclining above the entrance. Here live the greater number of his wives and children. In the companion residence adjacent, called Beehive House, live at least two more wives. Additionally, wives and children live at his farm and several other residences at Great Salt Lake City or within an easy ride thereof. I gather that others yet live in residences in remote parts of the Territory.

Though gentiles luridly imagine otherwise, the atmosphere of Lion House is not voluptuous as the harem of a sultan, conducive to carnal fantasy, or even in the slightest sensual. A male is apt to feel smothered by the femininity of the furnishings, and neutered by the sober and stark spirit of devotion. After inhab-

iting there for several days, I easily believed that the Prophet, as he declared of himself, "never entered into the order of plurality of wives to gratify passion." His purpose is purely and simply to "raise up a righteous generation."

(As an aside I will say that Americans generally and Mormons in particular are as misguided as we English in their view of female sexuality. In England the word is, "Lie still and think of Empire." In America in general and Utah in particular it is, "Men have orgasms and women have children.")

An unmistakable pecking order reigns. Emmeline Free is the queen bee. Handsome, tall, graceful, of fair complexion, she is the mother of eight of the Prophet's children. At dinner she sits at Brother Young's right hand at the head table, and he favors her with his conversation, his smiles, and his glances. At his left sits Eliza R. Snow, a former wife of Joseph Smith himself and therefore much honored in Deseret and in Lion House. Guests are also favored with the head table, except for Sun Moon, Asie, and me. Wishing to avoid dangerous gossip, he placed us at one of the two lower tables, as though we were guests of one of his lesser wives. I am grateful for his perspicacity, for some sense reminds me that we are not safe. (No, not safe, though the faces of my companions show a touching longing for sanctuary.)

At long tables running away from the head table sit most of the other wives and children, and the childless wives. Their menus are plainer than those at the same meal at the head table. Though I have been unable, even by devious questioning, to determine how many wives the Lion has taken to himself, nearly twenty made their appearance at dinner at one time or another during our stay, and so presumably live in Lion House or the adjacent residences, Beehive House and White House . . .

4

"*CAPTAIN BURTON?*" *THE* speaker was a tall woman with a waspish mouth.

Burton got to his feet, inconspicuously closing his notebook and concealing it in a pocket.

"I'd . . . I'm Harriet Washer, the fourth wife."

She identifies herself by a number! He inclined his head as a way of accepting this self-introduction. "Would you speak with my son Oswald a little?"

The lad stepped up alongside his mother. He was fourteen or fifteen from appearance, strong-looking, and of bestial aspect, and now of downcast expression. Burton regarded the mother. She had the demeanor of a woman who has endured much, none of it in silence.

"Sit down, lad," and Burton took his chair again. "What do you wish?"

The boy slouched up to Burton's writing table, pulled out a chair grumpily, and clomped his bottom down onto it. He radiated ill spirit so strongly Burton could have bagged it and sold it by the pound. "Ma says I oughta find out about the real world from you."

"Real world?" Burton refused to glance up at the mother.

She intruded anyway. "The world outside Lion House, outside Mormonism, outside Deseret. The normal world. I grew up in New York, I know what I'm talking about."

Burton regarded her. She looked like she knew her own mind, at least, and that perhaps to a fault. "Madam, will you sit with us?" He indicated another hard-backed chair with a nod. She took it.

"What would you like to know, Oswald?"

The lad shrugged. Finding out about the "real world" certainly wasn't his idea. He ambled his eyes sideways at his mother, and her look reprimanded him. "Wha's it like, the rest of the world? Special the big cities?"

"What do you think it's like?"

"The old man says it's all whoring."

"The old man?" Burton was scarcely prepared to believe . . .

"Brother Young," put in the mother.

"Tha's what I call him," said the lad, "the old man. To his face."

"What does he call you?"

"Reprobate," replied the lad quickly.

Burton wondered whether Oswald knew what the word meant, or how to spell it. *And in the mind of an adolescent lad, does a land of whoring sound like hell or heaven?* "Um-m-m," said Burton. *What the devil?* "Is that all of Brother Young's description?"

"Whoring, sleeping with other men's wives, and divorcing."

Burton raised an eyebrow.

"And gambling, robbing, and murdering," Oswald added.

Burton nodded. The lad had adopted Brother Young's custom of never using a circumspect word where a blunt one would do. The Prophet's sermons sometimes scandalized the more delicate members of his flock.

Good God, what a question! What is the world like? Burton recalled the teaching of his Dharma masters. "The spectacle of life is vast and varied," he said. "It has everything you can imagine in it—fidelity and adultery, generosity and robbery, self-sacrifice and murder, loyalty and betrayal, love and hate, creation through art and destruction by war. The Wheel of Life, some wise men have called it."

The lad gave a look of disgust at his mother—wondrously unalloyed, twenty-four-karat disgust. Burton sat in admiration of so pure and riotous a feeling.

"Oswald needs to hear about books, poetry, culture, the theater, music, philosophy. You are an author," Harriet Washer said baldly.

Burton eyed Oswald. The lad didn't give a damn, the mother was owed nothing, but perhaps there was something to learn. . . . He cast his voice into a tone of quotation:

> " 'This goodly frame, the earth, seems to me a sterile promontory; this most excellent canopy, the air, look you, this brave o'er-hanging firmament, this majestical roof fretted with golden fire, why, it appears no other thing to me but a foul and pestilent congregation of vapors.' "

"That's an odd thing to quote to Oswald. Ugly, it is."

Burton sighed. "Why have you come to me, Madam?"

"My boy needs to know there's more, more than this." She looked around her with contempt.

An impertinent question arose. However, Burton was first of all a writer. "Are you not content here, Madam?"

"Content?" The word sounded like a whoop in her throat. "Humbug. Mormonism, polygamy, the whole of it, the lot of it, humbug." She sneered, showing long teeth, like a horse's.

Burton sat stupefied.

"Are you shocked? Poor gentile. Poor John Bull that knows nothing.

Do you think none of us can see beyond the tip of Brother Young's nose? Everyone in this house knows what I think."

"Are many of your"—Burton searched for the word—"sisters of similar mind?"

"Pshaw, no, he's got 'em all bamboozled."

"You, um, are a skeptic now, Madam. Were you always?"

Harriet Washer looked sheepish. "No. I didn't know any better at first. They don't educate women, and they don't want us to think for ourselves. But after a while a brain just naturally sets to work."

The lad Oswald was staring out the window. *Not that lad's brain, I'll wager.*

"So your sisters are true to the faith."

Harriet Washer nodded yes. "Which don't mean they put up with Brigham. Not necessarily. Emmeline Free does. Lucy and Clara Decker do. They make babies like factories, every two or three years. But some of us can't stand him."

"Us, Madam?"

"Brigham Young hasn't been in my bedroom since Oswald was born. Nine months before, matter of fact."

"Why do you not go elsewhere with your son?"

She eyed him mockingly. "You know darn well. The Danites. Hear you had a run-in with Porter Rockwell yourself."

Burton stood to dismiss them. *Damn all.* The hairs on his back and bottom prickled with the sense of danger. *To die in battle would be one thing, but to be assassinated, perhaps in sleep . . .*

"You're a spy yourself, ain't you?" said Mrs. Washer with a clever look.

Damn all! Burton opened his mouth to speak rudely. He believed in the saying, "A gentleman is never rude unintentionally," but now he felt sufficient cause.

Words from the opposite hall stopped him. "Captain Burton!"

Two young ladies and a chap, with Asie and Sun Moon in tow. Burton was trapped.

"I am Gracie Johnson Young." As she spoke, her eyes slapped Harriet Washer's face. Mrs. Washer tried to look amused. "This is my sister Ima Herbert Young and her friend Harold Jackson."

The wife and daughter dropped their duel of eyes, neither the victor. What about this young man—was he a suitor?

"We just . . . wanted to meet you." Ima Young giggled as she spoke.

Burton gave the ladies a shallow bow and shook the lad's hand. Burton judged them as about sixteen. *Ripe for marriage, by the standards of the Saints. Brother Young's daughters. My, wouldn't that increase eligibility?*

"Pleased to make your acquaintance."

"Would you care to see the garden?" said Harold. "Our people are especially interested in horticulture."

Burton eyed Sun Moon and Asie. The two had not ventured from the rooms since they arrived, except for meals. They consented with their glances. "Delighted."

Gracie Johnson Young led the way, Burton at the rear. He sighed inaudibly. He was more interested in the management of the harem than in flowers.

SUN MOON WANTED very much to walk in the flower garden. She had looked and looked at it from the windows of her bedroom. Compared to her home country, the America she had seen was dry, hard, barren of life. The plains of Kham were a land of snowy mountains and verdant grasslands. Miles and miles of it were marsh, impassable to strangers. Summer was the season the convent permitted her and other young aspirants to go home and be with their families, and that was when the grasslands were a sea of wildflowers, vibrant reds, strong purples, rich yellows, delicate pinks and whites, an exuberance of color, Earth showing off her extravagant fecundity. Sun Moon felt homesick.

She had never seen a formal garden of flowers, though. She swallowed hard, and forbade herself to remember. At the monastery in Chengdu, the capital of Sichuan, just a week from her family's summer camp, were celebrated flower gardens. So she had persuaded her parents . . .

No! she told herself, and felt the iron band within her throat tighten.

She followed the Mormons into the garden, Sir Richard just behind. The August sun slapped her like a half-rough hand. It was harsh, this sun. This country seemed poor beside her home. Dry earth, dry skies. Barren plains surrounded by barren mountains. The Mormons had learned to grow flowers and vegetables by diverting the creeks through ditches along their streets and onto their gardens, which was admirable, but the land did not seem to want to be fruitful.

She reached out to a rose. The petals were so soft, the fragrance so full. *Compassion for all sentient beings.* All monks and nuns dedicated their lives to such compassion. She had always felt herself deficient in this feeling. However splendidly she mastered learning, her compassion stayed more a precept of the mind than an inclination of the heart.

She imagined the struggles of this flower, to break out of the hard shell of the seed, to lie still in the cold ground, to soften in water and expand, to form a slender stem, to accept the sunlight and convert it somehow into strength, to endure the drying, buffeting winds, to reach upward and upward and upward and finally to express the joy of living in a blossom.

She imagined all that, rehearsed it in her mind. Yet she knew she did not powerfully feel kinship with the flower, or other creatures, or other people, even herself. For the young girl who entered the convent, who spent long hours memorizing, who was often cold, who sometimes longed to be touched and never was, she felt impatience, intolerance of weakness. For the young woman who was abducted, drugged, shipped abroad, enslaved, she felt . . . the iron band.

She reached out stiffly and cupped the rose in her hands. She wondered what it was like to send out pollen, to receive pollen, to bring forth new creatures, to make seeds and send them out into the world, to germinate and grow. Her mind felt for her womb, her unused womb, but could not find it. *And I have no feelings about that.*

She looked at the two young Mormon women chatting with Sir Richard, girls really. They would marry soon, they would procreate, they would act as vessels for the journeys of souls back into this world. They would act as the instruments of life.

I will never find out how it feels. Her vow of chastity was sufficient reason, one of the five first vows every monk or nun takes. Now she had another reason. *Mahakala, teach me that destruction is creation.*

She breathed in the essence of the rose. She noticed her breath, just as she did in meditation. With the same fine attention she noticed the scent. It felt not only sweet but moist, fruitful. *Fertile.*

Something in her belly pulsed.

"*I AM ESPECIALLY* fond of roses," said Gracie. I was all a-jump at getting to walk through the garden. Few Saints had ever been Gracie-ed with this privilege. Even when I'd been a sort-of Saint, I was a dirty

Injun, and dee-definitely not a candidate for a tour of Brother Young's roses conducted personally by his daughters. Sun Moon wouldn't have been one either, because she wasn't any more white and delightsome than me. So we were up against white-folkism again. Sir Richard was white. British. A man of rank. Important with a capital I. They escorted him, they showed him, and we tagged along.

Gracie pointed out the highlights to us. I never paid half attention, stuff about blooms under two inches or over four inches or in between. All the different colors, red, pink, yellow, white, lavender, and how they were mixed together to delight the eye. The Youngs had roses that were shrubs or little trees, roses that climbed on trellises, roses that were hedges, every kind you can imagine and then some.

Gracie did tickle me. She set out to explain how hybrids are made, especially some called hybrid perpetuals, which were the latest item on the block. "You cross roses by taking two blossoms . . ." And here she got stumped. I couldn't figure why until Harold pitched in.

"The gardener designates one as male and the other female, one male one female, it doesn't matter which." I could see by the wild light in Harold's that the words "male" and "female" were just too indelicate for Gracie's dainty lips. Harold was as tickled by this as me, and I recognized a kindred spirit. He went on. "Remove the petals and stamens from the female. When the male produces pollen, you transfer it by hand to the female. Result? Something new under the sun." He said it like a new kind of rose was the finest thing you could imagine. But I had never eaten a flower (I've eat far stranger since, by your lights) and had no plans to try.

"Stamens?" asked Sun Moon. She didn't usually speak up.

"The male part," said Harold.

"In Sanskrit the *lingam,*" put in Sir Richard. I don't think any of us knew what that meant. "In Tibetan the *dorje.*"

"Pollen?" Sun Moon went on, which was real inquisitive for her.

"What comes out that does the fertilizing," said Harold. Now he was antsy.

And I was antsy. Not for the same reason. Gracie pointed off somewhere and said something gay to Sir Richard, I didn't hear what. They started that way. I turned in front of Sun Moon and held her eye. I nodded my head sideways. We were beginning to get our signals down pretty well by then. She nodded yes, and we wandered off, looking for all the world like we were just turning to another bush of flowers. *It was time.* Or so I thought.

"WHAT DO YOU think about that?" I asked, stalling. My legs had the willy-woollies. Those funny pains were saying, "No, no, don't try it."

Sun Moon smiled at me. God, I loved her smile. She didn't mean to get drawn into small talk, which was part of what I loved about her. Right now that love was bothering me. My body was near panting. Maybe that talk about stamens and pollen and breeding had hotted me up. Near feverish, I blurted it out. "Sun Moon, I am powerful drawn to you."

Something Jeehosaphat funny happened in her eyes. What she said was, "I am a nun."

That put a foot in my chest, hard. "I, I . . ." I couldn't bring myself to look at her. I stared at the ground in front of my feet where we were trundling along. I couldn't help thinking, *You are a nun, but are you a virgin? Do you have experience of what Sir Richard calls* lingams? *Do you want to? Or do you want to shrivel and die an old maid?* I was and am ashamed of those thoughts.

I flicked my eyes sideways at her and right back down. I gave myself a lecture. Probably she didn't want any experience of *lingams.* Sure bet she didn't.

Maybe she special doesn't like the idea of mine. Which seemed natural enough. It's a peculiar-looking thing. No reason to think it might please anyone besides me, and pleasing me was a secret.

"I just wanted you to know," I said.

"I am going back to my home," she said in a stiffish tone.

Somehow in those words I took a hint of hope. "I have feelings for you," I said.

Now she just walked along silent. Silence was one of the things Sun Moon was best at. My eyes slithered sideways like filings will slide toward a magnet. Somehow I couldn't turn hope all the way out of my mind. Which just goes to show how foolishness will persist.

At that moment the others came back for us. "Will you join us at dinner?" Gracie asked. "Harold is coming."

Burton looked at Sun Moon and me. We nodded yes. "We'd be grateful," he told Gracie.

CHAPTER ELEVEN

1

BURTON OBSERVED THAT "Us" consisted of Gracie's mother, Corrine Johnson, and three sisters. Burton was seated on Mrs. Johnson Young's left, next to Harold. Asie and Sun Moon sat on the other side of their hostess. Everyone was in place on time, perhaps forty in all. When Brother Young saw that all was to his satisfaction, he said grace.

While large platters of food were being served (Mrs. Twiss acted as housekeeper and another wife as her assistant, or servant), Mrs. Johnson Young held forth verbally like a gusty wind. "Darn nice today." "The corn is fine this year." (Indian corn, that is—Americans call corn "wheat.") "Well, those Neilsons will . . ." (This with an affronted eye on the Johnson clan.) "Did you know Harold is being set up for West Point?" "That Oswald." "Green beans again." None of this was directed at Burton or her other guests, or her children, or anyone in particular. A wind does not care what sail it fills, or whether it fills any. She simply tossed out these remarks at large, and let the world receive them as it would, gazing inscrutably into the distance as she did so.

However, the captain pursued one comment. "West Point?" It was the American Sandhurst, so Harold must have come from an important family of Saints. "Is that so, Harold?"

He nodded. "The Governor is arranging it, I think." So. The United

States in its wisdom had seen fit to replace Brother Young as Governor of Utah Territory, and had put its own, secular man in place of the ecclesiastical man. Then it took the politic course and offered the Saints one of the privileges reserved to rank, a place for a son of a leading family at the leading military academy. Burton noted for the sake of his government that Brigham Young was building bridges toward the U.S., not burning them.

"Do you want to be a soldier?"

"You bet," said Harold. *Ah, the ubiquitous affirmation of the American West.*

"For the United States?"

Now he became slightly more guarded. "We Mormons respect authority. We know the necessity of self-defense. As long as I'm not called on to march against my own people . . ."

He helped himself to meat—there were beef and mutton—and set to eating in a hearty way.

Burton offered, "If there's aught I can tell you, as an old soldier . . ."

FROM BURTON'S JOURNAL:

> *The rest of the repast consisted of baked potatoes, corn meal mush, the detested green beans, cheese, bread, and milk. The meals tended to be much the same. Each morning as family and guests walked downstairs to breakfast, Young children could be heard chanting, "Peach sauce, peach sauce," in protest, because it was served every day. Brother Young, however, was reported to be indifferent or impatient with such complaints. If food nourishes the body, in his judgment, that is enough to ask. Teasing tongues in the family note that he himself does not eat the peach sauce for he takes his breakfast alone in Bee Hive House, a boiled egg, milk, cream, bread, and fruit. The egg out of duty, for Brother Young believes it increases fertility.*
>
> *The meal was overcooked, but no worse in this respect than what passes for good English cooking. As we were nearing the end of the main part, before dishes were cleared for dessert, came an untoward event. Suddenly in the room rose a hush loud as a roaring wind. One of the childless wives, a frail nothing of a woman of sour face and self-effacing demeanor, rose from her*

seat and started toward the head table, plate in hand. Every eye in the room followed her. What does she want? *everyone wondered, meaning,* what delicacy from the head table that is withheld from us? *When she arrived, she dared not raise her eyes to her husband's. His glare would have felled an elephant. She helped herself to some dish she coveted (I heard later it was rhubarb) and returned to her seat.*

The room waited. After a long interval of staring, the Prophet returned to his meal. The children broke into scandalized whispers. I overheard a wife to my left say, "I'll bet he fixes her so she don't do that again." Mrs. Johnson Young looked like she would gladly do the fixing herself. After the prayer meeting Brother Young did summon the transgressor into his office. She came out later like a mouse scurrying for a hole.

Dinner is followed by an hour of rest, then prayer meeting. First the family sings several hymns, of the low-church sort and with some infusion of Welsh spirit. Brother Young then reads prayers from the Bible. Though I know him to be utterly sincere, I did sometimes get the impression that he was not so much entreating the Divinity as talking things over, one great man to another. Sometimes he even seemed to give advice. After the prayer meeting the family lingers for an hour of domestic felicity. Having wearied of the company (I have endured my share of prayer and unction from English rectors), I retired to our rooms to write in this notebook.

2

"WANT TO SEE something?" Harold had a hint of a crazy smile, and I knew he'd picked me out as a kindred spirit. Without any notion of what he had in mind, I said yes. He nodded toward some chairs, and we sat.

The family talk that came after the prayer meeting was breaking up, and wives and children were heading back to their rooms, or bedroom suites, as they were called (in those days I thought it was spelled sweets). Brother Young was just perching there in his big stuffed chair, answering a question for this one or that, dispensing and withholding, male of the pride.

"Boobledy boo boo," said Harold.

I gave him a queer look.

"Boobledy boobledy," he said again, that glint in his eye.

"Heckahoy," I answered.

He turned to a distant horizon, clicked his heels, and saluted smartly. "Ahoy, heck!"

"Heck?" says I, scrambling to my feet.

"Heck," he confirmed, pointing.

"I fear the fires of heck, but I didn't expect them this close."

Both of us chuckled a bit, and looked around for some more fun.

Brother Young stood and looked around like a man who doesn't know what to do with himself. He fished in a coat pocket for something and brought it out in a white handkerchief, all the while looking distracted, like he was really doing something else—you know how a man taking a pee will look around like he's doing something else? Then he fidgeted for a minute and set out down one hall.

There were two halls, the left visible and the right out of sight. Brother Young headed down the one where we could see. "I thought so," says Harold. "Watch this!" He sounded like it must be better than ice cream on a sultry day.

Brother Young wandered along the hall, that white handkerchief tucked up in one hand and one end dangling. There were doors on the right and the left, doors of main bedrooms where wives slept, sitting rooms, and kids' rooms. A couple of times, when a door was open, Brother Young spoke softly to someone inside. Seemed like the words must have been kindly, but the way he stood was kind of cramped, like a man who's uneasy with what he's going to do. He went clear to the end door, looked in briefly, moved his lips, and came back our way.

Harold was tight as a fiddle string—you could have twanged him. But he kept on trying to sit relaxed and idle, like we were just two young fellas enjoying a social hour. At last Brother Young came back into the parlor and passed into the other hall. "Evening, Brother Young," said Harold. The Lion of the Lord gave a flicker of an eyebrow as he walked by, but you couldn't have said whether it was a greeting or not.

"Damn," said Harold. "I thought he'd go for Mary."

Not yet daring to guess what Harold meant, I just tried to keep the expression on my face from looking stupid.

"C'mon!"

He jumped up, but after two steps began to creep. I followed, tiptoeing along like a thief. We got up to a big urn at the corner of the hall. *You idjit, you spy on the man who gives you sanctuary?* That's what I was screaming inside my head. Harold stationed himself close behind the urn and motioned me behind him. *He won't just condemn you to heck, he'll call Porter Rockwell to escort you!* I'd have run, but fear turned my legs to noodles.

"Know what that is in his hand?" whispers Harold.

I shook my head, though Harold couldn't see it.

Brother Young ambled down the hall, hesitating now and then, cocking his head upward like he was checking out the sky straight through the ceiling.

"It's chalk!"

I didn't get it.

Brother Young acted for all the world like a man making some sort of big show or playacting. *But why?*

"He's picking out THE one. Of the night."

Finally Brother Young kind of sidled over to one door, turned his back to it, looked about while acting like he wasn't, turned toward the door again, and touched it with that handkerchief. I couldn't see if it left a chalk mark. What I remembered later was what a whipped and hangdog air he had.

Harold whirled on me. His eyes were huge. For a second I thought he was going to pounce. "Alice!" he practically screamed in a whisper. And he ran off, going, "It's A-a-alice!" and giggling like a maniac.

I ran right with him. I'd spent my life scooting away from Mormon churchmen, and Brigham Young was the churchiest of 'em all. But I wasn't every bit as fast as I might have been. What Harold had said had given me carnal thoughts, and my thing was a little heavy there in front, wagging back and forth.

Sitting on his small daybed, Richard Burton continued his journal by candlelight.

> *Human curiosity is such that readers will want to know just how the conjugal aspects of Mormon polygamy are conducted.*

As far as this observer can tell, every manner conceivable may be employed. The imagination of the gentiles, though, is much inflamed by speculation. This is the sort of anecdote some spread:

"One Mormon husband and his three wives were obliged every night to sleep in the same room. The first wife required her husband to sleep with her in an upper bunk, the second and third being relegated to the lower. When the husband felt desire for the second or third wife, he simply said so. The wife gave her permission, as long as he returned to her bunk when finished. He performed the copulation and slept the rest of the night with wife number one."

This is manifestly nothing more than an example of the preoccupation of puritanical American culture with concupiscence. The crowing tone of the anecdote gives it away.

First-hand observation indicates than the Lion of the Lord and other husbands in celestial marriages provide their plural wives with separate bedrooms or living suites, often with separate residences, sometimes with faraway residences. The matter of a wife's husband's intimacy with her "sister" seems to be dealt with decorously. My guess is that conflicts inspired by jealousy are few. In countries of Asia where polygamy is practiced they are uncommon.

Asie and Harold came spinning up through the door, slammed it, and threw themselves on the floor, panting. "Sir Richard! Sir Richard!"

Burton couldn't tell which lad was talking when, the way they babbled his name.

"We, we . . . ," said Harold breathlessly. The lads looked at each other merrily and burst into laughter.

Asie had the courage. "We watched the bull inspect the cows and *choose one.*" Gales of laughter.

As they told the story by turns, interrupting each other, Burton's delight spiraled from his belly to his head. It was a good story, regardless of what Brother Young was really doing.

"Sweet gizzards," exclaimed Asie when they'd blurted it all out.

Burton regarded them with a broad smile. "So. Concubine of the night," said Burton.

"I wouldn't say that," mouthed Harold, and a hint of steel edged his youthful voice.

Stupid to put it so bluntly. Harold Jackson might be an independent-minded Mormon, but he was no traitor.

Burton the man felt for Harold Jackson. Burton the writer knew an opportunity when he saw it. "When he goes to one of his wives, does he stay the night?"

How much are you willing to say, young lad?

Burton watched the mind hesitate. It flipped, flopped, and flipped over again. Harold came to disclosure. He shook his head. "Never." A moment's pause. "He sleeps alone in a bedroom next to his office in Bee Hive House."

So why are you talking to an outsider? What do you want to say, o ye son of the great?

"I am a Saint, you know. Genuine."

"Of course."

"I wouldn't want you to think I'm a jack Mormon."

Burton nodded sagely. When you didn't have a clue what to say, a sage nod was always a good trick.

"But I don't want to have a plural marriage." The young man reddened.

"Ah."

The young man looked hard at the ground. Up at Burton. Back at the ground. "I believe God meant man and woman to feel *passion* for one another."

Burton regarded the young man. *Yes, you are newly launched into the hot-blooded years.* "Your father and his wives . . . ?"

Harold just hung his head.

"My observation," Burton put in, "is that Brother Young's house has a spirit not of passion but of piety and duty. It is cool, bloodless, diligent."

"*Yes.* What the gentiles imagine . . ." The lad shrugged in frustration.

"Do you think . . . ?"

Harold interrupted. "I shouldn't be talking about this. At all." He gave forth a veritable compendium of the body language of being ill at ease, head down, hands wringing, torso twisting, feet shuffling. "There is something I should mention to you, though. It's about Porter Rockwell."

"Is he here?" asked Sun Moon.

She stood in the doorway of her room. She seemed so vibrant I wondered how I had not felt her presence, even if I didn't hear her open the door.

"No, Ma'am," muttered Harold, "he's not. It's something else." Harold looked from her at Sir Richard queerly. "Father opposes the Danites. Brother Young opposes the Danites." He looked sidewise at me and Sun Moon. "He respects Porter Rockwell but opposes the Danites."

"Is that so?" says Sir Richard.

"Of course," said Harold. "They were *essential,* a necessary evil in the early days of the Church. *Rabble,* those were *rabble* that hounded us in Missouri and Illinois. Armed self-protection? Absolutely essential. Anything else, suicide."

My mind was going goosey loops. *So why is the Prophet helping us? Or is he?*

"Now, though, we Saints are safe." I wasn't so sure about that. "We're established here. Our enemies lie a thousand miles away to the east or west. *The Danites are a throwback."*

Sir Richard smiled, and I could see he didn't want to seem patronizing, which always made him seem patronizing. "Can even the Prophet always control the Danites?"

Harold pulled a slow nod. "They are stubborn, especially Orrin Porter Rockwell. He is a legend among my people, feared and admired. He fought wisely in the Utah War. He's hard to curb. Even for . . ."

Sun Moon spoke softly. "Do you know Porter Rockwell?"

Harold looked at her, flushed, and cast his eyes downward. "He's a family friend. Way back."

"What sort of man is he?"

Harold flashed his eyes up at her face. "I don't know why Port would want . . . You're so decent." His face turned sheepish.

"Why does Porter Rockwell give himself to violence?"

She could push, Sun Moon, in her way.

"He don't. I mean . . . You know what happened to him, to Port? You know about Joseph?"

Sun Moon shook her head. "Tell me, please." I could feel her mind open to him to like palms, ready to receive.

Sun Moon concentrated on the young man. She became attentiveness.

"Port loved Joseph. From when Port was a kid and they were neighbors, I mean. He looked up to Joseph." Harold twisted his legs together, then untwisted them. "Joseph had the countenance of a prophet, fire in his heart, and a holy light in his eyes. Port saw that, and knew he weren't nothing like that inside his self, and he loved Joseph for it. In that way Joseph drew Port to the Church and unto himself.

"Port helped Joseph. Eventually that help became protection. Gentiles cast themselves into opposition to Joseph. Governments raised their hands against him. Mobbers craved the blood of Saints, Joseph's most of all. So Port became one of the Sons of Dan, the men who protected us against the rabble of Missouri and Illinois. When Joseph required particular protection, Port acted as his guardian angel."

Sun Moon drank the young man with her eyes.

"Until the day he went to the Carthage jail. Joseph knew what would happen to him. In the prime of life he was offered up into the hands of his enemies. He went in peace, and he stayed the hand of Porter Rockwell. He ordered Port to stay back, to let him go undefended, a lamb to the slaughter."

She heard the pathos, but she also heard simplicity and truth.

"Port took Joseph's death hard, and his failure to shield his leader harder. Anger became a holy rage. If any of the rumors about him striking out at the gentiles are true, it would have been at that time. He may have shed blood, but I doubt that it was innocent.

"I hear Port did some drinking in those years, and his anger festered in him, not abating even here, with the founding of Deseret. When the Sons of Dan acted again in their wrath, Port was one of the leaders. Blood was let, the blood of apostates.

"That's when the change come. At some time in those years as a destroying angel, Port came to believe he had violated Joseph's law: The sins which shall not be forgiven are the shedding of innocent blood and adultery.

"What blood is innocent? Only the Lord God knows. Did Porter Rockwell shed innocent blood? What counts is, he believes he did. And in believing so, he has condemned himself to a hell on Earth. He lives in the shadow of guilt. He believes he sinned and sinned, until he has put himself beyond even the mercy of the all-merciful God."

Harold Jackson's aspect changed. He brought truth to Sun Moon. "Has he threatened you? They say so. Therefore, I ask you, I entreat you, do for Porter Rockwell what he cannot do for himself. Forgive him."

Sun Moon felt the iron band ease on her throat.

CAPTAIN BURTON THRILLED at this drama. He believed the young chap's story, for it fit the man he knew. It fit the despair, the bitterness, the blackness of spirit.

Harold stopped, evidently wondering if he'd said too much, the youth in him desperate to say more, to explain, to justify. He stood. He shuffled his feet. He started to speak and held back. At last he said, "It's the social hour inside. Maybe you two would like to meet some of my friends?"

Burton deferred to Asie with his eyes. Asie considered. "Sure," he said. He offered his arm to Sun Moon. After hesitating, she took it.

"I wish to write a little more, and will join you soon."

In fact, Captain Richard Burton wanted to pray and then to transport himself to the land of Xanadu. He waited for the lads to close the door and performed his evening duty, the fourth prayer of the day. Then he lifted a stoppered flask to his lips, and drank deep. He sat back on the bench. It would not take long. Meanwhile he would watch the sun set beyond the Salt Lake to the west. It was a melodramatic sight, bloody as the Old Testament. *Tomorrow I must send out to the chemist for more laudanum.* A necessity for travelers, he would say.

And when will we be traveling? Burton sighed deeply. They would leave soon. A place between his shoulder blades was itching often now, a feeling he knew well. It meant, watch your back. If Brother Young had an apostate wife in his household, he bloody well might have a spy. *All the way to San Francisco with some sort of deception.* It was a forbidding prospect, and he would have to face it. Tomorrow.

He looked toward the window and shifted his feet so he faced precisely toward Mecca. As he knelt, he could already taste the laudanum.

3

"CAPTAIN BURTON!" THE lass came toward him, arms extended. Burton took her hands politely. "I'm Clarissa Angesley Young, and I'm so glad you came." Normally, it would have seemed an exaggerated welcome, an adolescent trying to be a womanly hostess. In Burton's Kubla

Khanish state it became a mad parody. The lass was raven-haired, her skin fair and perfect as paper untouched by any pen. He imagined the poems of love waiting to be written on her face, on her bosom, on her thighs and between. The sensuous lines came to him in flowing Arabic, more beautiful than the music of water flowing in desert fountains.

Clarissa led him by one hand toward the rosewood piano. She was radiant, she shone with an exotic fire. Her shining innocence only made her in Burton's eyes more erotic.

I'm squiffed, Burton told himself loudly in his mind but to no avail, *squiffed by the laudanum. Every woman is a siren in my eyes. I must take care.*

The long parlor was speckled with pairs of adolescent lads and lasses, two on a sofa here, seated on a bench here, standing by a window there. Burton saw Asie seated at the piano, Sun Moon beside him. Burton recognized most of the lasses from the dining room. *The men must be Young sons and the suitors of Young daughters*—la crème de la crème *of Mormon society.* Some were going so far as to hold hands. The only light came from a bright lamp on the table in the middle of the room. He wanted to make a lilting song of it—la crème de la crème de la quim. *A bawdy song.*

Asie clattered a tune out from the keys. *Oh, the schottische. One, two, three, hop!* Burton noticed that the lad had the gift—this schottische had a lilt! *One, two, three, hop!*

Asie was playing some sort of dance music, Sun Moon knew. She had seen and heard enough dancing at Tarim's tavern. She had begun to hear some sense in the music. It was crude, though, beside the music of the zithers, flutes, and great lamaist brass horns. The dance was vigorous but lacking in subtlety. Yet she could see that Asie spirit entered into the song like a proud dancer, and kicked up its heels handsomely.

The girl with hair the color of a raven, Clarissa, led Sir Richard into the dance. He was graceful in the turns, but she recognized the mad agility of the drunk. Clarissa whirled, faced him, whirled a time and a half, and back into his arms with a gleaming smile.

Courting, they called it in English. She remembered the courting in her own country, funny, joyful, sometimes bawdy. Tibetan women were not demure, nor chaste. That was why their sexiness was legendary among Chinese men. *Which is why Tarim wanted me.* The iron band choked off that line of thought.

She herself had never been courted. She entered the convent before puberty. She had watched, she had heard her sisters tell stories . . . Some monks and nuns returned to their families periodically and lived ordinary, uncelibate lives. Sun Moon had held herself to the highest standards, had never so indulged.

She turned back to Asie. His face was enraptured, transported. He was living in a reality other than the usual one, a reality resplendent with sounds, a reality flowing from his fingers, his own creation, his own collaboration with the fine energies of the universe. She had always loved the rapture of musicians. She loved it in Asie now.

Her body tingled. A sensual feeling of her girlhood flowed back to her, the first time she touched herself and felt arousal . . .

It slipped into her mind unwelcome—the warmth in her body when . . . She felt her body entwined with Asie's on the sand. Her skin prickled.

ALBERT WATCHED THE John Bull captain, trying to be discreet. He wondered what Brother Rockwell actually wanted. "Intelligence," Rockwell had said, "everything."

He supposed that included the information that Captain Burton danced with Brother Young's daughters with too intimate an expression on his face, and too much insinuation of body. It did not matter that Clarissa was a Young daughter he fancied himself.

Albert had been flattered to be trusted with this task. His father had fought with "Port" in the Utah War, and admired no man more than Brother Rockwell. "Brother Young is the brains of Deseret," he said, "our women are the heart, and Porter Rockwell is the hard muscle."

But what exactly did Brother Rockwell want to know? To be sure the fugitives were here—that was solved. Probably to know what rooms they were in. And especially to get some idea of their plans. "Renegades," Brother Rockwell had called them. Raised through the tribulation of inner conflict and apostasy, Albert knew what that meant, the trials it brought the Church. "They cannot hide in Brother Young's house forever," Brother Rockwell said with a look. Something in the look made Albert feel he would follow Porter Rockwell into hell itself. As his father had felt.

How to discover their plans?

He got to his feet and strode straight toward the dancing pair. His heart tripped as lightly as their feet. Clarissa's face turned toward him, and the look gave him pause. He forced his feet onward, smiled, and lifted a hand to her.

With a cold and brittle smile Clarissa Young joined hands with the young Saint. He saw her eyes stay on Captain Burton as they danced away, pining.

Anger pulsed in Albert, and he used it to push out questions. "Who is that odd-looking man?" Silence. "I hear he's staying in Lion House—can that be true?" Silence. "I hope he and his friends go soon. Outsiders contaminate Deseret." But Clarissa did not answer, did not even look at Albert. When the song ended, she whirled and walked back toward Captain Burton.

And Albert came to knowledge of jealousy.

Gradually the light dropped by half. Burton saw that one of the older lasses had stacked books high around the lamp as a shield. He kept chatting with Clarissa as though he noticed nothing.

Asie changed music. It was something . . . Burton couldn't say, but it inspired reverie rather than dancing. The dancers, as by consensus, disappeared into shadowed corners.

"Let me show you something," said Clarissa. She led him by the hand to a high, slender window. She seemed to walk on air, and he to fly lightly behind her, a balloon trailing from her hand. "Look," she said. Far to the northwest a last ribbon of light touched the barren ridges of the Hogup Mountains. Above it, in the plush half darkness, an arc of moon was already setting. Clarissa looked up into Burton's eyes. It was as though she gently pulled the balloon to her face. "Captain, when the moon . . ."

Richard Burton inclined his head slightly and moved to brush her lips with his. She turned her head, so that he touched her hair instead. "My, Captain!" she murmured low.

She took both his hands and held him at arm's length. She pivoted into one arm, stepped back, and looked up. He found her lips a hairbreadth from his. He took full advantage.

And then Burton slipped his left hand past the hem of a bodice and found a delicate breast. The lady gasped. He caressed the small, hard nipple.

Oh, enchanting madness.

The parlor door rasped. By a deft movement of shoulders Clarissa slipped away from Burton's palm. She turned to face Burton again, flashing a brittle smile.

A set of candelabra loomed in the doorway. Beneath it materialized the stout form of the Prophet.

On the piano bench Sun Moon trembled. *A powerful man is angry.*

The Lion of the Lord peered about himself fiercely. Unmistakably, he could see well enough. "The girls will go upstairs to their rooms," Brigham Young declared, "and I will say good night to the young men."

Clarissa walked away without looking back. Sun Moon had watched her closely with Sir Richard, had seen her in his arms at the window, had witnessed the furtive caress. The sight had made her feel her own arousal. She avoided looking at Asie on the bench next to her.

The young men stood foolish and hangdog. Burton rocked on the balls of his feet queasily.

This is odd. What is the harm in courting?

Burton's feet carried him along the back wall, and his body followed with a wobble, Sun Moon thought. He turned the knob on a side door.

"Captain Burton," snapped the Lion of the Lord, "will you come to my office at nine o'clock in the morning?"

Terror played its fingers up and down Sun Moon's body. Pictures of flight crashed through her mind. With the iron band Sun Moon controlled herself.

"Nine o'clock sharp," Brother Young repeated. His face didn't look brotherly.

"Of course," said Sir Richard.

Sun Moon suppressed quivers. *I despise being at the mercy of men.*

PART THREE

ON THE ROAD

CHAPTER TWELVE

THE DOOR TO our bedroom cracked open. A figure darkened the crack. Harold Jackson whispered, "We're getting outta here. *Now!*" It was a good trick, making a whisper sound like a bullwhip, but he did it. He was standing still, but like a dust spout stands still while it's spinning like fury.

Sir Richard jumped up like he'd been flushed from cover. Heckahoy! I'd been worried about him last night—seemed like he'd fought the popskull whisky and lost. Big and wild-eyed as he was, that angry scar on his cheek, he looked like that Frankenstein you hear about.

"Move! We've got trouble!"

I tapped on Sun Moon's door, and she opened it in a flash, plumb dressed. She and I, seemed like, were getting used to skedaddling fast with the devil screeching at our hind parts.

"Vamoose!"

Clarissa came bursting in, the Prophet's daughter that Sir Richard had been sparking last night, and she cared nothing that I was still pulling up my pants. She eyed Sir Richard greedily, but he was covered up by his nightshirt. (He always slept covered head to toe, but I never thought anything of it until later.)

"Ready," she tossed at Harold. He pushed Sir Richard's trunk toward her. She and one of her brothers hoisted it and ran off like spooked pack mules.

That was how our holiday at Brigham Young's fine home ended—us stampeding down the back stairs like sheep fleeing a wolf. If I saw what I thought I saw between Clarissa and Sir Richard last night, we were. That man had a plain crazy streak in him that was hard to beat. Even after I knew about the opium, I saw the craziness riding it like a wild horse, and using the whip.

Harold rode point and got us out a back door, along some hedges, through a cut, behind some more hedges, and onto the street. It was plumb dark—no moon at all—and I pitched forward right onto my face once. The possible sack in my arms kept me from getting bunged up.

Two wagons loomed in the street, their shapes darker than the night dark. I could see black somethings sticking up that musta been the mule skinners, and somebody else on the board seat. The mules were clomping and wheezing.

"In!" said Harold, gesturing at the behind wagon.

We jumped in slickety-doo, and he roar-whispered, "All the way down!" When we were flat as ribbons, he threw some stuff on top of us—a lot of it, and he kept stacking it up. Found out later it was shirts, dresses, and blankets made by Mormon women. Best dressed I been before or since.

"Don't make a peep!" said Harold's voice. "On your lives, not a peep! No matter what happens!"

We were between a trunk and some gun cases, which later turned out to be Sir Richard's traveling arsenal, which was substantial. Sun Moon and I didn't have any trunks nor valises nor the like.

The wagon rocked and settled, which I figured was Harold climbing up. Then it rocked and settled again. "Clarissa, get down!" snapped Harold.

"Will not!"

"Will!"

More bouncing of the wagon, a lot more. The sound of shoes scuffling. A *whump!*, like a stiff hand hard on a bottom. A whimper. "Brother Young would send the Legion after you," snapped Harold. Some more whining, getting farther off, and footsteps running away. So ended Sir Richard's career as a seducer of Mormon women, far as I know. That night ended mine, too, and I never got started.

"Gaddup!" came the cry, and again. The wagon jolted, mules' hoofs clomped. "Gaddup!" from both skinners. Now the crack of the bullwhips, too. We were off, no telling where to. I wiggled and tried to get my back comfortable on the hard planks of the wagon bed. They kept banging back at me.

So I took a deep breath and told myself fighting it wasn't going to make things easier. I was going wherever the mule skinners were going, heavens or hell or any octave in between. Most of me thought, *Just as long as we get clear of Deseret.*

Sweet gizzards, but hadn't this whole journey gone strange. Set out for the Alpha farm but got tossed into the river, which took me on a side trip. Next set out for California or Tibet with a nun. Near got killed by Porter Rockwell but instead hid in Brigham Young's harem. It all seemed like a good idea at the time.

It did all put me in mind of what the old Shoshone told me about the rabbit path. It strikes out at a queer angle, stops, doubles back, loops around, and general goes crazy-like. Regardless of anyhow, you must follow it. So this crazy trip all over the West, it was just my rabbit path. Even in the back of that wagon, I was headed right where I needed to go.

"*RIGHT HERE WILL* do!"

We'd been Mexican jumping beans in the wagon bed for I don't know how long. My back felt like the wheels had run over me. The sun had been up a good spell—I could see light through the cracks dancing madly on every bounce. Like Sun Moon and Sir Richard, I suffered in silence. Maybe they were quiet because fear was running in wide, wavy yellow streaks up and down their backs, like it was mine.

When I heard the shout the second time—"Right here will do!"—my fear jumped over the moon. I recognized the voice. That was the roar of the Lion of the Lord.

"You can sit up," said Harold.

We did.

First thing I took in was the freight goods stacked all around us, full loads. Second was sons of Brigham Young surrounding us on their mounts, scatterguns laying casual-like across their saddle horns. At that range we didn't have the chance of fool hens. Third was the Prophet himself on a big black gelding, unarmed, glaring like the Lord on Judgment Day. He was sitting that horse a little uphill from us, looking down. Man like that, I told myself, he's the judge that hands down the sentence, but he's not the executioner. No need for a great man to get his hands dirty with a common of work.

"Captain Burton," he said in a big voice, "it's past 9:00 A.M." I bet the words of the Burning Bush came out sounding just like that. "You have put your hands on my daughter's tits. You are a fool. Did you think to deceive me? Did you think to thwart my will? Did you think to pluck my innocent flower?"

Sir Richard just stared back. He was wrong, he did it, but he wasn't one to say he did wrong. He'd die first. Question in my mind was, Who snitched to Brother Young? Because he never had a chance to see Sir Richard's hands, not where he was. The second and more important question was, Would me and Sun Moon die, too?

Heckahoy, there wasn't anything he could do. Sir Richard probably had his hands on his pistol and that big African knife—he always kept 'em close as he kept his personal equipment—but the scatterguns were cocks of the walk this time.

"Before I pass sentence, do you have aught to say for yourself?"

Sir Richard just kept staring. I looked around at the sons. Never saw such a collection of grim faces in my life. Finally, Sir Richard said, "Spare my companions, Brother Young. They have no fault here."

"I would not harm Sister Sun Moon. Brother Taylor, did you indulge in like foolishness?"

"No, Sir. I was playing the piano."

His eyes licked at me like low flames. "Take me seriously, Brother Taylor. My mind is firm on this."

I don't know what got into me next. The words came out, but I never planned them. "Brother Young, I never touched your daughters. I had carnal thoughts, plenty of 'em. If that's a crime, I'll go with Sir Richard. He is my friend, and I'm right proud to go wherever he does."

The Prophet's eyes gleamed. Now I was in the outhouse, way down in. "Lasses, too, have fantasies," said Brother Young. "My daughters, however, will keep theirs in thrall to their wills. If they don't, as I told Clarissa last night, they can whore it in California. We will have no whores in Deseret."

If he'd banish his own daughter, I had no doubt about what he would do to us.

"Harold," said the Lion of the Lord, and gave a signal with his head. Harold dropped a noose over Sir Richard's shoulders and pulled him back against some grain sacks hard.

"Double-crosser," I whispered. He turned his face away from me.

Afore I knew it a like noose dropped over me and pinned my arms to my chest, and over Sun Moon. We were trussed like turkeys and yanked back hard, away from Sir Richard.

"It is said, Captain Burton," declared the Prophet, "that you have worshiped the many gods of the Hindoos, the gods of the Persians, and the one God of the Arabs. Call upon them now and see if they save your life. Or call upon the name of Jehovah. He will not save your life—that belongs to me!—but He offers mercy to your soul."

Brigham Young now raised a heavy pistol, a cap-and-ball weapon. He leveled it at Sir Richard's chest and set the trigger. Steady, very steady. "Have you any last words, Captain Burton?"

Sir Richard just looked at Brother Young. "None," said Sir Richard. I studied his face for a twitch or a tremor. All I saw was El Ayn, his evil-eye stare. The Prophet stared back with the two eyes of his head and the single eye of his muzzle. This time Sir Richard was outgazed.

Brigham Young squeezed the trigger. Smoke belched out of the barrel, and it kicked upward.

Sir Richard didn't stir.

Brigham Young began to laugh.

Sir Richard looked down at his chest. Instead of blood, he saw a wad of cloth. He flicked it away with one hand.

Brigham Young had shot wadding at Sir Richard!

I let out a little cackle without meaning to, like a belch.

Brother Young commenced seriously to laugh now. He was guffawing. He was roaring. He was slapping his thighs. The laughter bubbled out of him like water from a big spring, and the sound echoed like in a deep well. It was a once-in-a-lifetime, boy-ain't-this-fine laugh.

The sons, though, kept their grim expressions. I tried to stifle my own cackling, which sounded childish to my ears.

Finally, Brother Young sobered up. Sir Richard had glared at him all along, stony silent. When Brother Young got quiet, Sir Richard says, "Mr. President, I apologize. I abused your hospitality."

Brother Young nodded. Nodded again. "You did. I can understand lust and how hot it runs. I have myself looked at titties with desire, particularly young and innocent ones. I know my sons do the same." He cast his eyes around at them. "But you asked me for sanctuary and then . . ." The two looked at each other, and finally Sir Richard lowered his eyes. He was wrong, good and wrong.

"That is not why you were shipped out, however. You are four hundredweight in wagons belonging to Brother Jackson's freighting company—maybe Harold's father should charge you freight rates." The Prophet smiled at the world. Likely he was trying for a joke. "No, I asked you to come to my office this morning for a reason you did not guess." He gave a pause here, as a good orator will do, making us wait. "I had intelligence that Porter Rockwell was laying plans. Even the refuge of my home, it seems, is merely a challenge to his ingenuity . . ."

From above a voice called, "It was easy to plant that intelligence, Brother Young. Sure did work, too."

Porter Rockwell rose up black and massive from behind a boulder uphill of Brigham Young, and two others beside him. They had us all covered with rifles.

Brigham Young took a big breath, and it seemed to make him not only wider but taller. "Brother Rockwell," he said, "put your gun down. You are endangering your immortal soul."

"Did that long time past, Brother Young."

Now Brigham Young spoke with an edge. "We have discussed this. Your services to the Church have not smudged your soul." He sounded short-tempered.

Porter Rockwell gave a crooked smile over the barrel of his carbine. "May be there is other matters, Brother Young."

"I cannot answer for that," said the Prophet. "You will, in the fullness of time."

Rockwell nodded. "Right at this here time, Brother Young," he said with sweet mockery, "the whore and her friends will answer." His tone changed sharp now. "Oblige me by breaking those side-by-sides open and turning your horses back to the city, all of you." The sons looked at Brother Young. At a wiggle of his eyebrows they broke the shotguns open. "You drivers can take the wagons on. I ain't no thief. Just four hundredweight will stay here. Permanent-like."

"Brother Rockwell," said the Lion of the Lord, "you've been the Destroying Angel of the Lord. Now you're becoming the instrument of the devil. You will pay the ultimate price."

"I 'spect so," said Rockwell. "You know, you don't head back real quick, you oughta stand out of the line of fire. I ain't shed no blood of Saints yet." He grinned. "I'd guess Brother Taylor qualifies as an apostate."

Brother Young looked back at us in the wagon bed, then up the hill at Rockwell and his side men. He looked all around at his sons. Everyone knew what he was thinking. Rockwell said, "No, Brother Young. Those scatterguns at this range will feel like raindrops. Our rifles will shoot you in one side and out the other."

I could see Brigham Young figuring it, too. He didn't like the sum he got. Me neither.

The Prophet nodded to himself, stepped down out of the saddle, and handed the reins to one of his sons. He nodded to himself again, confirming whatever it was. Then he began to walk.

Up that dusty, rocky ridge he walked, straight toward Porter Rockwell. It was a steep walk, and he was a man with a lot of heft. He did it graceful, though—he had more than fat in those thick legs—chugged on up there like an engine. Never once looked up at Porter Rockwell, or back at any of us. I expect his inner eye was checking out the country beyond the Great Divide right then. Only a fool would trust Porter Rockwell. Hell, Rockwell couldn't predict himself.

This time he snugged that carbine tighter into his shoulder, pressed his cheek down harder on the stock, and squinted a bit more keen. And held his fire. Or did until he could near choose between Brigham Young's chest hairs in his sights.

"Give me the rifle, Brother Rockwell."

The Destroying Angel didn't move, didn't stir, didn't shift, didn't waver.

I took a deep breath. Seconds went by. I ordered myself to let it out, but it wouldn't go. Minutes went by, seemed like. Rockwell's sidekicks kept their sights on Brigham Young's sons, waiting, waiting, waiting for the main man to decide.

Brigham looked right past the muzzle and into Rockwell's eye.

I think I felt it before I saw it. Like a wind settling down, Rockwell's spirit eased off. Some tension slacked out of his shoulders.

Sudden-like, he lowered the rifle. I could see by the way he looked at Brother Young, and the contrary way he held his head, the wind could kick back up at any moment.

Brigham Young held both arms straight out, palms up. "Give me the rifle, Brother Rockwell," he commanded.

Rockwell done it.

"Tell your men to pull the caps off."

Rockwell nodded at them, and they popped 'em, which turned their rifles into mere clubs.

"Come with me." The Prophet turned and clomped his way back down the hill. His shoulders sagged, and he looked like an old man now—he never done so going up.

Rockwell walked behind him, but not hangdog. Somehow he'd given in without feeling whipped. He must have still had considerable Saint in there somewhere.

His two sidekicks walked down, too, acting real casual. Saint or gentile either one, I wouldn't have been relaxed myself, not when I'd been holding a gun on Brigham Young and his boys.

"Brother Rockwell," said the Prophet, "can we proceed on trust?"

Rockwell was glaring at Sun Moon, giving her the evil eye. She gave it right back to him. Somehow it doesn't look the same from a hundred-pound woman as a two-hundred-and-more-pound man.

"I wouldn't trust me," said Rockwell, straight at Sun Moon.

"Agreed," said Brigham Young. "What about your . . . confederates?"

"They ain't nothing to do with it."

"Fine. I'm going to arrange for you to spend a week in the lockup. Even a deposed governor, I believe, can muster that much power. I'll think of a charge." He turned to Harold. "Enough?"

"Two weeks," said Harold.

"Three weeks," said Sir Richard.

"A month," said Asie.

Sun Moon just stared at Rockwell. When Brother Young raised an eyebrow, she gave a tiny nod.

"I'll keep him occupied for a month."

"He'll never find her after that," put in the lead skinner. "In San Francisco, she kin go in with her kind. Even in Dayton and Virginia City, they's Chinese."

The Prophet nodded curtly. He didn't like talkiness.

Myself, I eyed Sun Moon to see how she took to being called Chinese. Her face was unreadable.

They rode back toward the city, Brigham Young and his sons. Porter Rockwell and his badmen brought up the rear.

The skinners clucked and our wagons headed the other way. Sir Richard said casual-like to Sun Moon, "So you can't go for that hideout gun even when you need it. It isn't you, Sister."

Not till then did I see her hand was inside her jacket the whole time, stuck. Her head hung.

I turned to watch the Mormons ride back toward the city. I'd grown up thereabouts, but figured to be done with the place for good this time. They were good and bad, the Saints—good as Brigham Young, bad as Porter Rockwell. Speaking of him, as far as I could see and maybe farther, Rockwell kept his head turned back, glaring at us, no doubt especial at Sun Moon. She never let herself glance his way, but she watched him in her mind's eye, and felt afraid.

CHAPTER THIRTEEN

Toward noon, far out of rifle range from Orrin Porter Rockwell, Burton brought up what the skinner said. "Virginia City!" he exclaimed.

Harold Jackson nodded. Seemed less than civil as a way for a youth to answer a captain of the Queen's army, Burton thought, but Americans ran to such foolishness—their drivel about equality and all that. Besides, the dust and the heat had obliterated all manners.

Virginia City, queen of the Comstock! To use an Americanism, it set the blood a-jangle!

Several years earlier the Comstock Lode had been discovered, richest vein of silver ore on Earth, they claimed. Of course, everything in America was the biggest, richest, deepest, highest, or most of whatever it was. Americans seemed to have cornered the market on grandiosity. People poured into the Washo District, which was the name of all the country around those parts, coming from everywhere, especially California. A lot of miners and prospectors were disgusted with California. Washo was the comer. An influential man had even told Burton in confidence—every secret in the nation was available over cigars and whisky if you dressed respectably—that the silver and gold from the new Territory of Nevada was financing the War Between the States. Where there was nothing but dust and Digger Indians three years before!

Wherever two people gathered together on the Oregon and California Trails, or even a drunk and a prairie dog gathered, their talk was Washo ahead and the War of the Rebellion behind. Jeehosaphat (Burton was enjoying making fun of American speech in his mind), in Virginia City, word was, every man was rich. Feller could spend a dollar for breakfast and two for dinner, drink champagne, and keep a Chinee to do his laundry by day and his pleasure by night.

Burton winced when those last words came to his mind, and glanced sideways at Sun Moon. In the Occidental view, women of color were little but an opportunity for sexual indulgence. He himself had carried such an attitude to India, and all his experience in the East and in Africa strengthened it. Having spent entirely too much time in Deseret, he found the fantasy of any woman appealing. *Oh, Isabel!*

Most Mormons would have no truck with Virginia City, however. The city by the Great Salt Lake might have emptied, Saints flowing West like a raging river, but for Brother Young's injunction against mining. Work of the devil, he said. So the Mormons steered clear, except when the prospect of profit appeared. Thus these wagons, the captain was sure. The best sort of sin is the one that yields a buck.

"IS THIS THE Pony Express route?" queried Burton. The one he'd taken two years before.

"No, when the telegraph come in, the stage stations on that route dried up and blew away. This is the old California Trail. It has better grass anyhow."

Harold turned away, and Burton regarded his back. The wagon bumped. The midday August sun was brutal, the dust choking. Sun Moon and Asie rode with their lids half-shut, their minds doubtless in a better place. Burton decided conversation was preferable to boredom.

"So. We are on *safariy.* With little preparation."

"What's suh-far-ee?" says Harold.

"A desert journey. An Arabic word." When this brought no response, Burton plunged on. "Virginia City offers good commerce?"

"We used to trade just to Mormon Station, emigrant trade. Since the boom on the Comstock, even California cannot keep up with the demands, and in winter the passes to California close. More than ten thousand souls in Virginia City, about like Salt Lake City. The demand is great."

" 'hat ain't the only kind of calico trade," said the skinner. "Veritable."

"Our guests are higher-minded than you, Muley," said Harold.

The skinner turned to them, and Burton saw how he earned his name. He had a face long as a mule's, blue-gray with stubble from the cheekbones down, and front teeth big as thumbs.

"Is the captain high-minded?" queried Muley in a high, whining voice. "I wouldn'a said so. I'd a bet the captain is a man veritable fond a' calico." Burton had once seen a parrot's eye whirl in circles. Muley's eye did something like this now.

Calico, yes, that's what they call it.

"Muley!"

The skinner shook his head and stuck out his horsey teeth. "Save your tongue to me, I ain't none of your Saint."

"Even a gentile can tell when there are ladies present," said Harold.

Muley turned his head around and moved it back and forth in little jerks, like a rooster. His eye stopped sharp on everyone, including Sun Moon. "Don' see me no ladies. Veritable see me some yaller calico!" He stood up and waggled his arse.

"Enough, Muley," said Burton equably. He looked at Sun Moon and saw by her eyes that she understood and was miffed. *Yes, that slang she would know.*

The skinner turned back and attended to the mules. "Oh, the gentlemen is offended at Muley's tongue, is they? Then let them be offended by *this.*" He broke into his own version of the California Trail song "O, Susannah."

"We're sons of whoring fathers, boys,
And mothers drunk on brew,
Who whispered as they wrung our necks,
'God curse and condemn you.'
Thieves, capitalists, and all their friends,
They wish us hearty speed,
Behold the world will steal from us
If our steps to fortune lead.

"Oh, California!
Thou land of broken dreams,
Where worthless mud and yellow piss
Are found in all thy streams!

"The lot of us—have we not left
The best of life for this?
To give our youth and all our strength
For whores and gamblers' bliss!
So drop your cocks and grab your socks!
With hopes by fancy led,
Go where the Sacramento flows
O'er its swindling bed!

"Oh, California!
Thou land of broken dreams,
Where worthless mud and yellow piss
Are found in all thy streams!"

"Muley," said Harold crossly, "Father doesn't have to hire you."

"No fear 'bout that," said the skinner. "You kin pay some other fool sumbitch drive you back."

"Muley?"

"This be my wagon and my mules. I'm for Washo, veritable, like them other fools."

Burton couldn't help intruding. "Why, Muley? If miners only get robbed by thieves, gamblers, and whores?"

"And capitalists," said Muley. "Don't forget them capitalists. Bonanza ain't in the cricks or the earth. It's in selling grub and clothes for five times their worth! Veritable! I aim to be a capitalist, just like Harold, here, and his father. If I get real lucky, I'll be a monopolist."

Not bloody likely. Muley wore an undershirt for a shirt, pants of osnaburg, and boots that looked like a hide scavenged by vultures. His stubble was tobacco-stained. His speech was crude in the extreme. *Americans are nearly as particular as we British about keeping profit where it belongs, among the mannerly and well dressed.*

"What was your father, Muley?"

"Preacher man," said Muley. "Hardshell Baptist."

Burton's mind did a twirl. *Yes, in America vicars may be uneducated. They read scripture on their own. Maybe that's where "veritable" comes from.* "Is your father still living?"

"My pap?" said Muley. "Same as dead. Runned off and j'ined them Shakers. Lucky for me he waited, veritable. No place to put his pecker now!" Muley cackled.

"I ought to dismiss you," said Harold.

"Mebbe Porter Rockwell ull dismiss us both first." Muley didn't even look back at Harold, but just flicked the reins. The mules ignored him—it was too hot.

Burton looked around warily. The wagons were passing around the north end of the Great Salt Lake, where the country was broken, and every hillock and gully offered a hiding place for a rifleman. On the occasional flats, even the scrub gave cover enough for any bushwhacker. *Good show Rockwell is in custody.*

Burton pictured Virginia City in his mind. *Yes, a chance to see the celebrated carnival of greed. A chance at whisky, and by report even fine brandies. Chinese there. A chance of opium.*

And Porter Rockwell? Burton didn't think so, not with a month's start. And yet. *A whiff of danger makes a man alive.*

Captain Burton felt envious. His own actions were circumscribed by the rule of *takiyyah,* concealment of everything to do with faith, history, and customs. He even had to perform his prayers out of everyone's sight. Sun Moon, however, meditated openly in camp every evening, gazing at her small altar, singing and chanting softly. She could be open and private at once because everyone knew she was just a superstitious heathen, and naturally had heathenish practices, which no white man would inquire about.

Burton, however, was aflame with curiosity. He had studied the secrets of Hinduism, had in fact been initiated as a Naga Brahmin. He was acquainted with the esotericism of the Tantras. He was devoted to his own mystical practice, Sufism. Though he knew something of lamaist Buddhism, to him Sun Moon represented an *avis* very *rara* indeed. A nun of the lamas, practicing before his very eyes. His mind spun with questions. The prospect of answers, theological discussions, made him dizzy. So dizzy that he held his tongue: He had plenty of time, and hardly knew how to begin.

Those chants, though, pushed him beyond the limits of his patience. *Why Mahakala? Mahakala, the Tibetan equivalent of Kali, the goddess-monster?*

He watched as she rose from the lotus position and put the altar away.

"Sister?" Burton began, speaking in Tibetan. He knew she loved to speak her own language.

She looked at him in silence. It was evening, and the sun, setting on the rims of the mountains to the west, cast a reddish gold light on her features. Burton thought again how lovely her face and form were, only enhanced by the scar, and how much he regretted their loss to celibacy.

"Sister, I fear impertinence. Please forgive any offense. Among your vows, as I understand it, is neither to kill nor commit other violence." Burton well knew, in fact, that the other four beginning vows were to be celibate, not to drink to intoxication, and neither to steal nor to lie. He heard that novice monks took thirty-one more vows, and full monks 253 more still. Presumably nuns took similar vows. "Why then do you make offerings to Mahakala?"

Burton's very breath was curiosity. Among the Hindus he was acquainted with, Kali was a horrific figure. He knew the story of her birth. Kali sprang forth from the brow of the Great Goddess Devi *in extremis* of battle against demons. Wearing a tiger skin, armed with a sword and a noose, she laid waste all around her. The demons saw that she was garlanded with human heads, carried a staff with a skull handle, and used as ear pendants the corpses of infants. Her third eye gleamed scarlet. She decapitated and crushed her enemies, laughing, and drank their blood.

Burton had seen hundreds of images of this deity. Her skin was black, her face gaunt, her eyes red and sunken. Her mouth gaped, her tongue lolled, her skin was emaciated. She was an inspiration not to Hindus of compassion but to the assassins known as the Phansigars, or Thuggees. *So why a lamaist nun making offerings to such an ogre?*

He saw Sun Moon's uncertainty. He saw emotions tug at her beautiful face—he imagined on one hand they were the desire for privacy about matters of the spirit, and on the other hand compassion, the duty to teach, the need for understanding. He was wise enough to let her decide for herself in silence.

"Do you know Tantrism? Left-handed, esoteric Tantrism?"

"Yes, Sister, a little." Seekers of the truth through Tantrism walked paradoxical paths. In their view, if celibacy and honesty are virtues, it is also true that all opposites are the same, all dualities one—celibacy is lechery, honesty is lying. Burton knew that some practitioners of Tantrism sought enlightenment not through chastity but through extreme indulgence. He accepted these paths, and at the same time felt mystified by them.

"Mahakala is neither male nor female. She is time who devours all. She is the source of all, Creatrix, Protectress, and Destroyer."

Burton nodded, but he felt uncertain.

"Like Shiva, her consort," Sun Moon went on, "she dances eternally, at the same moment bringing the world into being and destroying it. She lives in a cremation ground yet is the Mother of Life. She kills yet she protects. She is merciless but is all mercy."

I wish we were speaking English, or Hindustani. Burton understood the doctrine of the unity of dualities, though sometimes its practical forms seemed daunting.

"I have not done Tantric studies myself, but I know the rudiments. The practitioner seeks unity in opposites. As death, Mahakala is the essence of what is forbidden. Thus the practitioner goes toward her to assimilate and overcome death, to transform it into a vehicle of redemption." Sun Moon paused, regarding him attentively.

If only she would speak not of doctrine but of herself.

Sun Moon spoke very softly now, as though deliberately requiring effort by the listener. "Mahakala is not only death but triumph over death. The practitioner masters her and so himself."

Burton looked at her. *This is theology. Where is your truth? How do you feel about your enemies—love through hatred?*

He looked long at the woman in front of him. *How lovely you are.* He saw courage in her face, and determination. He could picture her fighting Porter Rockwell, twice, and again in the future. He could not picture her winning.

"Thank you, Sun Moon," he said, "for your kind answers."

"Would you give me something in return?"

He nodded.

"Teach me to shoot." She took out the derringer.

"We'll use my smaller handgun," he said. "I have plenty of cartridges for it, and I suspect you're short." Burton looked toward the hillock behind the camp. "Asie," he called, "would you care to join us shooting?"

I WAS WHISTLING the evening away, and enjoying it. Heckahoy, whistling never felt like *just* whistling, not to me.

I skittered down the hill.

Sir Richard set us up some rocks, which were what the country had most of. He had a high-old-time expression on his face, and I knew he was reveling in teaching a nun to fight. Anything that was mad, it just thrilled him.

He checked her derringer and its loads. He had her shoot them and reload. "Now you have taken the first step," he says.

He went over the mechanics of his handgun with both of us, and we shot at the rocks, which were fist-sized, tearing up the nearby dirt considerably. He told us we were doing fine, though. You didn't aim at any exact spot with a handgun, that was his theory. You didn't aim at all. You drew and pointed and hit a general area.

It felt good. I had never shot a handgun afore.

Then he began his real teaching. "The secret to fighting is that it is not a physical endeavor," he lectured, "but mental and spiritual. The winner is always he who has the willingness to win, the passion to win. Or she. Violence, you must commit yourself to inflicting violence, to utter destruction."

He whirled of a sudden and fired. One of the rocks shot into splinters.

"Practice is necessary, physical practice. Your weapon becomes second nature to you."

He shot without looking, it seemed like, and another rock blew up. "What is more than necessary, however, is preparation of the spirit. Sit quietly. Search within yourself for your fury—all men have it, all! And women! When you find your fury, picture an enemy, any enemy. In your mind heap destruction upon him. Descend upon him like a storm. Commit mayhem upon him. Dismember him. That is the essential preparation of a warrior."

He leapt his gun at the rocks and fired three times. Three rocks exploded into pebbles and dust.

"You must become Bashi Bazouks!"

He looked at us triumphantly.

OK, I was willing to look ignorant. "What's a Bashi Bazouk?"

Sir Richard smiled delightedly. "In the Crimean War I was detached to Turkic regiments who fought like true and fine berserkers. They rode gloriously into the jaws of death, they galloped into the mouth of hell as into the bosom of Abraham. Never have I known such true-spirited fighters. Bashi Bazouk! The very words sing the spirit of warriors!"

I was past patience with him. "Sir Richard," I said, "Sun Moon is no Bashi Bazouk, nor no nun is. It's ain't monastery stuff. For that matter, I druther whistle than fight myself."

Sir Richard pounced and caught me. "I was hoping you would say so.

I'm not sure you're right. Sun Moon *might* find the martial spirit through sufficient supplication to Kali. You *might* find it if circumstance pressed you sorely.

"But let us assume you cannot, or are not ready." He hit me a blow with his evil eye. "Then do not have the arrogance to oppose Porter Rockwell, or any other true warrior. You would be no more than a fly to his whisk."

I gave him some eye back. "I don't guess we have Porter Rockwell to worry about no more."

Sudden-like Sun Moon spoke up. "I think we do."

Sir Richard looked on her curiously. "How so, Sister?"

She cast her eyes down, unable to answer, and spoke softer. "I just think we do."

Sir Richard took it in, then nodded. "And I am confident we do not. For which I give thanks."

CHAPTER FOURTEEN

1

We were camped at Deep Creek, more than halfway from Salt Lake City to where the California Trail split off from the Oregon Road. You wanted to camp by water, not just to let the stock drink but because you'd spent the whole day getting parched. Nothing is as hot or arid as the deserts of western Utah and eastern Nevada in summer. The mountains were hard and dry as cracked walnut shells. The leaves of trees and bushes were brittle as paper left weeks in the sun. The air scorched. All day long the mule skinners drove hard, and the dust sailed straight from the mules' hoofs into your lungs and parched them. Even the water wasn't hardly wet.

Until sundown. At sundown everything changed. The desert colors turned from dust and dirt to purple and pink. Around the creeks and water holes the air sweetened. A few animals came to water, coyotes, foxes, sometimes deer and antelope. The birds eased my spirit with their abundance. Swallows afloat in the evening. Nighthawks, owls, seagulls, sage hens, sandpipers, sometimes herons and egrets.

I sat out away from camp that evening and called to them. They weren't the birds I was used to. That night we couldn't get any music going, for they didn't know I wanted to be part of their song.

All of a sudden Sun Moon appeared there next to me. In her direct way she says, "We build your drum." Muley'd shot a mule deer, and she'd got the hide off him and soaked it for the purpose. She'd borrowed a crosscut saw from Harold. She took me in tow and showed me a hollow log of cottonwood. She had it all worked out.

I cut off a round like she wanted. Those days, though, I knew nothing about working with hide. We had to get Carlson to show us how to stretch it over the open ends of the log, poke holes in the hide, and lace it and pull it tight. He did it in silence, like everything he did.

Meanwhile, she cut off a couple of pieces of hide, I didn't know how come.

Carlson was the other skinner, the one we never rode with, a young fella maybe my age. He was a stalwart-built young man, had a red beard and a good-looking face, but he set his features stubborn all the time. Plus he never said anything. Heckahoy, I mean *nothing.* The only thing came out of his mouth was tobacco juice. Nor did he meet anyone's eyes. Just went about his business like jobs of work was all there was in the world, or anyways there weren't any people. He didn't actually show us how to stretch the drum but just done it for us and walked away without a word.

"You play," she said. Then I saw what she was holding out to me, a stick to beat with. Wooden handle, deerhide cover . . . What was it stuffed with?

Then I saw. She'd cut off part of her braids to stuff the head of my drumstick.

"Gift," she said. "Gift say thank you. You do much for me. I want help you music."

If she hadn't been so standoffish, I'd have hugged her. "Thank you, Sun Moon. You honor me."

"You play after some days." Yeah, it had to dry before it could get thumped on. "Thank you," I said again.

I was grateful, but also uncomfortable. Seemed like she wanted me to beat a drum, to be an Indian. I was an Indian, sort of, and maybe wanted to be. But the notion of beating a drum made me feel like a fool.

"You make sacred music. You maybe a *pawo.*"

"What the beJesus is a pah woh?"

Her face set stubborn then. She looked all around like the answer was somewhere out there in the desert.

I just waited. I'd found out that was the way with Sun Moon.

"*Pawo* man cross over, come back. Bön-po way in Tibet. Cross over, come back."

The cat took my tongue. A *what?* Me?

"You fall in river," she said. "You fall in, see and hear other side."

I got it then. It had been prowling around in my head since it happened. The waves came for me that day and swept me away somewhere else and I heard things you don't hear in this world. Every day since, truth to tell, had been peculiar, trying not to think about it, like sitting in a room with a griz and telling jokes and carrying on and pretending lah-dee-dah there isn't no silvertip here. When the bear is all you can think about.

"Yeah," I said. "Yeah, I did."

"I know some about people cross to other side and come back. They bring wisdom. I learn in books. Book know only. You have gift maybe. Your people maybe know how cross over."

I just looked at her. Half of me was mad. If I was going to be an Indian, and maybe my people were out there ahead somewhere, I didn't mean to be one that crossed from one side to the other and back. Other side of *what?* Common sense said there wasn't any such thing.

Yet I had been there. I had heard the music. Music more beautiful far than any I'd ever heard or would hear on this earth, with these mortal ears. I knew the music over there was way, way more real than any music here. I just didn't have any explanation for it.

A thump on the head, you say? You think I knocked my head on a rock in the bottom of that river and heard music like people get thunked and see stars? Well, I can just picture Handel and Beethoven beating their heads on rocks to get the music to come. Besides, I started hearing the music minutes before I went into the water. And those waves, they *came* for me.

Maybe you don't know. But I do. I know where my ass is planted on the Earth, and I know whether I'm warm or cold, and I know what I heard in the river. Knew it even that day at Deep Creek. So I couldn't nay-say Sun Moon.

"What do people see on the other side?" I didn't even have the guts to say *hear.*

She shrugged.

"What do they bring back?"

She shrugged. Finally, she said, "Do not matter what they see, hear, do, bring back. Matter what *you* see, hear, bring back."

So Sun Moon thinks I'm a pah woh, I says to myself. *I talk to birds, and once I heard song lyrics in a language I don't know. That crazy I am. But Bon Poh pah woh? Loony. Even the sounds is loony—Bon Poh pah woh.*

It bothered me. Ever since that day, I'd been half-afraid I was crazy. Which was worse? To be crazy? Or to be a cross-over-and-backer?

The good part was, I didn't feel so desirous of Sun Moon now. Who wants to romance with someone thinks you're a Bon Poh Pah Woh?

2

We were worried about Digger Indians, so Muley said. We took turns at night guard. Their main practice, so Muley told me, was running off with the horses. As second choice they would stick the critters so full of arrows you had to leave 'em behind.

Muley told us all this the first time he asked for night guard. He did it without a blink, a wiggling eyebrow, or any other sign that one of the folks he was telling about "those rotten Indians" was an Indian. I didn't know whether to be insulted or flattered by his attitude. Insulted at what he said, flattered that he didn't seem to include me. Or insulted that he didn't include me. One night I gave thought to running off with the horses myself and joining up with the Digger Indians. Been just Muley and Carlson, I would have done it.

"Why are they called Diggers?" says Sir Richard.

Muley just gave a disgusted look. "They eat roots. And bugs."

Carlson snickered.

"What tribes inhabit this country?" he pushed on, ever the scientist.

Muley shrugged. Carlson's mouth worked, and for a moment I thought he was going to break his record by saying something. After a big show of lips flagging up and down, jaw working from side to side, and chin wagging, he only spat. "Tribes," says Muley. "I guess that's like herds or flocks. You best learn their ways afore you hunt 'em."

He and Carlson both gave ugly chuckles. "Skinny bastards. Waste a' bullets, not enough meat." More chuckles, louder this time. Then Muley gave Sir Richard what passed as a serious look with him. "These critters is really the A-rabs of America. They is thieves, nothing satisfies 'em, and no amount short of *all* will do. Their hand is agin every man, and every man's hand is agin them."

Sir Richard gave him the evil eye, and I pondered that Sir Richard was half A-rab hisself, or more. Muley and Carlson got up and moved off, so they could share each other's ugly company. I smirked at Sir Richard. "You don't look for nuggets in a chamber pot," he said.

I TOOK MY turn on guard like everybody else. Against Indians. I told myself that if I was from one tribe, I'd be willing to stand guard against another tribe.

One night Sir Richard sat up with me. Among his madnesses sometimes, seemed like, was not being able to sleep.

He just sat by me companion-like. He was a good companion, Sir Richard. He had his faults. For one, sometimes I could tell he was drunk, visiting never-never land with some drug, or by other means not in proper occupation of his mind. For another fault, he was sneaky. I'd seen him once, on his knees, bowing all the way down. I suspect he did that every day and kept it from us. His secret was safe with me. The man's big fault, and virtue, was that he surely did believe in books. He was always diving into some notebook and writing every fact down, or getting lost in reading some tome he'd brought. He was the damnedest man for writing and the written. It was like all of God's creation was only a preliminary sketch. The final draft was the published version, especially when penned by Sir Richard.

We had none of us seen hide nor hair of any horse thieves. Muley said that was because we fired two or three times into the air fast when we changed guard, let 'em know we were awake and watching and had repeating weapons. I didn't say it, but the air was the only thing I was going to shoot at. For sure not any Indian. Shooting your relatives isn't right.

After he sat awhile, Sir Richard got started talking. "I understand Digger is not a tribal designation." He was sure telling this from some of his researches. "The tribes are Pah-Ute, Shoshone, and perhaps others." He hesitated like he sometimes did, thinking. I could feel his mind circling something, restless, questing. "Each valley, each basin, each desert may have its own tribe. Perhaps each tribe has its own, separate language. I'm told this is so in California."

That wasn't what he was circling toward.

Finally he came out with it. "Do you ever think that the Diggers are perhaps your people?"

I looked at him sideways. *Well, I don't know whether I want to talk about it.*

"The bond of blood is powerful," said Sir Richard. He was one smart man. Right now I couldn't read his face—too dark. With that big old stare and the piratical scar on his cheek, his face never told much about his insides anyway.

We just sat there. The wind ran gently by, maybe bearing music we couldn't hear. The stars moved a smidgeon. I wondered if there was such a thing as the music of the spheres. "I don't know nothing about 'em," I said.

"You must have tried to find out. What do you think?"

He already knew the story of how old Taylor picked me up somewhere on the trail. I pondered a moment. "Don' know."

More sitting, more wind-listening, more stargazing. Sir Richard knew when to just let things be.

"I've wondered everything you can imagine," I said.

"Why did you start this journey?" asked Sir Richard. "What do you hope to find?"

I listened for the music of the spheres and heard silence. Or maybe I was just stalling. "Main thing was, I was just done with the old life," I said.

I let that sit, but it didn't do me any good. "There's something else," I said. "Something the Mormons don't know about, maybe something white people don't know about." Then I took thought of who I was talking to. "Most white people," I amended. "That's what happened the day I fell in the river." I hesitated. "I heard things." I looked sideways at him. He knew the story, the outside of the story.

"Words?" he prompted.

"Words, yeah, but more music. Song. Most glorious singing you ever heard, what the heavenly choirs must sound like."

After a bit, he says, "The words didn't matter?"

"I didn't know what they was. I can't tell if I didn't honest hear 'em or whether they was in a language strange to me." I stared at my fingers. "I knew what they was saying, praises to God, such as that. Just couldn't get the actual words."

"Did you have the thought that the words might be in your native tongue?"

I worked my fingers. "Yeah, I did. But they might have been anything. Saints speak in tongues, you know."

All of a sudden I felt like a fool. "Or maybe I just hit my head on a rock."

"I don't think so," said Sir Richard, "and neither do you." I couldn't help smiling in the dark. "I could teach you about mysticism," he said. "Even about speaking in tongues, which I assure you is authentic. We could talk now. Or I could send you books from England."

I shook my head. "Not my way to learn things out of books."

He nodded, because he knew that.

"Maybe I'll go to Tibet with Sun Moon. They know about mysticism."

He nodded yes. "Is that what you want?" he murmured, more to himself than me. We sat quiet for a while.

"Sometimes," I started, "I have a kind of dream. It's an awake dream, really, but I have to be half-asleep, or feeling toward that, to have it. In the dream I came into a narrow valley, good grass along a creek, lots of evergreen trees on the slopes, high mountains above. Very beautiful and somehow very familiar. I walk slowly into the valley, fascinated.

"In the middle of the valley is a tepee, smoke easing out the top. Feeling strange—eager but nervous—I walk toward the tepee. When I get close, a young woman comes out to tend to a cook fire in front. She sees me and smiles, easy, like it's natural I should be here, and welcomes me by the name Sima Untuasie. Her man comes out and says hello like I was there only yesterday. They ask me to eat with them. I sit down, some kids sit next to me, and I stay."

Neither of us said a word. I looked into the desert at all the shadows the moon made.

"That's it. That's the whole dream. It can't be my people. Indians out here don't live in tepees. That comes from pictures in kids' books, pro'ly. And I don' believe there's no alpine country with good water, grass, and trees in Washo, not anywhere." I indicated the barren desert with one hand. "That's it," I repeated. "Except that sometimes I see a blue, hazy shimmer upriver, like a lake there."

After a while, Richard said, "Does it seem like she's speaking English?"

"I only speak English," I said, a little sharply.

Sir Richard nodded. "Sometimes in dreams people know they're hearing a different language and can understand it."

"I don't speak any Indian," I said. "Old Taylor wanted me to be a white man, way it looks. Pfeffers sure did. I've learned to sign, that's it."

"You don't remember any at all? A four-year-old, the devil, a two-year-old would have been talking. Have you heard Snake, Ute, and Pah-Ute?"

I shook my head no. "Indians, breeds, interpreters, when they came into the store, I used to ask 'em to say a few words in Indian for me. But I never recognized nothing. Even the sounds, they was . . . just sounded foreign."

I looked at Sir Richard, thinking of the twenty-nine languages he spoke, or some such number. I wondered how that felt. I wondered what tongue I ought to be speaking. I tried to remember the words I heard at the bottom of the river.

"Do you think you may be remembering the valley in the dream?"

I pondered it. "Don' know," I said.

"Sun Moon's people believe you've lived many lives. You might recognize a place from a previous life. Though you didn't know what it was, you might have a strong feeling about it."

I shrugged. This was too far into guessing for me.

"Old Taylor gave no hint of your origin?"

"Others told my names, either Sima Untuasie or Rock Child." I shrugged.

"You must have wondered what Rock Child means."

I looked into his eyes, then back down at the ground, and shrugged. "Yeah. I asked a lot of Indians and breeds and interpreters. Nobody knows anything about it."

We sat in the dark for a while, sort of companions.

"Journeys," murmured Sir Richard.

At the City of Rocks, after we split off toward California, three Indians came into camp. In the evening, after supper, they just appeared. Felt spooky. One minute they were not there and the next they were, like now there's mist, now the air is clear. They didn't make a sound, much less say a word.

Harold invited them on in, an older man and two less than my age. He poured coffee, stirred lots of sugar in it, and handed them our big tin cups full. They stood, didn't sit, and I could see they were uncomfortable.

Heckahoy, no wonder, look how we acted toward them. Muley and Carlson moved back and leaned against the wagons like guards. Harold played the smiley host, but the cat took hold of his tongue. Me and Sun Moon and Sir Richard just kind of gawked.

Sir Richard broke the silence, addressing the oldest, the one about his age. "Good evening," he said, "what tribe do you belong to?"

When he got no answer, he repeated, "Tribe?"

"Shoshone," said the man.

I saw my chance. I signed to him, "Root Eater?"

He nodded yes.

The Shoshones were divided into different outfits according to where they lived and what they ate, which was more or less the same thing—Root Eaters, Buffalo Eaters, Salmon Eaters, like that. They were way, way different, and these were the first Root Eaters I'd met.

So I tried to start a conversation. "Where do your people live?"

He looked at me funny, and I later thought maybe he understood me to be asking where their camp was, which he wouldn't want to tell. So he signed, "The Goose Creek Road is good," meaning that part of the California Trail.

"Many whites on the Trail?" I asked him.

"No. Two years almost no one on this road." That was since the Pony Express set a new route across Nevada to the south and the stages had followed.

"Tell him the Saints offer him respect," said Harold. "Brigham Young is his great white father, and we would be glad to trade with him."

I did it, feeling bad.

The man just nodded.

I hesitated, not knowing what to say, and he didn't seem to want to say anything.

"Ask him if he know what Rock Child means," put in Sir Richard.

I pondered. Couldn't hurt. The Shoshones back in Deseret didn't know those words, but they were Buffalo Eaters, different. Still, I hesitated. I felt kind of twisty inside about it. Finally, I signed, "What is" and spoke the strange term "Rock Child?"

He shrugged his shoulders.

"Where is Rock Child?"

A shrug.

"Who is Rock Child?"

He set his coffee cup down and looked at Harold. "Food?" he said in English.

Harold gave him a hundred-pound sack of flour. One of the young men took it in his arms, and I guess they traded off, because these weren't horse Indians. They didn't look happy. Later we found out it wasn't because of the weight. When folks gave Diggers flour, they dumped it on the sand and used the sacks for dresses.

AT GOOSE CREEK we came on the first company we'd seen in the week since we'd left Salt Lake, hustling like leaves on a big wind. The wind was our uneasiness about Porter Rockwell, and Salt Lake City was over two hundred miles behind us.

The company was three wagons of the prairie schooner sort. Families were set up washing clothes, making dinner, and putting the camp right. I thought maybe we'd have company regularly from here on out. Hoped so.

"I'm gonna take a day to rest the team," Muley said when he'd whoaed the mules.

"We have a schedule," Harold put up.

Muley didn't pay him no mind, just got down and began to unharness them, and Carlson done the same.

"We have a schedule," repeated Harold. He was trying to sound like one of those that just say something and folks snap to. Maybe that worked if you were Brigham Young.

Muley turned his back eloquent-like. He could actually do that—turn his back in a way that said, Go to hell with all your ancestors and descendants in a thimble.

"Muley!" said Harold.

Without even looking around, Muley said, "These mules is this child's nest egg." Meaning they were his stake for however he was going to get rich in Virginia City, and he didn't mean to get them there slat-ribbed. The grass in the bluff-lined valley of this creek was good. He went on with his unhitching.

"Well, too-ra-loo-ra-loo," said Harold Jackson, and waggled his ass at Muley.

After dinner we were invited over to the other camp for coffee, and all of us went, us three mismatched pilgrims, Harold, and the two skinners.

The people in the wagons were all related, DeSelie by name. M. DeSelie and his wife, handsome French-Canadian folks in middle years, took on like they were in charge. Reeshaw and Root, they told us to call them, which I later found out was a Frenchy way of saying Richard and Ruth. Two grown sons of theirs with wives and little ones, all name of De-

Selie. Plus Root's nephew and his wife, probably in their thirties, and their kids. Frenchy is what they were, Métis, they called it, half-bloods from Canada. You could see it easy in the way they were decked out, red sashes, embroidered coats, and other fancy stuff, even on the trail.

What got quick on my mind was the DeSelie daughter, Annabelle. She was the tiniest creature, a willow branch of a girl, maybe seventeen or eighteen. She wore a black dress with a scarlet sash, her hair was the color of onyx, her skin the color of wet sand. What stood out about her was none of that, not hair nor face nor figure, only one feature. She had eyes that glowed like she had a bonfire of spirit inside. I couldn't keep my eyes off her, which Sun Moon noticed. I couldn't tell whether the nun gave a damn or not.

Reeshaw was full curious about the road ahead and Californy. I thought maybe they were headed to the Golden Shore to make their fortunes as farmers—you could grow crops all year long, the way folks told it. But when I said this to Reeshaw, he just chuckled at me. "I go to Californy 'cause I go to Californy. Métis, me."

Muley spat. Carlson spat, too.

Root and Reeshaw was worried about getting over Donner Pass before the snows. What happened to the Donners some years back still preyed on everyone's minds. "Tell us about t'e road ahead," Reeshaw urged, looking hard at our drivers.

Muley grinned and waggled his head. "Ain't hard, that's the thing. Easy. But all the same, day after day. Grass hard by the river only. Them hillsides is desert like a good God ud never made, my pa woulda said. Dry stuff, stony, and hoodoo shapes. Hoo-oo-oo-doo-oo. You walk and you walk and you walk and then you walk and last you walk some more. Nothing but mirages and shapes of hoo-oo-oo-doo-oo. To the sink."

"How long?" queried Reeshaw. He was holding forth for good sense.

"For you? A month. For us? Ten days." Though I could tell Muley was bragging, it made me count. Porter Rockwell would not be out of a jail before we reached the sink.

"From the sink we go south to Virginia City. You gonna go the way of them crazy Donners?" He spat. Carlson spat amen.

Reeshaw looked long at his wife and daughter, one to t'other. Root looked back. She had gray hair still flecked with rust, like some mixed-blood people do. It hung in long braids. Her carriage was like a queen's. Never saw a woman as good-looking at mebbe fifty. He had thick, luxuriant black hair, made him look younger than his years. "What you t'inking, Reeshaw?"

He shrugged his shoulders in that Frenchy way. "Well, Root," says he, "I'm looking to get out my fiddle, me. I see a lot of dancing partners hardly been used."

"Formidable!" said Annabelle in Frenchy talk, the first words I'd heard from her. She had high voice, sweet as a fife.

That fiddle just jumped into Reeshaw's hands. He ran his bow on the rosin next to the bridge and set horsehair to catgut. A tune popped out like a jack-in-the-box and began to dance.

So did everyone else. You never saw feet start hopping and jumping and kicking front and back like then. Root and Reeshaw's sons and their wives together, Muley and Carlson with the little daughters, Root with Sir Richard, and . . . I took the hands of Annabelle and gave my legs, body, and soul to the music.

SIR RICHARD CUT in after the first dance. Which was just as well. In the first place, I was bamboozled as a baby by Annabelle, her flashing smile, her luminous eyes, and her dancing feet. In the second, I could see Sun Moon staring at me. She was the only female in the place not dancing. She wouldn't know how, of course. Plus none of the men would ask a heathen Chinee. I wondered if she would want to, being a nun and all.

I watched Annabelle turn and twirl guided by Sir Richard's hands, her full skirts flaring. I felt envy, I did, and something else stronger. I was jealous, jealous of Reeshaw and that fiddle.

What happened next made me think Root was a mind reader, and maybe she was. She stuck her head in one of the wagons and came out with a banjo in her hands. She held it out to me. "By t'e Virgin I know you play music, me. I see it in your eyes."

IN HIS MIND Richard Burton danced with his wife Isabel. Ah, the young Annabelle touching his hands, allemanding, promenading, do-si-doing, turning at his touch—she was lovely, winning enough for a night's pleasure, or a week's, but she was not Isabel Arundell Burton, his Isabel, his wife. From his own Isabel he still wanted everything a man can imagine. He dreamed of pleasures of the body, the heart, and of the spirit that were rare, very rare, evanescent, perhaps illusion. *Now she knows me, she will reject me.*

Pain from an old wound stiffened his back. Pain of a thousand slights made his arms rigid, and his attractive partner hesitated, frowned. Burton forced his attention to his dancing. He made his body spin gracefully, supple and strong at once. He held the lady's hands with his own. He dived into the dance. He ached for his Isabel.

Tonight after prayers. Yes, tonight I will transport myself. Sweet opium!

I CAN PICK. Always could. Got a used banjo with the first dollars I ever earned. Worked it out by myself right quick. If the Pfeffers hadn't thought I was loco for playing the banjo and whistling at the same time, I might be a Saint yet.

I didn't know Reeshaw's Frenchy canoe songs, but my gift is for picking music up quick. After one verse I was strumming out those thwanging paddle rhythms strong as him. We mounted up high and flew into the chorus. We came around about another way through one more verse. When we hit the chorus this time, we were sailing, riding the big wave of sound. We stroked through the rapids and rode the current home.

The dancers were right pleased. Reeshaw gave me a gleam—he could feel the music too. He jumped right then into another slappety-go paddling song, and we brought her home hot and hard.

That was when I decided to go for a change. A slow song, sad, "The Dying Californian." True, the banjo is picked, but you can flow better than a fiddle, with a feathery touch and sliding your fingers. And I had another tactic that was flow as all get out—whistling along with picking.

I am no musician,

Sir Richard wrote in his journal later that night,

> *but immediately I and everyone present felt ourselves in the presence of the muses. Richard DeSelie harmonized and gave Asie a pulse in rhythm. The lad strummed a melody on that banjo so dulcet, so poignant . . . All was heart-stirring. What was extraordinary was a high, floating harmony he whistled above all the other notes. It reached in, stroked the soul, and made it purr.*
>
> *That was when I began to understand. All along the lad had borne himself like a man with a secret, not a secret of fact, which is known thoroughly, but a secret sense, an inner feeling which*

imbues his whole being. Yet he does not know how to express this feeling to another, does not even understand it himself, but merely bears it, delicately, like a golden bowl of precious liquid that must not be spilled.

Here surely was Asie's secret, or a large part thereof: His native language was music. To my inquiries later he offered confirmation: He hears music in his mind every day of his life, when awakening, or alone, or traveling through the countryside. Birdsong is particularly inspiring to him, and he cannot hear it without harmonizing, elaborating, imagining more birds and a symphony of calls. His whistling had its origin here, in imitating birdsong or harmonizing with it.

He is a virtuoso whistler, capable of rapid scales, trills, turns, volumes loud and soft, tones piercingly brilliant, gently soothing. Perhaps the ladies who thought Niccolò Paganini the devil for his fiendish skill on the strings of the violin would be as much astounded by my young half-blood friend. His effects are no less impressive when the natural limitations of his instrument, two lips, are considered. Less dazzling, they are more soulful.

After two verses and choruses, Annabelle DeSelie sang the words of the song, and showed how earthbound and crude are words in expressing the nuances of the heart, compared to music alone. The story of the song is simple, even primitive: A man bound for California but dying of fever asks his brother to hold him, then says final words by turns to his wife and children, and expresses deep faith at finding a home in the arms of God. The words are merely sentimental, dipped deep in pathos. Yet the eloquence of the fiddle, banjo, and especially the whistling made all poignant, heart-rending, beautiful beyond description.

I ask myself, To what end? A mixed-blood lad living in the wasteland of the American interior, enfranchised neither among white or red, quite homeless, far, far from the great cities where music is loved—where can such a young man give expression to his genius? This circumstance alone might undo the complacent English notion that the Divinity sets us providentially upon the Earth and thenceforth takes care of us. True, I have seen a few employments for musicians in the West: They may act as pianists or organists in church, fiddlers in camp, or performers on the piano or hurdy-gurdy in whorehouses. Which end for Asie,

I ask, would be more ghastly? Oh, one more employment: He might beat the drum and give voice to bizarre caterwauling at the dances of the native peoples. It is an appalling dilemma.

We were lucky—the DeSelies also intended to stay over a day and rest their animals. We all looked forward to a second night of dancing and singing and general music-making, too.

After breakfast Sir Richard, he did me a great service. "You're grand on that banjo. Would you like to have it?"

"Do one-legged ducks swim in circles?"

"Perhaps Reeshaw would take the Hawkin in exchange for it. If so, I'll make you a gift of the muzzleloader. The music in camp will be worth it."

Reeshaw was a woodsman, knew the rifle would feed his family, and traded me the banjo gladly.

Sir Richard's gift made me feel tremendous. Sometimes I'd felt like Sir Richard was Sun Moon's protection on this journey, and I didn't have anything to do. Of course, music is not as practical as a good gun, as Reeshaw could tell you.

3

That afternoon Annabelle and me walked out along the creek together and talked. Truth to tell, we even held hands. In this small courting I felt the approval of Root and Reeshaw, or at least their tolerance. Maybe it was only because we would hitch up and head out tomorrow morning and never see the DeSelies again. But I thought there was more than that to it. The Saints kept their girls away from me because I am not white and delightsome. When I went to make a match, my choices would probably have been among half-breed women, or other Lamanites getting the benefit of Saintly rearing. If I'd been really good, I might eventually have had a chance at a white girl, but only from the poorer families.

Root and Reeshaw, though, were mixed-bloods themselves. Those Métis went way back, the way they told it. Reeshaw's words were, Before the memories of the oldest grandfathers. Root said, Since the first Frenchmen came into the country hunting furs. A long time anyhow.

And all that time the white and red blood had been mixed, till no one knew or cared who had how much of what color. The Métis even made their own way of talking, their own way of being Catholic, their own way of hunting, their own way of dividing up land, according to Root and Reeshaw. Whether you courted full red, full white, or mixed didn't mean a damn. (Except to some white women that came into the country later, said Root.) So Root and Reeshaw, I think, just looked at me as a man, not an Indian. It felt good.

Annabelle, she felt good and not good all at once. She looked scrumptious and smelt grand, just jimmy-joomy. When I looked close, even more when I touched her hand, I felt desire. Up to then I'd hardly even held hands with anybody, and nothing more atall. I was in my twenties and powerful hungry for a woman, as you might guess. Walking along, sitting on a log, talking, and all else I did with Annabelle that day, sure, I felt like slipping her clothes right off her body and slipping myself in. But I couldn't get started.

For one thing, even while I was flirting with Annabelle, pictures of Sun Moon kept popping into my head, and sounds of her voice. It drove me half-crazy, touching and feeling one woman while seeing and hearing another, like being two men in two places at once. In later years I heard of a split personality. That's what I was that day.

A lot of times in my life one half of me has blundered into trouble, and later I've wondered where was the other half, the wiser, smarter, altogether better half. When we went wading in the creek, it turned into one of those times.

We were looking for minnows. They are favorites of mine. Instead of critters of matter like the rest of us, they look like little flashes of sunlight in the water. So delicate, so fast, so quicksilver.

"Let's catch some," said Annabelle. She took hold of her skirt and tucked the bottom up so the cloth ballooned down about halfway.

I'd never actually caught any. In the Pfeffer family we didn't hold with hunting, fishing, or just roaming around in nature. I felt kinda afraid Annabelle would show me up at this catching 'em.

She did, too. She waded in calf-deep where she saw them, bent low, and put in her hands halfway down in the water. Then she stood still as anything you ever saw. That girl took a crazy-kid grin on her face and turned herself into a rock.

After a long while the minnows would start swimming around just like before—they'd accepted her as a log that fell into the creek or some such. They began to pass right over her hand like it was a stick. She grinned even bigger and waited. Instead of being impatient, she seemed to wait longer than she needed to, just to show.

She moved swift as a hawk. Her hands shot straight on up, the minnow soared into the air above, and sparkling drops of water showered up with it. I could hardly see which gleam was minnow and which was droplet. Then both fell back into the creek, and the air was empty of all but sunlight.

"Crackajack," says I, and clapped my hands sincerely. It was smart as a circus act.

"Let me show you how," she says. So we did it together, side by side, touching hips sometimes and smiling like we had a secret. She did it twice more, and I loved seeing the fish fly. But they were quicker than me, and I came up empty.

"Let's go over t'ere!" says she. We started splashing across the creek. Water might have been cold some times of years, coming out of the mountains to the southwest, but in summer it felt nice. Annabelle trotted ankle-deep to a log half in the water and started scrambling up. "Help me," she says. I took her hand and supported her while she got onto her feet. "I want to stand all t'e way up," she says, indicating her waist with her hands. I straddled the log and held her there.

She thrust her arms into the sky and let loose a call, long and lonely and beautiful. A loon call it was, she told me later, but I'd never been to the northern lake country and never heard a loon, before or since. She sounded to me like a mysterious and hauntingly beautiful bird that was looking for company. I wanted to call back, or whistle back, but I hesitated.

She shuffled to her right, got hold of a limb, and says, "Come on!"

I stood up next to her. She took my hand, let go the limb, raised her arms and mine to the sky, and stiff as a plank slowly toppled forward.

It was a hole. I came up flailing, and Annabelle was thrashing around beneath the surface.

I grabbed her under the back and the knees, turned, and hauled her up onto the sandy shore. I knelt and set her down but kept my arms underneath.

My feelings were doing loop-de-loops. *What the hell are you doing? Don't you know . . . ?*

Then I saw her thighs shiny wet, gleaming in the sun. Since she wasn't wearing any bloomers, I saw them right up to where they stopped being thighs and turned into something else. I looked at her eyes, laughing. I looked at her smile, sparkling. I looked at her nipples, poking up against her thin bodice.

I slipped my hands out from underneath and put both my hands on her breasts and caressed them through the cloth. "Not here," she said, "over t'ere. I saw a place."

She hopped up and ran off. With no idea where we were going, I panted along behind.

YOU KNOW WHAT my fantasies were. They went beyond the most direct thing you think of. Lying around in the raw, too, letting the sun warm our bodies. Making love again. Walking our fingers everywhere, stroking our palms everywhere. Making love again.

Still at a trot, she headed up a little hill. I followed, clutching at her. Just before we got to the bushes at the top, I caught her. I pulled her to me and kissed her hard, with all the twisties you can put in a kiss.

She grabbed my hand and pulled me on. It was a cave she was aiming at, a long, low slit in the bluff.

I stopped cold, and resisted her tug. Cold wriggled in my belly. My mind churned with premonition. My eyes worked the darkness of the cave. They said, "No, Porter Rockwell isn't in there." My throat squeezed and said, "Yes he is."

Annabelle looked questioningly into my eyes. The warmth of her hand melted my fear, and desire defeated the fear of death. I laughed aloud.

We dived in, wrapped our arms around each other, giggling, and rolled until I ended up on top. I looked into her eyes. The moment had arrived.

A voice said gently, "Annabelle."

Root's voice.

We looked deeper into the cave and saw Root and Reeshaw. They were in about the same position as us. Only Reeshaw's trousers was already down, and Root's legs were showing up to you know where.

NEVER DID I lose my enthusiasm for anything in such a hurry. I sat back, stood up, and clunked my head. Annabelle looked at me queer-like, stood up, and clunked her head. We took each other's hands and pulled each other down, sitting, to keep it from happening again.

Reeshaw began to chuckle.

"Would you two wait for us outside?" asked Root.

Reeshaw was laughing but trying to keep it quiet.

We scurried like crabs to the entrance and halfway down the slope. Pretty quick they came out.

"You see cave," he said, "t'ink maybe good place to . . ." He gave a Frenchy shrug. "Make love." They looked at us, they looked at each other, and they plumb lost control laughing.

"Too late!" says Reeshaw between guffaws. He slapped his knees. Root did the same. They shook. They laughed. "Too late!" Reeshaw roared. "We walk, we see same, we t'ink same. Cave in use!"

"Sandy bottom of a cave," Root said. She looked into Isabelle's eyes. "Good idea, daughter." They whooped again.

I blurted it out. "Sir, I'll marry her. I will, I swear." Wonderful what a fella will say when his legs are jumping to run, isn't it?

Reeshaw gaped at me. Then at Annabelle. Then he shook his head at Root, eyes laughing. Then his hands were laughing, too, and chest, and belly. *"Marry!"* he exclaimed. "A dalliance in a cave, incomplete, and marry!" He pronounced it dah-lee-awnse. "Hoo-hoo-hah!"

Not only were they were both laughing, Annabelle was grinning at me. She slipped her arm through mine and gripped my hand warmly again.

"Me when young like you," said Root, "I do my dalliances. If marry all, make husbands like army."

They got lost in whooping again.

Sweet gizzards.

Sun Moon didn't think it was so funny.

Nobody told her, of course, or told anyone, but she had eyes. The young DeSelie girl took Asie's hand when she felt like it, smiled at him possessively, put her arm around his waist. He obviously liked it. Loved it. Worst of all, they had that moony look new lovers get.

New travelers had rolled into camp, and the people treated Asie and Annabelle as a couple. All the Americans were excited. Tonight the desert air would burst with music. Everyone would dance. Asie and Annabelle would dance together, their eyes so locked on one another that their gazes would be like ropes intertwining.

Sun Moon was disgusted. With him, with herself, with everyone. *Lingam* and *yoni* might be drawn to each other, but they were base energies, mere appetites. Asie ought to be pouring his energy into something more important, like his drumming.

When Asie walked toward the creek with a bucket, Sun Moon followed him. She spoke to his back as he dipped the bucket for water. "You go with them? Stay with DeSelie woman?"

Asie straightened up and looked at her. "What are you talking about?"

"The DeSelie woman. You go with her? With them? Or you stay with us?"

Asie stepped around her with difficulty, pulled down on one side by the heavy bucket. "Sun Moon, you and I and Sir Richard are crossing the desert to Californy. That's that." He kept walking.

"I think . . ."

Asie set the bucket down and turned back. "I know what you think. It ain't so."

She looked into his face. She couldn't help wondering, *Would it be so if I didn't speak up? Were you thinking of it?* She blinked, and hoped the deep twilight kept him from seeing the hurt on her face. *Am I not as pretty? Do you hate my scar? Why would you take great trouble to help a foreigner like me?*

Asie turned his back, hoisted the bucket, and lumbered off.

Sun Moon watched. *What am I doing? I feel jealous—I can't deny the feeling—and why? I don't want Asie for myself. I am desperate, desperate to remain celibate the rest of my life.*

She shrugged it off. Sometimes she didn't understand herself. After meditation she didn't understand better in her head, but she felt free of the negative feelings that got hold of her, like jealousy.

She walked into some boulders. Here she could be out of sight, private, to do her meditation and do the *puja.* She set the altar on a rock, put cedar and sage on it, and lit them with a match. She had discovered that cedar and sage made not a bad incense. She smelled the thick, rich odor of the plants and sat in the lotus position.

She spoke in a formal tone:

"O Mahakala! Thou art fond of cremation grounds; so I have turned my heart into one
That Thou, a resident of cremation grounds, may dance there unceasingly."

Sun Moon did not merely repeat words lazily, but made herself think of their meaning. *My very heart is the fire of a funeral pyre,* she went on silently, in her mind. *It is littered with the ashes of bodies. Trample the conqueror of death, and come dancing into my heart.*

Sun Moon breathed in deep, and let all the air out. It was always hard for her to pray for the embrace of death. Yet if she were to pass beyond her fear of death, if she were to attain understanding that death and life are one, that destruction and creation are one, that mother and murderer are one, she must. Every day she prayed with half a heart, hoping that affirmation lay somewhere beyond.

She lowered her eyes to the dust at the foot of the boulder and began to pay attention to her breathing. After a few breaths the words came without her willing them: *Om mani padme hung . . .*

As usual, Sun Moon came to the fire for food only at the end of supper. Burton always disliked that, the way she kept herself apart. In his opinion it was both arrogance and self-effacement. Sun Moon put herself last. None of the white people took exception—the natural way of things, the way they saw it. They never realized that Sun Moon was testing, noticing, and judging. He watched her start her pot of tea. Every evening she made tea from a plant called ephedra and known commonly as Mormon tea. Long since she had learned that no one else would drink it. When the pot was on the fire, she helped herself to stew.

The stew was a great relief to Burton. Every night they ate the very salty jerked meat brought from Salt Lake City, which Burton detested. Tonight the DeSelies added prairie turnips (a root vegetable), fresh wild onions, and other vegetables. Harold gave a few pounds of potatoes. The DeSelies professed themselves grateful for the meat, which the captain thought scarcely credible, and Burton found himself cringingly grateful for anything other than briny meat.

Sun Moon sat alone on a low boulder, holding herself apart with the language of body and eyes. How graceful she was! Burton never tired of watching her. Her eyes spoke of serenity, her scar of violence.

"Sister," he said in the Tibetan language, "may I join you?"

She smiled at him, and Burton sat on her rock.

"Sister," he began, "I believe we will get to California. Three weeks to Virginia City, a rest, and from there a stagecoach to San Francisco. It doesn't look difficult."

"Porter Rockwell," she said simply, eyeing Burton like a foolish child.

"Yes, I understand. After Brother Young keeps him a month, though, he'll never catch us. If he even tries."

She looked off into the twilight, her face unreadable. *What has happened to this woman?* Burton wondered. It was more than his fertile mind could imagine—the convent as a mere girl, a decade of learning, then the madness. Abduction, definitely. Rape? Probably. Shipment to Canton and across the Pacific. More rape? Perhaps. Escape. And now the journey back? Even a fanciful mind couldn't wrap itself around all that.

I admire you.

"When we get to San Francisco, I will give you money. Passage to China is not an imposing sum. I see it as tribute your spirit commands."

She looked at him, and he saw her mind move behind her dark eyes. Though she had a few coins, doubtless stolen, the amount was piddling. "Thank you very much, Sir Richard," she said.

They held each other's eyes.

At last she went on, "Would passage to India be possible?"

"Whatever you prefer. Where?"

"Calcutta," she said.

Yes, the mouth of the Ganges. She was thinking of it as a pilgrimage. He wondered how good a conception her scholar's mind held of the journey done that way. Calcutta, north through mountains to Bhutan, north again across the highest mountains in the world. Then Lhasa. Yes, he understood, she wanted to visit the holy city of her people, perhaps to see the Dalai Lama. But then a long journey eastward to Kham, her home country. More difficult than going through China.

She spoke with an edge he'd never heard. "I will not go near the Chinese." Hatred. Yes, hatred. Fascinating. Burton gave thanks in his mind to Allah for the endless fascination that is the world. So a longer journey, but safer, and far more consoling to the spirit.

"I will give you funds, Sister." In the firelight he thought he saw tears shine in eyes long dry. She turned away. So many ways to keep privacy, so many ways to avoid human contact, so many ways to hide the soul . . .

Burton didn't know why, but he wondered whether she would go to Calcutta, Lhasa, and her home, the convent at Zorgai. So far, so many occasions for missteps, so many choices—opportunities as wide as the world itself. From Tibet to America, halfway around the globe—that was wildly improbable, more a fantasy even than the tales of Arabian nights he loved. Return trip? That pushed the mind from fascination to skepticism. He could not imagine it.

The fiddle struck the first notes. It called to the legs, "Come dance!"

CHAPTER FIFTEEN

I EYED THE newcomers. They were all men, a horseback outfit heading back to the States fast, everyone broke and dissatisfied. One of 'em said to me, "If I can ever get back to Missouri, I'll gladly eat out of the trough with my hogs."

Folks going West on the trail those years held Californy as a golden land, a place of fulfillment of dreams. You didn't hear many good words about the place from the folks headed back East. Grumble, grumble, bitch, bitch. Why did the ones headed West keep going? Why didn't they set themselves down, right there in camp, have a good think, and turn around? The country between the deserts and Missouri was thick with buffalo—nobody would have starved going back. And plenty of good places between here and there to settle down.

It was partly the War Between the States. The talk of the West in those years was one of two subjects, war in the East, gold and silver in the West.

What I noticed was that people see dreams larger than what's in front of their faces. Dreams have a powerful hold on us human creatures, for good and for bad. Jesus of Nazareth had a dream, they say. So did Joseph Smith. So did Genghis Khan. The question is, what's the dream? What human feeling does it come from? I think Jesus' dream came from love. Old Khan's came from the lust for power. The California rush for gold and Washo rush for silver came from greed. That made all the difference.

At the time, though, I told myself us mismatched three were different. We were sensible.

Later I laughed at myself. No, the engines of our trip weren't dreams. Sun Moon was only looking for a way to go home to Tibet. I was only looking to find the people I was born to, or figure where and how I belonged on this Earth. Sir Richard was only trying to get known as a big-time author and explorer. No dreams there!

WHEN REESHAW STRUCK up the music, I grabbed my new banjo, new to me, and dived in with a frenzy of notes. Come! Get those feet going! Hoof it! Let's have a big time!

Everybody cut it up handsome. Since the newcomers were all male, there was a right shortage of females. Every woman had a partner waiting for the next dance. Some of the men tied bandannas on their sleeves and danced the female part temporary-like. Annabelle was Jeehosaphat popular, of course, and didn't she look jimmy-joomy! Second was Root. Instead of slowing her down, her years seemed to give her a kind of dignity and strength. Root had something that her daughter-in-laws hadn't risen up to yet.

Reeshaw and I took turns trying to shine. He'd do a fiddle tune, usually one of his Frenchy paddlin' songs, and I'd back him up. Then we'd switch and I'd take the lead. I went strictly for tunes everybody knew, "Dinah Had a Wooden Leg," "Irish Washer Woman," "Tulsy Waltz," "Fort Smith Rag," and all like that. It was hard to watch Annabelle waltzing with another man during "Tulsy." But heckahoy, I druther play with sounds in my mind than bounce around on my legs. Which has been fateful for me.

When I started on one ballad, "The Little Log Cabin in the Lane," Reeshaw slid over and got Root. They spun slow, they allemanded, they do-si-doed, they promenaded, they dipped, and they rose through the night air, lit handsome by the fire. Reeshaw's fine, long, thick, black hair shone in the flames, and Root looked statuesque. He danced like he was proud to show her off, and she danced like she was proud to be led by such a man. It made me feel better about the upshot of marriage than ever I had, up to then.

I headed straight into another ballad, thinking I'd enjoy watching them again. Reeshaw had other ideas, though. He bounded over and offered a hand to Sun Moon.

She drew back—actually, drew back without moving, in that way she had.

His hand rose and banged back to level again, inviting, demanding. He smiled like a sun.

She hesitated.

Reeshaw picked her up by the waist, held her high in his big hands, and set on her the dance ground.

She followed his lead.

Root clapped her hands. I think everybody was watching, on the sly or straight on.

Reeshaw just swept her along, not allowing any mistakes. Sun Moon moved her tiny feet, and after a bit I saw that she was right in rhythm, and nimble.

Then I beheld the looks on the faces of the others. Our folks—Harold, Muley, Carlson—were embarrassed. Sun Moon didn't really figure in their world. They generally acted like she wasn't around. Reeshaw putting her in the center threw them off.

The newcomers, though, they were tickled. Kept trying not to grin at each other, at the same time avoiding Root's eyes. Then I caught on. Back in Californy, if a white man danced with a Chinee woman, it meant only one thing, whoop-dee-doo in a back room right quick. They'd likely done it themselves.

That made me mad. When I finished the tune, I nodded Reeshaw toward his fiddle, set down the banjo, and took both of Sun Moon's hands. Reeshaw sashayed into a slow waltz. I was a not-bad dancer, and I think Sun Moon and I got through it with our dignity in place. It wasn't until we were through that I noticed everyone had stopped dancing and was just watching us. So I kept her hands and waited for the next tune.

Imagine my surprise when it came from the banjo. One of the Missouri-bound fellas was pickin', a lanky youth with a homely face that was all nose and Adam's apple. His fingers just naturally set feet to flying, and right quick every grown-up in the place was whirling and twirling. I jumped around with Sun Moon, and we bumped each other hard only once. She laughed, which was a pleasure to see.

That picker was good to hear, a real music man.

At the tune's end he says, "Here's a Spanyard song I heerd in Californy." After that he had a Basque song, a German song, even a Danish song. By that time he'd wore us out, and everyone was setting on the ground. He sang the fine old song "John Anderson, My Jo." It was too beautiful to do anything but listen anyway. At the end he said softly, "Irish."

Said Sun Moon into the silence, "How about Chinese?"

Well, heckahoy. It got quiet enough to hear the earth breathe. Chinese? Outrageous! I could see the looks around the fire. Give one of those yellow skins an inch and they'll act like damn fools.

The picker was not flabbergasted. He did look hard at Sun Moon first. "B'lieve I got one," he says soft-like.

It was the same tune he'd just picked, only the words were changed.

"John Chinaman, my jo, John
You're coming precious fast.
Each ship that sails from Shanghai brings
An increase on the last.
And when you'll stop invading us
I'm blest, now, if I know.
You'll outnumber us poor Yankees,
John Chinaman, my jo."

Everybody was ashamed to look at each other or at Sun Moon. She had that glazed look on her face that came sometimes, like she didn't want to know what was going on, she refused to credit what was right there. I felt for her.

There were other verses, but the picker didn't go on. His heart didn't seem that mean. Instead he flabbergasted everyone by saying, "They's a lot of songs *about* the Chinese in Californy, Ma'am. Some of 'em are meant funny, mostly poking fun at queues, so maybe not funny to your ears. Some of 'em are meant harsh, 'cause Chinamen takes white men's jobs. There's one I know as is sympathetic, 'John Chinaman's Appeal.' "

We were all still struck silent, and in the silence he launched into the old tune "Umbrella Courtship," with new words.

"American, now mind my song,
If you would but hear me sing,
And I will tell you of the wrong
That happened unto Gee Sing.
In fifty-two I left my home—
I bid farewell to Hong Kong—
I started with Cup Gee to roam
To the land where they use the long tom."

Then came a chorus that was silly but fun and not meant to hurt.

"O ching hi ku tong me ching ching
O ching hi ku tong chi do,
Cup Gee hi ku tong mo ching ching,
Then what could Gee or I do?"

It went on to tell the story of how Gee Sing came to San Francisco. Starving, he ate a dog and got arrested and fined. He went to the goldfields and got chased off. Went to another mining camp and the Know Nothings wouldn't let him stay. Went to Weaverville and got driven off by other Chinamen. Went to Yreka, set up a laundry, and went broke. Finally went home:

"Oh, now, my friends, I'm going away
From this infernal place, Sir;
The balance of my days I'll stay
With the celestial race, Sir.
I'll go to raising rice and tea;
I'll be a heathen ever,
For Christians all have treated me
As men should be used never."

At this awkward moment the dance broke up. People acted sheepish and wandered off to their wagons to sleep. The only one made any gesture toward Sun Moon was Root, who walked right up and gave her a hug. Being of another race herself, probably, Root understood. Reeshaw gave Sun Moon a touch on the shoulder, too. Sun Moon stood stiffish, not knowing how to react to this Frenchy affection.

Then I noticed Annabelle walking quiet into the bushes. With the picker. My heart twisted on itself. I let my breath out, and it eased some. Guess I'd known all along how Annabelle was.

I sat on a rock and moped. After a while I decided to turn my mind to something useful. Never mind what I felt about the picker right now. What must Sun Moon's feelings be? He had meant both kind and unkind, seemed like, songs on both sides. Even his notion of kind, of course, wasn't much kind—yeah, it's not fair, but the best thing to do is get your carcass off this continent and go back to your own.

Part of the strangeness, naturally, was that Sun Moon wasn't Chinese.

She hated the Chinese, or at least some Chinese, and she had way more reason than anyone here for that hatred. Yet all her time in America she'd been treated like one of the race she hated. I wondered how that made her feel about hate.

Life was getting me used to strange, that's for sure. It's kept doing that in the decades since. O strange, O wondrous, O enchantment! O Flabbergastonia!

Well, since thinking is not living, I got up and went over to her. She looked up into my face, her eyes big as moons, excuse the expression. "I'm sorry," I said.

She nodded. Sorry wasn't an idea she spent a lot of time on. She held my look for a moment, and I guess that was her way of showing acceptance. "Drum dry now," she said.

Peculiar. I was worrying about her, and she had a thought for me.

Yep, the drum. *I owe you that. Guess I owe us that.*

The hide felt good and tight. I pushed at it with my fingers, then a flat hand. It was springy. I walked away from the fire so I could see into the darkness, Moon behind me. I didn't know where I wanted to sit to beat the drum. Above camp I could see a rock jutting up like a thumb, short, thick, and stubby. That looked right to me.

The moon lent me plenty of light to pick my way up there among the sagebrushes and other scrub—it was full, perfectly round, no nibbled part at the lower left showing it hadn't quite arrived, nor no nibbled part on the upper right showing it had just passed full. It was *full.*

Halfway I noticed Sun Moon was still a few steps behind. "I need to do this alone," I said. *I'm not any Bon Poh pah woh.* She nodded and turned back. I knew she could hear the drum in camp, and would listen, but I still wanted to make the music by myself.

I chuckled. I thought, *Two bits somebody will complain at me tomorrow morning for making devil drum all night, keeping decent folk awake with heathen stuff.* I won the bet, because that's what happened. It was Muley complained.

At first I felt awkward and self-conscious. Plenty quick that sloughed off, though. Didn't matter what I did with the drum, 'cept whatever I felt like. I tried things out. Boom-boom-bOOm-BOOM, each one getting louder, then repeating the four. Tappety-tappety-tappety-tappety real fast, almost like a rattle. TUM-tuh-tuh, TUM-tuh-tuh, TUM-tuh-tuh, a three-beat rhythm. For a while I put down the beater Sun Moon gave me and tried it with my hands. Turned out, though, I wanted the beater—wanted to send those sounds right out across the desert in all four directions, right down to the center of the Earth, right up to the sky.

I tried some more rhythms. I shifted beat in the middle of things, went back, circled around, crossed in a new rhythm taking turns with my bare hand and the beater, came home to the first rhythm, stronger. Fooling around with rhythms was fun. More than fun.

I looked up at the moon and held my eyes there. *Maybe,* I thought, *I can send my beat all the way to the moon.* I've always liked to imagine the music we make never stops. It goes from here to there in the sky, and further, and further, fast but still using up time. I imagine the sounds pushing the air, invisible as wind, and singing when it arrives at the moon and the stars. Where does the music ever stop? Nowhere. Wind pushes wherever there's a sky, and that goes on forever. Maybe the moon is magic, and if I could go up there, I'd hear all the music ever made, whispering round and round the moon, moon, moon.

So I sent my rhythms to the sky. I thought of my heartbeat and sent that. I thought of the heartbeats of everyone in camp and sent them. I thought of all the heartbeats of all the people in the world, about one every second, and I heard them all in my imagination, one big life, beating, beating, beating. I sent them all to the full moon. After a while all the heartbeats of all the animals joined in, hurling the head of my stick onto that vibrating skin. For a while I imagined the whole earth was beating, beating, beating, sending the thump of its life to the moon.

I did that for a long time, and a long time, and a long, long time.

It wasn't until later that I thought it was kind of like the music I heard in the river. No voices of women, children, and angels this time, though, nor of trumpets, flutes, and violins. No cries of birds, nor sounds of the spirits of sky, wind, flowing waters. Just a beat. A simple thump. Thump, thump, thump, thump, to all eternity. Somehow felt like everything was in that one sound.

CHAPTER SIXTEEN

From the journal of Captain Richard Burton:

The Humboldt River is a humbug river is a Humboldt River is a humbug river.

Traveling along the Humboldt in summer is the blastedest blastedest blastedest blastedest . . .

One walks, naturally. Muley's mules, his nest egg, must not lose flesh or fat. Therefore people must. Muley and Carlson drive. Sun Moon, Asie, Harold Jackson, and I walk—walk all day for three days, until Muley hears our complaints about the heat. Then we walk all night and try to sleep during the day. We switch back to walking during the day, back to night, and spend the rest of the trip quarreling about which is worse.

Is it hot? My thermometer spends its days in the vicinity of 100–110 Fahrenheit. Fahrenheit, however, has lost its meaning. Instead of looking at the thermometer, I contemplate all the words for hot *I can think of. Fiery, roasting, frying, white-hot, red-hot, scorching, boiling, piping hot . . . I set these words to a martial drum in my head and the beat of my boots against the ground: right foot burning, left foot blistering, right searing, left scalding, right steaming, left simmering, right torrid, left sweltering. Then I realize I should have left out the words that imply water, for water there is none. Therefore, add right foot dry, left foot parched, right arid, left . . .*

One cannot count the Humbug River as water. It is horse piss spiced with alkali and salt. It is the muddiest, filthiest, meanest stream in all creation. I walk along it in fantasy, dreaming of pure, clear, sweet water that may be found in the Sierra Nevada, promised somewhere ahead. Though I have spent much of my life in hot places, this time I swear repeatedly that never again will I endure foul water and wretched heat. I can not swear fancifully, however, for my brain is baked. (If fortune attends me, I shall find haven from my wanderlust in the arms of Isabel. Through her nurturing, I shall tame my demons. Through her love, I shall conquer my cravings.)

Walk, walk, walk, morning, noon, evening, midnight. Get across this desert. Walk, walk, walk, morning, noon, evening, midnight. Somehow, some way, get across.

Then there is the dust, which is also alkali. It is also manure gone to powder. It is also ash, volcanic ash. Immediately one learns to walk out in front of the wagons, to be in advance of the clouds of dust. Even so the stuff puffs up upon every plop of the foot.

The dust surrounds one. It swirls and envelops one. It wraps one, cloaks one, drapes one, hugs one. It invades one. It turns your skin gray-brown. It grays your hair. It dries your eyes until the lids scratch like sandpaper. It gets between your teeth. It coats your tongue. It follows your breath up your nose until the insides parch hard as baked earth. (What a blessing a dripping nose would be in this country!) When at last the cool of evening comes, and one takes a rest for a meal, your supper is gritty with dust.

The next morning one discovers the true insidiousness of this dust-manure-alkali-ash. It has worked its way into every fold of clothing and every crevice of the body. What moves, scratches. What doesn't move, itches.

It is therefore necessary to bathe. The river is surprisingly cold. Its brisk blessings are apparent, however, when the legs move without grinding. Occasionally the river offers another blessing, a pond of hot water to bathe in. What a devil of a coun-

try, where the very boons of the land are hot springs, boiling and sulfurous.

Not long ago tens of thousands of people thronged across this trail to California, in fact 50,000 and more in the summers of 1849 and 1850, lusting for gold. Yet that was only a small part of the migration of living beings. Many travelers, says one of the diaries of that time, "never tie up their bedclothes in the daytime. It is astonishing to contemplate how many millions of living creatures must be emigrating to California in close contact and partnership" with these sojourners. I fear Muley and Carlson are adding greatly to this migration.

Yet I have not mentioned the worst part of traveling along the Humboldt. It is the boredom. Sandy plains rise toward sage-covered hills which rise toward bare-arsed mountains. A few miles further on, sandy plains rise toward sage-covered hills which rise toward bare-arsed mountains. A few miles further on, sandy plains rise toward sage-covered hills which rise toward bare-arsed mountains. And you have the benefit of knowing that tomorrow sandy plains will rise toward sage-covered hills which rise toward bare-arsed mountains. So tomorrow and tomorrow and tomorrow creep in this petty pace from day to day.

It is appalling to think of the emigrants of the 1840s and 1850s taking more than a month on the 365 miles of the Humbug River. Then to end one's journey at a sink, a spot where the river is simply gobbled up by the earth, and nought but burning sands stretch ahead. The DeSelies presumably will take a month. I would half wager it dries up even the hearts of those generous people. Then Asie would find the lips of his inamorata *dry and uninviting.*

At each rest I relieve the boredom by writing in this journal. One day Harold Jackson, who is crossing this desert for the first time, upbraided me: "My God, Burton, why do you write about this trip so you can remember it? All I hope is to get home alive as soon as possible so I can forget it!"

Desert at twilight. Sun Moon liked to look at the desert when the sun was nearly gone and the shadows long. Never could she love desert—love was the special place in her heart for the fertility of her native country. But she liked to look at the desert in the evening, to watch the colors changing in the shadows, to see the sun-glow on red rock, to drink in the big masses of dark and light, shade and sun.

This was one of her secrets. She took time after meditating to watch the desertscape.

Another was that she avoided the campfire. She would not have built a fire each evening, more heat after boiling all day, but it seemed a ritual with the whites to kill meat and cook it. She had never seen so much killing in all her life. Tibetan people avoided killing, left the slaughter of animals for food to foreigners. White people relished killing animals. It made her feel squeamish.

She looked to the west. A long valley stretched hazily into blue shadow in that direction, and a line smudged the horizon. One day, before long, that line would become the mountains of California. Beyond those mountains would be a ship to the Orient, but she had hopes in the meantime, hopes that the mountains would be like her native Kham, well watered, bursting with life, snowy peaks in the background, grasses and flowers underfoot.

Mountain water. What she missed most in the desert was the pure, sweet taste of mountain water. She had not tasted truly pure mountain water since she left home.

Movement. A shifting of shadows down by the river. Deer, probably, come to drink in the evening. Though she liked animals, the mysterious shifting always seemed vaguely disquieting to her. She was glad she could not hear the creatures. She had sat right by the creek once and watched them come to water, and they were silent, utterly silent.

Skitter-skitter-CRACK!

Sun Moon jumped. Scrambling to her feet, she banged her knee. *Ouch!* She nearly stumbled as she whirled around. The words quavered in her mind. *Why did a rock clatter?*

"E-e-e-ek!" she squeaked.

Above her on a boulder loomed Porter Rockwell. His features and figures were black with shadow, but the lowering sun rimed his edges in gold.

Now she screamed. "AI-E-E-E-O-EE!"

"Sister!"

She drew breath for another scream, then held it in. The voice was . . . ?

"Sister, it's me!"

The voice was Sir Richard's.

The figure dropped down off the boulder into the shade. Now that he wasn't lit from behind by the sun, she could see his face clearly. "Sir Richard," she said, "you scared me."

"I'm sorry, Sister. I didn't see you. I was looking for my own quiet place."

"I thought you were Porter Rockwell."

Sir Richard regarded her. "You still fear him?"

"Yes."

He looked at her surprised. "Porter Rockwell is taken care of. Will be for another ten days. He'd never catch us."

Sun Moon nodded. She knew that Sir Richard looked at things only with his mind. Though she admired Sir Richard's brain, which worked fast and accurately as an abacus, she found his heart deficient. *Like mine. Unlike Asie's.* Her heart knew about Porter Rockwell.

She composed herself to answer. "Thank you, Sir Richard, for giving me your protection."

"You are very welcome." A look of inquiry came into his eyes. "Younger Sister, will you do something for me?"

She waited, still shaky.

"Tell how me you came here, halfway around the world. Tell it more fully." Sir Richard looked at Sun Moon with a huge, dazzling, gentleman's smile, self-delighted, conquering and conspiratorial at once. She felt hesitant. True, during the nights and days of flight she had seen beyond the blackness of his spirit. But only by force of will did he make it serve goodness. She had never seen such indomitable will in a human being. *Careful,* she told herself. *Will is not as trustworthy as serenity of spirit achieved through meditation . . .* She held his dark eyes.

"Come, Younger Sister, it is time."

Trust came hard to her. She wanted to keep her secrets, to control her life, to put nothing in the hands of others. *This is my single greatest fault, this desire to control, this willfulness.*

Sir Richard breathed in and out conspicuously. It was one of the tricks of white men to show impatience with women and people of color, their inferiors.

To begin to correct my fault I will.

"Yes, Elder Brother, tonight," she said. "You and Asie only."

"*I, THE INSIGNIFICANT* nun Dechen Tsering, was born near Zorgai, a great city on the plains of Kham. My birth name was Nima Lhamo. My parents were Norgay and Pasang Lhamo, and all our family were herdsmen and traders. They traveled far. The men of Kham are nomads, skilled horsemen, known widely for the fierceness of their warrior spirit. My ancestors were Khampas in every way, and I am proud of them.

"My parents gave me to the convent at Zorgai at the age of nine to be raised to work for *moksha,* the liberation of all sentient beings, the highest purpose a human being can devote his life to. I took the basic vows—to remain celibate, not to kill or commit other violence, not to indulge in intoxicating drink, not to steal, and not to lie. I began my studies in the Tibetan tradition of the Great Exposition School, *Sarvāstivada.* Soon I underwent rigorous training in the five academic subjects, logic, canon law, monastic discipline, Mahayana philosophy, and psychology. Later I began study of the Bön tradition and especially their teachings of *Dzog-chen,* the Great Perfection, and also *Mahamudra,* the Great Seal. It was my ambition to come to a position as teacher in the college at Zorgai.

"It is the custom of the monastery to permit monks and nuns to join their families during the summer, if they choose. In the spring of last year, I took leave to travel with my family to Chengdu, in Sichuan. Though it is not customary for women to go on trading trips, this was a journey I asked for, a special treat. I wanted to see the formal flower garden at the monastery in Chengdu. My mother joined us. As usual, the men of our family provided strength against all hazards, my brothers, uncles, and cousins.

"On the third night the bandits attacked. Normally they would simply have run off our horse herd. However, the leader had an unusual commission, to steal a nun. He was eager. Chinese men think that Tibetan women are especially attractive sexually, easily available, and fond of acts Chinese women will not commit. The idea of a nun being forced into such acts inflamed this man. And he was promised a great deal of money."

She hesitated, reluctant. "Though my relatives fought back courageously, we were overwhelmed. I saw them all killed."

She looked into the faces of her listeners. And she hated what she saw there, an odd avidity. *Even Asie and Sir Richard are greedy to hear what happened to my body, what happened to me sexually.* Her breath caught on an angry spot. She made herself breathe in and out, and reminded herself that she owed them compassion. But she didn't want to go on.

"You know the rest of the story. I was treated as chattel, shipped against my will to America for purposes of prostitution, transported to Hard Rock City, and sold to Tarim as a whore."

She hoped the last word slapped them.

"I must rest now," she said. She rose and went to her blankets.

Made me think of home, that's what Sun Moon's words did. I walked over to the wagon and got my drum. Halfway up a hill I found a rock that looked good. If I beat on it light and sang a song soft, or whistled, it wouldn't wreck nobody's sleep.

I sang to that valley I dreamed of. I named the stream Home Creek and called its canyon Peace Valley. I made up a song about how I'd feel if I ever got there. At first I gave it words, but then they seemed not enough to me. Words are clumsy next to what you can say with a melody, a change of chord, a slide on a fiddle string anyhow. So I dropped the words and just made the music. I sung it over and over, half the night. I didn't know where the valley was, or even whether it was. But I knew how fine it would feel to walk into such a place, breathe the air, and say, "Hello, Home Creek."

The Humboldt Sink pleased her companions, Sun Moon could not see why. Here the river followed so tediously for mile after mile after mile—365 miles, the white people said—was gobbled up by the desert. It ran into a hole and didn't come out. True, the hole was a vast marsh, a low spot in a still more vast expanse of desert, and you couldn't see from any one place that the water got lost. But it did.

From here your choices were to cross westward for forty miles across terrible, waterless desert to a river coming from the west, or cross southward across terrible, waterless desert to a river coming from the south, she forgot the names. Apparently, even in recent times the drive had been a formidable *jornada,* as they called waterless stretches of travel. No more, said Muley, not for light wagons pulled by mules, plenty of water aboard.

A blue shadow marked the horizon on the west. The mountains of California. The two rivers came from those mountains. Yes, they also ran into the desert and didn't come out. You could walk up the rivers, though, into the mountains. Grass, trees, birds. Crisp air in the mornings and evenings. Cold, clear water to drink. Wildflowers, some times of year.

She thought especially of the wildflowers, and felt homesick. She pictured in her mind the Flower-Viewing Festival, the grasslands spread out like beautiful carpets, green but laced with floral colors. They reached in every direction to snowy mountains under a high, infinitely blue sky. From those mountains gushed water, measureless water, bringing life to the grasslands, supporting plants, birds, horses, yaks, every kind of animal you could imagine. Marshes so fertile with life you could smell it—fecundity, creation, the fruitfulness of life teeming, swarming, bursting, singing its song over and over, I am, I am . . .

The Humboldt Sink was marshy, too, but its life was thin and poor, compared to her homeland. Deer, coyotes, foxes, birds that ran on the ground and were good to eat, and pack rats. The one pulse of life was lots and lots of water birds. This virtue seemed to Sun Moon undone, though, by the many vultures, creatures that fed on death. All around lay the signs of their scavenging.

The trail leading to and from the sink, and around the sink, was littered with thousands of carcasses, now no more than bleached bones and a few pieces of dried, hairy hide, too ruined even to offer anything to the vultures. The carcasses had once been horses, mules, oxen, and cattle. People had crossed the trail to California, but their animals had died of thirst, starvation, or exhaustion. It nearly amounted to killing animals, and it turned Sun Moon's stomach.

Mahakala, she said to herself, *in your honor I should learn to love these birds that take the flesh of death into their bodies, and live on it.* But she could not, not yet. Her homeland was fruitful with life, and her heart still loved it.

At a stand of stagnant-looking water stood a low, mean-looking hut. Here goods could be bought, all the usual sorts of trading-post items, Sun Moon supposed. Sir Richard and Harold marched in excited as children, to see what they might acquire. She was not interested in buying anything herself. She'd deciding working in Tarim's store that white people's interest in things-things-things-things was their most foolish notion. Harold emerged with a compass, and Sir Richard a bottle of whisky. Then they made camp in a spot with good grass a few hundred yards from the hut, near a single emigrant wagon and a single milk cow, grazing.

There Sun Moon heard it right away, the low moaning, the sound of human misery. She looked at her male companions. They barged on with setting up the camp, aware of nothing but stakes, hobbles, a cook fire, and tasks. She walked across to the other camp, toward the lone wagon.

A middle-aged man and three youths were gathered at the front of the wagon, shuffling their feet and looking helpless. They brought their eyes up to look at her as she approached, some uncertain, some hard. She slipped around them, pulled the curtain away, and looked inside, knowing what she would find.

Her eyes took a moment to adjust from the harsh desert sunlight to the shadowed wagon bed. A slight creature who looked just past the age of monthly bleeding, half-girl and half-woman, sprawled on thin ticking. Her legs were spread wide, skirt above her knees, trunk curled forward in pain. She clasped her swollen belly. She moaned like a wounded and angry beast, then suddenly stopped. Her eyes raised toward Sun Moon. Sun Moon felt a pain in her own belly, where the eyes stabbed her.

"Can you help us, Ma'am?"

She felt a flash of anger but didn't look back. These men standing in the sunlight were helpless, all their muscles and their brains weak as damp paper, because a woman was giving birth and maybe in trouble. They assumed that because Sun Moon was a woman, she would know everything—how to bear a child, how to deliver one, how to preserve the life of the mother, how to bring breath to the child, how to clean up, how to make everything safe and healthy, how to bring the goodness of the spirits to this place, this event, these people. *But I am a nun. You submit to the endless circle of procreation. I stand outside it.*

She refused to look at the speaker. Her feet wanted to move away, to take her away from this shadowed birth. Before her yawned the grossly corporeal. Another way to put it was, Before her yawned the pain of becoming. *Do I want to leap into the sea of blood and birth fluids?* Enmeshment, it felt like. Not so much enmeshment in the tortured feelings of all these people as in a process both awful and awe-inspiring, a soul's strapping onto the Wheel of Life, coming into the world to suffer all the turnings of another incarnation. Her feet wanted out.

The woman's eyes held on Sun Moon's belly. Sun Moon held her breath against the pain the eyes caused. They protruded, as though trying to leap at Sun Moon. They looked straight into her barren belly, yet they didn't seem to see it or anything of Sun Moon but something beyond her, something invisible to anyone but the becoming-mother. The eyes spoke fear and they spoke pain, great pain, the pain of physical existence itself. Somehow they transported that pain into Sun Moon's gut.

I must stay. Compassion. Compassion for all sentient beings, understanding of suffering, a fundament of the Buddha's way of seeing human existence. Compassion, yes, and something more held her, something . . . whatever.

She climbed into the wagon.

"Can you help us, Ma'am?"

She turned, blanking the anger out of her face. The voice sounded educated, as she understood American voices, but it was also pathetic. This middle-aged man had fading red hair and a pointy goatee. "I'm Rutherford Swaney of Lynchburg, Tennessee, Marybelle's husband. I'd be beholden for anything you can do."

Sun Moon closed the curtain on him. *Husband? That old man?* "Marybelle?" she said into the shadows.

The girl just crouched there. She was slender, wispy, and the deep shadow made her look more insubstantial. Sun Moon wondered whether her hips were so narrow they'd make things hard.

Sun Moon had never seen a baby delivered. Since she had gone to the convent as a child, she lacked the experience most nomad women would have. The proper mantra had not been said for this birth several weeks ago, as it should have been said. If anything went wrong, life would leak through her hands like blood. *But I am not as helpless as those oafs outside.*

She looked into the woman-child's eyes. Two pairs of eyes met, held, negotiated, reached agreement, recognition.

Suddenly the eye clasp broke. "Ooh-oh-o-o-oh-oh-o-o-oh-oh-oh-oh-oh." The bearer of life hunched over hard, gripping herself, moaning, endlessly moaning.

"Marybelle," said Sun Moon, "get on your feet. On your feet."

The bearer hunched motionless, moaning.

"Marybelle, on your feet, squat."

No movement, only endless moaning.

Sun Moon bent, trying to look directly into the eyes, to make contact. Impossible. Marybelle's head was down, eyes open but focused on nothing, or something beyond everything.

Sun Moon clasped Marybelle's elbows and tried to raise her. No response. She lifted hard. The child-woman was far too heavy. *I must get her on her feet. The lying position is too difficult.* Another pull didn't help. Moaning, endless moaning.

Sun Moon sat down beside Marybelle and hugged her with both arms. The child-woman seemed not to notice. Sun Moon held her firmly, as though forever.

Moaning, endless moaning.

Sun Moon thought of the breach through which life would enter. *Mahakala dancing eternally,* she thought, *conveying life into death, and back to life.*

The moaning stopped. Marybelle's body softened. Sun Moon held her closer. Perhaps Marybelle's muscles became a little pliable, and her body took a little comfort from Sun Moon's.

After a long while Sun Moon said, "You must get onto your feet." Marybelle stirred. She shifted her feet around. Sun Moon pushed on her shoulders, and the weight rolled forward. "There," said Sun Moon. "Now we can do it."

She made sure Marybelle was steady. Then she opened the curtain and spoke to the circles of males congregated there. "I need a small piece of butter."

They looked at her as though stupefied.

"Isn't the cow giving milk? I need one bite of butter."

"Of course," said Mr. Swaney. He jerked his head at one of the young men, and the fellow ran off.

SUN MOON WAS concerned. She knew the *nakmar* but had never said it. The child-woman would have no faith in its power. The butter did not even come from a yak.

She held the soft mound to her mouth and blew on it. Slowly, ritually, she murmured the words of the mantra in her own language, blessing the butter, letting herself feel spiritual power as she spoke.

She held it out to Marybelle. "Here, eat this."

Passively, Marybelle opened her mouth. Sun Moon put the butter on her tongue. Starting to chew, Marybelle made an awful face. "Yech!"

Sun Moon caught the butter as Marybelle spat it out. "You must eat it," she said. "It will help the birth." She put the yellow glob back into the girl's mouth.

Marybelle closed her mouth, worked her jaw, swallowed.

Sun Moon nodded to herself. She wondered whether the butter would pass through the mother and emerge on top of the baby's head, unmelted, as it should. Or would the mother's lack of faith undo the blessing.

I have done what I can.

TIME CIRCLED IN its forever way. The sun moved from high to low. People walked, stooped, sat, worked, rested. Insects whirred and buzzed. Plants breathed. Animals waited for the cool of evening.

Outside the wagon under the desert sky a man approaching old age waited, sometimes with companions.

In the wagon, in the half dark, two young women waited. The older held the younger. Bronze hands helped a white body to rise onto splayed feet, knees askew, and to lie back. Silence alternated with moans, vast laments issuing forth, sometimes sounding like primordial wails, sometimes barbaric yawps. In the silence their breathing synchronized, so the twain were one. During the moans the breathings were two, and Sun Moon could not help.

The heat eased a little. Trees painted shadows on the white canvas. Sun Moon thought how the air would redden the canvas as the sun set, and then turn it gray-blue as evening came.

The change came indetectably. Marybelle was squatted, bottom hanging between her feet, moaning. Suddenly she said her first word, or Sun Moon thought she did. The moan changed quality a little, transforming itself from OH to OW. *"Now,"* thought Sun Moon, *she's saying "now."*

Pain twisted in Sun Moon's belly, like hands wringing blood from her guts.

"Push," urged Sun Moon. This single word constituted nearly her entire fund of knowledge about how to bear a child—push it out. Marybelle grimaced, pushed, and groaned louder. "Now" wasn't right—it was in fact not yet. "Push!" hissed Sun Moon. Her own belly ached sharply.

The time seemed not to be yet. The sun sank from its zenith. Behind its brilliance the stars crossed the sky invisibly. The moon circled on the dark side of the globe. For some further ticks in the motions of the universe, pushing was not enough.

Finally, it was. Sun Moon put her hands onto the breach and felt a hard, fuzzy ball. "Push!" she cried. Though spoken softly, in intensity the word was a shout. Sun Moon watched Marybelle grimace, groan, and focus all her being on expulsion, on thrust.

A form emerged from the breach. Miraculously, the ache in Sun Moon's gut eased.

Mystery, thought Sun Moon. Her own breaths rushed, intoxicating as wine. *Mystery, come into my hands.*

In this fullness of time the mystery came forth, and displayed itself in the shape of a boy-child.

Sun Moon helped to draw it forth the last inches into mortality. She held it high for Marybelle to behold, and for herself to see. It was bloody. It was wet with exotic liquids. It was alive.

Sun Moon breathed from her mouth into the boy-child's nose. No response. She breathed into him again, and again. On the fourth time she saw the tiny chest heave, and could nearly see the air flow into the lungs. Once more she murmured the blessing of the *nakmar* in the Tibetan language.

She looked at the top of the baby's head, and saw no butter.

She handed the boy-child to Marybelle.

Now the girl-woman's eyes changed. They refocused from eternity to the here and now, to her son. Her arms opened gentle as flower petals. With infinite tenderness they folded and brought him to her bosom. She looked into his face and received the blessings of his being, like a gift of rain from an infinite river of sky.

Sun Moon cut the cord and tied it.

She lifted the draping cloth and stepped out onto the wagon seat and to the ground. Rutherford Swaney looked at her clothes and arms and hands, and then up into her face with a world of question.

Sun Moon saw that she was bloody, fabric and flesh drenched in crimson. She felt exhausted, sweaty, brought to earth.

Swaney bolted by her without a word. In a moment she heard his exclamation of delight, and the soft, affirming response.

Sun Moon faced the setting sun. It colored the sky ruby, maroon, and orange. She held her arms up into the evening air, and they added yet one more red, scarlet. She beheld. With her eyes she saw that she was part of the sunset. In its wild colors she pictured the child-woman, bloody of leg, bloody of belly, bloody of breach. For once in her life Sun Moon thought no words, she only looked. And looked, and felt.

Since such was her nature, she thought the words later, and made them part of her evening prayer. "Vehicle. This small, half-grown woman is a vehicle. Mystery transpired within her. Mystery manifested itself from within her flesh, between her legs. Spirit into flesh, eternity into time. This is how life dances forever, a dance awful and sublime." Sun Moon paused before murmuring the next words. "Thank you, Mahakala."

Her gut twisted, not hard enough to hurt, only a reminder.

THEY CELEBRATED.

First the three Swaney sons went hunting, Burton with them. The marsh here at the sink was a haven for waterfowl, swarming thick as bugs on a May evening. Late in the afternoon they came back with armloads of geese and ducks. A long, narrow fire was built and three spits set up. Burton saw the Swaneys look at Sun Moon like she ought to do something, but she slipped away. He could hear her thinking, *Do your own deuced plucking and cooking.*

He asked himself, *Will you meditate? You're right. People don't make you part of things except as a servant.*

While the fowls cooked, Sir Richard and Rutherford Swaney sat together and talked. A certain sense was in the air—we two are alike and must flock together. Burton amused himself by considering what Sun Moon or Asie would be thinking—middle-aged white men together? Or was it white men who are fatherlike together? He himself was amused by the ways of his culture sometimes.

Swaney was no witless backwoodsman. "Our cattle are getting so poor it takes two to make a shadow," he said. The man had attended the University of North Carolina—he got out his copies of Lord Chesterfield's letters and Byron's poems to show proudly to Burton. "Of an evening I read a little," he said. "It elevates the mind"—he glanced toward the wasteland surrounding them—"in circumstances where elevation is badly wanted."

Mr. Swaney actually rang a dinner bell—*clang-clang-clang-clang-clang!*—which seemed to Burton a quaint expression of his authority as *paterfamilias.* The three Swaney lads shambled up. *How odd,* Burton thought, three sons nearly grown and now a fourth, no daughters. One son of about twenty helped the new mother to a seat, holding her child. She looked wan, happy, and dazed. To Burton's eyes the young man's expression was utterly unreadable. He let her go and sat down across the fire without an upward glance.

Harold Jackson, Muley, and Carlson joined the dining circle. By instinct Asie and Sun Moon hung to the rear, like shadows.

Swaney went to his wagon and brought forth a jug, surely preserved with care in anticipation of this moment. "In honor of Emerson Judd

Swaney," he said, lifting the jug high in a toast. Until that moment Burton had not heard the newborn's name. Swaney handed the jug to Burton, who repeated the toast and drank in the peculiar way Americans had, jug against upper arm, elbow tilting it up. The whisky circled the group. Marybelle shook her head no. It was not offered to Asie and Sun Moon, sitting behind. *Bizarre,* thought Burton sadly.

Suddenly he took thought and offered them the jug himself. Asie took a swallow.

Turned on a spit, the goose was delicious, dripping with juice. Eaters tore at the flesh eagerly and tossed the bones over their shoulders into the desert behind. Burton wondered whether the unnoticed Asie and Sun Moon were actually in the line of fire, but no. Swaney carried on amiably to Burton, taking little note of his wife, his new child, or his older sons. His conversation was littered with proverbs from the Latin: A blind man cannot judge colors. A cock is bold on his own dunghill. A liar is not believed when he speaks the truth. Better be envied than pitied, which Burton noted was Greek rather than Latin, like the rest.

When the meat was gone, they spoke of the road ahead for the Swaneys, the old route, the one taken by the Donners, a name still spoken in a hush. First came the dry drive to the Truckee River, a stretch of forty miles. Then up the river to Donner Lake and Donner Pass.

"Rest your stock, get 'em well watered, carry plenty of water, you won't have no trouble," said Muley. "No trouble, less'n ye're afraid of ghosts." He grinned toothily. "Steep, bugger steep, but a go. Folks didn't switch on account of the route. Account of the ghosts."

Burton regarded them. *All unspoken, but tangible, and bitter as cold wind in the face.* The Donner story. Lateness. Early snow. The winter camp at the lake. Human beings eating one another. The rescue, in time for some, too late for others, and too late for self-respect. Sometimes Burton thought the failure of America was lack of imagination, a failure to grasp what strange creatures human beings can be. A failure of the British, too.

"We are afraid of guns, not ghosts," Swaney said to Burton, like it wasn't Muley who'd been talking.

"Is that why you are taking your family to California?"

"From Egypt's persecution into the Promised Land," intoned Swaney.

Burton cursed himself for his curiosity, but it pushed him on. He eyed Swaney and nodded ambiguously. *A Southerner. Tennessee.* "A Secessionist then?" This was daring. The War Between the States was far more inflammatory as a topic of conversation than religion.

"Secessionist? What an appellation for those who simply wish to live their lives in their own way. We secede from tyranny."

To tyrannize others, thought Burton. His gullet burned, but he asserted his impeccable self-control. From the corner of his eye he saw Sun Moon and Asie walking off, and was relieved they wouldn't hear any more.

"You don't think the South will win?"

"The world favors the strong over the righteous."

To the devil with it, Burton decided. He took a moment to frame his question simply but bluntly. "Do you think Negroes your inferiors?"

"A black plum is never as sweet as a white," quoted Swaney. "That, however, is not the issue. Mr. Lincoln is right. The issue enjoined in the Great War is not slavery but union. The question being decided is whether the South must live as the North wills."

Burton let the man see his evil eye for a long moment, then stood and walked off without a word. In the opinion of Richard Burton, Captain of Her Majesty's Army, being a gentleman meant never giving offense *unintentionally.*

CHAPTER SEVENTEEN

Sun Moon stood on the river's edge, looking into the dark water. No moon shone on it, no stars, no firelight. It was black. Black as . . . *Black* black. It could be felt, only felt, not known to the eyes.

She'd walked a half mile above the camp, above where the river bled into the marsh. She wanted a bath and had seen the hot spring here. She'd washed the blood off her hands earlier, and washed her clothes. But she felt the need for . . . She didn't have words for it.

The bank by the spring was treacherously soft, muddy, slick, salt-wet. She would wade into the river below and walk upstream into the hot water. From here she could see the steam rising off the waters, gray intertwined with the blackness of the unknown.

She stripped off her pants, her shirt, and, last, her shoes. She stood beside the river naked. She had never river-bathed naked before. Though the night air was warm, she shivered. Her skin trembled.

She put her left foot in, and the river was cool. She put her right foot forward and felt hard, smooth river rock. She stepped gingerly on,

calf-deep,

and on farther,

knee-deep.

The rock bottom turned back to sand. The river turned from cool to cold. A big shiver shook her skin.

She turned upriver, toward the rising steam. She made herself wade, one foot in front of the other, steadily, stubbornly. The river got deeper,

thigh-deep.

A thought came, *I cannot swim,* and it passed. A thought came, *the unknown,* and it passed. She felt her nipples grow bumps and ridges.

She waded forward into darkness. Now she had lost her sense of place, and perhaps of time. The river was the dark night sky. It was the space between the stars. It was all waters, it was the waters of the snows of the Himalayas, it was the holy lakes of her country, it was Lhamoe Latso, it was all the mothers of life.

Instinctively, she turned toward the middle of this river of all waters. Without will she stepped forward into the unknown and unknowable liquid. She found swift, cold fluid, the current, the energy of riverflow.

She turned upstream again, and the liquid swirled around her *yoni,* first the hairs, then the flesh. It foamed and frothed. She felt a thrill in her belly. Delicately, she imagined the water issuing its vitality into her.

She walked forward and the river deepened. It reached

her navel,

her waist,

her ribs.

She lowered her arms into the water, hands, forearms, elbows.

She walked forward.

Black liquid to the small mounds of her breasts, then to her nipples.

She felt them shudder.

She walked forward. Cold water to

her armpits, her collarbone, her throat.

Riverflow, cold and black and mysterious and alive.

She walked forward.

Water to her throat, her chin, her mouth.

Its sweetness licked her lips. She opened her mouth, let a little of the water run onto her tongue, and swallowed it down to her belly. It had changed—she felt it warm now, salty, earthy.

Something primeval swelled in her belly. She turned into the warmer water coming from the bank. She let it lift her gently in its embrace.

Her body floated upward, and she rose into the liquid energy. She opened her legs to the flowing water. Gently, she imagined the liquid surging into her *yoni,* life-bearing. Its warmth lifted her to the surface, a white lotus upon the darkness of the waters, and she surrendered.

WHEN SUN MOON came back to her normal self, or usual self, she was sitting nude in a few inches of river. She felt unsure how she'd gotten there. She did not know how much time had passed between the moment of her surrender to riverflow and this time in this place. She stood up and looked around and listened. She breathed in, her senses open, her very flesh a sponge. The air, warm and dry. The night sounds. The moonlight. She absorbed them.

She bent, put cupped hands into the stream, and lifted up water. She turned her hands toward the moon and raised them until they reflected the pure, white light. *Moon and stars,* she said reverently in her mind, *what shall I do?* She heard no words, and the light only glistened at her, self-possessed. She drank deep. It was cool and sweet.

She did not know how much time passed before the words came from behind her. "Sun Moon."

Her name was spoken softly, but not in a whisper. Asie's voice.

She started to turn, then remembered her nakedness. "Asie," she said. "You are alone?"

In answer he stepped from the dark willows onto the sandy beach, twenty steps away, not quite shadow, not quite man.

He saw it all.

She didn't care.

He saw me naked.

She didn't care.

He sees me naked.

She didn't care.

She rose. She faced him. She showed him her flesh. She opened her arms.

He came simply, neither fast nor slow. He touched her. He brushed her skin. He touched her intimately.

After a few moments they lay down on the sand and found their way into each other. In their love she felt again the warmth of the hot spring within her. She saw the two of them floating on the river, twin lotuses joined by the tendrils of arm and hand, *lingam* and *yoni,* eye and eye, spirit and spirit.

PART FOUR

TREASURE HUNT

CHAPTER EIGHTEEN

Sun Moon got crazy smack in the middle of the Forty Mile Desert.

That night after we made love there by the hot spring, we walked slowly back to the camp. I was thinking that naturally we'd get our bedrolls out of the wagon and go off somewhere and be alone together. Alone together, and probably do it again, the way I felt, and again a hundred more times.

We were holding hands as we walked along, me feeling unsure of myself, at the same time happy as a mule in mud, and my mind prancing hither and yon and everywhither. Heckahoy, what had happened, that makes a man's mind prance, and his feelings prance, too. I did say a man.

Of a sudden I noticed she was gone, not gone physically, but still gone, not with me. Somewhere else, like she'd transported herself back to the convent without taking her body. Don't know how I knew it, or how she did it, but it was so.

Fifty steps from the camp she stops and looks at me. In the dark I can't see what's in her eyes, if there's anything, or just emptiness.

"I want to be alone." That's all she says, and takes her hand back. When she lets mine go, I can feel all the dryness of that desert right there in my skin.

She walks away into the darkness and disappears.

That woman had a way of surprising a man. Matter of fact, she was one big flabbergastonia all by herself.

At that moment, standing in the desert empty-handed, I marked a big step in becoming a man. I stood there in the emptiness and opened my arms and shuffled in a slow circle, offering or asking. I looked up to the sky, with stars like tinny little grace notes, and reached and reached. Nothing came. I didn't know what I wanted. I was happy and sad at once. Happy because, well—a fellow doesn't come to his first carnal knowledge of woman but once in his life. And beyond happy and sad I had a gigantic sense of . . . maybe it was strangeness.

I went down around the shore of a marshy pond and made my way to an empty nest of some of my friends the fish hawks. I sat on a rock two dozen steps away and looked.

I felt lonely, I felt fulfilled. In my mind I dit-dotted a cry to the bird. I asked it every question and heard every answer. Its yawps were the wisdom of the universe, and they were nursery rhymes and silly limericks. And somehow, nothing to do with any imaginary words the bird sang, I learned one whicheversomething that is a big piece of growing up:

Another person stands there right next to you, or with her arms around you, and doesn't see what you see, or not the way you see it. You see fun, she sees folly. You want to embrace, she wants to run. Or vice versa.

You can't ever quite say why. It nags at you, even tortures you. Why doesn't my lover, or my brother, feel like me?

You can question, but the answers will always be a little off. However you twist around and look from behind her shoulder, however many miles you walk in her robes, I swear to you, it will never quite rhyme, the way you see things and the way she does.

Then, just because the sun comes up fine and the air is fresh, all that won't matter. Sweet gizzards . . .

Later that day you'll say to yourself, By God, that just doesn't make sense.

Why's she different?

This is all flibbertigibbet.

Right then, if you can remember these words, you'll find a world of help. It's a flabbergastonia, that's the way of it, and the wonder. And sense just isn't what it makes. But it does make a reason to chuckle, and jig your feet, and whistle a tune.

That's what I did that night. I made a dit-dotting call in my mind to the birds of the empty nest, birds that were probably back in the Rocky Mountains I came from. I called, Where-WHere-WHEre-WHERE-WHERE-WHere-where-where-where-where-where? Two or three times I did it, Where-WHere-WHEre-WHERE-WHERE-WHere-where-where-where-where-where? Finally, from deep in my mind or wherever, the birds answered back. Here-HEre-HERe-HERE-HERE-HEre-Here-here-here-here-here.

I called again and got the answer again. But my growing up wasn't far enough along yet to understand that one.

After dark the second evening, when we started the crossing of the Forty Mile Desert, was where she went crazy.

It was a hard crossing, but not so big a job as in earlier years. Now everybody knew the how-to. We carried all the water we could, for there wasn't a drop. Walked all night, rested, and walked all day until the heat got bad. Found some shade and rested there, some of us slept.

Sun Moon spent that midday rest back in front of her altar, doing what she called a *puja,* I guess. Anyhow, off on her own way.

All afternoon, too, she never walked near me, nor near anyone else. She carried an invisible wall around her, and I knew better than try to go through.

Along about dark we rested and ate in the shade of some rocks. The idea was to get on to Carson Lake that night sometime, lest people and mules alike die of thirst. If you walked during the cool night, you didn't sweat out as much moisture.

She sat out by herself again, and after a while I couldn't stand it no longer. I gathered myself up and walked right over to her.

I'd kind of gone crazy in my own way already. Had been walking along in fantasies, pictures of her and me doing this and that, and mostly you know what. Between the desert sun and your mind you can get really hot.

She looked up at me wild. But I'd made up my mind I would speak. Heckahoy, I'd already set myself to cross the Pacific Ocean, climb the Himalaya Mountains, and otherwise go to the uttermost ends of the Earth for her. If my courage could move me halfway around the world for her, it surely could move my tongue.

I felt right foolish—proposing marriage to a person who won't look at you does that. I stopped my pacing, shoved my hands in my pockets, put on my finest casual slouch, and spoke. "Sun Moon, I love you. Will you . . . ?"

But I never got the big word out. She keeled over, flopped onto her back, and her eyes rolled up in her head.

SIR RICHARD PUT his hand on her forehead and said, "Fever. High fever."

He poured the contents of his own canteen onto her hair and her shirt—a generous act in that dry stretch. Then he made a place for her to lie unconscious in a wagon and commanded Muley to get going. When Muley started to give him a mulish look, Sir Richard said, "Her life is at stake, man."

Sir Richard and I clambered on, and Muley made those mules cover ground.

At Carson Lake we dipped her right in the lake, and she stirred a little for the first time.

Sir Richard said it wasn't my proposal, or anything else we done, that made her crazy. It was fever. And it was. But later I wondered. Sun Moon had broken her vow of chastity, and she took her religious vows seriously. I think a certain sort of person would rather have a fever, which blanks the mind, than remember what she had done.

We left a note for the others and hustled those mules on toward Carson City. Sun Moon dozed most of the way. Sometimes she thrashed her body and especially her head around in a way that scared me. She lost color. She stayed hot. Though I didn't know much about fevers, I knew she was in trouble.

A man on the road told us the nearest trustworthy sawbones was up in Virginia City. He'd lived in Carson City, but caught a fever himself, gold fever. Sir Richard ordered Muley to turn those mules up Six-Mile Canyon, and up Sun Mountain we went. An hour afore sundown on a hot day we rolled into Virginia City, queen of the Comstock.

I'D NEVER SEEN a mining camp before, and was caught off guard by the smell.

Heckahoy, I know smell isn't the word. It's a feeling, a sense, an atmosphere that fizzes into you from all directions at once. Something rotten. Whatever in human beings was appetite, was lust, was naked, raw, coarse, it was here. Money, booze, money, whores, money, gambling, money, violence. I felt a chill. At the same time I was intrigued. That atmosphere is dicey, it's loony, but it's kinda fun, too.

Then I looked at Sir Richard and saw his eyes wide, his lips aquiver, his face delighted. I started to think, *Madness,* and then corrected myself. My friend had told us he was a lover of cities—the crowds of Delhi, Cairo, Alexandria, the hubbub, the smells of food, dogs, human bodies. The corruptions—liquors, hashish, opium, fleshpots, all manner of deceptions. It was only natural his eyes should feast and his senses should crave. Natural, and dangerous.

Sun Moon was better for the moment, and we could scout the place. Muley kept asking where to go, and Sir Richard kept saying, "Onward, man, onward—let us see the town." Muley did. The layout was sloped steep, just like any mountainside. Some streets ran horizontal, others sharp up and down. Muley turned down the mountain and sort of rolled on down. Before long I smelled it and knew what it was before I even saw it. Though I hadn't seen a Chinatown, I recognized the aroma of ginger, sandalwood, angelica, and spices too mixed to sort out. Soon I could see it—an open-air market with chickens hanging by their feet and many vegetables and spices, yellow-skinned people milling about.

I looked back at Sun Moon, and was glad to see her awake. She looked around at the joss house. She stared at the queer writings of the Chinese on a window. (Next to that stuff it said in English, "Chinese Restaurant.") She cocked her ear toward the singsong of the language of people in the streets. Did she want to visit Chinatown, I wondered, so she could see folks of her own color? Buy the spices she liked on food? Or did she want to stay as far as she could from the kind that kidnapped her? She lay back in the wagon, her face a mystery to me.

The streets of Chinatown were narrow, and right quick Muley couldn't go forward. He spent some time getting into a side street and then cracked the blacksnake over the heads of the mules. They pulled uphill, and pulled, and pulled, taking us . . .

"To the hotel," said Sir Richard.

"Ain't no hotel," says I.

"There is," answered Sir Richard.

"Then they ain't gonna let me and Sun Moon in it."

I HAD FIGURED without the imperial arrogance of an officer of Her Majesty's Army.

"I shall require a suite of three connecting rooms, please," he said to the clerk at the desk.

The ends of the fellow's mustache twitched. I was standing to the rear, instructed to keep my eyes down.

The clerk flicked his eyes at me like a comment. Back to Sir Richard, he said, "You can pass through the walls easy enough, they're muslin."

Sir Richard swept on. "My servants will manage the baggage." Which was Sir Richard's war chest.

Now the clerk caught up with things. "How long will you be staying?"

"Perhaps a week, perhaps a month," he said carelessly, like he wasn't accustomed to answering to any of the clerk's ilk.

"A week in advance then?"

Sir Richard handed over some gold coins and I knew we were in.

"One of my servants requires a physician."

The clerk shut his eyelids halfway, a peculiar mannerism, and nodded. "I'll send the sawbones around."

We helped Sun Moon through the lobby up the stairs with our arms under her shoulders. She collapsed onto a bed like clothes with nothing inside. I stared at her fretfully, but Sir Richard said, "If my experience is any guide, the worst is past."

I pushed through the muslin and saw all our rooms, which were identical, cramped and bare. To think I'd imagined polished mahogany tables, marble fireplaces, ornate candelabra, brocaded chairs, and canopied four-posters.

I looked out window. Wagons jammed the street so tight they couldn't move. It was the busiest place you ever saw, full of people of every size, shape, language, and accent, all walking and talking peculiarly fast. There was money afoot, and every man meant to grab a share.

We had come to the home of the Comstock Lode, biggest silver strike that ever was. Men had come from the world over to feed at this trough, and some women. It was another part of Flabbergastonia. Despite my worry about Sun Moon, I was oddly happy.

Dr. Reagan strode in and started asking questions without a fare-thee-well. "How many days?" He was the spiffiest-looking doctor you ever saw, slicked-back gray hair, trim goatee, black coat, and white spats.

We counted on our fingers, and Sir Richard said, "Four."

"How high has her fever been?"

"High, I'd judge," answered Sir Richard.

"Chills?"

"Yes."

"Has she complained of aches in the muscles and joints?"

"No."

"Eruptions on the skin?"

"No."

All the while the doctor was getting out some instrument with tubes that stuck in his ears and came together in a sort of coin at the other end. He leaned over Sun Moon, half-conscious on the bed, and started to reach inside her shirt.

She clasped her elbows across her bosom, and I clasped my fingers around Dr. Reagan's elbow.

The doctor jerked his arm away, stood back up, and aimed his peculiar instrument at me. "This is a stethoscope. By amplifying volume," he said, in a tone like explaining two plus two to a baby, "it permits me to hear the heart and lungs."

"That's true," said Sir Richard. "It's a standard practice. He needs to place it here and here," indicating several spots around his upper breastbone.

The doctor glared at me. "Now may I examine her in private?"

We went into the next room. "Would he have reached inside the shirt of a white woman in front of us?" I asked.

"He would have asked us to leave," said Sir Richard.

After about five minutes the doctor stuck his head through the cloth and waved. We gathered around her. She was sleeping again.

"Probably she is beyond the gravest danger," said the doctor. "I cannot say what this fever is, there are so many in the West, and they haven't been studied. They come and go unpredictably. One I've treated seems to last about a week, another a month, and another returns over and over."

He picked up his little bag. "The prognosis is guarded. She needs rest. From time to time she may feel very well, and it would be good for her to go out into the fresh air and sunshine then. The most important part is this. After her fever has subsided, you must wait a week before continuing your journey. A week, to make sure it doesn't return." He looked at Sir Richard significantly.

"We understand," said Sir Richard.

"That will be three dollars. I'd like to see her again in a week. Do you know how to keep a fever down?"

"Cool the patient with water or ice," said Sir Richard, handing the doctor coins.

"If she has a crisis meanwhile, summon me immediately." Pushing the cloth of the wall aside, he turned back and repeated, "Immediately." Then he was gone.

There's some people, the way they act, it just makes me want to shake my head and say, "White people."

Soon as the doctor left, I says to Sir Richard, "It could be a long time. You don't have to wait, you know. Sun Moon and me will be OK."

I'm embarrassed, now, about saying that. I didn't have two bits, and we'd have been on the street without a thing to eat. Beyond that, I was half-afraid of being left alone with Sun Moon, half-afraid of being left alone in Washo, and half-afraid of my own quest, which adds up to one and a half and means swamped. Luckily, Sir Richard had a heart half as good as his brain and saved me from my own foolishness.

"I wouldn't think of it, my dear boy. I am devoted to the two of you." He smiled. "Besides, Virginia City looks . . . appetizing."

I didn't like to think what appetizing might mean to Sir Richard.

Came a soft rap on the door jamb. Sir Richard let in one of the cleaning women. "I have hired Bridget to sit with Sun Moon," says Sir Richard to me. "Will you permit me to take you to supper?"

We went to a fancy place called Nell's. I was worried. Heckahoy, I'd never eaten in a restaurant before, and I half figured the place wouldn't serve Indians, if they took me for an Indian. On the other hand, Harold had given me a bunch of new duds. The town seemed full of swarthy-skinned men who weren't treated like Indians. It was worth the chance.

A young man with a bush on his upper lip seemed to follow us through the streets, came right in after us, and took a table nearby. I was less worried about him than myself and bluffing through.

The waitress trotted over without a raised eyebrow, give her credit, and asked did we want to order. Sir Richard even let me go first. "Ham steak, mashed potatoes, green beans, coffee, and pie," I says. Welcome change from Muley and Carlson's cooking clear across the Great American Desert, fried bacon and beans three times a day. Sir Richard ordered eggs, sausages, and potatoes, which he claimed was the only edible American dish.

Next the waitress goes to Bush Lip at the nearby table, he looks around, and orders loud and clear, "Yes, Ma'am, one baked horned toad. Two broiled lizards on toast, with tarantula sauce. Stewed rattlesnake and poached scorpions. Very nice and well done, ever' bit of it." Then he surveyed the room with a toothsome grin, meeting everyone's eyes but ours.

Sir Richard's eyes was a-popping. "He's pulling our leg," I says. Sir Richard could be naive about some things. Bush Lip's loudness gave him away clean.

He turned and looked at us at last, his eyes full of mischief and devilment. And that is how I have after since thought of him, a man who sees the deviltry in life and revels in it. "I take it you gentlemen are new to Washo?" he says.

"Isn't everyone?" says Sir Richard.

"Captain Burton, if I'm not misinformed."

Sir Richard hesitates, and then answers, "There is truth in desk clerks. Sometimes."

Bush Lip stood up and handed Sir Richard a card. "I'm with the *Virginia City Territorial Enterprise,*" he says. "May I interview you? My newspaper is interested in Washo's distinguished visitors."

"Of which I am scarcely one. I'm simply a British traveler."

I suppose lying comes naturally to spies after a while.

"Our readers would like your impression of Washo land," said Bush Lip.

"Why don't you join us?" says Sir Richard.

Bush Lip grabbed a chair like a hawk attacking a mouse. Before sitting, he stuck out a big paw to each of us. "Sam Clemens," he says. "I write a little."

NOW YOU MAY object to me marching in Samuel Clemens, better known as Mark Twain, author of boys' adventure books, here in a Virginia City restaurant. First Sir Richard Burton, then Brigham Young, and now Mark Twain? Preposterous, you're muttering.

I understand. But all along here, on every page, I am telling you both fact and truth. You know how Sir Richard came to be in the West in 1862. It's well-known that Brother Brigham was king bee in the Deseret hive at the time we're speaking of. And Sam Clemens was right there in Virginia, writing little bits for that very newspaper. You can look it up in his book *Roughing It.* Washo was like that. If this story followed the Comstock Lode along very far, you'd be surprised at the famous folks as would appear. Jenny Lind, the Swedish nightingale, for instance, Drew Barrymore, and Oscar Wilde, the Irish poet and playwright.

Right now our dinners came. Sir Richard was amused, silently, that Sam's order turned out to be six eggs, fried potatoes, and toast with butter. "They're fresh out of scorpions today," says Sam.

"Dinner costs a dollar," I says to him. "How can laboring men afford that?"

"A dollar?" says Sam. "A *dollar?* Why, in Washo we are never short of dollars. Other places they breathe air, here we breathe lucre. In Washo a fellow sets out of a morning possessed of a hangover and a bottled start on his next hangover. He wanders out unsteadily across the mountainside, tips sideways, tumbles three or four hundred feet, and wakes up with his nose in a vein that assays a thousand dollars a ton. That's how our fair city was founded. The drunk, name of Old Virginny, properly James Finney, said when he fell, 'I baptize this ground Virginia.' "

I was struck by the way his telling worked. He didn't just say words, he made them bob and weave. It made you want to hear what he was going to say next.

We chatted along through dinner. Since Sir Richard and I had just come across Nevada Territory via the Humboldt and the Carson Rivers, both of those streams petering out in desert sinks, Sam favored us with an explanation of how it happens that all the rivers of Nevada run not into the sea but into the sand. He told it in the manner of an old mountaineer or prospector, for Sam was a first-class mimic:

"The way it came about was in this wise: The Almighty, at the time he was creatin' and fashionin' this here yearth, got along to this section late on Saturday evening. He had finished all the great lakes, like Superior, Michigan, Huron, Erie, and them—had made the Ohio, Missouri, and Mississippi Rivers, and, as a sort of windup, was about to make a river that would be far ahead of anything he had done yet in that line. So he started in and traced out Humboldt River, and Truckee River, and Walker River, and Reese River, and all the other rivers, and he was leadin' of them along, calkerlatin' to bring 'em all together in one big boss river and then lead that off and let it empty into the Gulf of Mexico or the Gulf of California, as might be most convenient. But as he was bringin' down and leadin' along the several branches—the Truckee, Humboldt, Carson, Walker, and them—it came on dark and instead of trying to carry out the original plan, he just tucked the lower ends of the several streams into the ground, whar they have remained from that day to this."

Sir Richard grinned like only a connoisseur of tale-telling can grin. He'd found a kindred spirit, though he couldn't admit to being a storyteller himself. "Perhaps you can also explain to us, then, the meaning and origin of the term *Washo Zephyr*."

Clemens put on a pooh-poohing look. "Why, as you might guess from the name, Suh, it is a sort of breeze that comes hereabouts, particularly in the spring and fall. Its remarkable aspect is that it comes from the direction of the Pacific Ocean"—he held one arm toward the west—"deposits its moisture in California, and arrives here in the spirit of a dry drunk—lots of devilment but nary a balming drop of rain. In a devilish spirit it delights in going up vigorously, down with a vengeance, then round and round in whirlwinds, and at last from every point of the compass at once.

"At such times the tin on half a dozen roofs may be seen flapping in the breeze in chorus, each section of roofing giving out a roar more startling than would be the combined sheet-iron thunder of a dozen country theaters of average enterprise.

"Not to exaggerate, I may say that at times such clouds of dust are raised, that, viewed from a distance, all there is to be seen is a steeple stickin' up here and there, a few scattering chimneys, an occasional poodle dog, and perhaps a stray infant drifting wrong end up, high above all the housetops. Down below in the darkness, gravel-stones are flying along the street like grapeshot, and all the people have taken refuge in the doorways.

"Out on the divide between here and Gold Hill, where the wind has a fair sweep, the air is filled with dust, rags, tin cans, empty packing cases, old cooking stoves, and similar rubbish. Hats! More hats are lost during the prevalence of a single zephyr than in any city in the Union on any election held in the last twenty years. These hats all go down the side of the mountain and land in Six-Mile Canyon, where drifts of hats fully fifteen feet in depth are to be seen in the bed of the canyon just named. All these hats are found and appropriated by the Paiute Indians, who always go down to the canyon the morning after a rousing and fruitful gale to gather in the hat crop. When the innocent and guileless children of the desert come back to town, each head is decorated with at least half a dozen hats of all kinds and colors—braves, squaws, and papooses are walking pyramids of hats."

Now Sir Richard was grinning with a slightly unfocused expression. I'd come to recognize it—it meant he was trying to remember the lines to write them down. Maybe it was Sam being interviewed and not the other way around, unbeknownst to him!

I had something else in mind, after the mention of Indians. "What do you know about the Paiutes? Where's their camp? Can I meet some?"

Sam regarded me with curiosity and delight. That was what made him Samuel Clemens, I would say, a mind roving restlessly and a sense of humor about all it beheld. "I am acquainted with the Paiutes," he allowed, "as few white men here are, and would be pleased to escort you on a tour of their camp and an elucidation of their ways." Now he clicked his eyes from me to Sir Richard. "Especially if Captain Burton would grant me an interview."

Sir Richard hesitated. He was willing enough, I knew, to talk to the press, which is to say to spin his own tall tales. But he had secrets to protect. He said, "Can we strike a bargain, Mr. Clemens? I will grant the interview if you will show us around your fair city."

As the three of them strolled the streets, Burton felt exhilarated by the very air. A mining camp reeked of . . . desire. Everywhere the thump of hammers, the rasp of saws, shouts, the rattle of wagons, the clop of hoofs, lads yelling out the headlines of their newspapers, posters trumpeting chances to get rich, bulletin boards declaring the latest prices of mine stocks—everything in the world rushing to become what it was not, as of yet.

Cravings churned within Burton. He knew that, against the precepts he had learned so diligently in the Orient, he had not changed himself. He suffered from desire and dissatisfaction with the present as much as any.

They strode on briskly. Burton loved his little charade with Clemens and was intrigued by what the newsman pointed out. Yet the attacks on his sense swept away his whole being. Opium. Women. Booze. Opium. Women. Booze. *Oh, Isabel.*

As they passed gambling houses, he felt pleased that he was no addict of the roulette wheel or the faro box. His first enchantment was women, and here they were aplenty. Painted women, some of them showing their legs and sneering provocatively, even in the early evening.

Women looking damaged, actually selling their pathos and helplessness. Elegant women of the *demimonde*, young, beautiful, dressed even better than their respectable counterparts in the latest San Francisco fashions. There were fancy respectable women, too—wives of the prosperous, many of them, out for shopping or for luncheon. Wealthy women, owners of land, investors in stock, about the town on business. Burton couldn't yet tell invariably which women were respectable and which not, but all the citizens would know.

He breathed in and out deeply. He might want one of these women, the high-class harlots. Or he might want one of their low sisters. Though it shamed him to admit it, he might especially want a Chinese woman and then opium.

For now he felt exhilarated. The desire was ripe for him to breathe. Desire for gold, desire for flesh, desire for power, desire for inebriation, desire for lotusland, desire for madness. He loved the feel of a mining camp.

He would indulge. Temporarily, that is. Burton well knew—hadn't he and Isabel talked about it for long hours? hadn't he made her promises?—yes, he well knew that for him wine, women, and opium were the road to madness. He could not indulge. Well, not more than briefly.

Clemens looked sharply at Burton. "Perhaps the great American enterprise is selling illusion," he said with a touch of asperity. The captain beheld a street blocked by wagons, and on the boardwalk a huckster of the typically American sort haranguing a small crowd. His speech and dress gave him away—both attempted an impression of substance, but a glance revealed that the man had no breeding. What compelled Burton's interest were a lad with spotted skin, a gargantuan snake, and a female dwarf.

"Gentlemen," the huckster began, "you will agree the creatures before you deserve both your pity and your generosity. Behold this wonderful spotted boy, captured in the wilds of Africa, the huge boa constructor, which you see him handle with the greatest possible freedom. And here is the wonderful little Fairy Queen, eighteen years of age, and only thirty-one inches in height. She was born in Grand Rapids, Wisconsin, has a thorough education, and possesses the graces and manners becoming a lady of the highest standing in society."

"Let us move on," said Burton. He felt revulsion for the show, for the illusion. Somehow the huckster would turn sympathy into tossed coins, and would hint that the diminutive Fairy Queen, possessed of such graces and manners, might be available after dark for unusual sexual experiences. Burton had seen it in a hundred cities.

They strode briskly past every kind of business, saloon, general store, restaurant, outfitter, assayer, nearly all in tent buildings with false fronts. They turned up a steep street—everything was aslant here—architecture, engineering, business, and of course morals. The breathless climb stopped even Clemens from his tour spiel until they turned back onto a horizontal road. Then he began a history of the Comstock Lode.

Burton knew the story well enough. Three and a half years ago a bunch of miners panning for gold, doubtless the usual riffraff, discovered by accident that the ground was bursting with another metal entirely, silver. Even the muck they were throwing away to get at the gold was silver ore. Silver that assayed at unheard-of prices. Bonanza!

The California gold rush was old and tired, the easy pickings gone. So over the Sierra Nevada swept hordes of gold rushers. They set up a tent village. The first winter they came deuced close to starving to death—supplies packed here soon ran out, and snows closed the mountain passes. Then the diggings turned out to be demanding. Instead of panning and washing, the miners had to probe far into the earth. This required many men, much labor, expensive equipment, and, most of all, it necessitated capital. Thus did big money come to Washo. The more independent-minded miners went elsewhere, and the others became employees or . . .

"Do you know by what means most men live here, Captain?" Ever a showman, Clemens was determined not to let his audience's attention wander far. "By our wits. You think by mining, or building, supplying lodging and meals, washing clothes, selling supplies, and it is so, for some people. John Chinaman concerns himself a good deal with woodcutting, laundering, cooking, and waiting on people. The Paiute devotes himself to physical labor. But the man of wit and enterprise, he casts his glance higher. If he starts by mining, he soon moves into high-grading. If gambling, he soon learns to play sharp. If prospecting, he learns to sell a worthless prospect. If investing in mining stocks, he develops sources of forbidden information. And if she came for love, naturally, she soon apprehends how to make love turn a profit. You never saw such a people for living by their wits.

"After all, we have money, money, money. Where there is plunder, there will be pirates. No one really minds. Money is happiest, they say, when it is running from pocket to pocket to pocket."

At this very moment an old codger approached Clemens and waved him into a doorway. Clemens went, smirking. The codger spoke, hesitantly, reluctantly, a look on his face that was a parody of secretiveness. After a few moments Clemens put on a very sincere look, indeed a falsely sincere look, and gave the man a few coins. The fellow gazed back into Clemens's eyes with a regal countenance, as though he were dispensing boons to the newsman, not the other way. He slipped a ledger from within his raggedy coat, produced a nub of a pencil, and made a few marks in the ledger, surely in an impenetrable code. Then the codger looked about as though for enemies, hid the coins upon his filthy person, and slunk away.

"What was that about?" said Asie.

"That old prospector, name of Fitzgerald," began Clemens in the way that indicated a delectable story was coming, "is one of our shrewder citizens at living by his wits. He sells shares in mines that don't exist."

Burton was tickled.

"Don't exist?" said Asie. "How does he get away with it?"

"Originally, he bought a mine of some worth and sold it," said Clemens, "establishing his bona fides, so to speak. Then he disappeared for a bit and came back with a story of a strike up in the Black Rock Desert. Naturally, he needed a good stake to develop this strike. He went about and gave a few of us the opportunity of coming in on the deal—just his special friends, except that we never saw him outside of bars. It was all very hush-hush, of course—if word got out, claim jumpers would be all over the place. He allowed us to invest twenty dollars each in his great enterprise."

"Twenty dollars wouldn't buy a fig," said Burton.

"That's why I was sure old Fitzgerald was running a blazer. Anyhow, when he'd raised enough, he headed out to do his proving-up work, so he said. No doubt he actually went to the pleasure palaces of San Francisco to reinvest our funds in personal delights. In a few weeks he returned with the sad news that the stake wasn't enough, he'd misjudged a little, and he needed more. Again, hush-hush, we invested our twenty dollars a head, and he marked down in his ledger how much of his great strike we owned.

"In due time he disappeared and returned once more. The strike was greater than even he had imagined. He had assays to prove it—why just look here at these papers, which of course he bribed from any assayer what needed money. Sixteen thousand dollars a ton! Eighteen! And the vein was much longer, three times, once he really got to working on it! He would need . . .

"Once again coins were exchanged for marks in a black ledger.

"On this climactic occasion, however, he has surpassed himself in imagination. Everything is in readiness, he says. When he goes back this time, he will finish the staking out and proving up and make an announcement. Why, this news will blow the lid right off Nevada!

"He has only one problem! Rumor threatens to undo him. If he leaves, he will be followed by gents who have heard of his bonanza, and rough gents, too! He must outwit them. So he must hire a man to wear his clothes and set out down the mountain with burros and wagons, to the northeast. He himself will buy a fast horse, disguise himself impeccably, and ride south to Carson City. When he's sure the disguise has fooled everyone, he will ride like the wind to the Black Rock Desert . . ." Clemens held up both arms and shrugged. His eyes told how much fun he was having. "He needs an additional investment of only ten dollars!"

"Won't you fellows catch him crooked?" said Asie.

"No, he'll buy that fast horse, sure, and use it to make for San Francisco."

"Why do you go along?" asked Burton.

"Actually," said Clemens, "I am a special case, his smallest investor, his gesture of friendship. And he gives me something for my money. Old Fitzgerald knows more about who's who in Virginia, and especially who's well fixed, than any mortal." Clemens looked brightly at Burton. "It was him that give me you, matter of fact. But he told me you was Richard Burton the explorer and author."

"That is Captain Richard Burton." He put a smile with the lie. "I am Captain Sir Richard Burton. It is a common name."

We walked along in silence a while after that, me feeling sheepish.

But I was excited, too. Virginia was like no other place on earth, mainly because of the people. Businessmen dressed like going to their clubs in San Francisco. Miners in overalls, caps, shoes, and no shirts. Mexicans, Italians, Greeks, South Americans, all swarthy. Germans, Serbians, Russians. Irish, with their musical accents. John Bulls. Backwoods

Americans. Yankees. Gentlemen of the South, and riffraff of the same place. Even Mormons. Most exotic were the queued Chinamen leading donkeys humped with firewood for sale, and the Paiutes in face paint, claw necklaces, feathers, and white men's shirts and trousers.

The streets were stuffed, and Sam said they were crowded in Virginia day and night alike. The mines worked in shifts, the miners wanted food, drink, gaming, and women when they emerged from the dark shafts, and the providers obliged, gladly, in return for coin.

The languages were babel. You never heard so many foreign ones, nor so many ways of talking English. Sam wrote a sketch of it in *Roughing It,* no need to repeat that here.

Physically, aside from the canvas buildings and the steep slant, its greatest peculiarity was that the village was tucked in among huge piles of rock debris—tailings from the mines, which made all human endeavor look dwarfish.

"Those who come to Washo," Sam went back to his tour-guiding, "have no need of hell. The devil himself is affrighted of visiting here. We supply our own devils, who call themselves badmen. They dress like gallants, wear a sidearm on each hip and another in each boot, and walk with the swagger of giants. Until you've shot your man, you can't be a badman, so many aspirants come belching flame. They kill the first man that annoys 'em, or strikes their fancy as a handsome corpse. That's why 'Dead man for breakfast' is the rule. Ever' day you wake up, there's a body in the streets, holes in it, but otherwise unaccounted for."

"Dead men for breakfast," said Burton. "Washo is a very dangerous place."

"Not just because of that," said Sam. "There are three main diseases at this altitude. The one ever'body talks about, lead poisoning, which is a considerable hazard. The second one, more dangerous, is greed. I scarce need to elaborate on that one," he commented, and then elaborated anyway. "I say the easiest mark in the world for a swindle is any man in Washo. Ever' one has conned himself before he got there, and merely awaits confirmation.

"The third disease? Why, that is illusion. True, this malady grows as a native the world over, but Washo is a case so conspicuous a man can hardly credit it. Ever' man here walks around imprisoned by his own dream of what he is about to become." Sam gave us the big eye, and the bush on his lip twitched. "Why, sultans and caliphs have no vaults of treasure nor any concubines to compare. Why . . ." He fell silent for a moment. “Boys,” he finally said, “I’m sorry to say I am defeated. The power of illusion in Washo, why, I can find no words big enough to serve it up true.”

So the party fell into a funk—defeat will do that. We walked along catching our breath for a little. Then Sam says, “Mebbe now that interview . . .”

“What could a traveler for pleasure like myself tell you?” says Sir Richard.

“Mebbe whether, like they say, the twenty-ninth language you speak is pornography.”

Sam grinned, and Sir Richard held out an arm that guided us into the Heritage.

CHAPTER NINETEEN

As we clinked through the half doors of the saloon, I heard the fine upright piano opposite the bar, singing and singing. Felt like someone grabbed me by the ears.

I did what I do sometimes, circled away from what had hold of my mind, pretending to look at something else, anything else. I hadn't seen anything like the Heritage before. It was a two-bit saloon, a place where everything—a beer, a whisky, a cigar—cost two bits. Ordinary saloons in Virginia, for workingmen, were bit places, where everything for sale cost one bit, twelve and half cents, or even a short bit, a dime. The Heritage was class, class, class: The front half of the room was small tables, the right side a polished bar with a grandly carved back bar. The whole rear was gaming—outfits for bucking the tiger, roulette wheels, chuck-a-luck layouts, and felt tables for poker, each manned by a tinhorn in a tuxedo. Oil lamps lit the house. The bar had a brass footrail. Brass spittoons served convenience everywhere. Mixologists—that's really what they called them—served up drinks with ice. Can you imagine ice in your drink, hauled all the way from Lake Tahoe and stored all summer long, in a town where they near starved to death three years before?

I stood there for a minute, beholding the finery and listening to the music. Then I noticed one of the mixologists was beholding me. When he looked down, I knew I was OK. In America fine duds can make dark skin acceptable, lots of the time.

I walked toward the piano against the far wall, away from the bar. By now I was so mesmerized, I bumped into chairs as I went. The tune was one I knew, "Didn't It Rain," an old spiritual. The pianist was giving it a different feel, though. He sped the tempo up fast till it made your feet itchy—now it was actually too fast to dance to. Did things with the melody, too, notes to give it a mournful feel, mournful but really alive. Most of all, though, he was fooling with the rhythm, giving the tune an off-the-beat bounce. Instead of BAH-bah-BAH-bah it was b'BA-ah! b'-BA-ah. I can't rightly tell you about it, but you would recognize that feel in a jiffy. What you would call it was colored people's music.

The piano player wasn't colored, though—alabaster white, with long, slick red-blond hair to his shoulders, skinny as a shovel handle. He didn't wear a tuxedo, but a vanilla-ice-cream suit with a pleated shirt and a wine-colored, velvet cravat tied up at his neck like a blossom. Made those tuxedoed tinhorns look like they were his stableboys. There was a brass-engraved sign on top of the piano, says GENTLEMAN DAN.

I sat down at the nearest table and turned my chair toward the piano bench. He gave me half a hooded flicker with his eyes, put a flourish into the end of "Didn't It Rain," and without missing a beat eased into a slow tune. This one aimed at your chest instead of your feet, plucking at those heartstrings. Because of my sorrow around Sun Moon, this music came into me like rain into the parched desert. It was all heartache, too, but somehow it blew up my grieving big and eased it all at once, made it seem like it was right, the way of things. I've had call to play that tune many a time since—it's called "Troubled in My Mind."

Toward the end of this piece one of the fancy-dressed girls, a dance-hall honey, came and gave him a cocked hip, foot-tapping, eye-rolling kind of look.

The Gentleman didn't pay her a bit of mind, for which I was grateful. Straight on he dived without a pause. His style this time was taking the tune apart and putting it together a new way. The right hand would say the melody up high kind of bright, and the left hand would echo it low and mournful—sounded like soloist and echoing chorus at church. The tune was the old reel "Uncle Joe." Gentleman Dan opened it way up, made it twice as long, switched the tempo from quick to slow, and generally made a nice little song into a big show.

I felt so much like applauding I did. Even gave out one hoot.

Gentleman Dan turned nothing but his head and looked at me

measuring-like. He had a long face made longer by a goatee so blond it was nearly white. In the middle were the eyes of a hawk.

Suddenly he looked behind me. It was the dance-hall gal come back with one of the mixologists.

"You're getting deep again, Dan," says the mixologist.

"Thanks, Daisy," says the Gentleman mockingly.

"Well, it hurts business," says Daisy.

Gentleman Dan cast his eyes elaborately about the room. The few men in the place sat at the bar, their backs to us, or were engrossed in losing their money to the tinhorns. "I see so many prospects for dancing," says he. His voice was Southern, in some how cultured, and almost too soft to hear.

"Fancy Dan," says the mixologist.

"Deep Dan," says Daisy.

"That's what makes it music," says the Gentleman.

I noticed now that Sir Richard and Sam had left. I guessed Sir Richard was negotiating for some way to keep Sam from writing about him.

"When you don't keep it simple and foot-tapping, I have to tell Delilah," says the mixologist. It was said matter-of-fact, and even friendly-like.

Gentleman Dan nodded like saying "I know," and said, "I'm taking a break after this one."

He put his fingers back to the keyboard. That was the first time I noticed them. The rest of his body was thin and weak-looking, like one of those lungers as comes to the desert to get healthy. His fingers, though gentlemanlike, were big and powerful. When I watched them play, they went after the notes fierce, like talons diving for fish.

This tune was a working song, a drivin', totin', haulin' son of a gun. Gentleman Dan sang the words in a voice that seemed impossible after the way he spoke—raw, coarse, and savage. They told about a mining man working a double jack, and in other verses digging out that hole, mucking out that rock, loading up that ore. He brought it up to a grand finish. Made my body ache to hear it, and my heart break.

Then he slid off the bench and without any never mind sat down next to me. The Gentleman's coming was that way, like a big old predator bird of a sudden lighting on your limb.

"Daniel," he says, and stuck out his hand. Lots of men in Washo don't tell their family names. Didn't find out Daniel's for a long while.

I took his hand. "Asie Taylor."

"Care for music?" he says.

I nodded yes.

He waited. I felt like he was going to pounce. Instead he lit up a thin little cigarillo. "Do you know those pieces?"

"All 'cept the last one," says I.

" 'John Henry,' " says he, and blew the smoke carefully away from me. "Miner's special."

Lots of times when he talked, Daniel spoke in a sort of short talk, words normal enough, but some meanings only he understood fully. Then he'd nod in a distracted sort of way, agreeing with himself. Listening to these self-talks, I learned a lot of what he was thinking, but not close to all.

"Where you from?" says I, making conversation.

He looked at me like I'd broken wind.

After a bit he says soft-like, "New Orleans." He blew out a gout of smoke and let it sit. I was willing to bet he hailed from some rich plantation family. But then he wouldn't be here, I told myself, not playing piano in a saloon.

"You?"

The question took me by surprise, made me remember I didn't know where I came from. I blurted out, "Utah Territory."

His eyes seemed lighter for a moment. I'd noticed people looked at you funny if they thought you were a Mormon, like you'd plugged every woman in the Territory. When as a matter of plain fact I was a virgin on leaving Salt Lake, and had good prospects for becoming one again. What he said was, "I was there. They have no music in Utah."

I felt a little miffed. "Mormons sing," I said, "particularly Welsh Mormons sing."

He regarded me. "You don't look Mormon," he said.

"I'm not, not that they didn't try. I'm half-Indian." *Half—does that make sense?*

He studied my half-dark face for a few beats. He blew smoke above our heads, and it hung like a dark cloud. Why don't they ever ask what kind of Indian?

"I didn't mean offense," he said.

I lunged into it. "What was it you did to those tunes?" I probably sounded like I was about to bust.

He smiled smallish, which I learned was as big as he went. Slowly he stubbed the cigarillo out in an ashtray. "Sit with me on the bench, and I'll show you."

I did. He strikes up "Troubled in My Mind" again. He says, "Key of E. This is the way you might hear white folks back home play it back." He runs it straight through, couple of verses. "Now listen to this," he says. He repeats it, and that feeling is back. "Flatted thirds and sevenths, diminished fifth chords," he says. "Syncopated rhythms." I didn't have any idea what he was talking about.

"Let's try another." He lit into "Bluetail Fly," rolling and rollicking. "Harmonies just however they feel," adding some notes in the left hand. How they felt was hip-slidin', shoulder-slippin', head-bobbin' . . . Well, if words could say it, we wouldn't have the music.

I stared at him. Then I said something completely out of line. "I got a banjo," I says. "Can I sit here and pick along? I can pick this."

He smiled with mouth and eyes at once, and that was surely the only time I saw that. "I'd be honored," he says.

Heckahoy, didn't I catch that brass ring this time!

"May I walk with you to get your instrument?" says he.

"Aren't you working?"

He took my arm and led me toward the bar. To the mixologist he says, "I'm taking my supper break."

"Just as well," says the barkeep.

Sir Richard was back in the rooms. Said he'd promised Sam Clemens a real story in exchange for keeping his identity secret. "We'll have to think of something," he said.

When Daniel and I left, he wanted to go listen to us make music. Which meant us leaving Sun Moon alone again.

I sat on the edge of the bed and touched her head. It was hot but not real hot. I took her hand. She opened her eyes, but they were glazy. After a little she withdrew the hand. "Go," she said. "I don't need company. When I feel good, I go with, hear you play." She waved us away, kind of, and the wave was the tiniest gesture you'll ever see.

"I'm worried about her," I said. "Can we get someone to sit with her?"

Sir Richard nodded, and on the way out arranged with the clerk for a companion for her.

I couldn't do else than make music with Daniel.

"Who is she?" says he in the street.

I felt all flummoxed. "Just someone."

Daniel pulled up short in the street. "Devil of a way to start a friendship," he says.

Sir Richard pitched in with, "She's my servingwoman."

"No," says I right quick. I knew what friendship required. "We've agreed to pass her and me off as servants, but we ain't."

"It's delicate to explain," Sir Richard says, "and perhaps dangerous." At least he straightened out quick. "She is Asian. Not a prostitute. We are protecting her."

Daniel nodded. I could see something in his hawk eyes about it, something big. He never said another word all the way back to the Heritage. I figured he was just fretting over how we got connected with an Asian woman, other than the one connection society accepted. Yes, accepted is the word. Turned out later I figured wrong.

The Heritage was slam-bang full of people now, after supper, and pandemonium reigned. We had to shove our way to the piano. While I was tuning, Sir Richard showed up with whiskys, three of 'em. Daniel flicked his eyes at Sir Richard in a way that said, "No, and hell no." I started to reach for one, uncertain-like, and Daniel says, "May I introduce you to a drink? If you don't especially care for strong spirits." He came back in a jiffy with what he called a sherbet, in this case blueberry juice poured over crushed ice. (Yes, Virginia, even far from water, was big on crushed ice.)

"Best drink I ever tasted," says I.

"It's a Turkish treat. Any fruit juice over crushed ice."

Meanwhile Sir Richard settled at a nearby table with a brilliant grin and whisky enough for a party. I began to wonder what kind of holiday Washo was going to be for him.

Daniel led the way with an oldie that would raise folks' spirits up, "The Gospel Train," now known as "When the Saints Go Marchin' In." This was a saloon, after all, and his job was to create good cheer. I was worried about being able to keep up my end, never having heard about those altered notes he'd mentioned. He came at it straight on, though, no flatting or diminishing, and I was able to join in strong. He loved big contrasts, high and loud echoed low and soft—WHEN THE SAINTS (when the saints) GO MARCHIN' IN (marchin' in). I hit the louds hard and laid all the way off the echoes. We grinned at each other like clowns (except Daniel never stretched those lips into a grin in his life). It sounded good.

Right off a bunch of folks jumped up and got to dancing.

For the next couple hours without a break we took a tour of country dance music, reels, gigs, schottisches, waltzes—you name it, we played it, and they danced it. All played straight, so as to lift those knees and inspire those feet. All the while we were getting acquainted, Daniel and I, learning each other's little ways, supporting the other fellow, then borrowing his style for a minute and tossing it back. That's how musicians do.

Though Daniel never looked at anything but the piano and me, I surveyed the room: gamblers, drinkers, and dancers. Felt funny sometimes to be helping people feel like doing such a bunch of rotten stuff (well, Brother Brigham called it rotten). In particular we were mating dancers together, and that was commerce, dance-hall girls and customers—the business of pushing 'em to drink or pullin' 'em into a crib, depending on the girl. I thought of Sun Moon and got a peculiar feeling about that.

We were making it sing out, though, and folks were hopping up and down and having a good time.

Finally we took a break to make chin talk with Sir Richard. Daniel lit up—I hardly recall ever seeing him eat or drink a thing. I ordered a sherbet of kiwi fruit, sherbets now being my favored treat.

"Native-accented music, I gather," starts Sir Richard.

"What do you mean, Sir?" inquires Daniel. I could whiff burned gunpowder already.

"Simply music of the people's sort with an American flavor." Well as I liked Sir Richard, I've never denied he was a snob.

"I thought perhaps native was a reference to people of color," says Daniel soft as you please. When these gentlemen go after each other, they do it with tiny, shiny blades.

"That as well," said Sir Richard. "What is the origin of the music?"

"Much of what we've been playing originated with the Negroes," Daniel said politely. "The white folks, at least Louisianans, took some of the songs as their own. We primmed them up in the process, straightened out the rhythms, and made the harmonies more conventional. To my ear that made them more regular and less interesting. I hope we'll return to a kind of Creole music, the white folks' versions given back some of their black spice. That's what I prefer to play."

"Creole?" said Sir Richard inquiringly. His voice sounded poised to jot it down in his notebook.

Daniel's eyes could look dangerous with hardly a change. "Really it means born of Old World parents in the New World," he said evenly. "People use it to mean mixed-blood."

"Black and white," said Sir Richard.

Daniel nodded.

"Red and white."

"Yes, mestizo," said Daniel.

"Black and red and white."

Daniel gave a little smile. "That too. In Louisiana we call such a person a redbone."

"Black and red?"

Daniel nodded once more. "Washinango," he murmured.

"So you Americans have many words for the mixtures of black blood and white."

I kept thinking one of them was going to slap down a glove and demand satisfaction at dawn.

"In the South," said Daniel with a soft edge, "in order of percentage of white blood, the words are mulatto, which is half, quadroon, octoroon, and griffe, a sixteenth. Full-bloods are called blacks, Africans, Africo-Americans, or, fancifully, blackamoors. Also negroes, as they say it in the North, nigras as we say in the South when pretending civility, and when being honest, niggers." His voice was coming up hard now. "Then there are the gradations of color, black, brown, olive, meriny, and high yaller." His pale face was broken out red, like measles spots. "Let us not forget the condescending terms—darky, Crow, Cuffee, Sambo, blueskin, Senegambian, and tarbrushed folk, or the offensive ones such as coon, smoke, snowball, kink, boogie, and Zulu." His wagon was rolling downhill fast now. "Tell me, I pray you, why we pick out black women with such names as negress and nigger wench, or designate their children affectionately as dinkey, pickaninny, and tar pot."

Seemed a miracle he didn't bust.

Sir Richard didn't interfere, protest, help, or do anything else. He just watched with an expression of high curiosity.

After a few breaths Daniel began to fold his wings and look a little less warlike.

"I have been much in Africa," said Sir Richard in an easy tone, "Arab Africa. I have seen the slave trade up close, and I abhor it. It debases white and black alike. I know not which is more repugnant, to be slave or master."

The color began to drain from Daniel's face, which meant he was back toward normal.

"I gather that you are similarly inclined."

Daniel nodded. He took a moment to get out one of those cigarillos and made a ceremony of lighting it. "Back home they call me a nigger lover."

Sir Richard nodded and regarded Daniel. He was using that power he had to hold people's eyes, command their full attention.

"Is that why you are not fighting the war?"

Daniel shook his head no. "The war has other causes than race," he said. I thought I saw an approving light in Sir Richard's eyes. "I do regret having run to a town like this, full of racialists. *Virginia* City," he said wryly.

I noticed his complaint wasn't "Secessionists," and I know Sir Richard did, too.

"Why did you," Sir Richard hesitated, "run at all?"

Daniel looked at him plenty put out. Guess it wasn't a question a gentleman would ask. But Sir Richard often said he wasn't a gentleman, he was a writer, and so never let manners curb his curiosity.

To both our surprise, Daniel began to tell it. "To keep from killing." Then he went on short and direct. "I fell in love with a woman of color. Very little color. We proposed to be married. She's now dead, by my foolishness, and my child dead within her."

His glare dared us to ask more.

To my amazement, Sir Richard did. "How did she die?"

Daniel's eyes turned cold and dark—I hope I never see a tunnel that cold and dark. Yet he began to speak. "I took her dancing in a place, a place for whites only. I should have known better. A fool challenged us. I acted belligerent. Knives appeared. Just when I thought we were going to set to, and I had every intention of killing him, he used the knife instead on . . . her. She died in my arms."

"I'm sorry," said Sir Richard.

"Me too," says I.

Sir Richard murmured, "Race in America . . ."

"Our destiny and our doom," said Daniel.

"Dan!" The word was yelled so loud and sharp it sounded like a shot. We all jumped. It came from the bar, the mixologist. He jerked his head toward the piano. We all sat there a minute, calming our nerves back down. "Perhaps a more pleasant conversation later," said Daniel, and rose to go to the piano.

Quick before we started in, Daniel took the banjo and real soft showed me how to flatten those certain notes and squeeze that certain chord. Then we made music, Daniel's new kind now. I fell in with his tricks quick enough, though I couldn't always make them sing handsome as he could. Hitting those off-the-beat rhythms hard made it really happen, I found out. That was fun.

We made music—made it white, made it Creole—for two more hours. Sir Richard was gone. I ate and drank a sherbet while Daniel smoked, and we went back to playing. This time Daniel suggested we switch instruments, and we did that. Worked out real fine. We picked and plunked until I don't know what hour of the morning. All I remember is that Daniel saw me home, seeming no more sleepy than he was ever hungry. I fell into bed so exhausted I couldn't even check on Sun Moon, asleep in the next room.

SUN MOON SAID to Asie, "Where's Sir Richard?"

He opened his eyes and blinked. She saw him absorb the fact that the sun was well up, then the fact that she was standing in his bedroom. He said, "What time is it?"

"Noon."

He shook his head slowly and sleepily. Then he jerked his face toward her. "Sweet gizzards," he said, "I'm supposed to play the dinner hour at the Heritage with Daniel, and I'm due there now."

"Where is Sir Richard?" she repeated softly. "He not come home last night."

"You sure?"

She nodded.

Asie swung his feet onto the floor and adopted an attitude of thinking. *Funny, how Americans tell things twice, once with words and once with bodies.* "Don' know," he said.

He threw off the sheet. She flinched before she realized he'd worn his pants to bed. She flinched again, inside, when she realized she'd wanted to see him stripped.

"All night?"

They also asked things twice, Americans.

She wondered what his thoughts were. Hers were simple—whores, whisky, or opium. Though she had learned to care for Sir Richard, and to see a certain magnificence in his spirit, she saw well his spirit's waywardness.

She stood up and turned all the way around the room twice. She wrung her hands. She pictured Sir Richard in a siege of dissipation in this strange city. Behind him, like a huge, black shadow, loomed Porter Rockwell. Without Sir Richard the shadow would turn into a killer. *Mother Mahakala, make my heart fierce.* She wondered why no one but her foresaw Rockwell's coming, and feared it. *Mahakala, give me courage.*

She said to Asie, "You going find Sir Richard."

He stood up close to her. "I gotta go to the Heritage." He looked at her solicitously. "You seem better."

"Yes," she said, "better today." She stepped back from him. "Please go. Find Sir Richard. We leave here soon."

"A week after your fever stops, that's what the doc said." He brushed back his black hair. She watched thoughts and emotions play on his face: *Yes, I do like your company.* He was almost like one of her people in his open face and simple, guileless manner. So different from most Americans and Europeans. His yearning to play music was direct, touching.

"Come with me," he said.

She shook her head no.

"Hey," says he, "I'm gonna pick." He pantomimed playing the banjo. "You like that."

"Next time."

"I'll bring you some dinner when I'm done," he said. "You'll be OK."

"You find Sir Richard, please."

"OK. If he ain't here. After work tonight."

He disappeared out the door. *You have no idea, none of you do.* A good heart, Asie, a grand heart, but no awareness of her world, her heart. Yes, she was better. But she was not well. She wasn't home. She was ill, she was homesick, she was scared, and she was on the run from a maniac and murderer. Besides all that, maybe she was with child.

"FINE," SAID DANIEL. "Let's look for him in Chinatown."

I scratched my head. I scratched my tail. I stretched my back. I felt queasy-like about going into Chinatown, especially way after midnight like this.

Daniel was already ambling downhill. Chinatown was below the rest of the town. I was making up excuses not to go. *In this high-mountain air,* I grumbled at myself, *we'll freeze just catching our breath.*

Oh, heckahoy, says I to myself—*Sun Moon says I look Tibetan, maybe I'll make Chinese friends.*

In Virginia during the day you saw Celestials (that's what everyone called 'em) all around town, mostly selling donkey loads of wood—"One dollah load," their cry was, crooking through the streets. They were also commonly employed as servants, cooks, laundrymen, and even physicians of a sort, going place to place with their herb and tea cures. What they might be at night in their own place, out of sight of white eyes, I didn't know. Half of me wanted to find out, and half had the cajoolies bad. Yellow demons, said that half. Even telling myself Sun Moon was yellow, too, didn't help none. Not after what the Celestials done to her.

As we got there, I could smell how it was Chinese better than see it. Charcoal fires. Blood, probably from some many chickens getting their heads cut off right in the street. Spices—ginger, garlic, red pepper, angelica, and I don't know what else. The smells of many kinds of tea. The sandalwood they burn for incense, strong odor of that. Smells I don't have no idea of, much as I've since been around Celestials. And the sweet aroma I later learned was opium.

Daniel led the way to a cut in a hillside, and within that a low door. Pulling it open, he said, "I don't expect to find him here, actually."

We went through into a dugout. Inside, a dim red lamp hung from the center of the ceiling. A man that looked to be in charge sat at a table jammed with paraphernalia—horn boxes of opium, pipes, scales, spatulas, wire probes, bones covered with black dots—all opium-smoking gear, but I don't know how some of it's used. Two walls were stacked with bunks, and every one was chock-full of smoker. They stretched out on grass mats or old blankets. In every bunk was a little alcohol lamp burning blue, every one had a little light used to light the opium pipe. Some smokers were propped on one elbow, others sleeping, others laying back with eyes open or part-closed. Now the sweet smell was strong as poison, and had a bitter tang. They say that opium makes the brain dreamy, misty. Everything in that half-lit room was like that.

Daniel spoke soft to the proprietor. "No white man here," the Celestial said. He spread his arms wide, like saying, "Look for yourselves." With his droopy sleeves he might have been a bat. I wanted to shrink away from him. Then I had a thought I didn't like. I wondered if this was what it meant to be what Daniel called a racialist, and I was one, too.

They exchanged a few more words in low tones, and Daniel led the way out. "We'll try somewhere else," he said. I thought of asking Daniel how he got so well acquainted in Chinatown. But I could feel that he didn't like being asked personal stuff.

The next opium den looked more like an ordinary business from the outside. Inside it was rigged about like the other one, bunks on bunks, each full of its own dreamer. Jumpin' Jeehosaphat, opium wasn't like liquor, it sure didn't seem to make folks sociable.

A couple of exchanges between Daniel and the head Celestial and we were on our way.

"What about a saloon?" I asked. "He might be boozing."

"Chinatown has no liquor establishments," says Daniel quiet-like.

The third place looked like a parlor in a pretty decent house, and they brought us green tea. After Daniel asked a couple times for the proprietor, a meek-looking middle-aged man wearing loose shirt, baggy pants, and skullcap came out.

"A white man, tall, with mustache?" Daniel inquired, slashing his own left cheek with a finger.

"As you see, no one here but yourselves," says Meek-Looking.

"In the back room, however," says Daniel, pointing, "there are opium smokers." It was true—the smell was strong.

"No, Sir."

"White people smoking," says Daniel.

"No, Sir."

They went another round or two in that line. Then Daniel says, "May I speak to Tommy, please?"

"Tommy? Who Tommy?"

A couple more rounds like that, the most polite lying you ever heard. Finally, Daniel slips something into Meek's palm, looked like a Spanish gold coin.

"The gentlemen wait, please," says Meek-Looking, bowing.

When the fellow went out, I says to Daniel, "We don't have to pay to find Sir Richard."

"I've been wanting to meet this fellow," says Daniel.

We waited and drank that bitter tea for maybe half an hour. Then in came a Chinaman, looked to be in his mid-twenties, no more, decked out in as handsome a business suit as you ever saw, gleaming silver, with scarlet silk cravat at the neck and a matching handkerchief. The stock exchange in San Francisco doesn't sport any better. "Good evening, gentlemen, I'm Tommy Kirk. How may I help you?" Here we were a-visiting Flabbergastonia again, for his English sported a plummy accent just like Sir Richard's.

Since he was offering his hand, I took it and said my first name. So did Daniel.

"We're looking for a gent," says Daniel. "Englishman, new to town. Strong fellow, heavy mustache, big scar here." Daniel drew a diagonal line across his left cheek.

"Captain Richard Burton," says Tommy.

Flabbergastonia some more.

He smiled a gentleman's smile. Except for the color of his skin, he neither looked nor sounded nor any way acted like a Chinaman.

Daniel nodded to show understanding. "You have good sources of information in Virginia."

Tommy nodded, too, taking it like a compliment.

I pushed in. "What about Sir Richard?"

Tommy Kirk frowned slightly. "I wasn't told he's Sir Richard, simply Captain Burton."

"It's a pet name for him," says Daniel.

Tommy looked at me in a kind of appraising way. I realized that he probably wasn't showing curiosity about us because he knew all about us. I shivered, supposing that included Sun Moon, where we were staying, and where she was alone and sick. *He's a whoremaster.*

"Can you help us find him?"

"I'm sorry, I cannot."

"He didn't come back to his rooms last night, nor so far tonight. He has . . . vices. We thought you might know."

"If I had any knowledge of his whereabouts, I could not divulge them." His smile could light up a room, but it didn't mean a thing. He had a peculiar effect, this Tommy Kirk. He made you all at once want to come hither and go thither. Outwardly he was affable and inviting. Yet you knew something about him was deadly, like an iron bar in winter—it looked normal, but if you touched it, your hand would stick to the cold and freeze there.

Daniel considered for a long moment. Finally he says, "I'm honored to meet you."

"Thank you," says Tommy, just sitting and waiting.

"I'm told you're a businessman."

"I invest in enterprises I believe will be profitable."

Another long moment.

"I have something in mind," says Daniel.

Tommy just smiled at him.

"Perhaps you'd join me for a drink tomorrow?"

"At the Heritage?" says Tommy, letting us know just how smart he was.

Daniel nodded.

"Three o'clock?"

They shook on it, and we got up to leave. Tommy was still beaming at us. Meek-Looking showed us out. At the door Daniel slipped him another coin, and in return got another bow.

Outside the stars were on fire, and so was I. "What's going on? Who is that coon? Why does he dress like that? Where'd he get that accent?"

Don't know how many questions I blurted out afore Daniel cut me off with some answers. "Tommy Kirk is a most curious character," says he. "The report is that he's half-Chinese, half-Brit. Born in Shanghai from a liaison between one of the British diplomats and a celebrated courtesan. That may be exaggerated." He gave me a sidelong look. "Much of this may be exaggerated. Got his schooling in the little enclave the Brits built to keep out local influence. Got his real education on the streets of one of the world's roughest seaports. Neither side likes him, they tell it, the white or the yellow. So Tommy's making his own way. His capital is the spirit of adventure and a complete lack of scruples."

Daniel shrugged and paused for breath. We were heaving back up the mountain to the respectable part of town. "What seems certain is that he's come to Virginia with some money and the intention to make more. He arrived with a dozen female slaves, age ten to fourteen. He built that opium den for white folks only, if you can imagine that. It's genteel. It's said he has several dozen regular customers, including a few women. It's also said he now owns other brothels in Chinatown, and opium dens and gambling hells, and aims to own everything."

Says I, "The world is most peculiar." Those days I was keeping my word flabbergastonia to myself.

Daniel chuckled. "And more than peculiar," says he, "and yet more."

"Sirs, Sirs!"

The voice came from behind us. We turned and saw a man as big and rough-looking as you'll ever see. Chinaman. We waited.

When he got within talking distance, the big fellow says, "Captain Burton is with lady. Safe. Home tomorrow." He had an earring looked like a question mark dangling from his left ear.

"Thank you," said Daniel, and held out a coin.

Question Mark just shook his head no. Then he says, "Captain Burton say I go with you. Lady need watching, he say."

I could have eaten a frog.

"I bodyguard," he said. He started walking back up the hill, and we fell in. "People call me Q Mark."

That's how Sun Moon gained a watcher. Any time Sir Richard wasn't there, Q Mark or another mean-looking Celestial was. I knew we should be more afraid of Porter Rockwell than Q Mark, but not by a lot.

When we walked into the room, she said, "Note came from Harold." I read it while Q Mark explained his duty to Sun Moon in Chinese.

> Dear Captain Burton, Asie, and Sun Moon—
>
> I am sorry, but I have set out for Salt Lake City. I looked for you twice at the hotel, after I figured out you were here. I have finished our business, and my father expects me back quickly.
>
> If you see Muley and Carlson, give them a raspberry for me!
>
> Thanks for your company—you made the trip dangerous and delightful. Would be pleasured to see any of you again. Asie, if ever you want a job, you have only to ask.
>
> Your friend,
Harold Jackson

Well, thanks for the offer, Harold, but my destiny is not Saintly.

One day at lunchtime Sir Richard and me met Sam Clemens up at the office of the Sergeant Mine to go down and have a look. I was moderately curious about how it was done, getting all that dirt and rock and ore out of a big hole in the ground. Or, as I learned, a little hole that opens into a huge tangle of holes, like a honeycomb.

I showed up with a sack lunch, and Sam put the kibosh on that right off. "You can't take that down," he informed me. "They keep down crumbs in the mine. Crumbs rot and stink, and the one thing a miner needs is to be able to smell."

We got into a little car set on a track and running down into the inclined shaft. It took miners down and brought ore up, Sam showed us, and ran by steam power. As we descended, there was considerable talk between Sam and Sir Richard on hoisting machinery, donkey engines, horsepower, and an eight-inch pump. I took little interest in it.

When we got off the car and started walking, my mind was grabbed by the huge empty boxes that seemed to hold the earth itself up. Down a ways big shafts ran off in different directions, and some of them were many stories high. (Sam spoke of ore bodies forty, fifty, sixty feet wide, but my mind is not drawn to those kinds of bodies.) The question I saw was, When you dig this mammoth bunch of ground out and haul it up, how do you keep the rest from falling on your head? I am pretty sure the miners had the same question.

The answer was, You build open boxes out of big timbers, boxes as tall as three men and just as broad. When that isn't high or broad enough, you put them side by side and stack them right to the top. Whole shafts were supported in this way, like some giant construction a kid might make. "Remarkable," said Sir Richard, and other upper-crusty exclamations of wonder.

When Sam began to talk of the money being taken out of the earth, I asked again about the miners. "How come you say the men get rich high-grading? What's high-grading?"

"I'll explain when you see the bridal chamber," says Sam.

Sam started one of his complicated explanations of how things work. He should have been a mining engineer, or a drummer for a mining association. Sir Richard asked questions I suppose were intelligent and got answers that passed for the same. Myself, I got to watching a miner sitting on a ledge, eating his lunch, and playing with a rat.

The critter sat on its hind legs, looking at the miner. The man's face, not his hand. Yet the hand was holding out scraps, bread and meat it looked like. Some sort of deal was being made between the rat and the miner. I eat, you don't whack me. I eat, you don't grab my tail. If you get tricky, I bite your finger. Or if you're nasty, gobble your eyes.

At least that's how I imagined it.

Sam and Sir Richard noticed my fascination and stopped to watch the rat and miner.

The rat waddled forward. It was fat, and as it came, its body swung in an S shape. It stopped. Scooted backward. Waddled forward. QUICK! made a dash for the goodies. SWOOSH! skiddooed off. Disappeared.

"They never kill rats in a mine," observed Sam. "Rats begin to run about queerly in advance of a cave-in. It's the only warning the men have. Also, they clean up the scraps of food the miners leave, which keeps the air clean of putrefaction. There's hardly a pint of air down here anyway. If you let food stink . . ."

"How do the men relieve themselves then?" asked Sir Richard.

"Can't do it just anywhere. The way the air is, no man could work below ground. So they have ore cars for shitters. They haul it up just like the rock and ore. Howsomever," said Sam with a grin, "that carload don't go to the assayer."

I was looking at the miner's face, which was burned blue in places. Sam noticed my look. He whispered, "Nothing more common than that in Washo. A mining fool tries to tamp his powder with an iron bar or the butt of a steel drill. Iron strikes a spark, powder flashes, and the poor bastard gets a tattoo designed by the god of chance."

The rat made a second entry. Slowly, ceremonially, it repeated the whole dance. Forward. Back. Forward and back again. The dash for the eats and the skiddledeedoo retreat.

The man looked up at us and gave an easy smile. "Napoleon," he said in an Irish brogue. "That's 'is name."

"He's just learning?" I asked.

"God love ya, no," says he. "We're mates. Been feeding Napoleon every shift for weeks. He's followed me right down this shaft, foot by foot. He's just shy."

The rat stuck its head back out and waddled back onto the ledge. "Almost erotic, that walk, is it not?" says Sir Richard. Which made me feel odd.

"Let's go ahead toward the bridal chamber," says Sam. We trudged and clambered down into the tunnel some more. "We're back onto the vein now," says Sam. We followed along where they'd dug and torn up until we came to where we could see another crew taking a lunch break. "We can't go any closer," says Sam, "they don't permit any outsiders to see this, even good friends like members of the press." Sam grinned. "Especially members of the press. Management is particular friendly to us, except where it counts. In the bridal chamber the digging is in new ground, what you might call it virgin territory—the point where country rock isn't being taken out for a look-see but actual ore is being excavated. I don't know how valuable this ore is. Afternoon, boys," he called out to the crew, "you in bonanza or borrasca here?" They just sort of snickered.

Sam led the way back up the tunnel and off into a side shaft. "They won't answer," says Sam. "That is a trusted outfit, any bridal-chamber crew is. Investors would pay many a buck to know whether they're into bonanza or borrasca." He took a sidetrack to explain that borrasca means the opposite of bonanza. He had a big interest in words, which is one of the ways writers is crazier than musicians, who know that words are mainly lame. "If the men in these outfits talk, they either do it very, very carefully, and make sure they get some of the stock profit, or they get fired. If word gets out and management can't figure which man talked, they all get fired.

"Them's the boys do the high-grading. Most of that ore they load onto the cars and hoist it out in the right and proper way. Now, it may assay three or four hundred dollars a ton, or three or four thousand, or more'n that. When they luck into high-grade ore, in the thousands, they cache it in their pockets or lunch pails or wherever. A man earning four dollars a day on some shifts may be able to high-grade a hundred. Nobody thinks of high-grading as stealing. Except the mine owners."

"Why don't they put a stop to it?" Sir Richard asked.

"No way to do it," says Sam. "No way."

He led us back up the shaft where we could get a lift out.

"So they just fly blind in here?" says I. "Digging in every direction?."

"It is not that haphazard," says Sam, "but they do have their blunders. For instance, last year two underground companies drifted into each other's works, which happens now and then. Right quick they tried to smoke each other out—the Chinese stink-pot plan, we called it in the paper. A pitch-pine bonfire was set by one, and the other nearly suffocated. The afflicted then turned the smoke back by covering the mouths of their shafts with boards and wet blankets, and flooded water down. It was a right little war, good as Pukes and Mormons."

Sir Richard nodded his approval.

We were coming into the light above. "So how do you like the mine?" says Sam.

"Splendid," says Sir Richard.

Me, I said, "I don't like me no giant holes in the ground."

BURTON WATCHED SUN Moon make the very contrary of an entrance. For one born a sovereign nomad, she caught on quickly to bearing herself like a servant. She was right—a low demeanor, shy, eagerness half-concealed by hesitation, and true servant's dress, modest, drab, self-effacing. She followed Burton to a table near the piano. He set the newspaper, carefully folded, on the table. At the waitress's solicitation he ordered whisky for himself and tea for the lady. Or rather, the servant.

He gazed admiringly at Sun Moon. Though the chief procurer of Chinatown knew of her presence, and the Heritage was full of whores, she was willing to walk about, protected by her guise. Burton loved audacity.

Burton enjoyed the surprise on Asie's face when the lad glanced up. He nearly missed a note there. It even made the odd Gentleman Dan look about. The expression on his face seemed rather more complicated. *So would mine do if a woman of color had been murdered for loving me.*

Burton quickly shut the door on the memory of the woman of color he himself had loved, the Persian . . . *Living in the past, no, that will never do.*

The music clinked through the single large room of the Heritage, from the bar with the footrail to the window tables to the dance floor to the gambling layouts, men everywhere. Burton had listened with care to the native music of half the world. At first he felt impatient of all of it, even the sacred songs of India when he studied Hinduism so deeply he became a Naga Brahmin. The first time any appealed to him was after he embraced the Moslem faith. Those calls to the spirit entered the heart. They converted him to a seeker of the doors of sound everywhere he went, a true listener to music.

In retrospect he had given consideration to Gentleman Dan's Caucasian *vis-à-vis* Creole renditions. He thought them both modestly eloquent, and preferred the wrigglesome Creole style. He heard Asie's enthusiasm for them. The lad's very spirit was music. Yet this music . . .

He looked around the room at the tinhorns, miners, businessmen, and whores. The more flamboyant whores were unmistakable, but the ones who teased his imagination were more difficult to identify—they wore the same San Francisco fashions (which was to say Paris fashions) as the respectable, wealthy women. The trick was to calculate by body language who had arrived alone, and might possibly be persuaded to depart in the company of the dashing Captain Burton.

His nerve endings tingled.

He took second thought. He felt the bitterness inside, and knew he must assuage it.

I am sorry, Isabel.

The music stopped, and Asie and the Professor joined them at the table. Asie was excited as a kid. *A supreme sign of the Jokester who made the world,* Burton thought, *that any man's lot should be to fall in love with a nun.* He fingered the edges of the newspaper.

"I am honor, Gentleman Dan," she said. "Delight hear you play, Asie."

Burton inspected her face. He suspected that American dance music was nothing to her. Yet her face looked sincere. He gave thought to the words she had actually said, and nodded to himself, admiring their discretion.

Burton ordered another whisky, a tea, and a sherbet. *The company of teetotalers,* he thought disgustedly.

When the Professor had enjoyed two deep drafts of his cigarillo, Burton judged the time ripe. He held up the newspaper. *Virginia City Territorial Enterprise,* the masthead said. Beneath that the bold, black headline, LINCOLN TO FREE SLAVES. The date was September 23, 1862.

The Professor accepted the proffered sheet and studied the columns of type. As he read, Burton saw no emotion in the man's face. When he set the paper down, his face was still a mask.

Burton explained to Asie and Sun Moon. "The President of the United States yesterday issued a proclamation. On the first day of the new year all those persons held as slaves in the rebellious states are declared free. Despite this great gesture, slaves in other states are unaffected by the proclamation."

He paused. "Evidently, Mr. Lincoln wishes to assure the continued loyalty of the border states not in rebellion. Thus he furthers his declared policy: He is fighting a war to preserve the Union, not to abolish slavery."

As he studied his friends' faces, he thought of Her Majesty's government getting the news from their offices in Washington City. They would not be pleased. Lincoln was taking too clever a course. If the government asked his counsel, he would say that the South must lose the war, both physically and in the minds of men.

"What is your opinion?" he asked the Professor.

"It is a cowardly and hypocritical act." *You do not mince words, Professor.* Burton liked that.

"Why so?"

"He is wrong both ways. Slavery must be abolished, without hesitation or equivocation, and forever. In *all* states."

"And the Union?"

"No state has a right to impose its will on another, even when the other is wrong."

Truly a Southerner, thought Burton.

"How does this affect the American destiny? Race is 'our destiny and our doom'—I believe those were your own words."

The Professor looked askance at their companions. Before Burton could point out the aptness of the topic to these very companions, Asie leapt in.

I DIDN'T ACTUALLY know what I wanted to say, just knew I was mad. "You know," I started, "it feels right peculiar to listen to you, friends of mine, talk about people of color right in front of me like that. I don't even know whether I'm a white man to you, or colored."

Truth to tell, for the first time I found myself thinking of them not as "my friends" but as "these white men."

I looked at them steady in their faces.

"I understand perfectly," said Daniel, "and apologize sincerely."

"Perhaps you may take it," said Sir Richard, "that while your color may prejudice most people in this room and in this city, it does not affect us."

Stars and cornicles, I wasn't reasoning out how to take it, I was just mad.

"I don't understand," put in Sun Moon.

I looked at Sir Richard and read his thoughts. *By God, their disguise as servants is ruined—they're so confounded independent.*

Daniel brought Sun Moon up to date. "Miss Moon," he said, "when Captain Burton opened the door to a discussion of the relations of the races in this country earlier, I spoke with asperity on the subject, and revealed that I myself was betrothed to a woman of color. She's now passed away, I regret to say."

I was amazed at Daniel's coolness. I'd have bet he hadn't volunteered this news thrice in his life.

"So, 'destiny and doom,' " Sir Richard pressed on. "Our friends need to hear your thoughts. They have no experience of the rest of this country."

"The fact of the slave trade," said Daniel. He hesitated. "The fact that our people were willing for two hundred years . . ." His eyes looked haunted. "We have been captors, masters, overlords. We have hated people for the color of their skin alone. In the dark of night we have cultivated and nurtured that hatred. We have persecuted them. We have destroyed lives, destroyed entire families." He paused dramatically. "We know our guilt. Can you see what that *does* inside?"

Sun Moon was looking at him disgustedly. I judged she was too polite to say, "What do you think it does to the slaves?"

"Racialism exacts a terrible but less insidious toll on its indirect victims. That includes your, uh, ward, Miss Sun Moon," said Daniel. "And our friend here," angling his head toward me.

"Is that so?" says Sir Richard.

Daniel said yes with his thick eyelids. "Her skin color is her fate. In this country Asie's skin color is his fate. Different from hers, and the same—fate in either case. Think what it is to be at the mercy of the lust of any white man you meet. Or his ill temper."

"I believe the hue of Asie's destiny is his spirit, nothing more or less."

"Oh, frog jump," says I, and only said that on account of I couldn't think of anything else. They were both in the ether. Again—"Frog jump!"

Everybody looked at me like I was a pig that laid a egg.

I PLUNGED AHEAD. "Every man of color in this country knows what it means. How could you feel it like us? I can play the piano in here, or tend the bar, or take care of white people any damn way. Half the places I try to buy a drink, I'd get kicked out of. The other half, I'd be twice as like to get cheated at cards, and ten times as like to get mugged on the way home."

I tried to give Sir Richard as good an evil eye as ever he gave me. "The Mormons would have kept their white and delightsome women from me, or at least the pick of 'em. Here I might be able to go to a white brothel if I was very well dressed, or maybe not. Do you know they have white, brown, and yellow brothels? In the good district, the bad district, and Chinatown? Two dollars, one dollar, and seventy-five cents? Do you know there's a law here against Chinese owning mining claims? Do you know they talk about 'a Chinaman's chance'? Which is the chance the Chinese have to find gold working the leftovers, the tailings?" My blood was right up, helped by stuff Daniel had told me, and I was ready to keep going.

Sir Richard jumped in, though. "Quite right, every word. I also know that it's embarrassing for you and Sun Moon, my dear friends and mates on *safariy,* to go about town disguised as my servants."

He looked us in the eye. It's true, naming stuff straight on takes the sting out.

But I was still full of it. "I'll make a hullabaloo not to be nobody else's nothing. One hell of a hullabaloo." I looked at Daniel and considered. "You don't know my whole story. I near drowned and came out of the river different as I went in. I set out on this big ramble to find something, I don't know what." I thought of their kind of words. "To find my own personal American destiny and doom, I guess. If I go astray, come up lame, shipwrecked, or whatever, I'm going to keep right on going my way, not nobody else's.

"What you be thinking? It's damned hard. Hard for anyone to know where to go and what to do with your life. When I figger it out, if I do, might be whole lotta white men intend to keep me from my way. Well, they best keep their hands covering their balls. I'll go where I want, do what I want, work at what I want."

Now Daniel pricked at me. "And marry who you want?"

That made me so angry, plus I was embarrassed at saying that word in front of Sun Moon, so angry my devil jumped up big. "You bet," I said. "You bet. If she'll have me." I fixed my eyes on the face of Sun Moon, which looked beautiful to me as a swan floating on sun-blasted water. "If you'll have me."

Sun Moon looked at Asie with her eyes carefully masked. She could scarcely let him know the truth, the truth she almost knew for sure: *I am bearing your child.*

She studied his face and knew how awful he felt, blundering out with it like that, right in front of everybody. She could also see he was waiting, waiting, hoping . . . *You can't know how hopeless it is.*

"I am a nun," she said softly and gently, and stopped. *Buddhist, scholar, teacher, chaste nun—I can give none of these up. Never could, and still less now. I will raise our child to dedicate his life to the* moksha *of all sentient beings.*

She met his eyes and saw him trying to read hers, but she kept the mask up. *So much I cannot say to you.* In her mind rose again, against her will, his touch, the time they lay entwined in each other's arms beside the river, legs entwined, too, and lips, and *lingam* and *yoni.* Intertwined it felt like then. Now she knew it was entangled. *Nothing that has happened has been a danger, except you. Not abduction, not slavery, only you. The danger is love.*

Now their gazes intertwined. She felt their lookings coming together gently and sensuously, like tendrils, delicately grasping. "I cannot," she said distinctly, and only to Asie.

Suddenly next to her Sir Richard was standing up and extending a hand toward . . .

"Mr. Kirk," said Sir Richard. "Thank you for coming."

Sun Moon forced her eyes away from Asie's, an act of violence. She swallowed hard.

Such terrible timing. Such a self-assured, predatory-looking Chinaman. She shivered. *Perhaps my fever is returning.* Then she acknowledged his deep bow with a small inclination of her head. He murmured, "I am honored."

She watched Tommy Kirk and not Asie while the courtesies were exchanged—she could not bear to look at Asie. Sir Richard brought a chair for the newcomer. He was costumed in a handsome suit of light blue silk, a man of impeccable appearance. *Appearance only,* of course.

Out of a corner of her eye she saw Q Mark standing against the wall, and acknowledged him with a nod. She had confidence in this man for hire, as long as he was on the payroll. Tommy Kirk was another matter.

AS EVERYONE BEGAN to chat (that's what those social sorts call it), I looked directly at Sun Moon until I got her eyes back. They grew soft and said to me, "I do care for you, and I'm sorry." Then they looked away.

My insides felt like twisting snakes. I didn't hear any of the conversation. Sun Moon wouldn't look at me again.

After a while Sir Richard prodded the talk toward where he wanted. "Mr. Kirk, we were discussing slavery. Do the Chinese practice slavery?"

"Who does not?"

"Based on race?"

"Not what Europeans and Americans call race," said Tommy Kirk, looking amused.

I brought my attention to Tommy Kirk. Again I felt that come-hither-get-thither split. Truth was, I'd been pondering on Tommy Kirk. Whole truth was, I'd been fantasizing. A man who owns women. (I'd actually been pondering on just what lecherous forms this ownership might take.) A man who owns half of Chinatown and means to own all. A man who corrupts others with vices and takes their money for himself, sometimes leaves them ruined.

Sir Richard kept chasing. "Based on notions of racial superiority?"

"That's a singularly American vice," said Tommy.

"How do people come into such misfortune?"

Tommy shrugged. "Often they are given by their families as guarantees against a debt. Then the debt goes unpaid."

"Or conquered by soldiers?"

"Sometimes." He smiled ironically. "Once upon a time."

My fantasies were churning. My fingers wanted to touch the silk of his coat, but my feet wanted to run.

"What sort of people hold slaves?" asked Sir Richard.

Now Tommy beamed all his teeth into a brilliant smile. "Whoever has the power," he said.

All the cajoolies in the world attacked me at once.

"*DANIEL!*" CAME THE cry. It was the mixologist. "Asie!" He gave a jerk of his head toward the piano.

Saved from Tommy Kirk. We went back at it.

Since we'd been hoping Sun Moon would hear us tonight, Daniel and I were ready to put our best foot forward, all our favorites done the way we liked 'em best together, plus something new—we were going to be a trio instead of a duet, because I was going to whistle.

It's tricky business, combining a pair of lips with eighty-eight piano keys and five banjo strings—the five and eighty-eight are a lot stronger. Lips go high, though, and high carries. I got in some sweet and lovely echoing and high harmony on several spirituals, particularly, I thought, on "Swing Low, Sweet Chariot."

Halfway through the playing I saw Tommy Kirk head out, Q Mark behind him. I thought the room felt warmer.

We jumped back into it, and went more for some driving rhythms. The drinkers in the Heritage like to dance, and that's sure what the courtesans want. So we gave 'em a lot of schottisches, quadrilles, and reels, stuff to make the feet jumping beans.

Something's niggling at me here, and I've got to say it. You notice I don't use the word *whore*. I say courtesan. I have known a good many women in the brothel trade in my life, and I have gotten to where I cannot say that other word. If *courtesan* is a damn fool word, there's no helping it.

Dan and me quit when we got tired, close on midnight, and to the devil with the courtesans' business. One last drink and cigar and we headed for home. Outside the Heritage Daniel starts to excuse himself and Sir Richard makes him pause. "Tommy said to tell you he's expecting you tonight. Any hour, he said," says Sir Richard.

I looked at Daniel right surprised. Daniel wasn't one for opium, gambling, nor courtesans, nor anything like that. Far as I could tell, he was a teetotaler for all vices, and didn't even eat.

I saw Sun Moon was keeping her eyes away from him, too, disappointed.

He looked nervously at Sun Moon and me and then glared at Sir Richard. After a bit of glaring, he says, "It's a business proposition." With that he strides off into the cold mountain night, body like a cornstalk and arms flapping like leaves.

As the three of us headed for our rooms, I says, "Don't like that Tommy Kirk."

Sir Richard looked at me with that kindly curiosity of his. "Tommy's keen to make money, lots of money."

"He's going for power," says I.

"He mistake what is power," said Sun Moon.

I stopped and looked at her queer. We were standing in front of the hotel now.

Sir Richard observed, "Oh, I assure you, if anyone understands power, it is Tommy Kirk. He means to have a great lot of it."

"There be no power that way, none," says Sun Moon.

I looked at her flabbergasted. If a fellow owns several dozen women who earn him money, if the gambling joints are his and the opium dens and the restaurants, and all the profits from them, if he's heading to be the main landlord in town, if he's reinvesting that money in owning pieces of the Comstock Lode, well, what he sure enough has is power, conniptions of it.

"He controls the lives of more people than any other man in Chinatown," says Sir Richard. "I suspect that before long he will in Virginia City as well."

Sun Moon smiled gently at Sir Richard. "A man who no control his lusts," she said, "his urge for acquire. A man who fears others so grasps for control of them." Her eyes sought my face in the darkness. "A man so great lust, so great fear, so little love. Where is his power?"

CHAPTER TWENTY

SAM SAID WE had to see the abandoned shafts—not the working shafts, where we'd already been, but the shafts that had been started, headed off somewhere, and came up with nothing. Sort of petered out, a graveyard of human hopes.

We left Sun Moon with Q Mark. She was a little feverish one day and OK the next, half-well, which wasn't well enough. The evening was cool and pleasant. Sam, Sir Richard, and me dressed in clothes we didn't mind getting dirty, which meant the only other pants and shirt I had. "You speak of your weird and wondrous places," says Sam. "No man has imagination sufficient unto the task." He was carrying a big coil of hemp rope, which kinda gave me the whirligigs in my belly.

Tramping about, we soon discovered that the entrances of these shafts were underfoot on the eastern face of Sun Mountain just about everywhere—some of them were even right in town. Trouble was, they were caved in halfway, or even caved in far enough you couldn't make 'em out at all, so they just looked like jumbled places on the hillside.

"These places are the first habitation of death in Virginia," said Sam. "More people die in them than at the hands of our badmen. You are thinking that I speak of the poor brutes who dug them by physical exertion, and so I am, for these holes cave in often enough, and carry the laborers to immortality. Afterward, surprisingly, they remain instruments of the grim reaper. Since they are difficult to spot, people fall into them."

Now Sam gave a sly, self-mocking smile. "That, however, is where God's grace enters. Goats wander around the mountain, looking for all omnium-gatherum of things goats eat, and end up making a kind of feather bed at the bottom of the shafts. Why, just last month a six-year-old boy and his canine sidekick disappeared. They were found two days later at the bottom of a shaft, lying on great pillows of goats, both in fine fettle."

Sir Richard smiled all the time around Sam. He found our friend's language fascinating, and our friend worked up his talk to delight Sir Richard.

I wondered if Sir Richard was remembering he had to come up with some kind of newspaper story for Sam, somehow someday.

He climbed up to a spot in the shade of a big ledge, threw the rope on the ground, and started fixing one end to a timber. "This is the biggest coyote hole around," he says merrily. I was staring at the timber he was fixing the rope to. We were going to let ourselves into the bowels of the earth with our lives tied to that? The notion gave me the willywoollies. There was a pulley hanging from the timber, though, and it must once have borne the weight of earth and rock being hauled up.

Sam led the way. "Just hold tight, boys," he said cheerfully.

I went second, thinking my willywoollies would be worse waiting up top. It was a hand-over-hand job at a sharp angle, too steep to climb but not a straight drop. My feet were on the ground the whole time—felt easy enough, as it's always easy to get *into* trouble.

Where it leveled out, Sam was standing and waiting. He halloed up for Sir Richard to come on down and lit the lantern. The coyote hole followed a seam in the rock or whatever will-o'-the-wisp the miners thought they saw. We headed along. I noticed a cool breeze blowing lightly at my back, brushing my fingers and ankles and the back of my neck like strands of hair of a phantom.

I yearned for topside. I also tried to imagine the madness of the men who dug it. Fevered, they must have been. They turned the sight of gold—not even the sight, the mere thought of gold—into a fever. It infected their minds, it bubbled through their blood, it charged through their arms and legs and emerged in the form of all this work—months of slavish labor, thrusting a hole into the earth with a shovel, clouting some rock with a pick, blasting other rock to smithereens, hauling the dirt and stone out in wheelbarrows and then buckets, timbering up to keep the sheer weight of Mother Earth from avalanching onto them, and doing the whole shebang again, and again, and again. All to chase after a yellow gleam that disappeared on a whim, like a swamp light.

Half of me says, "My stars and cornicles, this is the true madness."

The other half goes, "Heckahoy, it's Flabbergastonia."

"There are things here you have never imagined," says Sam, in the tone of a ghost story.

"Behold!" said Sam, and held the lantern high. Monsters. Monsters everywhere.

Not your commonplace monsters, such as your romance-spinners dream up, but growths of insane form—I would say like bushes, barbwire, beer bottles, all those and more, cashews, cabbages, and coons, except those are everyday things. This was nature run amok.

Sam took my hand and put it on a critter shaped like a tangle of string. It gave to my touch, and my hand jumped back. I tried again. It was wet, bendy, and creepy.

"Fungi," said Sir Richard.

"Funguses," agreed Sam.

Mushrooms! Gigantic mushrooms! Thinking of them that way made it seem not so bad. I took the lantern from Sam and went on an inspection tour. It was like the Lord had given some ogre of a kid a vat of taffy, and the kid went wild. There were slimy curtains of them, nests of squirming snakes, piles of ram's horns, beavertail cactuses, and every other shape. I came on a different one looked like a little statue sticking up out of the ground. Walking around it, I saw it was made of crystals, like salt, and formed like a berobed woman. "Mineral," says Sam. "I call it 'Lot's wife.' You know, she came down here and never got out."

Just then came the eeriest sound I'd ever heard, echoing around the rock walls. "OH-Oh-oh-ah-AH-oh-oh!" a cackle, interrupted by queer stops, like devilish hiccups. The cajoolies clawed at my stomach. The cackle paused and then doubled up, twice as loud, twice as long, twice as scary.

I knew what it was in an instant. Sir Richard's eyes said he did, too. Porter Rockwell had found us, and in the worst possible place.

"I'm pulling the rope u-u-up!" It was said in a mock child's voice, high and singsong.

I imagined I could hear the rope slithering up the rocks, barely shushing, like a dry snakeskin.

Suddenly I was aware that it was night outside, and dark, very dark, and even darker in here.

"What the hell?" says Sam.

"We know who it is," says I.

Sir Richard nodded.

"Porter Rockwell."

"Porter Rockwell? The Destroying Angel? The sinning Saint? Boys, we are in for it."

"Take me serious," says I. "Believe it. Porter Rockwell."

Came the cackle again, but now I could hear it was a wail, uninterrupted, a lost sound, soughing, circling round and round, soughing and soughing, the sound of an abandoned soul.

A change of aspect came to Sam's face. He was sober, nearly grim. "What will he do?"

Sir Richard said, "Kill us, probably. The question is, Will he leave us in this hole and go destroy Sun Moon? Or kill us first, then Sun Moon?"

"We gotta help her," says I, paying no attention to the fact that she had Q Mark to watch after her, and was in less trouble than we were.

"I don't know this Saint, but he ain't gonna kill this Missourian," said Sam. "I know another way out."

"Let's go," I said. Then I felt embarrassed about how eager I sounded.

"I don't know," drawled Sam. "I believe that boy could hear us walking off. He might know where the air shaft is. Probably does, if he's smart. He'd just wait for us there."

"What is your plan?" said Sir Richard.

"I'm armed," said Sam. "Are you?"

Sir Richard touched the hogleg he always carried.

"You boys move back toward the entrance. Don't expose yourselves, use the timbers and boulders, but don't be too quiet. Act like you was trying to be quiet and not getting the job done.

"Meanwhile, I'll ease out and come around behind the bastard." Sam flicked his eyes back and forth between us, excited. "It won't take me any more'n five minutes to get there, ten at the most. So," he considered, "after ten minutes you'll hear me shoot. Then you're in the clear."

I nodded. After a pause, Sir Richard did, too.

That ten minutes was the longest I ever waited in my life.

Except for the next five.

And the next five.

And the ten after that.

Since we didn't have a lantern, Sir Richard struck a match and checked his pocket watch. We both knew, but he said, "We'll wait five more minutes, by the clock."

When it was gone, we didn't need to talk about our situation. Something had happened to Sam, or maybe he had run off. Either way, we were abandoned to the malice of Porter Rockwell.

"Let's find the air shaft," says I.

We upped and moved down the tunnel. Every score of steps, Sir Richard would light a match and we would peer all around. And peer. And step. And peer.

Where that got us, after a while, was out of matches. Sam had taken the lantern. We sat in the darkest dark I had experienced. I let myself cry inside.

"The only way out," says Sir Richard, "is the way we came in."

I sighed loud enough for Rockwell to hear us.

Back near the entrance I noticed we could see a little. The entrance was a patch of half-light. It even had moon shadows.

We whispered. "See if you can climb up," says Sir Richard. "See if you can draw fire. When he appears, I'll shoot him."

I opened my mouth to protest.

"He'll be shooting at sound and sound alone," says Sir Richard. "Any hit would be luck."

Bad luck, my luck, thought I. But I started. What other chance did we have? What other chance did Sun Moon have?

I WILL NOT tell you it wasn't as hard as I thought. It was harder, scratching for handholds and footholds like a blind chicken. I'd find a spot for a hand, or a finger, and scrape my boot up and down, looking for an inch of ledge. Step up like a fool into darkness and nothingness, and try it again.

It was impossible to be quiet. Everything I did made noise. Scrape of sole. Brush of pant leg. Heave of breath. I even knocked half a dozen rocks off, and they rattle-crackled into the black hole. The one I was coming out of, not the one I was going into.

Every minute I expected the gunshot from above. In my imagination it never missed. But, dying, I got to hear the answering shots of Sir Richard below.

No shots came. No sounds at all.

I wondered whether Rockwell was waiting or not. Maybe . . .

I shivered.

Then I would picture my head climbing and climbing heroically and finally rising into the entrance, seeing and smelling the sweet night air.

Then Porter Rockwell would stick a barrel in my eye and make a black hole of my mind forever.

The shots didn't come.

No sounds came.

I pictured the barrel coming into my eye, and flinched. But it didn't come.

Eventually, gasping for breath, I got to where the angle of the rock eased, and went level.

In the half-light I saw the timber, and the rope coiled neatly below.

And then it came.

A chuckle.

A rip-snorting, hog-roaring, ain't-it-grand chuckle.

I sank to my knees, whipped.

Then came a giggle. A sweet, piping, childish giggle.

Then chuckle and giggle at once, from two directions.

I looked around.

A match scratched and flared. In its light was haloed a head. It was a flattish head, like it had been squashed by sledgehammers head and chin at the same time. It was dark-skinned and silver-haired. A feather stuck up from it. And it was grinning.

The head said something I didn't understand.

Another match spewed, and a lantern lit. In its glow grinned the big, mustachioed countenance of Sam Clemens. "Believe we got 'em this time, Joe."

The head giggled, and jiggled with pleasure. "Sure did. Sure did."

I took the lantern a little rough from Sam and set it where Sir Richard could see it from below. I didn't trust my tongue yet, I was so mad.

"Asie?" queried Sir Richard from below.

I threw the rope into the darkness.

"Come on up," says I. "Sam has had some fun with us."

I turned to him. "What did you do this for?"

Sam says, "You wanted to meet a Paiute." He held out the lantern to reveal the old fellow. His mouth was wide and set in a toothless smile. His eyes glinted like mischief. His face was ancient. "This is Paiute Joe," said

Sam. The body was dressed in raggedy white-man clothes, right down to a wisp of cravat. The friendly face was adorned with three lines zigzagging in parallel, like red, white, and black lightning.

Silver Head gave me the sweetest look I ever did see in my life. He opened his arms and whirled, embracing the world and giggling like a fool. As he came back to face me, he held out the arms to me. "Good you be here," he said. "Well come."

I decided I wasn't ready to be hugged, not right then.

Sir Richard arrived, panting worse even than I did. He looked hard at Sam. Sam says easy-like, "Well, you could consider we're even for that story you didn't give me."

"I will," says Sir Richard.

I spoke grumpily to the old man. "Say something in Paiute."

He gave me that sweet look again. It was enough to make you giggle forever. "Brggdly gmp," he said, or something to that effect.

"Something else," I prompted.

"RASS-yo chidle. Brggdly gmp."

That was enough for me. Whatever Paiute was, it was nothing like what I heard under the river. It was just a plain human language. "What did you say? In English what did you say?"

"I make sorry to you. Come eat home me." He giggled.

I looked at Sam, who shook his head no.

"Next day," said Paiute Joe. "Come next day."

"Sure," I said, "eat. Tomorrow."

With that Paiute Joe set off, walking backward, and flashing at us the angelic sweetness of his smile.

WE ATE OUR dinner in silence, uncertain, not having a good time or bad, eyes checking each other out. Besides Sir Richard and me and Sam, and Paiute Joe, there was a man introduced as his brother and two of his sons. We just sat around the fire spooning food out of our bowls and into our mouths. The women of Paiute Joe's family, all ages, and the kids ate off to the side. They had a good old regular time gabbing and laughing and paying us no mind.

Once in a while those of us at the fire would smile and nod to each other like we were friends, or were enjoying ourselves till we couldn't stand it, or knew what was going on. It was tough on account of none of the Paiutes hardly spoke English, except Joe, and he wasn't talking. We had too many languages and not enough of them in common.

So I decided. "I'm gonna give my river language a try anyway," I says to Sir Richard. He looked at me quizzical-like. "Hell," I says, "maybe my river talk is Paiute."

Sir Richard smooched his lips and eyebrows and said, "Carry on."

I was some worried, naturally, because I never had been sure of the words of my special talk, or even the syllables. My notion was just to start babbling, and maybe the right sounds would come out. My stomach felt all willywoolly, but I surely to goose had nothing to lose.

I cleared my throat. I put on my brightest smile. "Paiute Joe," I says, "kriggledy dap wash ack gono? Bah, wokewoke Paiute?" Felt not too bad for river talk. I meant, "Do you understand what I'm saying? Is this the Paiute language?"

Joe answered, "You trying to make our talk?"

My heart and stomach did acrobatics, one over the other.

Joe beamed. "Kwa, kwa?" he said, or something like that—I can't recall the exact foolishness he uttered. He giggled. "Bo wah gik gik. Burr, burr, gowsy gop." He turned and bellered at a dog, "Saminy gip!" The dog skittered off.

Then Sir Richard got in on the spirit of the thing. He recited,

" '*T'was brillig, and the slithy toves*
Did gyre and gimble in the wabe;
All mimsy were the borogoves
And the mome raths outgrabe.' "

(He explained to me after that this was a bit of nonsense from a forthcoming book by a fellow Oxford man, and later he sent me a copy of *Alice in Wonderland.*)

"Every man know play talk," said Joe, and embarked on another gaggle of baby babble and silly syllables.

Sam joined in with a cacophony of gibberish, and scratched his ribs like a monkey.

Joe's brother asked him something that must have been, "What's going on?" Joe answered in Paiute, and the brother and sons told each other and commented in Paiute and grinned like fools. What with them carrying on, and Joe, the two white men acting crazy, we had a regular babel.

And didn't I feel the idiot?

In the midst of all this word folly, and with a sinking feeling, I decided to go for completely idiocy and try the words my father left. "Rock Child. Does anybody know what Rock Child means?"

Somehow this stopped conversation. Everyone looked at me, smiling. Then Paiute Joe took off into song.

"Rock-a-bye-baby on the tree top.
When the wind blows the cradle will rock,
When the bough breaks the cradle will fall,
Down will come baby, cradle and all."

Heckahoy, I couldn't help it, I joined in myself, singing it straight but turning it into a round. Sir Richard launched in with me. Sam tried, but he only croaked.

We sang through it three times, enjoying ourselves thoroughly.

In the following silence, I said in Joe's direction, "Rock Child don't mean nothing to you?"

He shrugged. "It means a baby-rocking song of you people."

Fortunately one of Paiute Joe's wives took the edge off my embarrassment by holding out the ladle and offering me more to eat. Glad of the distraction, I accepted. After all, hadn't Sir Richard murmured to me on the way to camp, "You must eat every bite of the supper and ask for more. Among these people that is mere politeness"? (Him and his books again.)

"You like the stew?" says Sam, trying to slow down the comical twitches his thick eyebrows and bushy mustache were doing.

"Sure," says I, "I love it." This remark was just politeness, though I had no particular objection to it as yet. Mrs. Paiute Joe, who we hadn't actually been introduced to, so I didn't know her name, filled my bowl right up.

Sam's lips twisted. He leaned over, spat on the ground as a cover, and whispered, "It's boiled *garbage.*"

I looked in horror at the conglomeration. In it I saw T-bones with tooth marks on the meat, half cobs of corn, oysters, clams, rags of scrambled eggs, hunks of lettuce, and orange peels. My mind leapt to a picture of the garbage pails behind Virginia's restaurants.

I ran for the bushes and threw up. And did some more throwing up. In the end my job of throwing up was quite thorough.

Why hadn't I spotted the signs sooner? I am inclined to live in my dreams, and often fail to notice things. I have never had occasion to regret this defect more than at this moment.

Now I looked back at everybody sitting around the little fire. They just stared at me for a minute, Paiute Joe and Sam and Sir Richard. (The rest of the family was kindly off to themselves, and there was a flock of them.) I was scared. *If you're impolite to Paiutes, do they scalp?*

Then Sam lost control and began to hoot and holler and slap Sir Richard on the back. Even Sir Richard's severe countenance shook with merriment. Altogether they quite enjoyed the joke.

I walked back to the circle of my friends and looked at my bowl, which was spilled. I studied the cook pot. Cast my eyes back and forth, and sloshed around in my misery.

Then Joe jumps up in a clownish way and offers me more. I shake my head woefully.

Sir Richard says dryly, "You must not be a Paiute."

Joe let out a big, squealing giggle. (Of course, he'd heard and understood everything.) That did it—they all commenced to heehawing again.

I took the whole business a little unkindly. It doesn't ever feel good to be the butt of laughter, and there was something else: My feelings were tender. Sir Richard knew I didn't feel good about it, not being a Paiute.

Heckahoy, I'd thrown up their food. *Guess I'm not one.*

I drooped my bowl toward my feet, and my whole self drooped toward the ground.

After a little, Joe said in a kind tone, "You skin dark. You Indin?"

I nodded and shook at once. When I'd recovered from this confusion, I said, "Father white, mother Indian. Don't know what people. Can't remember my mother—she died." Sam was watching me right smart now. Sir Richard was paying attention, too. "She come from somewhere in Washo, I think, don't know where. Been hopin' to find 'em."

Paiute Joe nodded sagely. "Hope you find what want. Watch out, watch out, I say. No matter what, it surprise, it surprise what you find, whatever something you find."

I tried to nod sagely back.

"Maybe you should meet Sallee Joe," he said. He pondered that. "Yes sure, you should meet Sallee Joe. She white get be Paiute. You want?"

I nodded eagerly. Maybe I could turn this embarrassment to the good side yet.

"She gone gather nuts. Few days I send word, you come. OK? Few days I send word, you come."

CHAPTER TWENTY-ONE

SUN MOON PUT the *torma* before the altar and lit the cedar. As it sent up a waft of smoke, she knelt and began to pray. But even as she began, she was aware that it was not the same. For weeks her prayers had a different spirit. She was different. Odd . . .

Several times a day she meditated, as was now her practice, and several times she prayed. She continued to pray to Mahakala, her savior of the last year. She gave thanks to Mahakala for the anger she had discovered deep within her, the protest against those who mistreated her, those who . . . She worked her throat, tried to loosen it against the iron band. *Mahakala, you saved my body, my life, and my spirit.*

Once she had prayed for access to anger and what paradoxically lay beyond the anger—serenity.

Yet she felt different. Now as always in meditation she made herself aware first of the source of energy for meditation, the *tewa korlo,* behind and below the navel. As always when she prayed, she sent her prayers outward from that source. But now it was changed. It was the source of energy not only of her self but of two selves. In the same place in her belly, it felt like, grew the new life. Her prayers were not only hers but her child's. She and the child were the same.

And her life was being restored to her. In a new way she was being saved. The human incarnation growing within her, she seemed to nourish it less than it nourished her. It felt like a blessing to her, like a fountain of life-giving water. Each morning and each night, on waking and before sleeping, she simply lay in bed and felt the life in her belly, the life at the center of her body, the hint, essence that would become a human being. This was her center, not self but other, or both self and other.

Now, kneeling before the altar, she felt a little woozy. She went to the bed and stretched out. She breathed—closed her eyes and breathed. She put her left hand on her belly, her right hand on her heart. She felt the beat of the two hearts within her. Though her fingers couldn't detect the belly heartbeat physically, she knew it as truly as the other. Two heartbeats, the beat of life, the rhythm of the one great force on the Earth, live now, live now, live now. She was the channel of life. Like Asie's drum, like the great brass horns of the monks, she was a primordial resonance of existence, she was the cycle of incarnation after incarnation after incarnation. She felt this being a vehicle somehow more strongly, more clearly than anything in her life. It felt more real. She felt the beat with her fingers, heart in chest, heart in belly.

It is changing me.

She did not know yet just how the awareness of the beats was changing her. She did not permit herself to formulate thoughts or words about that. She simply pictured a bud opening, before anyone can see the kind of flower it is. She could feel the thrust of whatever rose up from the ground and into the stem and opened that bud. It felt like hope.

I dedicate my existence to the nurturing of the incarnation within me.

She drummed her fingers lightly on ribs and belly. *My carnal act with Asie, forbidden, condemned, was in truth a great blessing.*

She rubbed herself gently, ribs and belly. *That is why I now must find the courage to speak.*

WHILE THE HERITAGE was being cleaned one morning, before opening for lunch, Daniel and me would run over tunes. One day he put some sheet music in front of me at the piano. I didn't read music nearly as well as I played by ear then, but he showed me, and soon I got the hang of it. Snazzlely stuff it was, but nothing for the Heritage at all. Tunes by a fellow from Louisiana, says Daniel, name of Louis Gottschalk. I read through them pretty excited.

Then he put another one up, called "Nocturne." He played through it for me, and then I gave it a go. Subtle sounds like you can hardly imagine, moods quick on the wing, deep as a lake, shimmery as light on water.

I'd barely heard a glimmer of music like this.

"Chopin," he says, pointing to the composer's name at the upper right.

I looked at him with what must have seemed the gleaming eyes of a child.

"I'm going to take tomorrow morning off," he says. "Business. Maybe you want that time to practice."

My thought was, well, honest, I don't know what it was. This music somehow put me back in the river. Like then, I was tumbling upside down, right side up, upside down, and like then I was hearing things. But I couldn't see yet where I wanted to go. Couldn't *hear* yet.

"Play some more Chopin for me," I says.

He gave his small smile and did it. I sat there and let the music play me, that's what it felt like.

After a while he says, "Let me take you to lunch." Daniel never worried about money, seemed to have plenty, and sometimes had the way of a man of affairs. And a man of secrets. And always unpredictable. We did the lunch.

And I did something that surprised me. Over lunch I told him about getting swept away by the river. Hearing the music. Washing up and Sun Moon finding me. Sir Richard saving us both. About scouting for the people I was born to. Even about Rock Child.

"Rock Child?" he says in an odd tone.

I nodded and said it again. It did feel foolish, and not just because it was like a lullaby. "You ever hear of it?"

Daniel studied me. "I'll ask around," he says.

I thought, *Friends are the best things we have.*

PAIUTE JOE AND Sallee Joe, his adopted daughter, stopped by the Heritage one afternoon and wanted to know if I'd like to walk back to their camp with them. I did.

I looked at Sallee Joe and saw a dirty, dark-skinned, rotten-toothed Paiute woman of middle age, two little kids trailing behind. When I looked closer, I saw a white woman in her mid-twenties with skin that was tanned deep by the desert sun, brown hair full of dust, and pretty green eyes.

We headed down the road. "Tell you story," Joe urged her. As usual, he was beaming like the sun.

She began hesitantly. "I been with the people for fifteen, sixteen years," she says in a backwoods-sounding accent. She looked to Paiute

Joe for guidance, and he nodded her on. "My folks come across on the California Trail, I guess. Paiute Joe took me from them on the Carson River, says they killed one of his kids so he took me for even. Don't know anything else and can't remember one single, solitary thing before I come here." She looked up at Joe, but always kept her eyes down in front of me.

"No one single, solitary thing." She mused a little on that. "Seemed so peculiar I went to the doctor over to Virginia. He told me a big scare can do that to a kid, leave you with no memories."

She stopped. She didn't know something like that happened to me, and I couldn't remember either. My tongue was caught.

Hers seemed caught, too, and I didn't know how to get her going again. I wanted to know how she felt about things, I wanted to know . . . Everything.

She walked in silence, eyes cast down to the ground. I remembered what Sir Richard had said he would ask. "The way you see it, how are Indians different from white people?"

The eyes darted up and down my face and forced themselves down. "I don' hardly know nothing about white people."

I felt stymied. She lived next door to a whole town full of white people and saw them nearly every day. She lived with Paiutes, had a Paiute husband and Paiute children. How could she not know?

"Like how Paiute women live against how white women live?"

"Tell him," wheedled Joe.

She began to talk slowly. "White women, most whores," she said. "Far the most whores." She let that sink in. "No Paiute woman sell her body, none."

I checked this out later, and it was gospel. Some Indian women did, but not Paiutes.

We left the road for the footpath toward their camp.

"Some white women work for other white folks; cook, clean, bring food, wash clothes. When I come to the people, no Paiute woman work for someone, for money. Now some do such." She shrugged her regret.

"Some white women got families, children. But they have to fight to keep them. Divorce sometimes. Children orphans. Women widows, or divorced women alone."

She flicked her eyes straight into my face for an instant, and then shot them down. Sir Richard had explained about the respectful custom of not looking others directly in the face. "No Paiute children orphans. No go to big building far from home, live without parents, live without relatives, unhappy. Every Paiute child have parents, relatives, families connected to families."

She let me sit with that sobering thought before she went on. "No Paiute woman without family, not one. None but very old without husband. Your husband die, your sister's husband take you. No orphans, no widows."

I was uncomfortable. Hell, I didn't make orphans or widows or courtesans either. I wasn't even white. "I ain't exactly white," I said. *Besides, there isn't anything wrong with being white. Is there?*

She looked at me full on now. "You ain't what? Dressed like that? Playing piano in a bar? Living in a hotel? Living in a *ho-tel* with a John Bull lord?" The shy squaw was gone. She shook her head in disgust.

This must have been the way to act she learned from her real mother, I thought. I was kind of feeling distracted.

"Tell him vice," Joe said, happy as a clam.

"Vices," she said. "No whoring." I'd about had enough of that one. "No drinking. You never see a Paiute drunk." Turned out they were well-known for staying sober, but my back hairs were getting up.

"Vice," Joe repeated.

Sallee Joe threw a grin at the landscape. "Gambling," she said. "You got one thing you call vice we like, gambling. You never gave that to us, though. We had plenty of that all along."

I decided to stand up to her. "What do you want that the white man has to offer?" Half of me felt like a traitor and half like an ass. Don't know why I couldn't please at least half. "What good sense do you see in the white way?"

"*Sense?*" Now she put her hands on her hips and glared at me. "No sense, white people don't have no sense. Live off the labor of other men. No Paiute does that. Ever' one of our men works at jobs, you've seen it." True, I had.

"Not grub around in dark holes in the earth that cave in on you, or kill you with gas. Not hunt daylong nightlong for something don't do no good—go crazy for it." Her voice was getting an edge. "Kill each other. Steal from each other. Cheat each other. You'll never see a Paiute doing none of that."

My feet had the willywoollies now—they wanted to run away from being white.

"Destroy your own food. We used to eat well on the pine nuts that was all over this mountain. The white man used all the pine trees up for firewood. You think on that."

We had climbed to the top of the little divide between Virginia and the camp. Sallee Joe stopped and looked back toward the city. I looked down at the Indian camp and then back toward the city, comparing. Joe watched us both, tickled.

The camp houses were, well, got up from brush, odds and ends of canvas, scraps of lumber, calico, poles, everything you can imagine, except you can hardly imagine what they managed to make use of.

And you eat garbage.

"What you looking at?" she challenged me.

"One people builds fine brick houses. The other lives in scraps. One people eats steak, the other eats the leavings. One . . ."

"You get on," she said, good-humored now. "You see better'n that. Or you don't, come to camp, set down and look. Yes, they rich, we poor, you bet. Now. They miserable. Far away from families, men alone with other men, I know how they live. Go to whores, get drunk stay drunk days and days, rob each other, beat on each other, kill each other, kill themselves from misery and despair. I seen it, sure I seen it.

"Look at poor little me, then, crossed to the other side. I give up fancy houses, smooth sheets, and canned food, and for what? Lemme tell you for what. I got my family, I got my husband and kids, I got my brothers and sisters, aunts and uncles, grandpas and grandmas, nephews and nieces, I got everything." She nodded at me as though to repeat, Everything.

My heart did a little tap dance.

"How many men come here with they families? Where your family?" She pointed straight at me, and I could feel how rude the jutting finger was. "Where's that Sam's family? Back in Missouri. Where's that Sir Richard's family? Back in England. You all living like sailors come into port. I bet. Civilized? *We're* civilized, watch out for each other, make sure everybody treat each other OK. No Paiute goes too hungry, we get food together and share it. We don't let nobody end up naked, or get sick without being took care of. How much of that can you say? How many you men in Virginia watch out for each other? Or do you watch out see if somebody dies so you can get what's in his pockets?

"Last year a white man said he'd go and get me a job, I wanted to come back to town and live white. I laughed in his face. Why would I want to live white? Lose my husband, who takes care of me? Live alone, get preyed on by white men who see a lone woman as a target. If I fall into debt, go to jail or work like a slave or sell my body to pay it off. Be lonely every day, not know what I'm living for, not be able to offer my children anything to live for, 'cept get treated bad by white men think they're superior.

"I'm rich, and you men are all the way paupers.

"And here's the worse of it. Every day you white folks wake up and think, 'We're high and all other creation is low.' That's as what sticks in my craw. So I wake up every day and say, 'Praise God. Lord, you set things right, you made me red and not one of them whites.' "

On top of the divide there I turned back. They invited me to camp for dinner, but I felt like being alone. I noticed Paiute Joe just kindly smiled sweet and kind as we said our good-byes, and sure didn't say anything to correct what Sallee Joe had proclaimed, nor set her down for saying it.

My walk home was strange; I don't know how to tell you. I wasn't a white man, I wasn't a red man. Nor even knew which I wanted to be. I wasn't thinking Virginia City was a jimmy-joomy place, but I wasn't holding out for the Paiute camp either. I saw the truth in a lot of what Sallee Joe said, and could have added other unpleasant truths from my own experience. I started out on this big ramble partly to find out if maybe my soul was Indian.

So what was pushing my feet toward the town instead of the camp? I could have made a list of reasons, I suppose, but I wouldn't have believed it. Right then, I don't think it was anything fancier than, *My friends are in town. I'm traveling with these, not those. I know about this, not that. I speak English, I don't speak Paiute.*

I was feeling pretty subdued as I walked along. Didn't recover any of my spirits until Daniel and I started making music for the dinner crowd at the Heritage. Come quitting time, I stayed and played all through the night. Slow ballads, spirituals, sad, soulful songs. I fingered soft chords on the piano and whistled above them, high and slow and sweet. White-man music, that I did understand.

Richard Burton was shaving carefully. The scar on his cheek was always a nuisance to cut around, and he believed that he did it better than most barbers. A well-groomed appearance was important to him. After shaving and dressing, he would take his morning constitutional, have luncheon, and get down to writing.

The afternoons worked well for writing. Nights he spent enjoying himself—forbidden pleasures, in whatever moderation he could muster. Well before dawn he was in bed. During the forenoons he slept, then a substantial luncheon—one Virginia restaurant was not half-bad. Then write all afternoon. For some days of the journey he had only notes, and he filled these out into full and proper entries in his journal. He felt fitful when doing it. Would he ever be able to reveal to the reading public that he'd traveled in America a second time? And let the Unionists know Her Majesty's government had opposed them? Doubtful, very doubtful.

Sun Moon's fever was only occasional now—a spell of fever, say, every second or third day. Customarily, she went out to dinner with him. Sometimes she felt up to going out to luncheon as well, or for a short evening walk. In ten days she might be ready to travel. In that time he might have indulged himself sufficiently in Virginia's pleasures—or might not. Praise be, there was always San Francisco. What hurry should he feel to get back to the exile of Fernando Po?

When he had completed his toilette, he found Sun Moon waiting for him in the sitting room. "Please luncheon today here? I need talk."

Intrigued, Burton ordered food brought up. They exchanged small talk, which he normally hated, but took pleasure in with Sun Moon, as a way of showing her the social graces of the British and observing the social graces of Tibetans. He was gratified to see that she held back her particular object of conversation until they had set the dishes aside and poured the last of the coffee.

"I tell secret, you keep?"

Now Burton was intrigued. "Naturally."

"Promise."

"Yes." *My profession is secrets.*

"Thank you pay passage ship to Calcutta."

Burton was delightedly surprised. Sun Moon never discussed money. As a nun she had little occasion to use it. Now probably she found her financial dependence on him embarrassing. They both knew better than to add to her embarrassment with a vulgar discussion of dollars.

She looked at him over her cup and said baldly, "I need more money."

He waited. Life was infinitely amusing if you waited and observed.

She touched her belly. "I need help for my child."

Burton tilted his coffee right into his lap.

SUN MOON MANAGED not to smile at him. She waited patiently while he changed his trousers. When he returned, Sir Richard simply picked up where they had left off. "Your child?"

She moved her fingers gently against her belly and took strength from it. She had thought it out, but she must go slowly and thoughtfully. *What to tell, what to keep for myself. How to ask with dignity.*

With the power from her belly she quelled her desperation. That life in her belly, it kept saving her life. Now her position for meditation was left hand on the heart in her belly, right on the heart in her chest. Her mind sank into the point below and behind the navel that was the center of herself and the center of her child. *I am making a new it, it is making a new me.*

"I once think this plan. Leave San Francisco few weeks, sail Calcutta, arrive winter, stay convent. In spring travel through mountain passes with traders of my people, go Lhasa. Stay at holy city, meet other teachers at *ta ts'ang*"—she fumbled for the English word—"college." In summer travel east with traders to Kham, to Zorgai, to my convent, arrive autumn. One year."

She lifted a finger. "Was plan. No more. Now not safe."

She took thought. She must make him understand. "Child," she said, her eyes moving to the hand on her belly. "Daughter." *Can you understand I know it is a daughter? Can you understand she is my life?*

"In spring I am big in belly. Show not chaste, not like nun should be. No respect. Travel dangerous for me, dangerous for child." She let herself feel the life within her for a moment, enveloped, protected, nurtured, loved.

She opened her eyes at Burton. She looked her appeal into his heart. "Must have money. Not dress as nun. Dress as wealthy woman. Hire guides, servants. Much money. Must do. Else child—daughter—not safe."

She breathed in and out slowly, taking strength from her twin centers. "You help?"

BURTON FELT THE effort these words had cost her—even he felt exhausted. "Asie's child?"

She looked at him evenly, with great serenity, and did not reply.

But he knew. And he saw. He saw that the life within her was changing her spirit. It gave her the desire to live. He felt a pang of love.

He spoke gently. "I will be delighted to help. How much do you need?"

She named a sum in Tibetan silver *tamka.* Burton translated that in his head into rupees, then into pounds, last into dollars.

"Five hundred dollars should do it," he said. Actually, he'd doubled what she asked for.

She nodded. The sum must seem immense to her, who had never had access to money. For a Tibetan surely it was a vast sum.

"Sun Moon, I'm delighted to help you. Don't you think, though, that you should tell Asie? It strikes me that he has a right to know."

"You promise keep secret," she said sternly.

He nodded. "And so I shall. Don't you think, though . . ." He stopped his tongue. *Obviously you don't.*

"What kind of life will your daughter have?"

"She will be a nun of the convent at Zorgai, her life dedicated to *moksha.*"

Burton pictured the convent in his mind, the huge prayer wheels turning, the prayer flags ever fluttering, the deep, nasal sound of the great brass horns, the chant of the nuns in the Lhakhang, the glow of the butter lamps. The ruined mother, the impeccable child.

He looked at the autumn sunlight flooding in the window. He listened to the silence dancing around them, full of meaning and mystery.

"Money," she said hesitantly, "you have much?"

Burton nodded. Five hundred dollars would in fact pinch considerably, but he considered it a debt of honor.

"Sun Moon, you have both my affection and esteem. I will help you in every way possible."

She smiled, and in that moment he knew perfectly the meaning of the word *beatific.*

Asie, though. Asie had struggled to save not only Sun Moon's life but her spirit, her love of life. Now he was the instrument of her deliverance. Was he never to know?

I swore.

Sometimes Burton despised fate.

Daniel took the next two mornings off from teaching. I clunked along practicing Chopin and Gottschalk on my own. When he got back, he put a proposition to me.

"I have a job for you."

I looked at him peculiar. "What sort of job?" I mumbled. *The Heritage going to pay me to side you every noon and night? That's a full-time job already, without wage.*

"I'll pay fifty dollars a week."

"Fifty dollars a week? Robbing the ore shipments?" It was double what a miner got paid.

"At Western Union Telegraph Company," says he.

"At *the Telegraph Company?*" I squawked.

From Chopin to the Telegraph Company—how could you make those two play in the same key?

"So. Will you worm your way into the Virginia City Western Union Telegraph Company? Starting as soon as possible?"

Fifty a week? It was a stake. It was what a young half-breed wanderer needed to get a decent start in life. It had to be underhanded. "Until Sun Moon is healthy enough to go on," says I.

She was still well one day, down the next.

"Then we'll have tea with Tommy Kirk," says Daniel. "He'll explain."

It wasn't what Sir Richard described to me as a tea. Maybe it was more of a half-breed tea. Tommy had a cook that provided his eats the way he liked them, which was half from his father the John Bull diplomat and half from his mother the Shanghai courtesan. We had tea with scones and dim sum. Heckahoy, when I told Sir Richard, he thought it was funny as a dog with five legs. But to me it was new and fun.

When we'd done a few sips and munches and the socially proper time had passed, Daniel pitched in. "I have thought it out with care," he said. He commanded my attention with that hawk look of his. "What is most valuable in Washo is information, good information. If a man knows what wildcat mine is going to make a strike, or when the Gould and Curry, Mexican, Ophir, or Sergeant is going to open into a rich new vein, he can make money. Real money." The Ophir, Mexican, Sergeant, and Gould and Curry were the main outfits in Virginia at that time. "He would buy stock in those enterprises. Or sell it. When news of the strike became public, the stock would rise on the San Francisco Stock Exchange, and a man could take his profit."

Tommy gave his generous smile. "Nothing is so common as information about what strikes are coming along. And nothing so unreliable."

Daniel nodded. "I investigated paying for good information. Unfortunately, whatever the wildcatters tell you is blue sky. The managers know the truth but keep their mouths shut. The miners in the new shafts talk sometimes, for money. But you can't tell who's telling you righteous and who's not.

"After giving the problem considerable thought, and after discovering personally how difficult it is to make money trading stocks in the normal way, I have hit upon an approach.

"The principal owners of the four big mines live in San Francisco. The mine managers communicate with them constantly. By telegraph. They wire news of discoveries, news of busts. The owners wire back decisions to make announcements, to seek new capital, to buy new equipment, to expand or abandon shafts, and all other business ways."

The transcontinental telegraph was new those days, and businesses played with it like a new toy.

Daniel took a big breath and let it out. "Rumors are flying just now. The Mexican is supposed to be on the verge of a huge strike. The Gould and Curry is supposed to be discovering that its new shaft is a bust. They say it both ways about the Sergeant. Stocks have been rising and sinking for over a week on these reports. Bonanza is going long, borrasca is selling short. Guess right both ways and your fortune in stocks will be bigger than the one in the ground." Of course, no one knew yet the one in this lode was the biggest in the world.

He put his elbows on his knees and leaned forward toward me. "But why guess? Why not intercept the reports to and from the mine owners? And invest before the news becomes public."

"How?" I asks.

"That's where you come in."

CHAPTER TWENTY-TWO

It turned out easier than it sounded. I rambled round to the Company office and watched the operation. The fellow at the telegraph key wrote every message in dark pencil in block capital letters, then copied it out again and stuck it on a spike. The outgoing messages got stuck on another spike—a copy of every single message going out, a copy of every single message coming in, my snooping mind recorded.

Then he gave it to a kid, and a word on where to take it. In those days they didn't have messenger boys hooting around town wearing cute little cap and on bicycles (which hadn't even been thought of yet). No, those days boys hung around the telegraph office and carried the messages for tips. Right off I saw the sticky part—if I just hung out like those boys, I'd get just a portion of the messages that came in, and maybe not the ones we wanted.

So I lounged around the office and jawed with the operator, fellow name of Alvord Smith, about thirty, hair thick and stiff as a broom and totally gray. Main thing was the constant clatter of that fancy-looking key. Alvord could savvy its meaning without more than half-listening, but it didn't make any sense to me at all. The very idea of sense from that racket reminded me of the nonsense lines from that song about the Celestials we'd learned on the trail:

O ching hi ku tong me ching ching
O ching hi ku tong chi do,

Having got the hang of what was up and what was down in the operation of the office, though, pretty soon I had my idea. Alvord needed a backup operator, another hand to run that key, and wouldn't I be his boy!

Alvord, Sir, I think this telegraph business is just the jimmy-joomiest work I ever saw. What is Morse code anyhow? (Says Alvord, I happen to have a codebook right here.)

I don't hardly see how anybody can hear sense in all that commotion the key makes. (Aw, shucks.)

I don't hardly see how anybody can move fingers as fast as those code clicks and clacks go. (Aw shucks, aw shucks.)

Maybe, maybe, Alvord, Sir, could I just try tapping something? (Why, yes, try SOS. I happen to have a spare key in this cabinet.)

Clickety-clackety crash! Oh, Sir, it must take a devil of a fellow to do that.

That same afternoon I got apprenticed to learn the operating trade. Alvord didn't even have to pay me to get the training, and in return I was so grateful I'd deliver any messages he wanted, anywhere he wanted.

So I had three ways to steal information. Take a message to deliver and sneak off and copy it. Get hold of the copy Alvord made. Learn to decipher that clacking with my own ear.

Though I had pretty good ears, I wondered how long it would take to figure out that clickety-clack like Alvord did. That would be the unbeatable way.

I made doodledy sure I was in that telegraph office every minute it was open, unless I was carrying a message somewhere. I figured out how to grab the messages for the mine myself and foist the others off on the hang-around boys. I slipped back to our rooms and scribbled down copies of whatever telegraphese looked good. A promising one might say, SIXTEEN GEARS SHIPPED STOP EXPECT DELIVERY 9-28 STOP. A not-so-promising one read, DO NOT THINK YOU CAN EVER COME HOME. Fearing I might miss something important, I got Alvord's permission to come in at night and practice on the key. Then I read all of that day's copies, and copied off the good ones. Alvord trustingly gave me a door key for coming and going.

Infiltrating wasn't as much fun as playing piano, but it was kind of fascinating. I'd sit near the sleeping form of Sun Moon with my bootlegged copies and read happily. Wasn't I a regular spy, just like Sir Richard!

After some thought, I took a little talk with Sir Richard that very evening. We spies don't tell our conversation.

Had a good talk with my employers, too. After Daniel and I played through the late hours at the Heritage, we spent the extra-late hours visiting with Tommy Kirk in his office behind the opium den. We sorted and sorted the copies, and we read 'em and read 'em, and we surely did some learning.

Things were easier those days. Since the telegraph was brand-new, the Washo mine managements hadn't yet started sending information in code. Later some boys tried to run the trick again and got stumped. But these were the early days, and all the mines and some investors did business by telegraph.

At first the stuff seemed worthless. If you want to know the most boring stuff in the world, just look in on everybody's secrets. Soon, though, Daniel and Tommy taught me what to look for. If I saw the word "assay," I was to come running to Tommy's place quicker than peas. I was to go perk-alert also about a strike in a new shaft, or petering out in an old one. Facts about needing to hire more miners, or lay some off. Any facts indicating bonanza or borrasca. Any facts savvy investors would buy or sell on. When they found out, which was supposed to be after we found out.

Sorry to say, we didn't find anything like that the first couple of nights. I went home near dawn very sleepy, with a heart low in my chest and fifty bucks in gold in my pocket, which generally will improve a man's outlook.

The third day my fingers were running ahead of my ears—I could tap that key so it made some sense—maybe the lack of sleep affected my ears. The fourth day I could send a message on the wire slowly but accurately. And that night I gave Daniel and Tommy their first useful bit. The Sergeant was expecting a shipment of eight oversized cars in a week.

They knew enough to make sense of this information. The Sergeant had sunk an extrawide shaft in a new direction. They'd brought up oversized cars to haul out all the country rock while they were looking for a rich vein. If they were receiving more cars, it meant they intended to haul a lot more of something out and a lot faster. Daniel didn't think they'd make that investment without indications, damned good indications.

The next morning I watched the crowd outside the telegraph office when we posted the San Francisco Stock Exchange prices. The Sergeant opened slightly off, as folks in the stock game put it. Soon as everyone saw the prices, the curbside stock exchange got going, bidding, buying, selling, and the rest of it. Tommy bought two hundred shares of Sergeant, I didn't hear the price. I walked over to the Heritage with him and saw Daniel get half the stock certificates. So that was how they were working their end of the scam. Daniel was behind the scenes, Tommy out front. Daniel got hold of righteous information, Tommy put up the cash. They split the take. In the end Daniel would keep his windfall a secret, and Tommy would crow.

Watching them, I tucked my thumb in my pants and rubbed my gold coins. Last evening I'd split the waistband of my pants and sewed them in. I wondered, *When I get all my pay, should I buy Sergeant?*

After a week or so I got into a routine. I worked until the office closed, made music with Daniel at the Heritage for a couple of hours, and then slipped back to the telegraph office to check the day's messages, sort and copy, put them back on the spike to make things look right before Alvord missed them.

I was glad it was dark, though, when I left the office. What would I say after all, if someone caught me? What I was doing wasn't against any Washo law, nor any other. But it might run against the notions of a mining-camp jury, which is the hardest-hearted kind. So on that Saturday night I put Alvord's copies back on the spike, slipped my copies under my shirt, looked carefully out the window, and eased out of the door, nifty as you please. (Nifty was a mining-camp word, and I liked it.)

"I'll take them papers," says the voice.

First I felt a rush, a whooshing wind in my head that said, PORTER ROCKWELL.

Then the wind quieted, because Rockwell wouldn't have asked for the papers.

The demand came from a under a big, black bandanna on the face of a tall man with slitty eyes. He was dressed all in black, with a black slouch hat covering his features. I knew what must be in his gun hand, pointing straight at me. And something was peculiar about that voice—it gave me the willywoollies.

I made a quick calculation of my wages against my lifeblood and handed over the papers.

"Now, Asie," the voice said in a normal tone, "I'll buy you a drink and we'll look these over."

The gun hand opened and showed me what it held, just a piece of scrap board about the right size. Off came the slouch hat and the bandanna. Underneath was Sam Clemens, grinning like he'd cornered a rising market on fun.

I grabbed for those papers. He snatched 'em away and held 'em far back. I grabbed him like I was going to wrestle him down. Sam shook like a dog and threw me off. He was a big man. "Asie," he said, "I'm gonna have a look at these papers." I could see I'd got his dander up. "Regardless," he said.

We went to the hotel rooms, where the whole world couldn't look over our shoulders. I looked in on Sun Moon (it was one of her poor days) and turned the bodyguard loose.

When Sam had gone through the papers once, me steaming next to him, he leaned toward me and gleamed those eyes at me. I saw now that the gleam could give you a chuckle or the cajoolies, for he could put fun or malice in it. "Asie," says he, "I'm gonna save you some lyin'. I got a tip you and Gentleman Dan was up to something. I been watching you in the telegraph office evenings, and you ain't been practicing on that key. These papers are confidential information about the mines. You fellers got something going, a money-making scheme."

He paused for breath. "No harm in that, now. Hardly a man in Washo without a money-making scheme, 'less he's a sky pilot or a dimwit, and I'd judge you to be too smart for either."

He leaned back expansively, delighted with himself. "So let's not go circling around about morality or shame, which neither of us gives a fig for. Just come straight out with the truth."

Now he gleamed his teeth, too, and they shined even from behind the bush of mustache.

"I can't," says I. I was nervous that Sun Moon would wake up and want to know what was going on, or Sir Richard would walk in on us.

"You can't? You can't *not!*" says Sam Clemens. "You want me to tell Alvord Smith in the morning what I caught you at? You want me to take them papers you stole and hand 'em back to him?"

I considered Tommy Kirk. Sam didn't know about him. If I gave up the game, Daniel would merely be mad as a bear. Tommy Kirk might cut my jewels off with a wee dagger.

I shook my head. "I can't," I said.

"So," said Sam Clemens, "you'd sooner be cashiered and maybe run out of town than talk. So there's something you're more afraid of. What would that be?" He was talking to me, but his mind was off spinning notions, juggling possibilities like balls in the air. He hadn't found anything he liked yet. "What say," he started in, teasing out word after word, pulling me along with his style, "you tell me the truth and I keep my mouth shut until you've got the boodle?"

"I can't."

He tilted his chair back and regarded me from afar, between bushes of mustache and eyebrow.

I had the willywoollies. Maybe Sam and me were friends, but he was also after the news, and by God that makes a newsman crazy. It's like getting the story is a higher morality.

"Friend," he says, "you don't leave me a lot of choice." He nodded to himself awhile, cogitating. "OK. I'll tell everyone I've seen you with. Alvord, of course. Gentleman Dan. Captain Burton. The Tibetan woman. And the sovereign of Chinatown, Tommy Kirk."

The cajoolies did cartwheels in my belly.

BURTON'S MARTIAL ENERGIES rose as he strode. They saluted and stood at port arms. He loved danger.

They were walking downhill into Chinatown, Clemens on the left, the Missourian of easy manner and a quick but vulgar wit. Asie walked in the middle and Burton on the far side—it was Burton's task on this excursion to protect them. He cast his eyes about for trouble—rooftops, windows, corners, shadows. . . . He didn't expect difficulties yet. The sovereign of Chinatown wanted something, had asked for a meeting. If he chose, the bugger could simply have done Clemens in. Nothing was more common in Virginia than a dead man for breakfast.

That was how Burton had struck his deal. Instead of giving an interview, Burton would save Clemens's hide.

The captain wore a long coat, and under it held a pistol in one hand and his *assegai* in the other. He whirled about and gazed uphill, his eyes probing the darkness restlessly. At this absurd hour any movement would be suspicious.

He faced downhill again. He listened, which was often more informative than watching. He smelled. He sensed. He breathed the cold mountain air in and out. He was ready.

In a higher state of readiness than necessary, he thought. *If our fate is trouble, it will come on the return journey.*

The Missourian told a ribald story about the moon, then another about the Virgin Mary. Burton imagined him the first man in America in his storehouse of ribald stories, but the captain was busy running his eyes through the dark, hunting assassins.

As they came into Chinatown, Burton sucked the smells in deep, the spicy, alien aromas of Asia that to him always meant danger, drugs, sex, and delight.

Asie led the way around a corner, slipped down a narrow way to a door, and entered. Immediately Burton recognized the bittersweet odor made by the opium smokers. As they passed through the room, he worked his fingers on the hilt of the *assegai* within his coat. Men lay in every bunk, apparently in the lotus state. But any one, or any half dozen, might be ready to spring upon the visitors.

Asie led the way past the old man at the table with the smoking paraphernalia—Burton felt a pang at the sight—and to an obscure door and thus to a back room.

After all the men acknowledged Asie's introductions, a low voice spoke in Chinese behind them.

"Captain Burton," said Tommy Kirk in English, "will you set your weapons aside? You are among friends here."

Burton hesitated for effect and stared at the Celestial leaning against the wall, a villainous-looking thug, probably a mate of Q Mark's. Such men were loyal to whoever paid them.

Point made, he handed the *assegai* and pistol to an underling. His hope was to look bereft enough that they wouldn't think of the additional knife in his boot. Whether that worked or not, they were not bold enough to search his person.

At Tommy Kirk's gesture they took seats in front of the desk.

"Captain Burton," Tommy Kirk began, "may I inquire the nature of your business with me?"

"I have no business in Chinatown, Mr. Kirk, other than to assure the physical safety of my friends. The night is dark, the time late, the streets hazardous."

Tommy Kirk nodded, as though to himself. "I may be obliged to ask you for a word."

Burton nodded back.

Tommy turned his regard to Samuel Clemens. (Burton could not think of Clemens by the nickname "Sam." He found that American custom silly.)

"Mr. Clemens," said Tommy Kirk, "what is it you want?"

"I know our boy Asie has been snitching messages from the telegraph office. Since he's brought me here, I reckon this thievery is something to do with you.

"Mr. Kirk, you are a legend in this city. Though no one knows anything about you, everyone has stories. Diplomat father, beautiful mother, child of sin, king of Chinatown, all that sort of palaver. I want to whet people's curiosity with some truth and a few lies, and end up making them still more curious."

"What does this have to do with the telegraph messages?"

"If they're a clue to a bold and dashing enterprise, a clever scheme to make a few million bucks, that would make the story even better."

"Why?"

"For the amusement of the world, which loves rascally endeavor, and will pay to read it in the *Territorial Enterprise.*"

"What if I do not care to tell the world my business?"

Burton stiffened a little, and carefully did not let it show. If the American took a belligerent tack here, surely there would be dead men for breakfast.

Samuel Clemens shrugged. "I'll sing a song of how good it is for you."

Burton relaxed. Clemens was no fool. Although he was a newsman, which often meant foolhardy.

"We Chinese traditionally keep things to ourselves."

"You Brits conquer the world and brag about it."

"If I have schemes, as you suggest, perhaps I should maintain privacy."

"Man on a Mississippi riverboat explained this one to me. Charming cozener, he was, traveled up and down the river selling patent medicines. I believe they consisted variously of Missouri crick water and home-brewed whisky, Arkansas crick water and home-brewed whisky, Tennessee crick water and home-brewed whisky, and Louisiana crick water and home-brewed brandy, which was whisky with a Frenchy tang.

"I asked him how come people didn't catch on to his medicines and run him out of town on a rail.

" 'Sam,' says he, 'people want to be slickered. They love to be slickered. They crave to be slickered. But they want their slickerin' with style. I give 'em a show. I tell 'em how the secret of this potion came from the thirty-third caliph of Baghdad, handed down in his family through the centuries. It was given to my great-grandfather for a service a man can't hardly mention, but the thirty-third caliph was over seventy at the time, and he had twenty-one more children after that. In brief, I make sure they get their money's worth, and laughter is worth more than money any day."

Tommy Kirk smiled. Then he drummed his fingers on the desk and looked hard at Clemens. "If I say no to you now?"

"I'd be obliged to talk to Asie's supervisor, and the sheriff."

Excellent, thought Burton.

Tommy Kirk smiled, conceding a point gracefully. "That would be inconvenient," he said. "Suppose I were to explain this . . . maneuver to you later?"

"How much later?"

"At most a month. Perhaps less."

"Why should I trust you?"

"You have my word."

"I should trust you for an honest knave? Hell, I don't trust myself. If I got drunk, I'd cuckold me with my own mistress."

Kirk actually laughed. Then he drummed his fingers some more. "In that case I shall offer you a proposition. Invest fifty dollars with me tonight. In a month I shall return it with the dividends and an explanation of this maneuver. I count on doubling my investment, and hope to multiply it by five."

Clemens looked at Kirk appraisingly.

Tommy Kirk beamed. "I will even give you the fifty dollars to invest." He took a pouch from an inside coat pocket, extracted five ten-dollar gold pieces, and stacked them on the edge of the desk in front of Clemens.

Clemens slitted his eyes at the fifty.

Come, man, a writer is by nature a spy and complicitor.

Samuel Clemens reached out, put a forefinger on the coins, studied them, pushed them toward Tommy Kirk, and said, "OK, partners."

Business partners.

"I'll want the whole story," said Clemens. "Telling a good story is even more fun than making money."

"Naturally," said Tommy. He rose, and said gently to Asie, "Thank you for bringing Mr. Clemens. And Captain Burton." Burton's spine hairs lay down.

As the three left, Tommy sent Q Mark and a couple of other rough-looking Chinamen along with them, "to escort you safely." Burton was sure the Celestials would cut their throats quick as Tommy said so. Burton's lot labored back up the mountain to the Virginia business district. Burton, Asie, and Clemens bade their escorts good night. Asie said, "Now my cajoolies are settling down."

Sun Moon turned onto her right side. She squirmed in the bedclothes. She closed her eyes and opened them again.

To her fevered mind the hotel was unreal. Muslin walls caught and held the bright desert sunlight, so the world was squares of shine. During the day the guests were seldom in the hotel, and the building was silent. A dark, vertical line stood just beyond the hanging at the foot of her bed, and she knew Q Mark was on guard.

When her mind was clear, she thought that Q Mark gave her little safety, and might himself be a threat. A thug employed by a pimp . . .

When her mind was fevered, she dreamed about Q Mark, menacing. She hurried through endless dry creek beds to escape him. He padded silently after her, relentless, a hand on his knife. Somehow she knew that he did not want her body, or her enslavement as a whore, but her death, choking on her own blood. She walked, she ran, she hid, but she would never escape.

But she knew she would never persuade Sir Richard to get rid of her bodyguard.

Frustrated, she flung her left arm out, whapping the bed. She turned over onto that side. She was not so hot now. She might be able to sleep . . .

She dreamed. She was in San Francisco again, Chinatown. She slipped through a narrow street, watching over her shoulder. She saw nothing. Hopeful for a moment, she slipped into an alley. It was indistinguishable from a hundred other alleys in Chinatown, back doors onto businesses, piles of garbage, rats. Chinese men stood erect, arms crossed, watching her with avaricious eyes. She skittered down the alley and turned left into another.

This time she did not look back. She could feel the dark man pursuing her. Perhaps he was a block back, perhaps a mile. It made no difference. He was pursuing her, the engine of his life was relentless pursuit of her, he would always pursue her.

She turned into another alley, knowing the alleys were a maze, and she would never get out. She ran, she trotted, she walked, she crept.

She stifled her panic, put it back down into her belly, and held on to it. Onward, endlessly onward—flight, flight to nowhere, flight, flight, flight.

Panic.

She fled. She had been fleeing for days, weeks, years.

She pictured herself turning, slowly, seeing the dark Porter Rockwell. She walked toward him. She opened herself to his hatred. She opened her arms. She opened her throat, and drank in his knife.

Sun Moon whimpered, rolled over, fought the bedclothes.

Almost every day she dreamed the same, running, running, endlessly running.

Sometimes she wished for death, and then she thought of the baby.

Occasionally she pretended that the dark man in the dream was Q Mark, a fellow menacing enough, a ruffian . . .

She would again ask Sir Richard to dismiss him, and Sir Richard would explain once more why she needed protection.

She opened her eyes. The sun was setting. On fever days her sleep was more restful by night than day.

With the dark came the cool. She shivered in the wet bedclothes, and drew an extra blanket on. Soon she was dreaming again.

This time she saw the waterfront. Wharves, docks, great ships hovering, looming. It was dark, and foggy. Sun Moon knew that one ship had come from Canton, full of adolescent girls, destined to become hundred-men's-wives. She shivered in the chill.

She ran from that ship. In and out of patches of fog she ran, from gray night to black night to gray night. Sometimes she stopped and listened. She could not hear the dark man, but she knew he was there, following, tracking, hunting, nearing. Strange that for a big man he moved so silently. She sniffed the air. Salt. Wet. Fish. Oil. Peril.

PORTER ROCKWELL DREW the sea air into his lungs. He didn't like it. To him it felt like rot.

He stood on the shore of the west side of San Francisco and looked toward China. He saw nothing but night fog, did not even see blackness, the darkness of the sea that stretched thousands of miles to Asia. In that darkness ships plied their way westward.

He drew the fog in deep. *Are you out there?*

He blew it out, drew it in again. *Are you out there? Have you escaped me?*

The fog wisped here and there, bearing the answer.

He stared at it.

Porter Rockwell had bumped and banged 750 miles by stagecoach, moving day and night, scarcely sleeping, substituting whisky for wretched food, growling and angry as a tormented grizzly.

In one week he had reached San Francisco. Now he had no idea how to find her, of course. There were thousands of yellows in this city. It was what Brother Brigham described, a place of whoring, murdering, and pestilence.

Instinctively, he had come straight here, to the edge of the great ocean. And here he prowled, a great predator on the hunt. He did not use his mind but his nose. And his nose told them they were not out there, on the boundless sea. They were behind him somewhere. Within his grasp.

He looked into the nothingness of fog, and onto dark, unreadable waters.

It was merely a feeling, and was feeling good enough? All his life he had depended on instinct. His instinct said it was not over.

The fog stirred and took new, inscrutable shapes. No answers there, none.

He turned and faced east, to the interior of the land. He let his instinct grope for her. Yes, probably, she was behind, quarry still. Probably.

So. You didn't rush off the continent? Stupid of you. You missed your chance.

Why had she stopped? He didn't care. Where had she stopped? Where would the John Bull want to delay her?

Without analysis he knew.

Porter Rockwell would act carefully. He would check the San Francisco hotels for the John Bull. He would bribe the clerks of offices of steamship companies to look for a passenger with a British passport disembarking under the name Burton. He would check for female Celestials returning to China. He chuckled wickedly. He'd bet there weren't any of those.

He would also bet he'd find nothing here. And when he was sure, he would start on the back trail. The Comstock Lode was a little over two hundred miles back.

In a bed in a hotel in Virginia City, Nevada, a woman dreamed. Again she fled, fled forever, her life nothing but running. Fear brushed her face and hair, it was the fog, and hopelessness was the endless whisper of the surf.

She ran along a lonely beach on the western edge of San Francisco. In the cold sea her foot slipped. She stuck a hand out, and put it into a wind as cold as the void. She looked up and saw in the tendrils of fog a head, the head of Porter Rockwell, looking at her with eyes of congealed ice. The head was borne upon no body, but rode a whirlwind of cold.

Sun Moon cried out, and the cry woke her. She sat up. She remembered the dream, the one she could never escape. She looked into the darkness and saw nothing. But she knew. She knew. She mewled a little and lay back down, sleepless, shivering, whimpering.

Porter Rockwell, there on the beach, felt something stir in his chest. It was knowledge, a kind of knowledge. He was certain. She wasn't here. He would go back.

CHAPTER TWENTY-THREE

It was Tuesday of the third week we got our break. By that time the rattlety-rat of the telegraph key was music to my ears—I could hear meaning in it as easy as sass in a grace note. Like a lot of music, most of it had nothing to say a fellow would want to remember—SIX GROSS CALICO SHIPPED STOP BALANCE NEXT WEEK STOP or PLEASE SPECIFY QUANTITY STOP. A common one was, NO PAYMENT NO SHIPMENT STOP. A couple of the more interesting were, GO SET ON A CACTUS AND WIGGLE STOP and MEET ME AT TRAIN CARSON CITY OR I WILL MARRY WHO-EVER DOES STOP. Told Sam that one and he copied it down.

Our news came through loud and clear shortly before the office closed for lunch. The key rattlety-tapped out clear as a march strutting its stuff, addressed to the general manager of the Sergeant Mine. MC-GIVERNEY REPORTS 12295 PER STOP SEND RECOMMENDA-TIONS IMMEDIATELY STOP. Alvord scribbled it out.

Says I casual-like to him, "I'll walk that over to the Sergeant on my way." I didn't say my way was up sky-high, whoop-tee-doo, diddledy-doo. I didn't have to make no copy of this message—I'd never forget it.

Daniel had coached me carefully. Ore got hauled across the Sierras for assaying, at least for the major mines. The little assayers in Virginia couldn't be depended on for accurate figures, and could be depended on very well to tell every Tom, Dick, and Harry your good or bad news right quick. On the other hand, in San Francisco and Sacramento you might get a break of a day or two before everybody knew your luck. I'd memorized and memorized the assayers' names—heckahoy, I dreamed the lists of names. McGiverney was a respected one.

Twelve thousand a ton, stars and cornicles, four thousand would have been good news. The parlay of twelve thousand, McGiverney, and the Sergeant added up to a grand deduction for those who knew how to read the signals. The Sergeant's stockholders were going from borrasca to bonanza. A thermometer thrown in boiling water wouldn't go up any faster.

I got lucky at the Sergeant. Mr. John Mayes, the general manager, asked me to come back in an hour. I jawed with Sir Richard at the hotel, came back in half an hour to carry Mr. Mayes's important recommendations back to the telegraph office. And then straight to my secret employers.

THAT AFTERNOON I was at Virginia's stock exchange. Those days it was just a blackboard at the curb in front of the brokerage house. The brokers marked up the latest prices, sold, bid, and asked. They also posted the prices that came by telegraph from the San Francisco Exchange. People bought and sold in silence—it was the only place in Virginia what was quiet. Surprising kinds of men and women bought and sold—not only prosperous-looking investors but women of substance, some of the town's courtesans, widows who didn't look to have the price of a cup of coffee, the owners of every kind of business, plenty of miners, and even several Chinamen. Watching that spot, you'd eventually see every kind of human critter that populated Virginia except an Indian. The Paiutes came into the city daily for every kind of laboring job you can think of, but they never bought or sold mining stocks.

My task was simple. Buy $250 of Sergeant stock at the going price and register it in the office in Tommy Kirk's name, the same in Daniel's name, and $50 in the name of Samuel Clemens. Daniel knew its history: It had been issued at a dollar par about a year ago, had run up to over two dollars, dropped to seventy-five cents, and was still under a dollar yesterday. I did my job.

Then I went and found Sam at his favorite perch, the tavern, gangly form splayed out on the bar, foot on brass rail. I says to him, "Mr. Kirk wants to talk to you."

What the beaming Tommy Kirk had actually said was, "I wonder whether in these circumstances we might not be able to make good use of Mr. Clemens."

Sam ran his whisky down his gullet and then ran his legs down the hill to Chinatown with me. He was thinking to have a lot of his favorite kind of fun—dig up the lowdown, find out some skullduggery humans was up to, set it down in words in that comical way of his, and have a big old chuckle, kind of liking us rascally humans and teasing us at once. I'd made my peace with Sam since he tricked us in the coyote hole, and hoodwinked me with a fake gun. I regarded him as a friend, more or less. But I knew I needed to stand clear of his rage to write things down in the newspaper.

Right quick we were seated across from Tommy Kirk in Tommy's back room. I wondered whether I was steering off course, spending so much time in the back room of an opium den recently. Brother Young would have disapproved of that, and it made me uneasy, too.

Sam got disillusioned quick—he found out Tommy Kirk didn't mean to give him something but get something from him.

"Mr. Clemens," Tommy said, "we have news. Big news. A bonanza. At a major mine." His fingers toyed with the edges of the telegrams. There were four of them now, to and from San Francisco. Sam's eyes prowled over them, but they were blank side up. "I believe that is worth something to a gentleman of your persuasion."

Sam Clemens raised his eyes to Tommy and glowered. Good thing he and Sir Richard never got into a glowering contest, someone would have got killed. Sam, I expect, as the younger hand.

Sam also nodded, and Tommy Kirk took that as a green railway light. "Perhaps if I were to give you proof positive of this big news—I can see the headlines in your publication now—you would do us a favor in return."

"Crack the egg," says Sam. "I can't eat the shell."

Tommy registered that with a funny look and went on. "We know the situation with some clarity from these telegrams, which as you know Asie pinched. Read them."

Sam took his time and studied them thorough.

"We have taken a position, a substantial position. Yet more information might be useful."

"What information?"

"When the Sergeant plans to make the announcement and how they intend to finance the expanded operation."

"What's this to do with me?"

"With these telegrams you can beard the lion in his den. Then use whatever wiles you newspapermen have to seduce a fuller story out of Mr. Mayes."

"Why should I?"

"I'm sure you want a fuller story."

"But why should I tell you?"

"It's tit for tat." He took on a self-congratulatory expression, maybe from showing off such a common phrase. "And since you're one of my investors, you stand to gain with us."

He handed Sam a receipt for the stock in his name.

The gangly man grinned. He put the telegrams in his pocket. I believe he was as tickled at his own rascality as at ours.

SAM SPREAD THE telegrams on the desk with his fingers and looked up at Mr. John Mayes. He saw a big man with the nervous energy of a caged beast, who ate the telegrams with his eyes.

"Congratulations," said Sam. He paused. "On your strike. Your big strike. Your bonanza."

Mayes didn't pick the telegrams up, had no need to.

"Why, the whole town will benefit from your discovery, the whole territory."

When Sam waited long enough, Mayes said, "Those telegrams are private, Clemens. Where did you get them?" They'd been hail-fellow acquaintances before, but the pretense of cordiality was gone now.

"Respectfully enough, Mayes, that's none of your concern. I'm a newspaperman. My job is to gather information the public wants to know. I've done it."

"I'll report you to the sheriff."

"I've broken no law."

"Have you gotten close to my secretary?"

Sam pictured Asie and kept his smile to himself. He shrugged, hoping the woman could take care of herself.

"Enough of this folderol, then. Get to the point, Clemens."

So Sam put his cards on the table: The *Territorial Enterprise* had these excellent documents and was prepared to make immediate announcement of the bonanza—why, tomorrow wouldn't be a bit too soon—printing the news ahead of the competition was the main object.

Mayes just eyed him rudely.

"Yet it occurs to me, as a friend of the Sergeant and the Nevada mining industry, that the most prompt announcement from the newspaper's point of view might work some hardship on the company."

Now he had Mayes's full attention. It felt dangerous, like drawing a mountain cat's attention.

Sam explained how he was acquainted with the ways an expansion due to a big strike was usually financed. Some mines borrowed from banks, but the Sergeant didn't have the equity for that. Some borrowed from big entrepreneurs, but then the lenders ended up with the real profit. Sometimes companies floated a stock issue, which without the crucial information could easily fail. So the most advantageous way was for the company to buy up existing shares of its own stock at the current price, make the announcement, wait for the price to soar, and then sell. "Why, that's what I would do if I was the company. And for that a man would need a little time. A few days, at least."

"What do you want?" said Mayes, low like a growl.

"How do you intend to finance your expansion?"

"You know that."

"When do you plan to announce the strike?"

Mayes breathed in and out. "How long is the *Territorial Enterprise* willing to wait?"

Each man eased a little in his shoulders and hands. Now they didn't give the impression they might strike.

"Three days."

Mayes looked at Sam cynically. "You're not looking just to improve your story."

"Not just," Sam agreed amiably. They looked at each other, scoundrels both. Sam smiled to himself. He liked both the man across the desk and himself well enough. What they were doing was common, legal, the way smart men operated. He'd long since learned that the American economy was a large, impersonal machine, dispensing wealth whimsically. A wise man watched his chance, reached into the machinery, taking care not to get his hands caught in the gears, and helped himself. Sam himself had made a million and lost it already.

Mayes decided to talk. "We'll buy stock every day. Mostly in San Francisco. As quietly as we can, not stirring up the market more than we can help. We have a price limit in mind. When the stock goes that high, we'll announce. At a certain price above that we'll become a seller."

Sam nodded his understanding. "The *Territorial Enterprise* will decide when to break the news."

"I need a week," said Mayes.

"We can manage five days," said Sam. "And I need everything. Assays at different locations in the new shaft. Extent of the vein. How many men you intend to hire, at what wage. How much equipment you're ordering, from what companies. All of it. Revealed at the right time, this information will help you."

"You may have it Friday." Which was four days.

Sam nodded, tickled.

Mayes nodded, wary.

Sam stood, and they shook hands.

"Clemens, on your personal account, don't buy too much."

Sam grinned, thinking of Tommy Kirk. Mayes had no idea.

"You neither," said Sam, and left.

They both grinned. A little extra cash will make a man grin. A lot will keep him grinning a long while.

"*I* DON'T WANT a woman like that touching me," she said to Sir Richard. He was proposing to have a Chinese prostitute dress her and do her hair.

"Oh, pooh, what a snob." He turned on his heel to leave. "You need her," he said. "You must become an Asian grande dame. You know this perfectly. Else you will be a target for every schemer and seducer half the world round. She'll be here about five." He brushed through the cloth door confidently.

Sun Moon knew he was right. She had to play the grande dame on the stagecoach to San Francisco, from there on the sailing ship across the Pacific Ocean to India, and from there in the caravan across the Himalayas to the holy city of Lhasa. All the way she must play the great lady, dressed, coiffed, imperious, possessed of the manners that go with wealth. If she looked like a pregnant poor woman, or worse, a pregnant nun . . .

She also felt a pang of guilt. Sir Richard had these fine dresses made for her. She must not be ungrateful.

She looked at herself in the mirror. Could a great lady have such a scar?

Sir Richard opened the new hotel room door, and said, "Miss Sun Moon, Miss Polly," and closed it behind him.

The moment she saw the girl, Sun Moon was sorry for her attitude. China Polly was beautiful and elegantly dressed. Instead of an air of defeat there was a devil-may-care spirit in her eyes.

Polly came behind her and lifted her left braid. "Always wear hair in braid? Too bad, lovely."

Polly's rough, singsong English made Sun Moon feel strange. Fingers began undoing the braid.

"I must do so," Sun Moon said politely, watching herself in the mirror. Polly might not be acquainted with Buddhists in her part of China, or at least with convents. From girlhood until her abduction, Sun Moon had borne the short-cropped hair of the nun. After her abduction, it grew out, but she certainly hadn't wanted to make it look beautiful.

She forbade herself to remember too much. "What is your name?" she asked.

"China Polly." The answer was automatic.

Sun Moon switched to the Chinese language. "No, your true name. Your name in Chinese." Sun Moon had hated being called China Polly.

The girl gave Sun Moon a calculating look. "Ah Lo," she said in a neutral tone.

"I am Dechen Tsering, from Zorgai, in Kham," Sun Moon replied. She saw the puzzlement in Ah Lo's eyes. "Tibet."

Ah Lo nodded. Her fingers stripped the undone braid long. She switched back to English. "Women of Tibet very sexly," Ah Lo said in the tone of a compliment.

That classification again! Sun Moon felt her anger rise, watched it, let it pass.

Ah Lo undid the other braid rapidly.

"No, we are not erotic," Sun Moon said in Chinese. "I am a nun."

Ah Lo pulled back and looked at Sun Moon like a madwoman. She chuckled. "So you go now as disguise," she said in English. "I make you sexly."

Sun Moon watched in the mirror.

"Like this, I think," Ah Lo said in Chinese, as though conceding. She held the thick hair in a bun at the rear top of Sun Moon's head. Studying the mirror, Sun Moon thought, *I am sexly. Or I would be except for the scar.*

Her hair looked good. "Yes, thank you."

Ah Lo began pinning the hair in place with long ivory sticks.

Tonight, Sun Moon admitted to herself, *I want to look splendid.* She looked at the new dresses Sir Richard had had made for her, dresses fit for a real lady. One was a silk of robin's-egg blue, brocaded with silver and gold thread. Another was a light shade of jade silk, another a brilliant sun orange.

"You like it?" asked Ah Lo. Sun Moon turned her head from side to side in the mirror, studying the elaborate bun. "Thank you," she said, "it's lovely. Later will you show me how to pin it myself?"

"That's what friends are for. Wait see what else I have. First I'll make up your face."

Ah Lo came in front of Sun Moon with a flask and rubbed something creamy and soothing on Sun Moon's cheeks. Then she turned to a jar of white powder—rice powder, Sun Moon realized. The girl applied it liberally to Sun Moon's face, using a rabbit's foot for a brush. Sun Moon didn't like the idea of facial makeup, but Sir Richard had insisted. Then came rouge on her cheeks, then lip rouge.

Sun Moon used the mirror. She didn't like the whiteness of her skin, but felt pleased by both rouges. *This will be fun.*

Sun smiled broadly at herself. Ah Lo looked at her in the mirror, and cried, "Party tonight!"

Sun Moon didn't let herself think about what that might mean to the young whore. *Tonight I'm going to a party.* It was a victory celebration. For more than a month she had fought the fever. Doubts had raged in her mind like the heat in her body. *I am poor, I will never get home, my child will be born dead, I am deluding myself about getting back to Tibet, I will die in this foreign place and no one will read* The Book of the Dead *over me.* Which meant she would have a hard time in the forty-nine days between incarnations, and the next incarnation would be difficult. *Oh,* she thought despairing, *I have lost my way!*

She forced herself to say clearly in her mind exactly when she got lost. *The night I made love to Asie by the river.* The night she got pregnant.

Fever, pregnancy, fever, confusion, fever, loss of focus, fever, fear. Her spirit had been storm-tossed. She was clear about what saved her—a precious incarnation of a human being growing in her belly.

"These, you like?" Ah Lo asked. She held earrings of gold coins beside Sun Moon's ears.

"My ears aren't pierced!" Sun Moon cried.

"We'll take care of that," said Polly, and held up an awl.

Sun Moon grabbed for her earlobes. "No," she moaned. Her ears had been pierced, routinely, when she was a child, but had healed during her convent years.

"You must," said Polly. "You are to be a grand lady, and grand ladies wear fancy earrings."

Sun Moon looked at the earrings Sir Richard had bought her. They were not merely coins but inlaid subtly and beautifully with copper and silver. Against her complexion and hair the effect was remarkable.

"More gifts from Captain Burton," she said, waving toward a jangle of jewelry laid out on a piece of velvet.

"They're lovely," said Sun Moon, abashed. Sir Richard was being wonderful to her. She didn't dare let her eyes take in the abundance of gifts.

Quickly, Ah Lo held a wood block behind Sun Moon's right lobe and rammed the awl through. *Ouch!* She gasped for breath. She hoped the second would feel easier, but the pain was sharp. She held her breath while Polly slid the earrings on, and fastened them.

She thought of her great good fortune. *In great peril I trusted two men. Asie and Sir Richard.* Asie had given her so much, and the incarnation within her was the crowning gift. Sir Richard had helped her, supported her, saved her life physically, and now provided the means for her journey. Home.

I have won. No, that was premature. She still had half the world to cross. *I have done the hardest part.* She had survived abduction, survived being indentured as a prostitute, survived the escape, survived momentarily the attacks of that Mormon murderer, survived the journey across half the American continent, survived the fever. She had survived physically, emotionally, spiritually.

Actually, Porter Rockwell worried her more than traveling halfway around the world.

"Now we try little scent," said Ah Lo. She made it sound deliciously sinful.

"No," said Sun Moon. "No perfume." She associated perfumes with whores and peasant women, who wore them to cover the unwashed smell.

"OK. Shut eyes." Sun Moon started to object. "You say great lady, I make great lady," reprimanded Ah Lo. "You see."

Sun Moon let her eyelids close and behind them drifted in her mind. The scents of the room, silks, powders, ointments, reminded her of riches. She breathed deep and let the breath out slowly. The face of her dead mother floated into consciousness. She felt her mother's hands on her neck and shoulders. The delicate smoothness of her first silk dress came to her. Her only silk dress, the one she was presented to the convent in. Suddenly she thought she could smell the wildflowers, abundant on the grassy meadows in summer. The sound of her language drifted over her, and the smells of the rich foods prepared for the Flower-Viewing Festival.

"Look," said Ah Lo.

Sun Moon opened her eyes and tried to study the silvery color Ah Lo had put on her eyelids.

"You see?"

Sun Moon thought of her convent, and deliberately brought to mind the smell of the butter lamps. *I'm going home.*

"Very nice," Ah Lo said. "Please stand up."

Ah Lo helped Sun Moon into the brocaded jade cheongsam, sleeveless, full length, with a stand-up Mandarin collar. She fastened the frog closings, cords covered with fancy cloth which looped over toggles. "Now watch," she said. She hung a pair of somethings on the ivory pins holding the buns in Sun Moon's hair. Examining them in the mirror, Sun Moon saw that they were bird cages delicately wrought in brass. Inside, remarkably, were tiny golden birds with eyes of bright emerald.

Sun Moon gasped. Ah Lo clapped her hands.

Then the girl leapt for the door and flung it open. "Come," cried Ah Lo, and Sir Richard strode in. No matter how decorously he moved, he always seemed to Sun Moon a thunderstorm. He had gotten himself up handsomely. Even the scar on his cheek, a slash of violence, looked right on him.

"You look very lovely," he said merrily. "Well done, Polly." The girl bowed to him. For the first time Sun Moon thought, *Is she his whore?*

She looked into the mirror and studied her face to conceal her feelings. The effect of the makeup seemed to her extravagant but not unattractive. *Maybe it should be extravagant.*

Sir Richard seemed to look her over more carefully. "Splendid," he said. "Remarkable."

"Thank you very much for all this," Sun Moon said.

"Sun Moon, it is my pleasure," said Sir Richard. He sounded like he felt it was.

Ah Lo busied herself putting slippers on Sun Moon's feet, embroidered ones with turned-up toes. Sun Moon looked down and suppressed a smile. *Since my feet were never bound, Ah Lo must think them large and ungainly.*

"You still haven't told me how you got all the money," she said.

"It's not complicated," he said. "Tommy and Dan's little scheme served them well, went from less than a dollar to over nine. He and Gentleman Dan made, the way we figure, perhaps $9,000.

"So here's the good news. I invested a hundred for you, and made enough to get you home in style." Sir Richard grinned. He could be quite the pleased-with-himself boy sometimes.

"Asie make money, too?"

"Yes."

"Tommy Kirk angry?" Ah Lo made last-moment adjustments.

Sir Richard chuckled. "When we told him, he said, 'Of course you did, smart lads. As long as you don't nick too much."

"What will he do with his profit?" She worried about Asie.

Sir Richard shrugged. "When a man comes into a handsome piece of money, you may see in what he does next his dreams. Also what he thinks of himself, his fellows, and the world."

"Asie's dreams," she murmured. To find his mother's people? To find the real world glimpsed in his river vision?

"I don't know that money will help him," said Sir Richard, voicing Sun Moon's thoughts. He looked sideways at Ah Lo. "Though some believe that there is no ambition in the world money won't help."

"I have a dream," Sun Moon said. "To go home. Thank you, Sir Richard."

"I am delighted to be of service."

She nodded.

"Are you aware that Asie is planning to use his profit to accompany you on your journey to Tibet?"

That's what I'm afraid of.

"It wouldn't do either of you any harm."

Carefully, she shook her head no. *Impossible! Then he would know!*

"One more thing for beauty," said Ah Lo. She held out a small vial to Sun Moon. "Makes eyes big," said Ah Lo.

"Belladonna," said Sir Richard, "deadly nightshade, an innocent stimulus. Have some."

Sun Moon shook her head. *A drug that affects my consciousness, no, no.*

"I'll indulge," said Sir Richard. He took the vial from Ah Lo and helped himself. So did she. They smiled at each other conspiratorially. *Watch out,* Sun Moon told herself.

At that moment the door banged and Asie burst into the room. He often burst into places. "Everything's ready at the Heritage," he said. "It's time."

Then she saw him take her in, all of the dressed-up her. She thought she could see stars in his eyes.

"Miss Polly," said Sir Richard, "may I escort you to the party?"

Ah Lo slunk to him, brushed his hip with hers, and laughed.

Sun Moon and Asie looked at each other. She had to admit he looked smart in his new suit, and for tonight in one way they belonged together. "Miss Sun Moon," he said, "you look gorgeous." He held out his arm, and she took it.

CHAPTER TWENTY-FOUR

GENTLEMAN DAN HOISTED his sherbet in a toast. "Here's to doing better than four dollars a day," which were miners' wages.

Tommy Kirk cried, "Hear, hear!" We all joined him, me and Sun Moon, Sir Richard and his lady of the evening, Polly, Sam, and Tommy's other dinner guests.

There was the rub, the dinner guests. Since they weren't there, they were pretty well snubbing Tommy.

Tommy Kirk had bought the Heritage. Then he planned this big, big party to celebrate. He took an advertisement in the *Enterprise* and hung signs like banners across the front of the tavern. GRAND OPENING—ALL DRINKS FREE ALL NIGHT!!! He didn't have to say a word about being the new owner. That would be the talk of Washo, a Chinaman buying the classiest saloon and gambling house in the territory. Tommy understood that sometimes you don't have to say anything to make a statement.

Next Tommy cooked up a plan to host a small dinner on opening night, presenting Sir Richard to Washo society, who would certainly want to meet the author and explorer. Sir Richard saw Tommy's thinking, naturally. Despite the barrier of being half-caste, he wanted to be important enough to bring together the distinguished visitor and Washo's uppity-

uppity. Sir Richard loved such social and political games, and consented gladly.

It didn't work. Of the first dozen folks invited, bankers, mine owners, and the other first businessmen of Washo, none accepted, and some didn't even bother to respond. Tommy fell back to second and third invitation lists. You could about guess who showed up in the end, aside from Sir Richard, Sun Moon, me, Gentleman Dan, and Sam. There was the publisher and editor of the *Enterprise,* cajoled by Sam into coming (and for them it was halfway work). Two of Tommy's fellow proprietors of saloons and gambling houses, who probably wanted to check out the competition. One of the founders of the mining district, a backwoodsman extravagantly rich and liquored all the time, well beyond caring what anyone thought of him. And Jennifer Ward, a courtesan who worked independently and was revered by everyone in Washo. This was a very beautiful and elegant woman, invited as Tommy's dinner companion.

The grand opening was going better. From what we could hear of the drinkers, gamblers, and dancers out at the main rooms, it was a heckuva party.

So there we were sitting at the table of Tommy's failure. Guess all of us at that dinner had a better time than he did. Tommy put on a good face and made the champagne flow. Sam acted the life of the party, telling stories and playing the grandee, though he'd made the least money of us. Gentleman Dan was quietly swelled up with some kind of satisfaction—you hardly never knew what Dan was thinking. Sir Richard and Polly floated along on the wine bubbles. Sun Moon was happy on account of she got her passage to Asia, and I was lost in her.

Oh my stars and cornicles, yes, I was lost. I was trying to listen to the world's signals. First fate brought a woman from the far side of the world and set her down in a place to save my life and mesmerize my heart. Then it tossed me a bonanza big enough to sail me to Tibet with her, if she'd let me. Seemed like that's how the signals read, anyhow. Sweet gizzards and Jehu nimshi, Tibet. I was busy being flabbergasted by pictures in my head of a place as foreign as . . . Well, even Sir Richard's tales of the bizarre East couldn't hold anything to how queer Tibet must be.

Dinner went off handsomely, far as I could tell. Tommy had a crew of seductive-looking Chinese women to serve us (courtesans, for there were no other Chinese females in Washo). He conjured up a genuine white-man feast, no ginger or soy sauce about it. That night was a first for me with champagne and fresh oysters, and I wouldn't be looking for any second. Everybody laughed at everybody else's jokes.

My mind, though, couldn't get away from two things. The first was how this feast would feed Paiute Joe's whole family for days, and I wasn't all the way easy with feasting when they were empty-bellied. The second was Tommy's snubbing. Appeared to me a man of half-caste could buy things in Washo, could own a lot of Washo, but he couldn't never be a regular fellow. If they'd snubbed Tommy because he was a man who lived by selling women, gambling, and opium, I would have understood. But they didn't care anything for that. It was the way they treated heathen Chinee. Or niggers, or Injuns. Or halves, like Tommy and me. I marked that down in my head.

"*THIS IS NO* ordinary whore," Sun Moon heard Sam whisper loudly to Asie, "she's Tommy's mistress, and the mother of his children."

It was after dinner, while the Chinese women were serving around dainty desserts to be eaten with the fingers. Tommy Kirk stood at the head of the table and introduced the young woman as Lu Pu-wai. While Sun Moon was pondering what it meant to escort one woman and then introduce your children's mother, Lu Pu-wai made a graceful exit, returned bearing a zither, and sat down to play with the air of an artist.

The zither of Sun Moon's childhood was the Tibetan yak zither, a six-stringed instrument that accompanied dancing and singing. She was educated, though, and was acquainted with the *ch'in,* the seven-stringed Chinese zither. It was a more refined vehicle for music, and Lu Pu-wai's approach to it was elevated. She introduced her performance with words in her own language, and Tommy Kirk translated.

First he closed the door to the main rooms tight, to shut out the din of the big party.

"Music for us Chinese," Tommy repeated after her, "is a way for the mind to reconcile *yang* and *yin.*" He hesitated and translated, "The great universal opposites. Each time of year has its own fundamental tone. This is autumn, and the tone is F."

Here Lu Pu-wai played a five-note scale. Sun Moon watched Asie's face very carefully. *Will this reach his spirit?*

"F is the tone of the north," Tommy went on translating. "The planet associated with it is Mercury. Its element is wood, and its color is black." She noticed that Tommy Kirk spoke with an unaccustomed seriousness and a hint of reverence. For the first time she saw the noble part of him. "The piece she will play is well known in China, 'The Falling Leaf.' "

Lu Pu-wai's face took on the softness and blankness of high concentration. Her fingers moved over the fingerboard. The sounds she plucked were separate, distinct, like drops of water on a cymbal, or isolated pings on stone chimes. The effect was ethereal, shifting impressions.

Sometimes Sun Moon lost the spirit of the music and began to think. Then she noticed the small ways in which the artist ornamented the melody, and the several different kinds of vibrato she used to make the notes more expressive. Then Sun Moon lost herself in the poetry of the sounds once more, and was happy.

When the performance ended, she wanted to gush breath in and out. She wanted to embrace Asie and look truly into his eyes. She wanted to embrace Lu Pu-wai.

No one applauded. It felt like they were too stunned to applaud. The performer bowed deeply over her instrument.

Tommy leapt up, but before he could speak, a high, unearthly sound stopped him. It was the melody of Lu Pu-wai's song, the same melody, but like the ceaseless wind instead of separate plucks. For a long moment she did not guess where it came from, but thought it the breath of spirit itself, sounding and sounding.

I DIDN'T REALIZE at first I had started whistling.

Until my mind caught on, the tune just sounded exotic. Then I took hold, I heard the five-tone scale with its enchanting minor skips, its wonderful quality of suspension, of going nowhere because it was already at the center of everything. The melody became a stately dance, drifting, turning, lifting, sailing. I was mesmerized.

No, not my river music, not at all, but what a heavenly music. I yearned to live longer in the world of that dance, and I . . .

Before long, a phrase or two in, it occurred to me that someone might think me rude for taking Lu Pu-wai's song. I kept whistling, but in the uncertainty I nearly lost the lilt of the melody.

That was when I heard the zither. Lu Pu-wai was joining back in, not an accompanist but a dance partner. I whistled a phrase purely, she ornamented it. She danced forward to the next phrase, and I repeated the first as an obbligato, meaning it as lingering, haunting. Two voices rising into the air, spinning, playing, whirling, being.

I never knew how long the performance lasted. After a while I heard the zither hinting at farewell. I answered with longing. From a greater distance the zither said farewell, and I said the same in return, with quiet, with peace, with acceptance.

When we finished, I stood and bowed to Lu Pu-wai. After a hesitation, she bowed to me. In that moment I felt complete.

TOMMY KIRK LED a big round of applause now, and called for another round of champagne. Burton clapped enthusiastically—a rare treat, that duet, in his opinion. And he judged the wine excellent. He knew Kirk had paid dearly to have it freighted from San Francisco.

Kirk rose in the manner of proposing a toast, and said, "I am grateful to you all for honoring me with your presence here. As a way of saying thank you, I can tell you that I have consulted the oracle. The luck of every one of you is sure to be good at the gambling tables tonight. Therefore, let us toast, Good joss!"

Glancing around, Burton concluded that everyone took Tommy's meaning, that he had put in the word with his dealers. *I wager the Americans will take good advantage, and that Asie and Sun Moon have done all the capering with money they want, at least for a while.*

For himself, Burton wouldn't mind taking in a bit at gaming. If it could be only one part of an evening of gaiety. *And decadence?* he asked himself. *And debauchery?*

"To the tables!" Kirk cried.

The company made a hubbub, almost a small roar, and headed for the main rooms.

"Captain Burton," called Tommy Kirk quietly. Burton turned back. "I have a special treat for you." Burton's lady of the evening, Polly, must have known, for she was holding the door to the kitchen open for them.

The three walked briskly through the kitchen, which was hot, crowded, steamy, and thick with food smells. Burton noticed that he was a little squiffed on the wine. They exited into a half-lit room at the back. It took Burton a moment to recognize the ambience of the opium den. The dim red light, the sofas, daybeds, and lounging chairs, the blue alcohol lamps placed here and there, the table offering the paraphernalia of the smoker.

"I have created a special refuge here," Tommy said. "A few white people have discovered the dreamy delights of opium, and I believe more will do so. Even women." Burton could not make out Kirk's attitude in his voice, or his shadowed eyes.

A rustle from the corner. A dark figure floating toward the daybed, reclining. *Kirk's mistress. Lu Pu-wai. By God!*

"I thought perhaps as a connoisseur you would enjoy being first to indulge here. Perhaps you will also mention its delights to others in the white community."

Kirk extended his arm, taking in everything in the room. "Everyone and everything in this room is for your pleasure tonight, and yours alone. Whatever pleasures you fancy, whatever you dream of, I beg you to indulge yourself."

Kirk bowed slightly and backed out of the room, closing the door behind him.

Burton looked first at the opium and accoutrements. Then at the mischievous eyes of Polly. Lu Pu-wai glided toward him seductively.

By God!

SUN MOON AND I were thrilled, excited by the wine, the dinner, and hearing the zither. Out in the big rooms, though, it was a different kind of excitement. It was a ruckus. Some people celebrate, miners ruckus.

Since drinks were on the house, everyone was liquored up. Elbow room was little enough that elbows were constantly getting thrown. Activities ran to gambling, where everybody was giving Tommy back the cost of the drinks. Other activities were about evenly divided between dancing, arguing, and shoving, with the odd fight for spice.

The piano was clinking up front by the bar, and I wondered who Tommy had hired to play. In the back, where most of the gambling tables were, a hurdy-gurdy was going strong. I saw that Tommy had added a second spot for dancing back there.

Right away we saw his big novelty. All the women serving tables, drinking and dancing with customers, and enticing men to the upstairs rooms were Chinese. They weren't just crib girls either. These were decked-out courtesans—Tommy had spent a small fortune dressing them, some in the Chinese style of slinky silks, some in the latest Paris fashions via San Francisco. They looked jimmy-joomy.

At a glance, though, you could see that Tommy had only half thought through part of it. The girls didn't know the miners' dances. Since mining men just flung their partners around by main force, though, it didn't make much difference.

(I may as well say here that this new tactic of Tommy's didn't work out. The white courtesans refused to work at a place that hired Celestials, and so did the brown women. While white men might go with a China Polly for a few minutes, or even a night, they wouldn't put up with a saloon and gambling hall with nothing else. So the Chinese women had to go back to Chinatown, which goes to show.)

Most of us dinner guests stampeded for the tables, eager to take advantage of Tommy arranging things—Sam, his friends from the newspaper, the saloon men, and the rich drunk. Sun Moon, me, and Gentleman Dan stood there for a moment, twiddling our thumbs. "I want to talk with you," Dan said. "An idea about how to invest your money."

Every time I thought about that gold, half a year's wages put away free and clear, I got a little glow. One thing a man should get from a great adventuring is coin of the realm. "OK," says I, feeling uncertain. Then it came to me. "But first I wanna dance!"

I took Sun Moon gently by both hands and looked at her with the question in my face. She cried, "Dance!" We pulled each other toward the dance floor. Daniel headed for the piano, and called back, "By God, I'll give you some *good* tunes to dance to."

We faced each other just as Daniel gave us the introduction to a waltz. It was a Frenchy tune, the one Reeshaw played on the fiddle, which he called the "Red River Waltz," which I bet the Cajun folks of Louisiana called by some other name, but by the luck of our celebratin' evening, it was one of the few we both knew a little.

The miners didn't care for any waltz, so they left the dance floor to us.

I took her in my arms and she smiled wonderfully at me. In the last week or so, when she'd got healthy, Sun Moon just glowed at me sometimes, and it made me giddy. It wasn't glow enough to get her to listen to me about us going to Tibet together, but I loved it.

We launched out in that three-beat rhythm, circling the dance floor. We glided. We added an accent—up on beat three, vigorously back into the downbeat. I began to turn us slowly, and she followed right with me. Soon we were whirling as we circled, floating, soaring, waltzing. I fell in love with dancing at that moment.

I also loved Sun Moon. I looked into her eyes and saw love there, too, but I didn't know whether it was for me, for the moment, for the dance, or for all the hope she'd found the last week.

In loving to dance, Sun Moon was thoroughly Tibetan. On visits to her family she liked to do the *guozhuang*, which celebrated the harvest, the *xianzi,* and even to tap dance. This business of men and women dancing as couples was new to her, but tonight she was willing to cast off, to sail beyond the ways of her life and her people, to enter into a world of abandon.

She liked the waltz, which was graceful, elegant, and rhythmic at once. She liked moving in rhythm with another person, so that as a pair they became more than two individuals, a new being, one dancing creature. She liked being the center of attention of all the watching miners. She liked, for the moment, being touched by the father of her child.

She looked into Asie's eyes, she felt the growth in her belly, and she pictured herself and her child in front of her convent, looking out over the mountains and breathing deep into the exhilarating alpine air. She spun, she lifted, she sailed, she dreamed.

The voice roared loud as gunshots. "Sign says everybody invited," it boomed over the din. "I reckon that includes me."

Sun Moon stopped on the rising third beat of the waltz, as though poised on the edge of a cliff. The music stopped. She saw clearly. She fell to her death, floating like a scarf.

Porter Rockwell.

Suddenly she knew that she had been waiting for that voice every moment, as one waits always, skin prickled, for the cold breath of death.

The crowd of miners fell back. Still raised on her toes, waiting for the downbeat that now would never come, she looked sideways. He stood just inside near the door, dressed in black. He seemed not a dark presence but a horrible black hole in the world.

He lifted his pistol with one long, straight arm, right at Sun Moon. Shorn of the dance, she stood motionless, frozen.

Lightning flashed from the muzzle.

In the same instant she felt Asie lurch violently. The roar smashed all music forever.

Sun Moon thumped hard on the floor on her back. Asie rolled them over and over each other into the crowd. The gun roared again.

Pain exploded in Sun Moon's belly.

She felt for blood. She could not think of her own life, or of Asie's, only the child.

Her hands came away dry.

I SAW THE miners had closed around us. They weren't going to let Rockwell get another clear shot. They wouldn't stand still for murder.

I shoved Sun Moon onto her knees, pushed her butt, and hollered, "Run! Run!"

We jammed through the crowd toward the back room. Some people made way, some even fell to the ground getting out of the way. Behind I heard a clamor, the sound of a big bunch of angry men. We'd have a little time.

Into the room where Tommy held the dinner. Through it, knocking tables and chairs aside. Into the kitchen. Down its narrow aisles into the back room, I didn't know where in hell we were going.

We busted through the door and instantly I saw it was outfitted as an opium den. I shut the door behind us. On a kind of bed on the far side was what I wanted, Sir Richard. He was stretched out full, and now I saw he was stripped absolutely naked. Polly and Lu Pu-wai were propped at various angles, just as naked. The opium pipe stuck up from Sir Richard's belly like a you know what.

"That shooting was Porter Rockwell!" I bellered at Sir Richard from a foot away.

Sir Richard opened his eyes at me. "Thank you," he murmured. "Thank you very much," and closed his eyes dreamily.

The door busted open with a bang. I knocked Sun Moon to the floor and flopped on top of her.

"I'll help," said the voice of Gentleman Dan. "Sir Richard is useless. Let's go!"

PART FIVE

GOING HOME

CHAPTER TWENTY-FIVE

We ran. I mean *ran.* Without you being scorched by flame spat out of a gun barrel, you have never run.

Full tilt we bolted out of the Heritage the back way, huffed along behind the other buildings, foot-and-arm-flapped downhill, gasped along a level street, rushed into the scrub brush, and busted gut up the rough terrain of the dark mountain, following Daniel.

We had no hell nor heaven idea where Porter Rockwell was behind us, but we knew damn well he would be coming. Coming and coming and coming.

We didn't have time to wonder where Daniel was taking us. He led the way with a wonderful assurance, like a man whose poise embraced even fleeing headlong from destroying angels. I just had to accept that as Daniel. Also seemed like his lungs found more wind than mine. I could scarcely keep up, and Sun Moon was hanging on to my hand and heaving her chest up and down.

"Not much farther," said Daniel evenly. He knew the way so well the blackness of the night didn't even matter.

We followed him to a steep, jumbled, broken-up place. He pranced through the rocks nimbly. Turning around first to make sure we were right with him, he squatted, then duck-walked forward, and disappeared. This was his first surprise.

Sun Moon darted right in behind him. She must have had the cajoolies bad as me. But I grabbed a big breath, like it might be my last, and dived into the earth.

Light. Daniel already had a candle lit, which was his second surprise. "You're safe for the moment," he said, and led the way forward down a tunnel. We followed, but I didn't like it. I have never been one for bowels, bowels of the earth or any other kind, nor for closed-in places, nor for dark places. The shaft was all in one.

Pretty quick we came to a junction where a drift forked off to the left. In the mouth of this drift Daniel reached, got two more candles, lit them, stuck them on small ledges, and revealed his tiptop surprise. A tank of at least five gallons caught water from a trickle and held it. A tick mattress stretched out on the rock floor, with blankets tucked neatly around it, and a pillow. Several tins of oysters stood on a ledge, next to a drinking cup and some eating utensils. Books flanked these.

Water, food, light, a bed, and . . . Well, it felt like a tomb. If you find yourself in a tomb, however, water, food, light, and a bed are a good start.

Sun Moon and I sat down to catch our breath. I was keeping an eye on her, what with her fever and this hard running and all.

"How are you feeling?" Daniel asked.

"Terrified," said Sun Moon. Her breath caught as it came out, and I could hear the tears behind it.

"You are completely safe here." He must have decided we could use some easing of mind. "No one knows I have this place, no one at all. I like somewhere to be absolutely alone, to read, to think, just to be. This is it."

Well, that was Daniel. Seemed precious.

He opened both arms to include the whole area. "This mine belongs to me. It looks abandoned, but I prefer to think of it as lying in wait. I bought it for nothing. When the mountain's veins run this direction again, it will be worth something."

I was seeing a lot new about my friend.

He studied our faces. "So tell me about the shootist," he said.

"He wants to me kill me," said Sun Moon.

"I gathered that."

"By now he probably wants to kill *us,*" I added.

"He's been after me for nearly a year," she said.

"A *year?*"

"Porter Rockwell," says I.

Daniel arched an eyebrow toward us. "If you're going to have an assassin after you," he says, "you may as well get the best."

I KEPT QUIET while Sun Moon told her story. I had no idea how much she'd want to tell Daniel, and felt pleased she offered so much of it.

Her style was simple and truthful. She told briefly how she was abducted from her homeland, taken to Canton, shipped to the United States and then to Hard Rock City. How she'd been sold to Tarim for purposes of prostitution.

Daniel gave her all his attention.

"The first night Tarim drug me. Then men gamble be first to take me." Sun Moon made an effort to keep her voice soft and even. "As winner undress me, I wake up and kick, bloody his nose. It is Porter Rockwell. He cut me." She touched the scar on her face with one finger. "Tarim beg I be spared as valuable property. Rockwell swears if he sees me again ever, ever, he kills me."

She swallowed. "After months with Tarim I escape. Rockwell see me near the Great Salt Lake, try kill me once, then twice. The Mormons hold him in jail to keep him from kill me. They say I am escaped. Yet he travels a thousand miles to fulfill oath."

I saw shivers run up and down her little body.

"I sorry be trouble to you," she said.

Daniel answered evenly, "My fiancée was a prostitute. The one regret of my life is that I didn't protect her."

At that moment I saw into Daniel's soul, and the word came up for me again. Flabbergastonia. A rich man who was a musician. Who fell in love with mulatto prostitute. Ran away to Virginia City. Bought up a mine on the sly, maybe more than one. Kept a cave to be private in. Put his neck on the line to help us. Flabbergastonia.

"I'd best go," he said. My heart lurched a little—we were going to be left alone in this hole. "If I reappear soon at the Heritage, they may not realize I took you off. Everything you need is here. I will come back with intelligence and supplies in the morning."

"We can't stay here forever."

"No. When I return, I'll bring the means for us to flee Virginia City."

Sun Moon and I looked at each other. Would it never end? Skeedaddling, skipping town, blowing the place, running like hell, all we'd been doing for months.

I looked at Daniel. "Thank you for 'us.' " It was a comfort, but not enough.

"You're welcome. I'll get your things from the hotel."

We looked at each other, each wondering about our gold.

"I'll get everything we can carry," said Daniel pointedly.

"What about Sir Richard?" asked Sun Moon.

"I don't know," said Daniel. "If I can find him. If he's on his feet."

Then he was gone into the shadows of the shaft.

For some reason I felt we'd seen the last of Sir Richard, and that hurt. I gushed out my breath.

Sun Moon touched my hand.

What came into my mind was foolish, but I said it. "I wanna go home to bed."

She eyed me for a moment. "I don't think we know where home is any longer," she said. "Either of us."

THEY LISTENED TO Daniel's footfalls fade. When there was nothing but eerie silence, she supposed he'd slipped out into the night, into the kind of darkness she and Asie could not have. Daniel had the vast reaches of the stars. She and Asie were trapped in a dark hole.

Without a word Asie found some more candles and a forged holder with a point for sticking into cracks. Sun Moon helped him light and mount them. She felt the fear waving up and down in her chest. She thought of Asie's word for it, *willywoolly*, and smiled to herself. Even six candles made no difference—the dark still felt like something caught in her throat.

Partly to ease this feeling, she rummaged in the tinned food. Yes, there was something besides oysters, which she knew Asie hated. Tomatoes. He ate those, and Sun Moon picked at the slick creatures that came from shells. Funny, she thought. Tibet was as far as you can get on this planet from an ocean, but she liked oysters. Though she wasn't hungry, eating was a comfort.

Soon there was nothing to do but go to sleep. How else would the long hours go away? What else could do they do but lie still and listen for friend or enemy?

She looked at the narrow mattress, the thin blankets. Autumn was cold in the mountains, tonight would be chill in this shaft.

Asie followed her gaze. "I'll sleep here," he said, and lay down with his back to the ledge, his side on the hard stone floor, and his head on his hands for a pillow.

She smiled tenderly. "Let's both sleep on the bed," she said. She reached for his hand. He took it tentatively, searching her eyes. She had to smile. "No, no touching," she said.

She showed him. Both fully dressed, on their backs, blankets to the neck, not touching anywhere. She wiggled herself into a more comfortable position and felt him do the same. She took a deep breath, let it out, felt him do the same again. They waited.

At last she took his hand with hers. "No touching except for this," she said. "Good night, Asie."

She could sense his uncertainty. For a long time neither of them slept, neither moved, neither spoke. The touch of hands felt precious. *Tomorrow perhaps I will die. Or Asie will die. Tonight we touch each other in love.* She stirred without actually letting her body move. *Tonight I cradle the child in my belly.*

At last she felt his body relax and heard his breathing grow long and rhythmic. Then her body softened, and she slept lightly.

When she woke, she noticed first that their hands were still interlocked. She opened her eyes. The tunnel was not so dark. Not light, but perhaps half of twilight. She thought of the distance to the half-concealed entrance, not far. She listened and heard nothing, absolutely, except for Asie's breathing. She lay and heeded the silence.

Keeping hold of his hand, she turned onto her shoulder and looked at Asie. His eyes fluttered. He sighed. He turned toward her, and they looked into each other's eyes. From this short distance she could see all the colors in his irises, iridescent, brown with flecks of yellow and green. They were very beautiful, in a way a mandala. *I have looked into his eyes from so close twice before,* she thought. *This time is purer, better.* The irises pointed to the pupils, which opened to the pure consciousness. In their blackness she felt his inner being.

She said softly, "I love you, Asie. Whether death comes to me today in Washo, soon in California, or many years from now in Tibet, I will carry my love for you until that day, and cherish it."

She saw the movement of the eternal behind his eyes.

Her lips trembled. In their delicate quiver she could feel words forming. They were, *I am carrying your child. Our child.*

I cannot. I cannot. She stilled her lips by force of will.

I FELT GIDDY and confused. When Sun Moon said, "I love you," feelings washed over me like warm waves. When she spoke of death, I got the willywoollies. And now she was *not* saying something. But *what?*

I wanted to hear, "I will marry you." Or, "Come with me to Tibet." Or just, "I want to be with you." Or, "Make love to me."

But none of those was what I saw in her eyes. I didn't know what in kingdom come I was seeing.

Sound!

I came back to reality with a jolt. *Footsteps!* I listened to the rhythm, listened to the weight, listened for any clue. *Daniel? Or Rockwell?* We sat up and looked.

The steps came toward us, loud-soft, THUD-thud, like DAN-iel, ROCK-well, DAN-iel, ROCK-well. A long, long shadow played crazy-like on the shaft walls. DAN-iel, ROCK-well.

A tall, ominous shape loomed out of the darkness.

"Good morning," came the voice of Gentleman Dan. "It is a fine day to travel."

HE HAD TWO knapsacks dangling from one arm. When I opened the one he gave me, I saw my belongings. First I checked my only weapon—I'd used some of the money to buy me a fine hunting knife in a scabbard, for all the good a knife would do me against the likes of Porter Rockwell. Then I checked for the gold pieces. They were safe in the waistband of my pants and the split leather of my extra belt and the knife scabbard. When you're on the run, coin of the realm comes in handy.

There was also a miner's cap with a candle mounted for light.

Then I saw, I guess we both saw, that Daniel was eyeing us funny, in bed together, dressed or not. Or maybe it was because I was in my Sunday best and she was in her fancy gown and showy earrings. The bird cages in her hair had fallen off somewhere.

We turned out of bed in opposite directions. I saw Sun Moon making sure she had her gold coins, too. It was going to be what we got out of our weeks in Washo. A poor trade for getting into Porter Rockwell's gun sights.

"The man Rockwell is no braggart," Daniel said. "I found him at the Heritage still, drinking. He wasn't inclined to talk much, except to offer a reward for information on your whereabouts. I kept his glass full without getting anything in return."

"You talked to him?"

"Like a comrade," said Daniel. "He's a curious case, so dark of soul, so isolated, so miserable."

I wasn't inclined to hear anything made me feel sorry for the Destroying Angel.

"I did find out he's been all the way to San Francisco looking for the three of you. He's determined."

"Is he gonna chase down Sir Richard?" I must admit to hoping he would split off on that trail, which was a sorry way to feel.

Daniel smiled tightly. "Captain Burton is in Chinatown with Tommy Kirk, dallying in lotusland."

My heart sank. I'd been holding on to hope that Sir Richard, however disaccommodated he might be, would rally and stand with us.

"I made sure, in fact," Daniel went on, "that a scoundrel told Rockwell where Burton is. I also warned Tommy, who has put up a heavy guard. If Rockwell tries to get to Burton, that will be everyone's good fortune."

I'd got past the point where I believed in luck, excepting bad.

"No tricks work with Rockwell," said Sun Moon. She'd arranged everything in her knapsack and was closing it. "He come for me. Come, come, come. I know. I must face him."

I looked at her woefully. "And?"

She shrugged. "Don't know how come out. Must face."

I guess I looked hangdog at that.

"Now we go. He catch one day, now we go."

We put on our miners' caps and Daniel lit her candle. I wondered at men who would live their days or nights by such poor light as this. But for now there was nothing for it. Daniel struck a match and extended it toward my head.

A rock clattered. Just a little rock. Up toward the entrance. Then everything was quiet.

Sun Moon and I froze. Looked down the shaft, ready to run. Looked at each other and Daniel, still frozen.

Daniel reached to his underarm and drew out a small pistol. His long, musical fingers folded around it most peculiarly. He glided four or five steps up the shaft, still and subtle as a shadow. He stuck his head around a corner. He looked back at us, his face stricken.

"It's my fault," he whispered. "In my ignorance I led him here." He hesitated, like swallowing something that tasted terrible. "Run!" He made a shooting motion. "Run!"

The shaft filled with the roar of gunfire. In that small space it felt like the explosions was in my head, busting my ears.

Sun Moon lit out. I tried to do the same, but a bullet buzzing past my ear persuaded me to dive for dirt.

Daniel came scrambling my way, loosing shots to make Rockwell keep his head down. "Run!" he hollered. I scrambled to my feet and slipped and fell.

Daniel crab-hopped over to his knapsack and swung it onto his back. "Run!" he yelled.

I found my feet.

A shell whacked Daniel, and he sprawled in front of me.

I pounced on him, thinking to drag him to safety.

"It just got this!" he bellered in my ear, pointing to the knapsack. "RU-U-U-UN!"

I did it.

Then came Rockwell's yell, the sound of the killer, oozing lust for blood. "Ah-OOOOH-oooh! Rasp-rasp-rasp. A-a-a-anee, anee, anee. Ah-OOOOH-ooooh!"

Before it sounded awful and awesome, man as beast, raw, primitive, more murderous than any animal. Now it echoed and echoed. I could feel my back hairs slowly curling and uncurling. "Ah-OOOOH-oooh! Rasp-rasp-rasp. A-a-a-anee, anee, anee. Oh-OOOOH-ooooh!"

THE ONLY REASON we didn't get killed right off was Daniel. He hopped from rock to rock and corner to corner and slowed Rockwell down with bullets. Even Rockwell's flesh was mortal, even his head could get blown off, so he had to play it cagey.

Right off Sun Moon's face came back around the first corner, looking for us in the half-light. I realized her candlelight might help us, but it also helped Rockwell—it made her head a wonderful target. For a sorry moment I felt glad mine wasn't lit.

"Go!" I hollered, and she did. I followed, hell-bent. From time to time she came to a drift to the left, or a crosscut to the right, and she just scampered whatever way, just like she knew what she was doing.

What we were doing, in truth, was running toward deeper and darker places.

A while after we took one left where we mighta gone right, we came to a cave-in. *Cornered.* My heart dropped into the well and shattered like slate.

Sun Moon just scampered up top of the pile of rocks, though, found something, and called to me. When I caught up, she pointed, wanting to make sure I spotted the little crevice we were going to slip through. I stuck my head in and saw the blackest black ever there was, *black* black.

I thought there was good and bad in it. Bad was, Daniel might not find the hole and get trapped by Rockwell. Good was, Rockwell might not find it and we'd get away. Bad again was, who knew what in stars and cornicles was on the other side? A thousand-foot drop. A pit of snakes. Without Daniel, we'd just wander through these shafts until we died.

Needful was, take the plunge. Or die right here.

"Me first," I said.

I squeezed through the hole feet-first. My toes found rocks aplenty. The slide felt no steeper on this side than the other. I drew my trunk through the hole and stood near upright, propped on my hands.

Big rumble coming at me, that's how it started. Strange, it didn't get louder, it got whispier, and it whirled at my face in the dark. A thousand flutters circled my head. Desperate, I flung up my arms and waved them wildly. Odd anythings brushed at my fingers.

I nearly strangled myself on my own scream, but I held it back.

Sun Moon came through the crevice with her candle, and I saw them flying away. I realized, and whispered to Sun Moon, "Bats."

She stumbled and crashed into me. We went down in a tangle. Points of rock jumped out and stuck me.

"Are you OK?" says I. I fumbled and finally got to my feet by pushing on rocks, not her body.

"Yes." When I looked for her face, I realized. Her candle was out. "I've lost my cap," she said.

We found it in a jiffy, but we couldn't get the light back. We'd run off without any matches.

I can't say I got the cajoolies or the willywoollies then, because that wouldn't cover the case. Fear felt like a million tadpoles swimming up and down my back, flicking my spine with their tails.

I took my heart in my hands. Sun Moon needed me now. So I began to work my way down, hands and feet, backing through darkness toward wherever the bottom might be. I could sense more than hear her coming down above me.

Sometimes the rock felt wet, and I didn't like that. I would write songs to open spaces, dry air, and sunlight, not to any damp grottos nor dark catacombs nor such like. Besides, wet makes you slip.

When I got to what felt like the bottom—the rock pile was getting level—I began to feel the water. First I thought I sensed the water, then I felt it for sure, then I was up to my ankles in it. It was cold.

Fine, ankle-deep here, but what about there?

The darkness swallowed me up. What folks call dark isn't dark. I can see well enough to walk cross-country most any night. Even new-moon night isn't all the way dark. Nor is under the covers. Caves and mine shafts a hundred feet down and eleventy-nine crooks into the earth, *those* are dark.

For a second I had the crazy notion that there wasn't any me, nor Sun Moon, but just a blackness bigger than anybody ever imagined. Maybe I could swim off into it, and it would be like fog, and I would be fog, and . . . I felt of my body to find something solid, chest, hips, face, but still wasn't absolutely sure.

"We must *go!*" whispered Sun Moon fiercely.

So I started feeling my way across with my toes. Didn't have no notion of how deep this cold water might be, nor how far across nor wide.

I eased one foot out, felt for solid earth underneath the water, and then shifted forward. Did it again. Did it, stumbled—FELL!

Both knees into the water hard, getting cut. One elbow smashed into the rocky bottom and hollered out its hurt. One hand forward . . . onto a rocky slant.

I felt with both hands. Sweet gizzards, dry ground to step up onto. After only a dozen steps in the cold, black water! Relief, relief. My hands and arms went from tense to fluttery.

I reached out into the dark, got some handholds, pulled myself out of the water, cocked a leg onto the rocks, stood up, and put my hands onto the top of the rock pile.

I leaned on my hands, shifted one to take weight, and put it onto . . . PURE SQUISH!

I leapt back and tottered toward the water crying, "A-a-a-gh," trying to throttle my bellow of horror.

I hit the water full on my back, then the rocks just under the surface. Felt like a hundred hammers giving me a sharp WHACK! at once.

I jumped up, looked at my squishy-feeling hand, saw nothing, rubbed it on my pants, which did no good, and finally dunked it in the water and washed it.

Sun Moon touched my shoulder gently, wanting to know what happened. "I put my hand into something awful, awful squishy," I says. "It scared me." Now I felt like a fool.

"Maybe a . . . What you call them? Snail without shell?"

"Slug," I agreed. Maybe so.

Suddenly light appeared.

It beamed from the vicinity of the crevice we came through. A candle, I saw, surely on a miner's cap. Though it didn't shed a world of light, it shone on Daniel's face beneath the flame beautifully.

He picked up Sun Moon's cap, climbed down to us in silence, waded through the water, and said softly, "Let there be light." He fished in his knapsack and gave us each matches. We lit each other's caps. I wondered how many more miracles were in that knapsack. "Rest awhile. From that hole I can hold him off forever."

Daniel mounted the rock pile again, took off the miner's hat, and set it, candle still burning, in the hole. Bait for Rockwell.

Daniel found another crevice, just big enough for his arm and a line of sight, sat next to it, and stuck the hand with the pistol through.

Sun Moon slipped half-behind some rocks and started changing clothes. I realized this was a devil of an idea and did the same. I got rid of the party clothes for everyday stuff and put on all my hidden treasures—coins in waistband, belt, and scabbard, and the knife itself, which right now had more use than gold. Though neither had any at all.

Sun Moon came out without that fancy gown, back in her Chinese jacket and pants.

I smiled at her, she smiled at me. We held hands for a second or two, feeling close. The candles made the place seem right homey, considering it was a big, wet, dark hole in the ground.

Then I stretched out in a half-comfortable sort of way on the rock pile. I'd been scared till my skin turned inside out, and that is exhausting.

I rested. I think I may even have dozed off.

CLAP-CRASH-BOOM!

The noise blasted me straight into the air. First thing I saw was that candle skittering down the rock pile. Rockwell had shot Dan's cap, and it flew into the water.

Dan fired into the blackness, shooting at Rockwell's muzzle flashes.

Rockwell fired back with a heavier caliber, CLAP-CRASH-BOOM-

SKIDDED-CRACK-WHEE! That din was the closest thing to hell I ever hope to know.

Sun Moon took off down the shaft. She seemed to have a certain poise and calm in her running. Myself, I felt shambly as hell, dogging along behind. At least the thunder didn't seem quite as close, and my legs didn't want to crow-hop sideways on every boom. By my candle I could half see where I was going, and could see Sun Moon bobbing along ahead.

She took a left, took a right, ran wherever instinct told her. Right quick, though, we ran straight into another cave-in, and you could see this one wasn't a go, it was wall-to-wall rockjam.

Suddenly I noticed that the booming had stopped. The armed ones had stopped shooting at each other. Which meant Daniel was on his way here, and Rockwell would be following.

Now we had to walk back up the shaft, straight toward Porter Rockwell.

Sun Moon did a whirl-around. She doused her candle, and I did the same. Then she headed right back up the tunnel. *Stars and cornicles,* I says to myself, *she has no fear.* I looked at her shadowy back and behind, strutting right back toward Rockwell, and decided I'd rather die with her than cower behind a rock and wait.

At the first corner we came on Daniel, wearing his light. He jerked his arm hard back up tunnel, like, Hurry up, dammit.

We ran to the next corner and crouched behind him. He opened his mouth to speak but it was Rockwell's voice boomed out. "Miss Sun Moon, Sister Sun Moon, Your Holiness Sun Moon. You have come to a caved-in shaft."

We all doused our candles.

"Oh yes oh surely oh deliciously, a cave-in. Why else would you come back? Why else would I hear the pitter-patter of little feet? Why else see the glow at the corner? You are rats hunting a way off the ship. I am the tomcat hunting you. And now I have you cornered.

"Oh Your Holiness, I'm gonna put holes in you. I'm gonna cut off the top of your head and hold you up by your feet and drain the blood onto the ground, splot, splot, splot. Oh Your Holiness . . ."

Sun Moon whispered calmly, "What we do?"

Daniel answered firmly, and I couldn't make out Rockwell's taunts above the whispered words. "We have to take that last crosscut to the right," he said. "It's where the shaft bends left. Go the opposite way." He knew the shafts like he knew the keys of a piano. Heckahoy, maybe there were eighty-eight shafts.

"Hey, Brother Asie, Brother Daniel," cried Rockwell sweetly, "come on out. You can go. I have no business with you. I want her. I want Sister Moon, you know, the sweet little Buddhist that broke my nose. Come out. I'll let you go free. She, now, she has a debt to pay."

Daniel kept taking peeks up the tunnel. "I have no idea where he is," he admitted. What with all the echoes, you couldn't figure where a voice came from.

"How far is crosscut?" asks Sun Moon.

"Twenty or thirty strides," says Daniel.

"I go," she says.

"Wait!" squeaked Daniel. He considered. Then he fingered shells out of a side pocket and slipped them into the cylinder of the pistol till there was a full load. I saw it was a five-shooter.

Rockwell roared again. "Miss Sun Moon, don't worry, I don't no more wanna stick my thing in you. I got some'p'n else a stick in you. It don't go 'tween your legs, no. Somewheres to the rear. Then I light the fuse and run." His horse laugh ack-acked off the walls from every direction.

"I go *now!*" she whispered.

Daniel held her back with a hand on her shoulder. "We all go," he said. "First I fire two shots, then we all run, firing. Stay behind me."

He switched his eyes between the two of us, eyeball to eyeball. "It's the only way."

He snuffed out his candle, raised the pistol, looked at us like we were horses at a starting gate, and lit out, spacing his shots.

CLAP-CRASH-BOOM!

CLAP-CRASH-BOOM!

The roar of that gun in that little shaft felt like it would knock me off my feet. Then I saw I was behind the others and jumped like snapped by a bullwhip.

CLAP-CRASH-BOOM-SKIDDED-CRACK-WHEE! roared all around us.

In the lead, Daniel sent his smaller CLAP-CRASH-BOOM! again.

Rockwell answered CLAP-CRASH-BOOM-SKIDDED-CRACK-WHEE! Those bullets felt like they weren't bouncing around the stone sides of the shaft but around the inside of my skull bone.

We whipped around the corner and huddled together like we were freezing.

"Go!" ordered Daniel. "There's a half cave-in beyond there. Find some cover and wait for me!"

Daniel took a pose for keen listening.

We skeedaddled as best you can skeedaddle in pitch-dark. I went feet and hands, tail up. Kept thinking what people say, about getting your ass shot off.

I could hear Daniel wheedle mockingly at Rockwell behind us. "Come on, Brother Rockwell, is it Elder Rockwell, come let's have it out. Be my good deacon. You are a man of God, Porter, and of the devil. But not equal, no, the devil has the mastery of you. The devil makes you want my gift, want the black of a muzzle pointed between your eyes. You've been looking for it your whole life, my dear Apostle . . ."

THUNDERCLAP-CRASH-BOOM-SKIDDED-CRACK-WHEE!! rocketed through the tunnels, I can't say how many times. It sounded like a twenty-one-gun salute.

Rockwell's voice was still, and the silence felt sinister.

Daniel is dead. That thought flash-flooded into my mind. *Daniel is dead.* The words sounded louder than the noises of our hands and feet.

Then came Daniel's tense, teasing voice. "Good try! *Good* try! But you missed, my Apostle! You missed! I missed! Oh, Lordy, the Divinity must be tickled. How many . . ."

But by then the shaft so rattled the words off the walls that I couldn't make them out.

We crawled over the rubble of the half cave-in and scooched down. I could imagine the two men listening, listening, their ears pricked for any sound, a clue that the other man was moving. You *could* creep up on your enemy. And he could spot you creeping, and put an end to your troubles.

A shape came together in the darkness. The long, thin form of Daniel, wings folded. He picked his way silent over the rocks and perched next to us.

"One cartridge left," whispered Daniel, holding up the pistol.

I looked through the darkness into Sun Moon's face. It was steady.

Daniel shrugged off his knapsack and began working at the straps.

"How far we get out?" asked Sun Moon.

Without looking up, Daniel answered, "Long, long way. Time for desperate measures." He lit his candle. "I need light to work."

I could feel Sun Moon's hesitation. "Why you risk self for us?"

Daniel turned to her. "First," he said, "you are my friends. Second, my stupidity got you into this. I led him here." He shook her hands. "Third, you are my friends."

I could feel objection rise in her, like you feel something gush halfway up your gullet. For a moment I was sure she was going to insist on being a hero, and a martyr.

My guts churned.

Daniel took one of Sun Moon's hands tenderly. "Do you love life?" he asked.

"This human incarnation is precious, yes."

"Then let me help you. Help you where I could not help her."

She looked into his eyes a long moment. Then she put her hands on her belly, an odd gesture, and seemed to ponder. Finally, she said, "It is good. Thank you."

So Daniel drew his other hand out of the pack and held it up full of a dark shape.

"I have blasting powder," he said.

I busted out, "You'll kill us all."

"It's dicey," Daniel agreed. "When I didn't take a risk, however, I lost the woman I loved, and life hasn't tasted good since." He turned to Sun Moon. "What about you?"

"I willing do anything. I want live."

He smiled straight at her, and it was an odd smile. "Believe we'll have to blow this place up," he said.

She nodded. Nodded again. "Yes," she said.

Just then came the sound. Rockwell was whistling, and the whistle bounced off every rock in the place. His tune was "Dixie." As you'll remember if you run the tune through your mind, it has some piercing high notes—"look a-WAY! look a-WAY!" and "way down SOUTH in Dixie." Those high notes shrieked at us like banshees, and made my brain cells hurt.

"I never did like that song," said Daniel, not looking up from his work. He sang loud to the tune of the chorus,

"I'm glad I'm not in Dixie,
oh no! oh no!
In Washo land I'll take my stand—
I damn near died in Dixie."

It drowned out Rockwell's whistling. So then Rockwell starts to singing the verse at a roar.

"Oh, I wish I was in the land of poontang,
Old times there was nice when coons sang,
Sing away, sing away,
Sing away, Dixieland."

Daniel's work went on apace. It looked tricky as the devil. He had two powder cartridges and a length of Bickford fuse. "No drill," he muttered. "We'll have to use cracks."

There were two likelihoods, he explained softly under Rockwell's vulgar bellering. One was that we'd set them off and get nothing but a lot of noise. Rock walls don't shatter easy. The other was that we'd bring the whole mountain down on ourselves. "And last," he said, "there's some possibility that we can break enough rock to block this tunnel and not be under it when it comes down."

He worked fast, from time to time tossing out a chorus of "Dixie" to reassure Rockwell. He rammed the cartridges home and tied the fuses on, leaving a rattail hanging down the rock. We didn't have any clay to stem the hole. When he lit them, we'd SKEE-E-E-daddle.

I couldn't help thinking how short these fuses were. But the next corner was close.

Finally he says, "OK."

We looked at him, ready to see the spewing of those fuses, which would tell us how many inches we had left to live.

"I want you to get around that corner quietly," he whispers. "I'll say something, cover your footsteps. And I will try a little ruse."

He steps back near the top of the cave-in and of a sudden calls, "Rockwell, I want to talk."

Silence in the tunnel, ours and Rockwell's. Nobody could believe it.

Dan shooed us down the shaft. He pointed and mouthed, "Corner." We started creeping that way.

"Talk," Daniel called again. "Here's how. I'll set a candle up so you can see. Then I'll throw my gun out. Last I'll step out in the open. We'll meet halfway and talk."

Rockwell's voice was low and slinky, the way a cat moves. "What would we talk about, Sonny?"

Daniel looked at us hard. We decided to trust him and stole along faster.

"We don't all have to die here."

"No," said Rockwell. Now his voice was way too close. Sun Moon and I skittered a few steps, then turned around and listened. "Just you uns have to die."

Daniel lit a match and held it to a candle. When the candle lit, he set it atop the rubble.

He kept the match going and put it to the fuses. Sparks spewed into the air, and he began calling loud to Rockwell to cover the hiss. "Here's the candle," he hollers to Rockwell. "I'm getting my gun out . . .

Sun Moon and me ran. The last few steps we flew, and didn't hear anything.

Daniel screamed, and I saw his wings spread as he came.

A ruckus like the end of the world blew up in my head.

When I woke up, I was flat on my face, with my nose, lips, and left eye scrunched by rocks poking from different angles. I rolled over and found out my body was one big bruise. I had a dim memory of tumbling head over heels on the rock.

Now I felt Sun Moon trying to untangle her legs from mine. Somewhere nearby Daniel was groaning.

I sat up. The world shone with stars and lights, jiggered, came back straight, and went dark. In a second I realized the dark was because our candles were out. "Anybody dead?" says I.

"Concussion, I guess," says Daniel. "It must come around corners."

Something sure had slammed us into the mountain.

Sun Moon pushed against me enough to get room to sit up.

Daniel lit his candle.

She said, "Is he? . . ."

A low, soughing sound came, like the wind moaning. But tunnels are one place you don't find wind. The mournful sound came again, and after a while it changed into, "O-o-o-oh! O-o-o-oh!"

That went on for a bit. Our six eyes batted back and forth at each other, wondering.

After another while it shaped itself into words. "God, God, God. O-o-o-oh! O-o-o-oh! O-o-o-oh! God . . . God."

Finally the voice attempted to communicate with us. “Hurt, I’m hurt, I’m dying, I’m dying. Help me, help me.”

Then a while of silence while we looked at each other, trying to figure it out. “Don’t leave me like this. Please. Have mercy on me. Don’t leave me. Kill me, come kill me. God, God, God. O-o-o-oh! O-o-o-oh! O-o-o-oh! God, God.”

“I’ll have a look,” says Daniel.

“Me too,” says I. Because neither rock walls nor Rockwells shatter easy.

“No!” hissed Sun Moon. “He lives! He shoot you!”

Daniel put his candle out. “I’m gonna look,” says he.

“He can’t see us in this dark,” I whispered to Sun Moon.

We slipped out around the corner and crept up the shaft. Right quick we came to a wall of rocks. I heard Daniel start moving over it soft-like, and did the same myself. Got the cajoolies now—Rockwell might shoot at even a sound.

I crept around that wall of rock for a long time. It was solid, top to bottom.

Rockwell set in again. “Don’t leave me, have mercy, kill me. God, God. O-o-o-oh! God, God.” He kept it up all the while.

Scri-I-itch!

Behind a boulder Daniel had lit a match. Now he set the cap out where anyone could see it and lit the candle.

No shot.

In the half-light we could see the rubble that filled the tunnel. That hole was plugged tight. No one was going to shoot through that, much less crawl through it.

A touch!

I spun so fast I almost caught Sun Moon’s fingers in my teeth. She gave me a look that said, Sorry.

We combed that place for holes, but there weren’t any. A mountain of rock jammed between us and Rockwell. The only thing that penetrated was his eerie voice. “Don’t leave me, have mercy, kill me. God, God. O-o-o-oh! God, God.”

Daniel put his candle cap back on, and we all eased off stealthy-like into the shaft. We couldn’t hear our footpads over Rockwell’s voice. “O-o-o-oh! O-o-o-oh!” Sounded weaker now. When we rounded the corner, it got weaker yet, “O-o-o-oh! O-o-o-oh!,” and kept fading. I honestly didn’t know if Rockwell was telling true or faking.

Doesn't matter, I thought.

Daniel whispered gleefully, "We dropped the whole mountain on him!"

"Need a hundred men to muck that out," I agreed.

"Rockwell's a dead man."

"Then why are we whispering?" asked Sun Moon. It was one of the few times I'd heard her sound annoyed.

She touched my shoulder again. I stopped, and she lit a match for both our candles. Her eyes looked intently at me in the glow.

"He not dead," Sun Moon said. "Tunnel blocked, good. Rockwell alive."

"Why do you think so?" asked Daniel.

"Rockwell not go away unless *I* make him."

I saw she meant it.

"How can you do that?" I asked.

"Have no knowledge," she said.

"So what do we do now?"

"We exit the mountain," put in Daniel. "I've arranged a pleasant surprise."

He set off and we came along behind. I'd had all the surprises I wanted in the last twelve hours. Rockwell, a hidden mine, getting shot at, and blowing up a mountain. What could Daniel have to compare?

Then I got my sense back.

"Flabbergastonia," I whispered to myself.

It was snowing. We could see the flakes falling into the big hole, the shaft exit. The snow was lit up like a chandelier, every flake a candle.

It gave me the shivers. After all, Daniel's watch said it was the middle of a dark autumn night.

We had slept the rest of the day away, I guessed, and now came to a shaft existing upward into the dark. Except it glowed to show us the way, and show us to the world.

"Glorious," said Daniel.

"Beautiful," murmured Sun Moon.

"What is it?"

"Firedamp. I've heard it happens here but never seen it," he said.

Now it shifted and fancified. Colored lights played in among the flakes, making rainbows, shimmery and glisteny, the way oil looks on water.

"Like northern lights," says Sun Moon.

Gastonia, I thought.

Now a smell came, rank, stomach-turning.

"What in tarnation is firedamp?" I asked.

"Carbureted hydrogen gas in mines."

Which meant purely nothing to me.

Daniel walked forward into the light, and it got brighter, like a flame of pure white. He turned into a ghost, eerie white and unreal. He waved, kicked his legs into the air, danced. Snowflakes danced around him.

"Wonderful," said Sun Moon. Getting changed into light meant something to her, something to do with Buddhism. Now the light burned brighter once more, furnace-bright, but utterly without heat. Every pebble in the shaft, every splinter, every piece of fungus glowed dazzling.

Sun Moon and I stepped into the crazy light, too, swirling, playing. "I'm an angel," I says. I started whistling a waltz, and Sun Moon came to my arms. We did a few triple steps. Her eyes gleamed like white silk cloth, and every bit of her face glowed with a white flame, even each hair in her eyebrows.

I heard a clattering above, and something flashed into the light. A rope ladder.

It hung up on some rocks off the bottom. I scrambled up to grab it, which was easy. I was ready to get out of this hole in the ground.

Daniel wanted to go first. Sun Moon followed him, and I brought up the rear. As I rose, I pretended in my mind that we were celestial beings ascending. The awkwardness of a rope ladder kept saying it wasn't so. Yet we burned like supreme candles, pure light without heat.

When I got to the top, I stepped clumsily onto Earth again and looked around. Four Chinamen stood around, three holding horses, one bringing up the ladder. All was unnaturally bright in the burning gas, or whatever it was. Celestials, I said to myself, chuckling. We call 'em Celestials, and now they look it.

Then I saw the fifth Celestial, standing out in the dark, Q Mark eyeballing the darkness. He figured we were not safe yet.

I looked back at the great light. It rose fifty or sixty feet into the black sky. Snowflakes beamed, swirling down, and the colors of the northern lights seemed to rise into the sky.

I spoke to the closest Celestial. "Where's Sir Richard?" I asked.

He just looked at me. Speaking English wasn't any coin in this realm. "Where's Sir Richard?" I repeated foolishly.

A figure came out from behind the horses. "Tommy Kirk say Sir Richard no good. Sleep to tomorrow. Opium."

First I recognized the voice, then I recognized his sweet face. The head was tilted sideways onto folded hands to imitate sleep. An angelic smile lit the face. Paiute Joe.

He came to me and stuck out his hand. "I am your guide," he said.

I shook it.

CHAPTER TWENTY-SIX

"YOU WANNA GO back to town?" I was sick of gallivanting all over the country. And under it.

"No," she said quickly.

"I believe Rockwell's out of the picture," I said.

Paiute Joe put in, "What?"

"We blew up the mountain on Rockwell," said Daniel. "If we didn't kill him, he'll have to be dug out." He addressed Sun Moon. "Since it's my mine, that won't happen."

"No," she said, "we must go San Francisco." I knew better than to try to charm her out of that.

She looked around at our escort. I noticed with satisfaction that every man had at least two guns, rifle and pistol.

"No need run now," said Paiute Joe.

"Where were you planning to take us?" I asked Daniel.

"Truckee River."

"Truckee River?"

"Near Lake Tahoe," he said, shrugging. "Good place." A half smile said something was on his mind, but doodle if I could see what.

"We don' gotta," I told Sun Moon again. "Let's take the stage from Virginia City."

"No," she said. "Rockwell come for me."

Daniel told Sun Moon gently, "You can catch the stage from Tahoe."

My heart stirred. "How long do you think this will go on?"

"I must put ocean between him." I saw her face change. "Unless I confront him."

Now my heart sank.

"You need to go to Truckee River," said Daniel. Funny thing was, I got the idea he meant me, not us.

"How make safe?"

"First," said Daniel, "let's send someone back to find out if Rockwell's dead."

"He not," said Sun Moon.

Daniel fixed us with his hawk eyes. "Let's send someone back."

She nodded. "Yes. But we go away now."

Daniel agreed. He and Paiute Joe talked low with Q Mark. "Tell Tommy Kirk we need to know whether Rockwell is alive or dead. Meet us at Truckee Outlet."

Q Mark nodded at Daniel, saddled his horse, and rode off without a word toward Virginia City.

"Tommy Kirk?" I says.

"He is our savior," says Daniel with a grin. "For a price."

"We must go now," urged Sun Moon.

So we did. I didn't know where, except it was down. We weren't on the Gold Canyon road, weren't on the Six-Mile Canyon road, weren't on any road nor way nor trail nor even animal track I could see in the pitch-dark, just down Sun Mountain behind Paiute Joe.

I didn't like going without Sir Richard. Had a funny feeling we weren't doing right by him. Yet, when you think of it, it was him let us down, not the other way round.

Peculiar thing. Since I set out to explore the wide world and find myself a place in it that seemed right, I'd been running and hiding and playing nip and tuck with death. Near drowned in the river. Near got shot a couple of times by Porter Rockwell. Hid in Brigham Young's bedrooms. Near got blown to smithereens in a mine shaft. Now I was hightailing it down a desert mountain in the middle of night, trying to escape.

I was rightly sick of it. I wanted to stop running, whatever came, pick a spot or a person or a job, and imitate Brigham Young by saying, "This is the place." Then sit and stay put.

Didn't seem like that was in Sun Moon's plans.

We ran all night, forever it seemed like. Down, down, down the steep slopes. I saw by the stars that we were also circling around to the west side of Sun Mountain. Down, down, down. When it was still full dark, we dashed across a sandy plain to where a creek flowed into a desert lake.

"Washo Lake," says Daniel. We were too tired to answer.

The Chinamen took turns on watch. Sun Moon and I wrapped up in blankets and laid next to each other, like we did in the mine. We were becoming partners, in an innocent way, more innocent than I liked. But her face said it was what she wanted, and that was enough for me.

At midday I woke up and ate. Paiute Joe came and squatted on a rock above me, feet flat, bottom dropped between them, rifle across lap, eyes roaming the desert watchful-like. One of the Chinamen was on guard, too. After a while Joe volunteered, "Travel in dark."

"Why are we going to the Truckee River?"

He shrugged.

It was Daniel who answered, a gleam in his eyes. "You must see for yourself."

"You keeping secrets?"

"You'll see."

"And after?"

"When it's safe, you can go on. Whichever of you goes wherever."

I shrugged and gave up. Whatever it was, Daniel was mightily pleased himself, and I wasn't supposed to ask. My friend delighted in secrets and surprises. He was a sleight-of-hand man with hidden parts of himself.

I drifted over to Sun Moon, gave her some dried fruit, and asked what she was thinking.

"Some way Rockwell come. No way out."

I could see thinking on it had her buffaloed, and I didn't want to hear any more of that kind of talk. I felt buffaloed, too. Even if Rockwell was dead, we were running. And I had come to the end of my time with running. I felt ready to be done with skee-e-e-daddling, whatever devil was trying for my hindmost.

Other things were niggling at me too. Going to Tibet, for instance. Traveling halfway around the world. Wasn't that running? And other things yet were bothering me, maybe, but I couldn't tell what they were. I sat down and began to peel threads off a yucca. Before long I was tying them into odd shapes. At the same time I was tying my mind up in knots, and soon was completely frustrated.

Sun Moon meditated until she saw the sun was halfway down to the peaks of the Sierra Nevada Mountains to the west. Gently, she brought herself back to the ordinary world and looked around. Paiute Joe was distributing food. She walked back to the group and sat on a rock next to Asie. He looked at her and she saw thoughts in his head, unspoken thoughts.

Instead of saying what was on his mind, he handed her some jerked beef and dried apricots. "Pretty good dinner for people on the run," he said to Daniel.

"I paid Tommy Kirk well to take care of us," Daniel answered, and lowered his eyes. Sun Moon registered that Daniel never revealed more than he had to, and whatever Tommy Kirk did was for money.

"Thank you," she said. Daniel nodded but said nothing. She knew he was still blaming himself for leading Rockwell right to them.

After a little chewing, she swallowed the beef whole. She never liked dried meat. What she longed for was the *tsampa* of her homeland, roasted barley flour mixed into tea. Or *paak*, barley flour made into dough. The thought gave her a pang, and for an instant she could smell Tibetan tea, rich and buttery. With this memory she could wait for Asie to speak.

She put a dried apricot into her mouth and squeezed it gently between her back teeth. She turned her face into the cool westerly breeze. Nun or not, she loved touch and smell.

Asie said somberly, "I've decided about Rockwell. If he's alive, I'll get Sir Richard, and maybe Q Mark, and we'll kill him."

"No!" The word burst out. She pinched her lips together to keep more from coming out uncontrolled.

"No," she said more gently. If Asie took a human life, the karma would be with him for countless incarnations. "You not even think kill, please."

"I don't want to run the rest of my life," said Asie.

"Not run," she said. "Not kill. Face."

Asie spoke angrily. "How you gonna do that? Face and not kill? He'll kill you."

She shrugged. She looked at him and held his eyes.

"You mean to die?" he asked.

"No," she said. "This human incarnation is precious."

"How you gonna face down Rockwell?"

She looked at him. "Don't know." She could see the burn in his eyes.

"Let's wait for Q Mark," he said. "Maybe Rockwell's dead."

She shook her head. She rocked forward onto the balls of her feet, reached to him with both hands, and took hold of the cloth of the shoulders of his shirt. "We do right," she said. "All we can do."

Suddenly it hit her, the pain. It clubbed her. She rolled onto her back, clutching her belly.

I reached for her, but she rolled away from me and put her back to me, wailing, "No! No!"

She squeezed herself together like a fist, and pain twisted her face something awful. She rolled along the ground, gasping. When I touched her, she shoved my hand away and yelled, "No, no, I am OK."

Loss welled up in me, a sense of something torn away, gone forever.

I sat down in the dust to look at this woman I loved and all of a sudden, straight through what I saw, I got a strange, strange picture. As in a dream I saw me and the four or five people in the world I cared about. We were in the ocean, holding on to big pieces of splintered wood, like our boat had just been smashed to smithereens. I don't even know who the others were, or what they were to me, but they were the ones I cared about. We were split apart and floating away from each other. I could see we were just going to float away from each other, carried by the currents against our wills, float, every which direction, alone and alone and alone, to the uttermost ends of the earth.

I looked at Sun Moon's back and felt a slow, steady, strong wind of loneliness. It was chill and rolled over me from all directions at once, even from up and down. It was around me and it was within me and it was me. I knew with a terrible certainty that loneliness had always been the air I breathed, it was my soul, it was me.

I thought the words, *This is the worst feeling the world brings.*

I felt my soul shrivel.

My fingers ached for my banjo, back in a hotel in Virginia City.

Sun Moon thrashed on the ground right in front of me.

I shook my hands and forced myself to come back and get to helping Sun Moon.

I don't want to picture the whole thing for you, because it was ugly and I don't want to make myself see it again. First she panted and gasped and cried out and wailed for a long while, clutching herself double. Then she convulsed over and over. She shook, she flailed, and she screamed, the worse scream I'll ever have call to hear. Finally she curled into an even tighter ball and blood seeped into the seat of her pants.

She lay still for a while, gasping for breath. When her breathing got easier, she began to cry, soft but not easy. Her whole body shuddered.

All us men just stared, ignorant or stupefied.

Finally, she sat up in the dust and looked at us. I couldn't tell you whether she was seeing us, or her eyes were just pointed our direction, and I couldn't begin to describe that look. "Leave me alone," she said softly. No one moved. She said more firmly, "Please, I need be alone."

We got.

A long while passed. The sun eased behind the mountains. Finally she called my name and I went to her. She was in clean clothes, and her pants were spread out on a rock next to the spring, drying.

She came to me and took both my hands in hers. In the last of the light she looked for a long time into my eyes. Finally, she says, "I have lost our child."

She kept eyeballing me hard. What feelings she saw in me I cannot report, nor what feelings I remember. Shock, agony, grief, words aren't enough for feelings like that. Even music won't say 'em, not all the way.

"I'm sorry," she said.

My tongue was struck dumb.

"I wanted the child, I wanted . . ." She lost her voice in tears.

I was mute.

"I love you. I wanted our child."

She turned and walked off into the desert.

I WAS HELPLESS. I couldn't do anything for Sun Moon, I couldn't do anything for me. I just sat there. I started to figure what did it, most likely getting blasted by that black powder, but then I figured it didn't matter, it was done.

After a while I wished I had my drum and banjo. When Daniel picked up my belongings, he didn't bring them, as they wouldn't fit in the knapsack. So there I sat, feelings turning topsy-turvy inside and no way to get them out. Odd, I was hearing music, bits of it, my music, the songs my heart was making. Yet I had no way to play it, and no heart to sing or whistle it. Felt like wanting to weep and being too dry.

A *GOOD WHILE* after full dark Paiute Joe says quiet-like, "Time saddle up." We set to it. Joe disappears into the sagebrush and comes back with Sun Moon in tow.

Just then we heard hoofbeats, someone coming hard from the direction of Sun Mountain.

We looked around and saw the sentries were both getting their saddles on—no one was on watch!

I scrambled up the biggest boulder I could find and looked east. Paiute Joe was there ahead of me. Though his eyes were over fifty years old, he figured it out first. "Q Mark," he said.

In a couple of minutes the big Celestial came banging into camp, his mount lathered.

We all stood froze, waiting.

He swung down. He walked right up to Sun Moon. I looked into his eyes for feeling—gladness, alarm, compassion, or whatever. I saw only indifference.

"Porter Rockwell," he says to Sun Moon, "he dead."

Q Mark turned his back and strode off to take care of his horse.

She turned to me, her hands on her belly. "Yet he kills," she said. "Yet he kills."

CHAPTER TWENTY-SEVEN

SO WE RODE toward Truckee River through a moonless night, and the death between us made our minds blacker than the sky.

I was worried about Sun Moon, riding long after what happened to her. Daniel and I told her we could rest a day. She said, "I want get away from this place."

Besides, Sir Richard was to join us at Truckee River. That was Q Mark's other news.

We rode.

You may not think it matters, losing a child who hasn't come into life yet. A *mis*-carriage, we call it, meaning things just went wrong. We don't say tragedy. We don't even say dead.

It mattered to Sun Moon. Regardless, it just did. She explained it to me later this way: In the Buddhist way of seeing things, our child was a soul coming once more into the cycle of life and death, for one of the incarnations that go on until the soul is no longer so attached to human life. Not being attached, that's good, it's enlightenment. If our child didn't come in, maybe it wasn't so attached.

But Sun Moon thought maybe our child was attached, was seeking a human life, a higher incarnation. And it was murdered by Porter Rockwell. A human incarnation ended by violence, that is a terrible thing.

Later I knew for sure what she didn't tell me. How ever her theory went, she was a mother. She loved our child, and wanted it, wanted *our* child. She wanted to raise our child in the way of her truth. And she wanted to be part of what she called the cycle of life and death, part of life. But I didn't know all that for a while yet.

The blackness for me was sadness, bewilderment, and confusion. Sun Moon had carried our progeny. We had got the child that night on the bank of the Humboldt River, the one time in our lives either of us had made love. It had grown inside her, crossed the last of the desert in her, and suffered through her long fever time. It had danced with us that night in Virginia City, it had been shot at, it had run through the night, and then it had skittered every which way through that mine. It had survived the grand explosion. It had climbed with us through the fire-glowing snow into the open air again. Then, for whatever reason, it had died.

Until right then I never knew how much I wanted to take care of some living creature, to make it warm, get its belly full, keep it safe.

I felt like I had a hole in my heart.

Sun Moon and I won't be able to fill the hole together, that was the rest of the meaning.

She hadn't told me about our child. She was intending to get on a boat and go halfway around the world and hide in a convent where I never would be able to find her. She meant for me never to know, or to know only by a letter that would do me no good. Our child was to be her child. Our child was to be her secret.

For the first time I understood that we were going to spend the rest of our lives on opposite sides of the globe.

Like a thin gourd tromped by a horse, my heart broke into little pieces.

During that long ride I put it back together in the shape of anger. *Why didn't you tell me?*

In my mind I stuck out my hands in a kind of strangling motion, and worked the fingers. My heart fractured in those hands. I put it back together as anger. It came fractured in my hands again, and this time turned to wet pulp.

Sorrow, anger, grief. Anger.

As we rode through the night, circling a lake we had never seen and still couldn't, it began to drizzle. Later it turned to light snow which didn't stick nor do anything except make my feelings cold.

Cold we came at first light to the ridge looking down on the valley of the Truckee River, where it comes out of the lake. Daniel says, "Let's take a breather."

We swung down from the horses and sat. For a couple of minutes I kept my eyes as down as my spirits were. Then Daniel says softly, "Look."

I raised my eyes from the ruins within and beheld. Don't know I can describe to you, nor anybody, the sight before my eyes. Lake Tahoe stretched away to the east, north, and south, still, like a mirror shining the blue-gray sky at us. All around, four ways, were evergreen-timbered hills. To our backs, away from the lake, jumped up the crests of the Sierra Nevada, steep, icy, awesome. Below us lay little meadows. Through these inviting patches ran a small river, the Truckee, bordered by gold grasses and wine-colored bushes.

In the southeast the sky begins to color, and I hunker down to watch. Sky and lake shift slow from blue-gray to white, salmon, rose. The sun collects itself from a line to a ball the color of white-hot fire. Somehow the lake seems to take the colors more lively than the sky.

Then I notice further. This is the valley of my dream, where I see the tepee and meet my relatives. It is, yet it isn't. The valley of my dream was wide and majestic, this one is narrow and delicate. That was mostly grassy meadows and aspens and expanse, this is river and willows in a narrow crook. *It isn't the valley of my dream except in how it feels to me.*

More differences. There I'm hearing grand organ music, here it's light women's voices, a cappella. . . .

I nearly jumped to realize. *I'm hearing music in my head.* It seemed an indescribable gift. *At this dawn, after my night of greatest darkness, I discover a valley like my dream.*

A tear ran, maybe two.

I felt something at my side and looked sideways. Sun Moon was squatted down beside me, looking not at the sunrise but at my face. A couple more tears ran, one at a time.

She took my hand. A thought flicked through my mind. *How could I hurt so much last night and feel so much healing this morning?* I banished the thought, and all thought. For a long time we sat and looked together across Lake Tahoe at the dawn.

I've had a few days that were truly unforgettable. Like the day I fell in the river and heard voices, and the night I made love with Sun Moon. That first day at Lake Tahoe stands next to them all.

When we mounted up and started down the trail into the valley,

Daniel walked his horse alongside of me and Sun Moon, her between us. "I have a special reason for bringing you two here," he said gently. "Partly it's some people to meet."

"People?" Funny, from the ridge I'd looked and looked and thought I took in the whole scene, breathed it in precious as air. But I hadn't seen any people. The way Sun Moon was smiling at me, I figured she had.

Daniel chuckled and pointed into the timber, but now more trees were in the way.

"Washo," he said.

"Never heard of them."

"Just one family, maybe twenty people." He looked at Sun Moon. "If you need to hide, they'll take care of you."

He switched his eyes to me. "But I wanted you to come here for a completely different reason."

I could feel him wanting me to look into his face, so I did.

"Asie, I believe the Washo are the people you were born to."

I sailed along for a moment like I was riding a star through space. Finally I whispered, "How come you think so?"

Sun Moon gazed at me, back at Daniel, back at me.

"Your one clue, Rock Child. It's a rock near here. The Washo know about it."

I rode along with that for maybe one second or one eternity, I couldn't say which. Waves ran up and down my body, warm and cool. Thoughts whirled in my head, though I knew neither then nor now what they were. A tune of some kind sang in my ears, and the horses' hoofs beat out a slow, steady rhythm.

"Let's go see it," says I.

Daniel smiled. "Let's ask the Washo."

Just then we came out of the timber into the clear. To the left the lake shone strong and vibrant, like a great gong of polished brass. I looked across the tawny grasses and the blue-flecting river and into the trees on the far side and saw them. Stick lodges, set back in the shadows of the trees.

The tune in my head came clear, and I now remembered the words:

I'm just a poor, wayfaring stranger,
A-travelin' through this world of woe.
But there's no sickness, no toil nor danger,
In that bright world to which I go.

I look at Daniel, and his eyes are shining, too. I commence to sing, and he joins me in a high, floating harmony.

"I'm going there to see my father,
I'm going there no more to roam.
I'm just a-going over Jordan,
I'm just a-going over home."

We cross the meadow now, splash through the little stream, brush through more red willows and yellow grasses, toward the lodges among the evergreens. Everything has a glow for me, like halos. Maybe it comes from the rim of tears in my eyes.

The four or five homes were built of willows leaned together in the shape of tepees, facing east toward the lake. Somewhat back from them we left our horses with the Celestials and the four of us, Daniel, Sun Moon, Paiute Joe, and me, walked into camp.

I flicked the reins of my mind and started thinking just a little. Since my whole world had long since gone funny and peculiar, and since this place was even more strange than it was beautiful, I decided to act right at home. Then chuckled at myself. *Why not right at home?*

A couple of young men met us and exchanged some words with Paiute Joe, too low for me to hear. We followed them through the camp. Women were at work, drying strips of flesh, pounding pine nuts into flour, weaving baskets. They wore rabbit-skin dresses that maybe did better for warmth than decency. Children of all ages played everywhere. One old woman sat idle with her face turned to the morning sun, soaking it up. They were a short people, mostly round of face and body. I couldn't help thinking that I was, too. If a first impression meant anything, they were a cheerful bunch.

We walked up to a fire in front of a lodge and an old man who indicated with his arm that we were welcome to sit down. Even in my daze I managed to sit without falling. *Is this man my grandfather? Are any of these people my brothers or sisters? Aunts or uncles?*

The old man gave Sun Moon an odd look or two, and I didn't find out until later that it was against custom to bring a woman to a parley. He decided to make generous allowance for our barbarian ways and said a few words, friendly-like. I strained to hear each one clearly, and repeated those I could in my mind. But to my disappointment I didn't recognize a single word, nor did the general sound of the language seem familiar.

The old man's wife had put the coffeepot on the fire, and now she poured it into tin cups for us. I didn't find out until later that this was a significant gesture of hospitality, with coffee and cups given by Daniel.

When we'd sipped awhile, the old man signed, and Paiute Joe spoke his words to us. "His name is Giver," said Paiute Joe. "He is the grandfather of this family. He greets me and Daniel as friends, and offers his fire to you two." Paiute Joe signed and said some words and made a gesture toward Sun Moon and me. The old man regarded us each in turn. "If you need protection, he offers it to you."

"Thank you," we said. I added, "I believe we are safe now." I could hardly shove my mind back to Porter Rockwell, who wouldn't be doing any more killing from beyond the grave.

Paiute Joe signed to Giver whatever we said.

"Ask him," prompted Daniel.

Paiute Joe talked with his fingers. I could have done that, but was glad to watch. Giver answered in words and signs. The words still sounded as foreign as Sun Moon's Tibetan. Maybe I'd never lived with my people enough to learn the talk.

"It's OK," Paiute Joe told Daniel.

"Sun Moon, when you want to go to San Francisco," Daniel said, "Giver's sons and grandsons will escort you and Sir Richard to the stage on the Placerville Road."

"Thank you," said Sun Moon.

"I want to see the Rock Child," I said.

Paiute Joe answered, "How about after you sleep?"

Daniel was looking at me curiously.

I looked around. *Is this my place?* I couldn't tell. Maybe. *Did I come from here? Should I come back to here?* I looked into Sun Moon's face. *Maybe I can stay and she can go and it won't be heartbreak. Maybe.*

I sat real still and turned my head and looked in every direction, east toward the lake, west up the river valley, north to the timbered ridge, south across the rolling hills. The world shimmered.

This was the most beautiful place in the world. However many wonders there were, this was the most beautiful.

"*TIME FOR ANOTHER* surprise," said Daniel. "Come along?"

I got up, still more or less in a trance.

"You are invited to dinner tonight," said Daniel to Giver.

Dinner? We didn't have decent food, but at least it wouldn't be boiled garbage.

We rode down the valley and then south along the lakeshore. "What you are about to see is my true ambition," Daniel told us. "No one else has seen this."

Oh you friend of many secrets.

The lake was spanking bright. "It's a wonderful country," I says to Sun Moon.

"Like my home," she said. "Like my home." I realized all the mountain West she'd seen till now was dry. This country was extravagantly watered, by compare.

We turned right along the shore into a natural clearing, with giant pines set wide apart. There sat a fine two-story log house with a porch running across the whole front, facing the lake. "I have built a lodge," said Daniel. "Welcome." For once he sounded happy, and the hawk look of his eyes was softened.

We rode up to the hitching rails in front of the lodge, and I surveyed the spot. It was the handsomest place to live a man could ever lay his eyes on, and a handsome day to come to it, warm and sunny. "What in Gastonia?" I murmured.

Daniel grinned, the merriest expression I'd ever seen on his face. "I'll explain over breakfast," he says.

As we dismounted, a white man and a Paiute wearing white-man pants came out of the lodge. Paiute Joe spoke to his tribesman, and the fellow took our horses to some corrals out back. "This is my foreman, Splinter," said Daniel of the white man. He looked tickled that the world held someone named Splinter. "You'll meet his brother Andy. Splinter will show you to your rooms."

We carried our bedrolls inside and followed Splinter up the stairs. The whole second story appeared to be bedrooms, like in a hotel. They had ticking mattresses stacked against the walls, four and six to the room, but no bed frames yet. Maybe they were meant for bunks. The Celestials settled in one room, all of them together. When Splinter gave Sun Moon one and started me toward another, I said, "Sun Moon, I want to be with you."

She looked at me and her eyes were soft. "Yes," she said gently.

We put the mattresses on the floor close together and spread the blankets. I felt jimmy-joomy—we were going to spend our last nights near together. I wondered how many more nights there would be.

Daniel met us at the foot of the stairs and gave us the tour while breakfast was being whipped up. The kitchen was ample, outfitted with a stove, where brother Andy was making flapjacks. The dining room had four long tables with benches. On the other side of the hall and stairs was a single great room for sitting, lounging, talking, and drinking.

"One of my shipments has come in from San Francisco," said Daniel, leading the way to the middle of the spacious room.

Then I saw his prize. In the middle of the far end of the room, with a tidy dance floor around it, sat a grand piano.

Oh, Gastonia.

He plunked some keys. "Do you think we could make some music on this?" His eyes were alight.

Before I could head for the bench, Sun Moon said, "Let's rest a little before breakfast."

Seeing her eyes were tired, I realized I was worn-out, too.

We went upstairs and stretched close by each other. I half awoke at midday, saw Sun Moon near me, and went back to sleep.

KNOCK-KNOCK!

I rolled over.

Knock-knock!

We both sat up in bed. "Come in," Sun Moon said softly.

The door flung open and framed Sir Richard, brow thunderous and cheek scar flaming. He pushed into the room, eyes fixing on us. "I apologize," he said. "I failed you at the crucial time."

This admission sounded trumped-up to me.

Sun Moon stood up and showed generosity. "You save my life," she said. "You take me for protect when you no need. You big-hearted man to me, always so, I never forget."

Sir Richard's eyes softened, even if his jaw stayed hard, and I knew that her words were special to him.

I looked in my heart and saw that I wanted the apology he gave, and it might not be enough. Sir Richard in the grip of drink or drug was a madman. *I will never be able to depend on you.* Nothing more to say. Except that it hurt.

I looked at him and done my best. "I understand what happened."

He shifted his weight on his feet, and I knew the way he looked at himself was in my hands. "My self-regard," he would put it.

I took thought. I wondered, not for the first time, whether twenty years of alcohol, hashish, and opium, the pressure of spying, and especially his disappointments in getting fame and fortune had parched the soil of his heart and spirit. I wondered whether anything could grow there anymore. I didn't have anything more to say to him right then.

Sir Richard turned into the hall and came back with a surprise in each hand—my banjo and my drum.

"Let's play!" I shouted.

"Actually," answered Sir Richard, "I believe Daniel is expecting us downstairs for supper."

I looked out the window and saw that it was twilight. We'd slept the day away, and I hadn't got to the Rock Child. But I'd been sunset to sunset without food. "Is it ready? Let's eat!"

THE GUEST OF honor was Giver, and he brought one of his three wives, a granddaughter, and two great-grandsons, seven or eight years old. All the Washo but Giver looked foot-draggy, and I wondered whether eating with the white folks seemed to them like a treat or a punishment. White-man food wasn't much like theirs, and they wouldn't be able to join in the talk.

Daniel asked us to push two of the long tables together and seated Giver and family square in the middle, where they wouldn't miss anything. The other Indians, all Paiutes, he seated across from the Washos. I supposed the tribes weren't enemies, but they didn't seem to speak each other's language. I did feel fortunate the Celestials had gone back, or we would have had four outfits of people bumping elbows without being able to talk to each other.

Maggie, the Washo cook, served up what the whites thought princely camp food, fried deer tenderloin, fried potatoes, fried wild onions, coffee, and raspberry cobbler. It was every man for himself out of big serving bowls.

Sun Moon and Sir Richard ate fastidiously, but not me—I felt real white when it came to meat and potatoes. I noticed that you nearly had to fight for the serving spoon, everybody was gobbling it so good, the Washos, too. Though silverware was set by their plates, the grown-up Indians ate with their belt knives and the kids with their fingers. A couple of times Giver and I met eyes, and we nodded with smug smiles, like princes passing in a procession.

When the dessert came, Sir Richard says, "Well, you've had an adventure. Nothing is as good for the digestion as a rousing adventure story."

So we told it, right from when we went lickety-split out of the Heritage. Right off I thought, *Either our audience can be just Sir Richard or it can include all these Indians.* So I signed while we talked. Daniel and me took turns telling, for Sun Moon wouldn't join in, despite our urging.

Daniel told about owning an abandoned mine where he sometimes went, and that brought admiration. He looked hangdog when he had to admit he let Rockwell follow him back to us the next day.

The rest was a pure bang-bang, bad-guy-chases-the-good-guys tale, fun to tell and fun to hear. When we told about blowing up the mountain on Rockwell, Sir Richard actually clapped, which made me feel great.

I told the part about coming out into the magically lit snowstorm, and about fleeing to Lake Washo.

There I had a decision to make. When I held eyes with Sun Moon, it was easy. I hopped over the part about losing our baby. That was ours alone. I skipped straight to when Q Mark came back and told us Rockwell was dead.

Sir Richard sang out a strain of a funeral march—oh, he was in fine fettle tonight!

Then I studied Sir Richard and saw a certain look in his eye. He was hurting. And a word rose in my mind—compassion.

So I looked at him solemn, and said, "I know you wish you'd been there. It would have been fine to have you. To me you will always be *Sir* Richard Burton."

He nodded, thanking me, and his eyes said the thanks was deep.

Maggie brought out a second round of coffee. I noticed Giver was keen for it, and filled the cup about an inch with sugar.

I couldn't keep a stopper on my curiosity. I says, "Joe, will you ask Giver what he thinks of our story?"

Joe done that.

Giver came out with a good smile and a wagonload of words and signs, which Joe put into English.

"He says it is a fine story, and he honors those that keep it in the memory of the people and tell it so the people will understand.

"The Washo had a demon like Rockwell, name of Ong. Ong was a monstrous bird that nested in the middle of Lake Tahoe. From time to time he flew out and hauled people away to his nest and ate 'em."

When the old man talked about Ong, his voice trembled, and I imagined the monster bird rising out of the deep, dark waters to dramatic music. There was a tremolo in the bass, and the right hand pounced from note to note in the tritone, the devil's interval, trouble a-rising.

"Long time since Ong came against the people, but they not forget him," Joe went on for Giver. "Not forget either to act like true human beings and thank the gods and honor them, so that Ong does not get loose again."

I wasn't ready to switch to how they gave what for to Ong. I wanted more scary stuff.

"Giver, he tell you some stories of Ong, but it is not the time for telling stories—he means it isn't winter—and he has talked too much already."

That put a stop to my musical dream. I wished I could get a bunch of Ong stories, and write some Ong songs. Then I realized . . .

Like reading my mind, Daniel says, "How about some music?"

Everyone gathered around the piano, Indians included, and Daniel and I played four hands. He rolled out an introduction to a fine quadrille. Catching on that dancing would be just the thing, I joined right in, and we set the feet to moving. Sir Richard grabbed one of those Washo women and led her right through her paces. Giver and Joe partnered each other in the same style, though none could tell whether Giver or Joe was dancing the woman.

After the quadrille and a reel, we played a waltz. Sun Moon got to her feet and asked Giver to dance. The old fellow accepted. You couldn't say which shone more, his old face or her young one. I noticed how much they looked alike, bronze-skinned and black-haired, these children of opposite ends of the earth. Then I realized that Sun Moon, who had done some waltzing and liked to dance, was taking the man's part and leading Giver. Beaming, the chief of the Washo made an endearing old woman. And I was delighted to see Sun Moon just purely enjoying herself.

Then Daniel swung into Chopin and the dancers sat. He played two nocturnes. They sounded lovely, especially with the bigger sound of the grand piano. The applause was enthusiastic, and after a hesitation the Indians joined in it, looking at their hands and funny expressions on their faces.

Maggie brought a second round of dessert. Everybody piled into the big, comfortable chairs and ate.

"Who's your crew?" Sir Richard asked Daniel. He was always picking up information for those journals of his.

"Two Paiutes," Daniel says, "who are good carpenters, and several Washos, who are learning. Two whites, Splinter and Andy; Splinter's the foreman. Maggie is Andy's wife. She's Washo, does the cooking and cleaning."

I pondered that Maggie and Andy being married meant there were going to be some in-between children, like me.

"How do the Washo feel about having the Paiutes here?" In his interviewing mode, Sir Richard didn't miss a trick.

Daniel favored him with a small smile. "Lake Tahoe," he began, "is the center of Washo country, center for food, religion, everything. Normally they'd fight anyone who came in here. I'm paying them for the right to use their land." Daniel had some pride here, I could see. "I'm also paying the U.S. government a little for a preemption entry, courtesy of Mr. Lincoln's Homestead Act."

"So what do you mean to accomplish here?" Sir Richard kept his voice amiable.

Glancing over the rim of his coffee cup, Daniel said, "I am investing the fruit of my financial shenanigans in my personal dream."

I looked around and saw that everyone was interested. Paiute Joe was signing to the Indians.

"For a while this will be a wood ranch," Daniel went on. "The forests of the eastern Sierra Nevada are disappearing into the mines of the Comstock Lode," he said. "For more than a year the principal obstacle to shaft construction has been shortage of timbers. Thus Pray's mill at Glenbrook, across the lake."

He looked particularly at me. "You can't see it from this shore. On the east side, cuts ten thousand feet a day. They haul the boards to the divide on the east and flume them down to Carson City. A splendidly profitable enterprise.

"My location is excellent. Timber for miles and miles, untouched. This winter we'll cut. In the spring I'll float across to the mill. Success is assured."

Sir Richard said dryly to me, "Again, every man in Washo has a get-rich-quick scheme."

"Riches were never my dream," Daniel replied evenly. "I want to create a school." He got up and walked to the wide windows facing the lake, looking into the evening darkness. "The summer after next," he said carefully, "we will open for business as a music conservatory." He paused, and as he went on, pride filled up his voice. "There is culture in San Francisco, and will be in Virginia City. Within five years the transcontinental railroad will put us close to both. This a wonderful locale in the summer, inspiring. I'm confident we can draw young musicians. I hope we can draw serious players and composers, not mere amateurs."

We had all fallen silent. No one's mouth gaped, but I figured we all felt the same about it. We were looking at a dreamer.

"We will be a residence camp," Daniel went on, "for students in their teens, performance and composition. Every kind of music, classical, dance music, shaped-note music, Negro music, Acadian music—everything.

"I want to help create a real American music. Not copies of the European stuff but something that grows out of all our peoples and all our musical traditions. Something new."

I felt awed by his idealism, which was both beautiful and mad. I asked myself if he'd succeed, and answered myself, *It doesn't matter.*

"If you should fail?" said Sir Richard softly.

"Then I will have a marvelous home on the most beautiful lake in the world," he said, "where I can live far from the defilements of humanity and play the piano to my heart's content. And friendly Indians for neighbors."

"You don't expect other commerce on Lake Tahoe?" he queried.

"A few other madmen like myself, perhaps, in search of loveliness and solitude," said Daniel. "Otherwise, it's far too remote."

CHAPTER TWENTY-EIGHT

1

THE ROCK WAS the size of a house, maybe a three-story house. The Rock Child sat on its lap, and we had to climb to get there, and that was part of the story.

"We never come here," said Second Goat in signs as we stood at the bottom. "Not even the oldest people remember using this rock, if we ever did." Otherwise, he seemed to be saying, there would be a ladder.

The climb was an effort. I only cared about getting up, standing there, seeing the Rock Child, touching it, finding out . . .

I followed Second Goat, paying little heed to Sun Moon, Sir Richard, or Daniel. I knew that it was hard for Sun Moon to get up, but she wanted very much to be there.

Second Goat walked over and put a hand on the Rock Child. He was Giver's grandson, lent to us as a guide. Probably the old man thought that ten miles or so each way was more than he wanted to walk. Or ride.

Second Goat didn't talk much. Hadn't said a word all the way up. Now he just looked at us with a glint in his eyes, hand on the big piece of granite called the Rock Child. It was nearly as tall as a man, and wider than it was tall. A giant muscling up full strength couldn't have done what Second Goat did now. He pushed gently with one hand and the boulder rocked.

Though he didn't permit himself a smile, his eyes were wild with gleam. He stood back.

I tried it, with a ridiculously soft touch. The Rock Child swayed in my hand.

My mind swooped around in a whirl once and came back to the boulder. I pushed again, hard. The Rock Child swayed again, neither more nor less.

When I backed away, the Rock Child responded to Sir Richard's touch, to Daniel's, and to Sun Moon's.

"Tell us about it," I said.

"There is a story," said Second Goat, "I don't know about it. Many winters ago some people came here to hunt and fish and gather berries during the summer. Seeing this big rock with steep sides and a flat top, good for storage, they laid their meat and fish here to dry.

"One day when the hunters were away, a big flock of birds carried all the meat away.

"Fearing a hungry winter, the chief had a fire built on the rock. The people danced around it and prayed for mercy.

"Soon the wind began to blow, and storm clouds gathered. Encouraged, the people danced and prayed and beat their drums harder. Thunder and lightning answered the beat of the drum.

"Suddenly lightning bolted down from the sky and struck the flat top of the boulder.

"The people fell to their knees and wailed forth their supplications. As the smoke cleared from the boulder, they saw this new boulder, smaller, like a child. And in the wind, visibly, it swayed.

"The people gave thanks, and they soon discovered that the Rock Child, swaying in the slightest breeze, scared away the birds. So once more they had a place to dry their food, and store it."

When he fell silent, I asked, "Do people still store food here?"

"I know of no one who does," said Second Goat.

I wondered why the people neglected to use the gifts of the gods, but didn't ask.

We climbed down with scarcely a word. In silence we ate a picnic lunch fixed by Maggie, and rode home.

What the talk was I couldn't say. I was overwhelmed with my own thoughts. Was I named after this rock? Born near this rock? Was I a Washo?

The questions felt so big I couldn't open my mouth and let them out.

THE NEXT DAY I went hunting. I asked to spend the day in the Washo camp, but Giver signed that I must hunt deer. He sent Second Goat with me, who was also married to one of Paiute Joe's granddaughters, and His Sweetness, Paiute Joe himself.

Sir Richard loaned me his Enfield carbine. I wasn't keen to hunt. I did think, though, *Seems like it's what I'm supposed to do.*

Starting at first light with Maggie's biscuits in our pockets, we rode up into higher country for a couple of hours, heading for a place Goat knew, the foot of a little canyon. When we got there, Joe said, "Shoot, me," pointing with his battered Sharps rifle, and set out to climb the ridge to the head of the canyon. Goat and I staked the three horses and waited for Joe to get into place.

The view from where we sat was considerable, and I was curious but nervous. I took a deep breath and asked Goat in signs, "Where all do the Washo live?"

He pointed to the east and signed, "Sun Mountain." The mountain was a bump in the distance there beyond the ridge east of Lake Tahoe, and Virginia City difficult to imagine. *The Comstock Lode has naught to do with the life of these people,* which seemed like good news.

Goat swung his arm around to the south, toward some deserty hills. He signed, "Headwaters of Carson River." He pointed west and signed, "Summit of the mountains." Last he pointed north and signed, "Honey Lake," which meant nothing to me. Then he signed, "Center Lake Tahoe." As yet I had no idea how true that was, but I figured any people making Lake Tahoe their center had good sense.

Nothing to do but wait, so I asked more questions. "What time of year camp in the mountains, the desert, at the lake?"

Our fingers established a picture worth thinking about. The Washo started their year hungry, after a winter living on stored pine-nut flour, grass seeds, and dried meat. Before the snow was gone the young folks, men and women, came up to Lake Tahoe to catch whitefish. At the same time the women, down in those foothills, gathered wild lettuce, wild spinach, wild potatoes, and Indian sweet potatoes.

In the late spring everybody went up to Tahoe and fished the spawning creeks. "The fish is thick and many as grass," Goat said with his hands. "Very easy fishing, even children scoop fish. Broil them, dry them, main food."

In the middle of the summer, when everything was all the way melted, they went to the high country. Up there the men did fishing that needed a lot of skill, with spears, taking males only. The women dried fish eggs and collected and dried plants—sunflower seeds for flour, cattail roots, shoots and seeds, wild rhubarb, wild strawberries, and wild onions. I was thinking how good it sounded when he added, "We take the sap of sugar pine for candy."

In late summer the whole bunch trekked down to the foothills, did a lot more gathering, and seined minnows with baskets.

In the autumn all the people, all three branches of the Washo, Wel mel ti, Pau wa lu, and Hung a lel ti, gathered in the Pine Nut Hills east and south of the lake. They held a big ceremony for five days, and then spent a month or more gathering and preparing *tah gum,* pine-nut flour, the food that got them through the winter. Giver's family would usually have been in the Pine Nut Hills now, but they came back after the ceremony—Daniel was paying them good to work on his lodge.

They had to go down the mountain before long, Goat signed, the snow was coming. So far, the autumn was warm and dry, but Giver's part of the Washo, the Wel mel ti, would camp down at Truckee Meadows.

Of a sudden Goat stood up and motioned up the ridge. That seemed to mean Paiute Joe was in place. We started riding up the canyon, no more sign talk, like our silent fingers would scare the deer. I supposed that the autumn was given over, a lot of it at least, to hunting deer back up in the high country. I half hoped I'd need to use the Enfield, and half hoped I wouldn't. I'd never shot it.

I was worried by Goat's statement that the Washo finished the winter in hunger. *How hungry?* I thought, mind in my stomach. I had reason to find out, for truth to tell, I had one eye on staying with the Washos and finding out if they weren't my home. I was thinking maybe living with the Washos was what I'd been looking for since I washed out of that river. *Where I come from.*

I'd been nervous about eats on account of that Donner party. Daniel said the place they half starved to death and half cannibaled each other was just up the creek from the Rock Child. The Washo got through that winter that year just fine, though, not far downriver, below the snow, minding their own business.

My people. My home, maybe? *Some folks say man's home is where his mother comes from.*

I wondered why their talk didn't sound familiar to me. Maybe I wouldn't be able to understand it after all these years, but why didn't it sound . . . ? If I'd grown up with it. If even just my mother spoke it to me. *I wonder if she did. Or did she figure it's a new world and only talked English to me?* I didn't know, nor have any way to know, and it was irksome.

Our job was to flush the deer out of the canyon where Joe would have a shot. All we had to do for that was stir things up, make some noise. But Goat rode silent, and I followed his lead. We pushed through the bushes along the little creek. Goat looked around like he was soaking up things with his eyes. I had the feeling he would be able to tell you about every blade of brown grass later.

What kind of music do they have? I wondered. The sound of Daniel's grand piano last night floated through my mind, and then I got a truly queer picture. I was sitting at the grand piano, fingers making music, but the sounds were Indian music, hi-yi-ing voices over a drum that kept banging at you and at you. I chuckled at my foolishness, and felt a chill.

Boom!

I jumped, scared out of my daydream by the shot.

My horse jumped, too, and I thought how I couldn't shoot off his back.

Boom!

Goat hurried for higher ground, where we could see. I kicked my horse after him, and when we got there, slid out of the saddle, and propped the Enfield on a rock for rest, just in case. It felt like playing a kid's game, but Paiute Joe had needed to shoot twice.

Pretty quick I caught movement in the bushes along the creek, something coming quick. I watched sharp. Damned if it wasn't a black bear!

The critter was running like hell and then stopping to scratch at its belly. Once it rolled over and scratched hard. I knew it for gut-shot. No telling how far it would run before it died.

Goat took off sprinting, bow in one hand and arrows ready in the other.

I took off sprinting to save his ass. *A bow and arrow against a bear!*

When Goat got maybe a hundred yards off, he began to yell. "Hi-hi-hi, hi-yah!" and such as that, real loud.

The bear stood up and took a look around. Then it acted like it got stung in the belly and rolled all around again.

Goat ran closer. "Hi-hi-hi, hi-yah!" he bellowed.

The bear sniffed. It sniffed another direction.

Goat got on his knees in a clear spot and drew the bow. "Hi-hi-hi, hi-yah!" he bawled.

The bear half stood, searching.

I saw two glimmers.

The bear grabbed at its chest.

It roared terrible.

Then it trotted toward Goat.

My shot was not clear—Goat was half in the way.

The bear was caterwauling, you could hardly believe.

Goat raised the bow, still kneeling.

The bear charged Goat hard.

I saw two glimmers.

I shot at its heart.

The bear dropped like I'd blown its head off.

It lay in front of Goat like a rug. It didn't twitch or anything.

I trotted up.

Goat was just waiting for a little, maybe make sure the bear didn't have one more swipe in it. He looked irked. In a minute, though, he lifted his face up and began to chant. Anybody could tell he was praying, but afterwards I didn't have the heart to ask him why he prayed. Found out later no Washo would kill an animal without giving thanks and asking forgiveness for taking a life.

"Did I hit it in the heart?" I babbled, knowing I did.

Goat looked at me queer, and I remembered he didn't speak English. He signed back, "The bear was dead."

I looked at him weird.

He pointed at the gun and at his own head. "The bear was dead," he signed. "I was alive."

Then I got it. Some gratitude, when you save someone's life.

He motioned to me to help and we rolled the bear over. Damned if there weren't four arrows plumb center in that bear's chest.

Goat began to cut. He sliced the belly open, ribs to bottom, and motioned I should get the guts out. Then he pulled his arrows out, right back through the ribs.

When I was done with the guts, we split the bear's breastbone. Then I saw that three of those arrows were in the heart. So Goat would have killed the bear.

That's when I looked for my shot. And looked. And looked.

Finally Goat signed to me, "You missed."

A thorough inspection of the inside of the rib cage confirmed that fact.

Paiute Joe showed up pretty quick to help us quarter that bear out and get it on the horses. He was excited to get a bear—fat meat and lots of it.

When we got to camp, everybody made over Second Goat. He went around camp giving big pieces away, first to old folks, then to relatives. Joe gave a fine piece of backstrap to Giver, who was his in-law. Turned out, according to Joe, the Washo hardly ever hunted bear. Neither did Paiute, said Joe, until they got rifles. Dangerous. That's how come Second Goat was a big man today.

I was invited for dinner at Giver's lodge.

Well, I thought, *That's the rabbit path. You go hunting, damn near shoot your partner, he kills a bear when you wanted a deer, and you're all heroes.*

2

I WASHED OFF in the river, which was cold, put on my best clothes, and Sun Moon and me got ready to go to Giver's.

Downstairs Daniel and Sir Richard were both dressed and freshly shaven.

"Let's walk," says I. I wanted to put off getting to the camp. Tonight I was going to tell some folks they were my family, which was a way of asking if I could come home. I had the jitters.

My friends looked at each other, and Daniel said, "Why not?"

The way ran along the lakeshore a little, and then down the river. Though dark was a good while off, the sun was down behind the Sierra Nevada, huge above us to the west. One of the glories of this country is the long twilights the mountains give, day in day out, summer, fall, winter, spring.

The lake looked violet in the half-light, and perfectly still. The mountain air breathed crisp, not yet cold. We walked in delicate silence, Daniel first, then Sun Moon and me, Sir Richard bringing up the rear. I tried to pay more attention to the scene than the cajoolies cavorting in my stomach.

We followed the trail left through the giant pines toward the Truckee. When we came out into the river valley, I sucked in breath to hold the sight. The Truckee flowed like a shiny silk ribbon away from us, exactly the blue of the sky. Tawny grasses and wine-colored willows ran beside the river like grace. I thought, *Not a bad place to live. Mighty good-looking home.*

We kept the silence all the way to the camp, maybe quarter of an hour, and I bet everybody had serenity but me. As we came in, people smiled at us. We walked among the children, between the running dogs, amid the many, rich smells of a camp, a place where human beings live, breathe, cook, eat, sleep, and do all things that make human smells. I was eating it up with my eyes.

Giver was sitting behind a fire talking with Paiute Joe, and he bid us join him. We did. He passed the coffee in friendly fashion, and we sipped sociably.

The dinner came quick. Those of us around the fire were served where we sat, and the women and children ate behind. They treated Sun Moon like a man—she sat with us. We were complimented by being served first, a privilege usually reserved for elders.

The food was blood sausage made from deer and cooked on the coals, a kind of biscuit made of acorn flour, and a sweet paste of some kind. When I asked with quiet fingers, Joe said the paste was made of grass seeds. Told myself this was eating the fruits of the earth. And truth to tell, it tasted good.

When we were done, everybody looked at each other like, 'What comes next?' Making conversation with signs is slow and awkward, and takes the fun right out.

I was going to wait forever, but sudden-like Daniel ups and out with it. "We believe Asie here"—he nodded at me—"is a Washo."

The cajoolies scampered like mice in my belly.

Paiute Joe signed it.

I thought maybe Giver would roll his eyes, or laugh out loud, but he simply looked at me long with his kind eyes. Then he said some words to one of his wives. She called to another old man who came over. The old man sat in the circle, and the woman, too. Giver said, "We have some elders now who remember way back. Tell us the story, my friend."

I took a breath and let it out, and another. I decided to tell it full out, for the sake of my friends there, who hadn't heard it all. I knew Joe wouldn't sign what the Washo didn't need to hear.

"First I know for sure about me is when I was maybe seven. It was the year the Mormons came across the plains to the Great Salt Lake. On July 7, 1847, they stopped and camped at Fort Bridger. I know it was July 7 'cause my adopted folks ever after said that was my birthday, July 7, the day when I came into their family. And all the Mormon stories say they were at Fort Bridger July 7.

"Way it happened was this. A lot of mountain men and Indians were camped at Fort Bridger that day. One 'em, name of Taylor, was dying. Unconscious half the time already, and not making sense the rest of the time. He'd clamp his hands on his belly and moan once in a while, then he'd sleep, then he'd talk. But no one was ever sure what he was saying.

"I was with him. A Shoshone woman had been with him, with us, but she'd died before. When we came into Bridger, it was just the two of us. Some of the mountain men and their women knew the Shoshone woman, but she wasn't my mother anyhow, not my belly-button mother."

I took a pause for some deep breaths.

"That's what Mrs. Pfeffer called it, belly-button family, the one you was blood of.

"The Pfeffers wanted to take me in. Otherwise, what would I a done, a seven-year-old kid at Fort Bridger? Woulda been underfoot at the fort, and wors'n underfoot on a trapping expedition.

"The Pfeffers asked old Taylor if they could take me in. Nobody was sure what he answered, but everybody interpreted it as yes. The mountain men didn't know what to do with me anyhow. Way the Pfeffers saw it was, they were helping out, making a barbarian into a Saint. Mormons been doing that with Indians from the start.

"Nobody knew, though, even whether I was full-blood or half-blood. Some that the Pfeffers talked to said I was son of Taylor and a Digger woman.

"So I was a half-Digger, which could mean any of the tribes live in the desert."

I looked around the circle and saw that every eye was on me. No people are like Indians for letting you talk yourself all the way out, no interruptions.

"For a long while after the Pfeffers took me, I wouldn't talk to anybody, nothing, not a word. But after a few weeks I began to sing, Mrs. Pfeffer said—join in the hymns at the meetinghouse and the songs around home. So Mrs. Pfeffer set the family to singing real regular, to take my tongue back from the cat that got it, and in a coupla months I was talking. English. Way she told it, I never said a word in Indian.

"The Mormons speculated about this. Some said old Taylor hadn't let his woman talk Indian to me, so I never learned it. Some thought maybe something bad happened, I'd been stole away or the like, and the language got scared out of me.

"Anyhow I had no memory of it, and have none yet. Or recollection of anything that happened to me afore I was adopted at seven years old. My first memories are of the family singing together in Salt Lake City.

"Because I took to music, Mrs. Pfeffer encouraged me hard in that. She give me piano lessons right along with her kids, and made me a present of an ocarina one birthday and a wooden flute another. The Mormons love music, and I have always loved it.

"When I got old enough in their opinion, twelve, the Pfeffers told me about how they came to adopt me. I had never guessed it, that I was adopted, didn't know I wasn't blood kin. I knew I was different, 'cause I got treated different, worse, but I thought I was just a kinda black sheep.

"I got mad about them not telling me, and I stayed mad. Took to calling the Pfeffers Mr. and Mrs. instead of Mom and Dad. Dropped the name they called me, Earl Pfeffer, and took Taylor, after Old Taylor, and Asie, from the name his woman called me in Shoshone, Sima Untuasie. Afore long I started trying to find out who I was, or at least where I come from. Trouble was, didn't have much to start on, just the name Taylor, hints about Diggers, and two mystery words. I'll tell about those soon.

"Our family had a general store at Brigham City, and that was a good place to ask questions, 'cause everybody comes to a store sooner or later, even mountain men and some Indians. I guess one time or another somebody from every territory in the West came within range of my questions. I got keen about asking, even learned sign language so I could talk to any Indian that come by.

"I started with the Shoshones, the ones live on Bear River. What I found out from them made things a lot harder. Shoshones, they told me, were spread clear from the Wind River Valley east of the divide, north to the Clearwater, all the west to here at Washo, and even way south of here."

Giver and Joe nodded.

"So if I was Shoshone, I could be from anywhere. I learned the names of a bunch of different bands—Salmon Eaters, Root Eaters,

Buffalo Eaters. Even these names made me disheartened, 'cause they showed how many countries the Shoshones lived in, and how far-flung they were.

"If I was a Digger, that was worse. Turned out Digger wasn't even the name of a band of Indians, it was a name the whites gave all the Indians live between the Rocky Mountains and the Sierra Nevada, on account of they eat roots. Diggers even included Shoshones. Whites didn't understand these bunches was different Indians with different languages, Shoshones, Paiutes, Washos, and more.

"My questions didn't lead to nothin'. After a while, discouraged, I came up with two ideas. One was that someone would come into the store one day and speak an Indian language and I would know it. Just like that. From that day I asked every Indian to say a few words in his language, and mountain men to say a little in whatever language they knew. But I never recognized any of it.

"The other idea was that someone would recognize the mystery words. Rock Child, Taylor called me. Rock Child.

"Seemed odd, even for an Indian name. The Pfeffers thought maybe that was part of the name of my people, or where my people lived, or maybe something about them, but it being my name seemed the most likely thing. I would ask strangers what came in the store, 'You got any idea what these words mean?' No one ever did.

"Until Daniel. He did, and he told me on the way in here. You live near the Rock Child, and honor it as a miracle. To me that's wonderful."

I looked at them with my heart in my eyes. "So maybe I am yours."

Giver let it sit a long time, pondering. He looked back and forth at Paiute Joe several times. Finally he says a bunch of words I couldn't understand.

I just sit there, mute.

Giver spoke soft to Joe, and signed.

Joe says to me, "He gonna say something to you in his language. See maybe you understand anything."

Giver laid out a bunch more words, soft and kindly-like.

I shook my head. Heckahoy, I couldn'a told hello from good-bye.

Joe explained, "First he said, 'Can you call me Grandfather? Can you call him Father? Can you call her Mother?' Then he said, 'Do you know of Ong? Do you know of the Water Baby Spirit? Of the sacred cave in the great rock above the camp?' "

Joe just looked at me.

Finally I says, "I don't understand a word."

Giver explained gently. "My friend, it is a little difficult. Suppose you were born to a Washo woman and a white-man father. Suppose even you were born to Washo mother and father. You do not speak our language.

"Our language is far different from any other language." Paiute Joe paused in his translating to confirm that. He knew several Indian languages, and the little Washo he knew showed it was way different. "That is because it is the tongue of the spirits. They gave us these words that we may talk directly with them."

Giver looked at me kindly but oddly. "How strange, a Washo who could not speak with the spirits. I think such a person would not be a Washo."

We all sat in silence.

It was Sir Richard who finally spoke up. "It is possible to learn a language," he said softly.

"Yes," said Giver, and seemed to consider that seriously. "Would you do that?"

"Yes," says I.

Yet I had the feeling he was holding something back. Joe knew it, too. I could see it in his face.

"Your name," he says, "Asie. White-man name?"

"No," says I. "Shoshone. Short for Sima Untuasie, which means 'first son.' "

"Maybe he is Shoshone," Giver said to Joe.

Joe nodded. "Many Shoshone women call their first sons that," he said.

After a while Giver came out with, "What do you want, my friend? If you are Washo, or become Washo, what do you want?"

"I want to live here," says I. "I want to find out what my people are like. I want to be with you, one of you."

Giver nodded. Held silent. Nodded again. "Maybe you cannot go white and be Washo again." He just looked at me. "I don't know."

Finally he decided. "First, we will talk about it, the ones who remember back. I will send my grandsons to the Pine Nut Hills, ask questions. Maybe find your relatives. Then we talk more."

He let it sit again. "Six nights," he said, "you come to us again, eat supper, all of you, Asie and your friends. We talk then."

I stood up and looked at him, feeling naked. *Maybe he is going to give me a welcome-home feast.* My body tingled.

Sun Moon, Daniel, and Sir Richard got up, too, and we shuffled our feet and murmured things the way people saying good evening and thanks for supper do. Then we walked home through the cold night air, brilliant with stars, saying nary a word.

CHAPTER TWENTY-NINE

SIX DAYS FELT like a long time to wait. Lucky for me, Sun Moon said right off she would stay and rest up and not go on to San Francisco till after. Sir Richard said the same. That only left me, what had ants in my pants, bees in my bonnet, and willywoollies creeping around in my stomach.

Fortunately, Daniel had a project. "Asie," he said over the last coffee of that night, "some people are coming by stage tomorrow. As a favor to an acquaintance, I've agreed to give them accommodations and show them around. Would you be willing to help me?"

"Who?" says I.

Daniel smiled. "That's best a surprise. We will ride around a good deal of the lake and see many sights. Why not join us? It will take less than the six days."

"What acquaintance?" says I.

"Oh," Daniel says phony casual-like, "the man who was surveying here last summer. Surveying a possible route for the transcontinental railroad, in fact." He looked at me sharp. "A good man to do a favor, I thought. He said the railroad may go up the Truckee River and over Donner Pass. I'm sure he was pulling my leg. It will go the easy way, south of the lake."

Daniel and his schemes. Well, his visitors sounded curious, and I didn't want to go back to the Washo camp before they had answers for me. I was too nervous. So I says, "OK."

And the rabbit path took another zigzag worth remembering.

The Reverend Mr. Harrison Lake Thomas descended from the stage on the Placerville Road about noon with an air of being a sun with moons circling around him. His moons of the moment were Jane Wearing, who appeared to be an assistant, and a Japanese man named Kanaye, whose place I never did figure out. They were all intent on their reverence for the Reverend, and that troubled me.

Harrison Lake Thomas was a slight fellow, maybe forty, slender and pale. Yet he came equipped with a preacher's essential gear, massive eyebrows, penetrating eyes, patriarchal beard, and a booming voice. It struck me funny from the start, this reed of a man talking like the Burning Bush. His disciples had no such sense of humor.

They came, the lot of them, from San Francisco up through the gold country to our remote stage station, and quickly let us know that they had toured through hell by the name of the Isthmus of Panama to get to the West Coast.

Daniel had showed me Thomas's letter at breakfast. It said they were Christian communalists name of the Brotherhood of Life, with a colony on Lake Erie in New York State. "Having concluded that we shall not be permitted to live in the way God hath revealed to us in New York," the letter said, "and having determined to find a place far from prejudice, prying eyes, and gossiping tongues, we seek land in the unsettled regions of the Golden Shore."

"Utopians," Daniel said with a look of dry humor.

I said to myself that Brigham Young might have written something very like that letter. I'm sure he did, and got mocked as a utopian, too.

Mounting, the Reverend Harris gazed all around us and said from the summit of his horse, "Solitude and beauty." He could make anything look like a summit, and sound like a pulpit. "It is by probing the Mystery of Solitude that the Seeker finds, in the end, the path into the Spirit of Society." He also had a way of speaking in capital letters.

It was a day to appreciate solitude and beauty. Even now, with autumn getting on, the day had come warm, nearly seventy degrees on Sir Richard's Fahrenheit machine, and the air was alpine grace.

The Reverend announced that they wanted to head to the lodge, spend the rest of the day recovering from their journey, prepare during the "forenoon," and begin their "circumambulation" of the lake at noon tomorrow, looking for likely property. Those were roughly his words. As we rode along, he offered tidbits of oratorical wisdom, too, but I couldn't get my memory around them. By the time we got home, I was good and tired of sanctified company.

So was Daniel, but he'd promised them a tour of the lake, so we were stuck for several days.

I did have some curiosity. When Sun Moon walked down to the lakeshore to meditate, I went along and took with me a little booklet called *The Brotherhood of Life* the Reverend gave Daniel to explain the inner mysteries of his future utopia.

Heckahoy if it didn't turn out right curious. The Reverend was a Swedenborgian, whatever that was. Also a spiritualist, which I put together to mean a live person in direct communication with the dead. Also a communalist. After some puzzling through long sentences, I judged that meant that everybody in the utopia put all they owned into one common pot. Which naturally reminded me of the United Order of Enoch, Brigham Young's common ownership plan, so there was another similarity. The Reverend Thomas's version was called Theo-Socialism, and its goal was the New Harmonic Society.

The last principle of the Brotherhood of Life was one Brigham Young wouldn't subscribe to. It was celibacy. Though I was pretty sure I knew what the word meant, I did considerable reading before I let myself believe that's what the Reverend was actually talking about. In the end I was sure but stupefied. "Only when free from the libidinous urges of the body," wrote the Reverend, "are we free to approach God." He said God was bisexual (the first time I ever saw or heard that word) and that "God Himself is the only Bridegroom and God Herself the only Bride." He did allow marriage for those "not yet attained to the higher planes," which I thought was good of him. I supposed that with celibacy, his program for making new converts needed to be right pert, lest the Brotherhood die with the present generation. However, the booklet shed no light on that subject. Of course, I'd never sorted out my thoughts on even Sun Moon's celibacy.

There were two more points of particular interest. One was Divine Respiration. The Reverend had come up with some method of breathing supposed to bring the disciple to direct perception of God. I wondered if that was something like Sun Moon's meditation.

The other was the Pivotal Man. The Second Coming of Christ, said the Reverend, would be announced by the Pivotal Man, within whom the cosmic forces of good and evil did battle. I got a little lost here, but did note that the Pivotal Man was none other than Harrison Lake Thomas.

At supper I decided not to ask the Reverend any questions, for I was afraid of a marathon of elevated discourse. So the meal was taken in small talk, and I could breathe the Reverend's frustration in and out. Why talk, he felt, if you do not admonish, entreat, or exhort?

After supper, in the lounging room, I brought up to Sun Moon how some of me stuck in my craw. "I laugh at these folks," I said, "but I feel like a hypocrite. I lived with Mormons, who were utopians and weren't so bad. Were in fact better'n the gentiles that lived around 'em. I don't feel a bit like laughing at you, but I guess a convent is a pretty utopian place, and it surely has celibacy. And I don't laugh at myself, but I reckon musicians live in a world that seems ridiculous to others, even unto founding conservatories in the wilderness." I appealed to her with my eyes. "Am I a hypocrite?"

Sun Moon shook her head. "The Reverend Thomas," she said softly, "is a disturbed spirit. He has little compassion and no clarity. You are right to stay away from him."

Sir Richard didn't have to meet the Reverend and company, as he was late getting back from a ride and when he got back, the utopians had gone to bed. He solicited the booklet from Daniel and over a late supper read parts of it aloud. He got even more chuckles out of it than I did.

Over the last piece of Maggie's cobbler and coffee, Daniel broached the subject of *me* being the utopians' host tomorrow.

"Don't need no idealists wors'n Mormons," I replied.

Daniel gave me a sort of friendship-hath-no-meaning-in-this-modern-world look.

Sir Richard put his voice in. "I am possessed of an idea, or it possesses me. Daniel, you want to show these utopians around, making it look like sincere, not make them mad, yet get them to want to get gone and stay gone."

Daniel nodded. "God help me, they seek solitude and beauty. Why did they come during a time of perfect Indian summer!"

"Oh," says Sir Richard easy, "I believe we can get them to see things our way."

Daniel raised an eyebrow at him.

Sir Richard told his scheme.

"By God," says I.

"Perfect," said Daniel.

We worked out a plan. Daniel and I would be the hosts and Paiute Joe would be the guide. Sir Richard would be the villain, as the utopians hadn't seen him. The rest of our Paiutes would be supporting villains. We worked it out in delicious detail.

Sun Moon just looked at us in a way I couldn't fathom. I suppose she thought low of scalawags such as us.

When we started out the next noon, the day was so perfect, even the hint of breeze was warm. We were going to have to dis-persuade the utopians ourselves, because Lake Tahoe was going to do the opposite.

Sir Richard had gone early to the Washo camp "to make preparations," and I dreaded to think what these might be.

I'd hoped Miss Wearing would stay home, because I wouldn't have as much to feel guilty about. But here she was, perky as could be, and the Japanese fellow was staying home. Paiute Joe brought the horses around without a word. The Reverend eyed the critters suspiciously. "I don't believe Miss Wearing," he offered, "is accustomed to a Western saddle." Clearly he thought the forking indelicate, and there were her skirts to consider.

Daniel nodded, and I could see his mind working. "We'll use the freight wagon," he said. "Joe?"

Joe headed for the barn. He didn't care. He was getting five bucks for guiding and an extra five for going along with the ruse.

"We'll ride to Old Lousy Dollar's Point," said Daniel, "and have a picnic lunch. Then we'll camp at Carnelian Bay, which may be your spot."

"Is there a road that direction?" inquired the Reverend.

"You came in on the only road," said Daniel. "Thus our solitude."

"Perhaps we should inspect that direction."

"I think you'll want to see Carnelian Bay. It's perfect for your purposes."

Myself, I thought we had a bang-up chance of getting the wagon mired along the shore north. Maybe Daniel was hoping we would.

The Reverend nodded, accepting Daniel's advice, and we were off.

Sir Richard waited until we were all spread out eating what Maggie had packed for us, tinned oysters, cold boiled potatoes, onions, and cheese.

One second it was a waist-high boulder. The next it was a waist-high boulder with the biggest, meanest, most savage-looking Indian you ever seen on top of it, pointing a rifle straight at Daniel. The soldier who had disguised himself as an Arab trader, a Persian merchant, and a Tibetan lama was converted into an Injun on the warpath.

"Mug wump, SAR!" barks Sir Richard at Daniel. Sir Richard had stained his face dark with something, and wore a mishmash of Indian and white-man clothes, like Paiutes did. The crowning touch was two eagle feathers stuck up at the back of his head.

Daniel got to his feet, looking sheepishly at us. He stuck his hands in the air.

Now the other Injuns stepped out from behind rocks and trees and pointed arrows or spears at the captive white folks. They were the Paiutes and Washo that worked for Daniel at the lodge, acting fierce. I thought they looked embarrassed at their part in this charade.

"Boizle bombee!" yelled Sir Richard, or something like that, waving his rifle at the rest of us.

We all got up, the utopians looking water-boweled. I was Jeehosaphat scared myself, scared the Reverend would see through Sir Richard's ridiculous made-up words. I told myself he probably didn't even know the names Paiute and Washo, much less the languages.

Sir Richard addressed Paiute Joe now in a waterfall of words that made no sense at all. Later he himself in his learned way called his tirade "sound and fury, signifying nothing."

Paiute Joe listened soberly, and then translated. "He says we're on Washo land. Washos not let no Indians nor any more white people on their land. Daniel only. Leave now."

The utopians looked at each other.

Paiute Joe repeated louder, "NOW!"

Daniel put in, "This is a renegade, Two Faces. He's never liked me being here. The Washo people accept me. I saved the life of the chief's brother."

I flushed at this embarrassing fairy tale.

Paiute Joe marched on. "Go back to lodge, go road today, take stage, leave forever."

Sir Richard bombasted a couple more sentences in gibberish.

"But one thing stay here," Paiute Joe translated. "The woman. Two Faces take the woman, teach you not come here. Woman his now."

Sir Richard stepped forward with a hand out, like to grab Miss Wearing's arm.

The Reverend interposed himself heroically between brave and maiden, eager to sacrifice himself to save her from a fate worse than death.

Sir Richard slapped his face, which must have been most satisfying. The Reverend actually staggered.

This was more than Daniel could stand. "Enough!" he shouted, and I could hear real fear in his voice. He addressed Paiute Joe. "Tell Two Faces we're sorry. He's right, the Washo have not given permission to any white people to come here but me. I shouldn't have invited you. My fault completely."

Paiute Joe did it, in gibberish.

Sir Richard and the Reverend were still going at it eyeball-to-eyeball. I was feeling sorry for Miss Wearing.

Finally, the Reverend says with a quaver in his voice, "Tell him we'll leave *with* Miss Wearing. Otherwise, it's a fight to death."

Daniel overrode the Reverend. "Tell him it's a bad idea to take the woman. Many white men would come here from Virginia City and the gold camps to get her back. Lots of fighting, many dead, white and Washo. Bad."

Now Paiute Joe talked a bunch more gibberish, and I realized I couldn't tell if he was actually saying something in Paiute or Washo or was just making up more crazy stuff.

Sir Richard glared at the Reverend. Then he looked past her at Miss Wearing, looked her all up and down, like thinking about how she'd be in the blankets. Finally, he stepped back. Still eyeballing the Reverend hard, he muttered some foolishness to Paiute Joe.

"He says go now, he let woman alone. She look plenty funny anyhow, he says. You go, keep going, he watch to see if stop. Take belongings and go to stage today. If stop, he take woman."

The Reverend got up his best hero voice, and said, "Tell him we accede."

The packing up went real quick. Saddling too. Last I saw from my saddle was Sir Richard and the Paiutes starting on the boiled potatoes.

CHAPTER THIRTY

THAT TUESDAY MORNING opened warm and sunny. All of us looked at each other over Maggie's breakfast with the same thought. Any day might be the last warm day of the year at Lake Tahoe. Pretty quick would come the kind of winter that froze the bodies, minds, and morals of the Donner party. We were all going to be here one more day. Then Sun Moon and Sir Richard would be off to San Francisco, Daniel back to Virginia City, and me, well me maybe into another world, a Washo.

Daniel spoke for everyone. "How about a day of fun!"

"Angling," said Sir Richard. He had his eye on Daniel's rowboat.

"Lying in the sun," said Daniel.

"Bathing," said Sir Richard, which was his John Bull way of saying swimming.

All of them sounded good to me.

"You go," Sun Moon said. Her look said, You go act like boys.

OK, thinks I, *let's do.*

Sir Richard had brought a fly-fishing outfit to Lake Tahoe, one of those rigs where you cast a made-up fly. We put out onto the lake and rowed around and took turns casting those flies in every direction. I had a good time rowing and a good time looking into the amazing blue of the lake and getting near mesmerized. I wondered about those fish—what kind of critters would eat flies anyway, flies of hair or, worse, real flies. Luckily, we didn't catch any, or even see any, so our peace was perfect.

The big man watched the fishermen on the blue lake. He wore a black duster and a black slouch hat and stayed well in the shadows of the trees on the little rise and eyeballed the men and the boat. He didn't have a Dolland like the John Bull did, so he couldn't say if they were the ones. They probably were, if the Chinaman was telling the truth. A hundred bucks oughta buy good information from a Chinaman, but you never knew.

He looked at the lodge. Since he was a patient man, accustomed to waiting for quarry, he watched it for a long time. No sign of activity. Once in a while he watched the boat and the passengers, too, but they never came near the shore.

His instinct told him they were the ones. In a twenty-year career of killing, he had learned to trust his instinct.

It felt very good. He had traveled a thousand miles by coach, bumping over the worst roads in the country, to find these people. He had hunted in Utah, in Nevada, in California. He had endured the parching heat of the deserts and the foggy cold of San Francisco Bay. He had doubted himself, he had cursed himself. Now he had found them. It felt *very* good.

But where was the woman? She was his real quarry.

Porter Rockwell squirmed. A figure was walking out of the lodge. A woman. Not the woman, though. This one was heftier and older. She carried something by one hand, a basket, it looked like to Rockwell. She walked to the shore, set the basket down, and walked back into the lodge.

Where was the nun? In the lodge, probably, doing women's stuff. She hadn't left. The breed and the John Bull wouldn't have let her journey to San Francisco alone.

In a minute, while the men were still playing on the water, he would go down and slip into the lodge. If the nun was there, he would settle with her.

"*Let's eat!" says* I.

"Let's swim," says Daniel.

I rowed the boat toward the beach in front of the lodge.

"Let's swim and then eat," says Sir Richard.

"All right, all right. But I'm hungry."

"You're about to get hungrier," said Daniel.

The cove was shallow, and Daniel said that kept the water warmer. I shipped the oars, stood up in the rocking boat, and started to take off my clothes. I looked toward the lodge. Yeah, it was far enough for modesty. In a jiffy I stripped, teetered on my board seat, and jumped into the lake.

It was like jumping into sherbet.

I flailed all ten of my arms and legs and splashed back to the boat. As I grabbed the gunwales, I took thought. Daniel's ruse should not be spoiled. "Damn, it's good!" I spouted.

Sir Richard leapt into the sky and plummeted into the ice water. Surfacing, he shook his head madly and looked daggers at Daniel. But he kept up the spirit. "Splendid!" he exclaimed. "Nothing finer!"

By that time I was back in the boat, shaking like a trill on the keyboard.

To give Daniel credit, he jumped in, too, and grinned stupidly when he surfaced.

What the hell—I dived back in.

Sir Richard dived back in.

When Daniel got back into the boat, we turned it upside down.

Rockwell eased toward the lodge, quietly, from tree to tree, shadow to shadow.

The woman came out of the front door of the lodge, the nun. Right in the open he stopped still.

He tingled. Here she might see him, and no telling what she might do. He had long since learned, though, that movement is more easily seen than stillness. Better to stand stock still in the open than run for the shadows.

She turned left toward Rockwell!

He held his breath.

After a dozen steps she turned right again, along a huge pile of logs. She walked beside the pile, spread a blanket on some grass, and lay down.

Are you mocking me? Rockwell squeezed his throat down on his anger.

She rested there, easy. Maybe she even closed her eyes. The top of her head was toward him.

He looked at the double-barreled shotgun, wondering if he should have cocked the hammers. *No,* he thought, *too risky.*

The boat turned toward the shore, and Rockwell understood. The naked men would come to the basket left on the beach for them, probably a lunch. Sun Moon lay behind this pile of logs for the sake of modesty. The pile was huge. Gentleman Dan must be planning a fair bit of building.

Rockwell took a slow step backward. The nun didn't stir.

He stood very still. With his eyes he calculated how many steps sideways he would need to get a tree between them. Eight or ten. He did a shuffle step to the left. She didn't react. Another. She was still. Still facing her, he sidestepped behind a tree. Then, slowly, carefully, he crept backward, deeper and deeper into shadow.

Now he would circle behind and check out the lodge. He needed to know all the players in this game. No surprises.

We stretched out on the beach, bare skin to the sun. I only wished I could put back side and front side to the sun at once. I shivered in great ripples. I would always have a vivid memory of the cold of Tahoe water.

"I'm here on the other side," called Sun Moon.

"Where?" says I.

"On the other side of the logs."

We all looked at the pile and got it. "OK."

Still dripping and panting for breath, Sir Richard says to Daniel, "I will not forget how you played me for a greenhorn."

Daniel had no more breath than Sir Richard, but he kidded, "Appears to me you've lost your horn."

I looked around and saw we all three had lost our horns to the cold. Had Sun Moon peeked at us, she wouldn't have seen a male thing.

Daniel handed out the sandwiches. Anything would taste good. Anything except the big jar of cold lemonade I saw Maggie had included.

I lay on the grass, closed my eyes, slowly fed my face, and felt the sun on my skin. I wasn't going to move until my thing was warm enough to come back out.

A pretty picture, thought Rockwell. He was peering out the big windows at the front of the lodge. Behind him the cook who called herself Maggie was neatly bound, dismissed as a problem. Before him, like a beautifully spread table, lay what he most wanted in the world. The nun, the John Bull, the breed, and the man who blew up the mine shaft. Perfectly naked, the men. Some of them probably napping, or at least with their eyes closed. A picture to warm a man's heart.

He studied the layout, studied the log pile, and knew where he would stand to command the situation.

I WASN'T ASLEEP, exactly, but I was dreaming. I was in a feather bed, and Sun Moon was next to me, cuddled up innocently. I was feeling my own breathing and listening to hers. I could stay there forever.

Klick-kluck was what I heard.

I didn't register what it was until it snapped a second time. *Klick-kluck!* That was the ugliest sound on the Earth if you recognized it, the hammer on a percussion firearm being set. When it came twice, that meant that you were facing a double-barreled scattergun.

I forced my eyes open and edged them around slow, up to the log pile between us and Sun Moon. I expect all three pairs of male eyes headed there warily. And all three saw what was risen up there, black enough to throw a black shadow over a sunny day and a whole sunny life. Holding the klicking shotgun, surely loaded with buckshot, and grinning like a devil that's caught a clutch of sinners red-handed, stood Porter Rockwell.

"Howdy, boys," says he.

I heard Sun Moon gasp hoarse beyond the logs.

"Miss Holiness." Rockwell nodded in her direction. He kept both hands on the scattergun, but he didn't have any worries. No man was going to rush him, not naked into the face of buckshot, which they say makes an oozy corpse. We were caught with our pants down, no joke.

"I've come to finish a job," said Rockwell. "Sorry I couldn't get here sooner, I had me a problem." He stomped his left leg, and I saw now a green hide was shrunk tight on the shin—must have broke it in the blast.

He waved the double-barrel left and right. "I'll need one barrel in that direction," tipping the muzzle toward Sun Moon. "That'll leave me a full barrel for your direction, boys, plus the wallop in my belt," where at least one revolver stuck. "So I wouldn't get no ideas."

He looked back and forth from side to side and spread his stance. That left leg looked a little uncomfortable. "No need for more'n one person to die here. Unless I start recollecting what nuisances some of you has been. Which I likely will."

His eyes licked at us like a snake's tongue.

Rockwell surveyed them. He had caught them with nothing in their hands but their peckers, and them shriveled, all the way shriveled.

"We thought you were dead," said the man known as Gentleman Dan. The sucker Gentleman Dan, the blaster Gentleman Dan.

Rockwell nodded to himself. It felt satisfying, very satisfying. "I meant you to."

"You found us through Kirk?" Gentleman Dan demanded.

Rockwell grinned and nodded. "A man that's for sale is for sale to all."

Rockwell could near see the Gentleman and the John Bull settling in their mind to get square with Tommy Kirk. *Good! You buggers think on that. As long as I let you think at all.*

Asie got up. Rockwell tracked him with the scattergun as he backed off and eased sideways toward the log-pile divider. The gun followed the breed, but the gunman's eyes clicked back and forth from him to the others. *You ain't coming closer.* He knew that would get him killed in a jiffy. *What do you want?* Barefooted, the breed struggled to the top and tenderfooted on toward the woman. *The bitch.*

Rockwell smiled. "You think that'll be more comfortable for her, dying with a naked man close by?" He chuckled. "You think them buckshot will feel any different tearing through the skin and ribs and lungs and heart if you're near? Or the blood will spill out slower?"

Sun Moon got to her feet. Rockwell pointed the shotgun at her, and said, "That's far enough."

The breed kept moving toward her. Now Rockwell understood. "You wanna stand in front of her? You wanna die with her? You wanna hold her and both of you die?"

Rockwell uttered a laugh so low and growly he thrilled at the menace of it. "Wha' for? You ain't even humped her. She don't let nobody have that precious pussy. That pussy is give up to Buddha or whoever. Ain't none other gonna have none of it."

He watched them, but their faces stayed blank. *The little bastard better not have had her.* The beast rage rose up, turned once in his belly, and settled back down, watching.

Sun Moon held up a hand toward the breed, gentle-like. He stepped back onto the pile.

Rockwell cackled. "You wanna fight me alone, little lady? You gonna keep big bad Porter from hurting you?"

He flung the shotgun to his shoulder and KA-BOOMED!

SHE FLINCHED AT the sound. Dirt and rock flew up at her feet, and stung her shins. She looked down and saw her loose cotton pants were torn. She knew thin streaks of blood ran down her shins. She was struggling to regain the balance in her mind, after the explosion.

I know the way. It may be my death, I can't know that, but I know the way. And it is the truth. She looked inside herself and considered Porter Rockwell, a man. She told herself, *This is what it means, compassion for all sentient beings.*

Knowing, she began. "No," she said, "I am not going to fight you. And I am not going to run. I am not going to resist in any way. Perhaps you will kill me."

"Perha-a-ps!" he drawled mockingly.

He switched the scattergun to his left hand, drew the revolver in his belt, and fired—WHAM!

She heard the death metal whip past her ear.

The noise jangles me. If I fail, if I lose my truth, it will be the noise.

She took a moment to focus. *I am filled with compassion for all sentient beings. That includes Asie, our friends, myself, and Porter Rockwell.*

"I going tell you the truth," she said.

Now Rockwell howls with laughter. "The TROO-OO-OOT?" In a flash he rearranged his face into a sinister scowl. " 'Pilate said unto him, "What is truth?" ' "

She looked at him neutrally, not knowing that name.

"I going tell you the naked truth," she said, and started lifting her blouse. *This is what I must do, show the truth, tell the truth. I accept death, and I live the truth.*

PORTER ROCKWELL WAS eating her with his eyes now. Strange feelings raged in him. *And not lust,* he noted, teasing himself.

She pulled her blouse off. Her breasts were small, and the rosy nipples looked terribly vulnerable. She shivered.

"The truth," she said, "is that your spirit is alive. The truth is that you are in agony. And the truth is, I can feel your pain."

She threw the blouse on the ground.

"Su-u-u-ure you can," he mocked. He didn't sound quite convincing to himself. To buck up, he lifted the revolver and—SCHLAM!

She quivered, and slipped out of her shoes.

"The truth is, you didn't save the man you loved. The truth is, it wasn't your fault, and it didn't kill you."

She bent and pushed her trousers to her knees. There was nothing under them. *Look at her perky little bush,* he told himself, but it didn't feel convincing.

"The truth is, you killed when they told you to. The truth is, every person you killed was you."

She stepped out of her trousers and stood in the sunlight, stark naked, facing Porter Rockwell.

"The truth is, you hate yourself. And that is killing you."

Now she started padding toward him. A step. Three beats of stillness. A step. Two beats of stillness.

"The truth is, what you shoot out of your gun barrels is your hatred of yourself."

Three steps. Four.

"The truth is, when you shoot, the person you shoot is you. Every time."

Seven steps. Eight.

Rockwell slipped the revolver into his belt. He raised the shotgun.

Ten steps. Halfway.

"The truth is, the Church didn't care about you. They told you to kill. They asked you to become a murderer."

Rockwell snugged his eye tight on his shoulder, looking down the barrel. She was still walking.

"So every day, in your anger, you despise yourself."

Sun Moon's bare flesh filled his vision. Sun Moon's words filled his mind. His finger stroked the trigger up and down.

"Every day you hate me, every day you hate the people you killed, every day you hate the Church, every day you hate yourself."

Sun Moon started up the logs, and her chest filled his eyes. His caressing finger stilled on the trigger, and tightened. "Porter Rockwell, you are drowning in hatred. You can stop. You can save yourself. *Only* you can save yourself."

He raised the barrels until they trained on her neck.

She stepped forward, and he felt the nudge through the shotgun. The flesh of her neck was actually touching the muzzle. *How cold does it feel, the metal of your death?*

"Porter Rockwell," she said evenly, "I feel compassion for all sentient beings. I love every creature that lives. I love myself. I love you."

He looked up into her eyes. He wondered what those words had cost her. He imagined exactly how her head would look, flying backward off her body, spurting blood.

"In the name of your love for yourself I ask you. Save yourself."

He straightened up. He held her eyes with his.

He pulled the trigger.

KA-BLOOM!

For an instant I saw what I feared to see, blood and gore.

Then I saw that they were still gazing at each other, the man in black, huge, and the small, naked woman.

Rockwell had shifted the barrel off to the side.

The gun was empty!

I took one running step. Sun Moon held up both hands—STOP!

I saw Sir Richard had sprinted a couple of steps, too, but he stopped.

Within reach those two, nun and killer, gazed at each other.

Porter Rockwell put the muzzle back in her face. He shaped the words clearly in his mind, saw them clear as on a sign. *You're crazy beyond crazy with your talk of love. But all the armies of the world ain't got as much guts as you.*

He smiled lightly, thinking he could still kill her anyway. *Courage is a rare thing.*

He dropped the shotgun. It clattered idly on the rocks.

He looked at her a little more. Without any gesture, even a nod, he stalked off. He walked down the log pile and into the trees.

I ran up to the logs to Sun Moon. We watched Porter Rockwell walk away. Somewhere in the watching she took my hand. It never struck me until later that we were perfectly naked, all of us. The last we ever saw of Porter Rockwell was the black of his duster fading into the shadows.

Porter, if you're still out there, I wish you well.

CHAPTER THIRTY-ONE

SUN MOON WALKED slowly toward her clothes. Every man of us done likewise. We dressed in no hurry but silent. Before long we climbed up the log pile and looked at each other. We looked deep into Sun Moon's eyes, and she into ours. Then, still silent, we walked toward the lodge.

We left the shotgun laying where it was. I don't know who ever did pick it up.

Us men went inside to have coffee. Sun Moon went somewhere to meditate. In a few minutes my nerves began to unwind. A while after that I actually laughed. And a while after that I remembered tonight was when Giver was to give me the big news. I guessed my nerves were loose enough for anything now.

GIVER MADE ME wait to hear it. We drank sociable coffee first. Then we ate. Then we drank coffee again. It was all I could do to hold my water.

Will they own me as a Washo or not?

And, *"Do I want to be a Washo or not?"*

Appeared to me Sun Moon, Sir Richard, and Daniel were nervous as me. Of the supper guests, nobody was relaxed but Paiute Joe, who was sweetly unreadable.

Finally the pot ran dry. Giver shook the last grounds onto the grass and set his cup down. I wished the coffee cup was like the Indian pipe—if you smoked it, you couldn't tell anything but the truth.

Giver signed to Paiute Joe, and I read the signs themselves, "My friend, we do not think you are a Washo."

A squish of feelings came over me, no way to describe them.

He regarded me with gentle eyes. "It is not just because you do not speak our language, or recognize it, when any Washo mother would have given her child her tongue from the moment of birth. It is more than that."

He took thought for a moment. "It is more because no one remembers a woman who went to the whites. We are a small band, a few main families only. I do not know the name of every Washo, but I think I recognize them all. If a woman went to the whites, we would know. Yet my grandsons went to the head of each band, and no one remembers such a thing. No family has lost anyone to the whites, especially not a woman of the age to bear children. We would remember. Our women are precious, and our children are precious."

Now he turned to Daniel. "My friend, I think there is a mistake here, a mistake not hard to understand. You heard our friend say his mystery words are 'Rock Child.' And you recognized them, true, as the Rocking Stone where Donner Creek flows into the Truckee River.

"It is a sacred place, a place where the gods of the winds speak. But you believe it to be a place especially sacred to the Washo, a place we tell a story about.

"This is not so. We know the story, but it is not ours. The stone is a well-known spot on the trail from Truckee Meadows to the other side of the mountains, where all the gold hunters are. We use it, but so do the Miwok, the Maidu, the Patwin, the Shoshone, the Paiute, and others. Maybe the story is theirs. All these peoples know the tale.

"If I guessed, though, I would guess that the story comes from the people who came before us, the ancient ones first here. Maybe, maybe not. I don't know."

He looked back at me. "I see that you have a good heart. You are always welcome at my fire. You are always welcome in my camp. But I think you are not a Washo."

CHAPTER THIRTY-TWO

So I set out on an odyssey across the mountains and deserts of the West, searching, seeking, dreaming about the discovery of what I never had, a home. And my imaginary oasis, a family, a people that would show me the way to live, turned out to be . . . a mirage.

These were my thoughts as we walked silent back to the lodge that night. Nothing needed saying. My one clue was spoiled, pointing evenlike at bunches of tribes. I was fresh out of directions for odysseys, and desire.

I felt tired, tired beyond tired. And one truth is, I felt relieved. Maybe if I'd been raised with my mother's people, I could have gone Indian and been happy. But I wasn't. Maybe a man who's taken to sherbets and pianos can't go back.

Sun Moon and I sat on the front steps of the lodge, silent, and I thought about what I wanted. After a while I said, "Tomorrow I'm gonna go for a walk. I'm gonna look at the lake, and look and look. I need that." Tomorrow she and Richard were to get the stage, and the next day they would be in San Francisco, so I was abandoning her. "I'm sorry."

"May I go with you?"

Her words took me aback.

She took my hands lightly and looked up into my face and waited. "Sure," I said. "Sure you can."

We went up to bed together. That night we slept spooned, holding each other, each by each.

Indian summer was gone. The early morning was cold when we left the lodge, and the day stayed snappy cool. Felt good.

I didn't know where I wanted to go or what I wanted to do. Walk. Look. Walk. See. Walk. Sit. Walk.

Funny how all those doings turned into *hear, hear, hear.*

Sun Moon and I just ambled right along the shore of the lake, heading north. I didn't have anything to say, I was all thought out and worded out. She was more of a think-it-out person than me. I was letting myself feel it out. She seemed content with silence, and that let me do the hearing.

From somewhere there was music in my head. I'd step onto a big slab of rock and hear something brassy. I'd look from there onto the lake and the evergreens on its shores and the string instruments would slide in soft, gentle, and ethereal. I saw a grouse and tossed a few notes at it out loud, musical croaks and gobbles. To a chipmunk I sang a few off-the-beat plunks. Once I saw a blue-gray rock with stone the red of pipestone inlaid. The red was in whorls, and suggested to my mind winged horses. For them I made up a song and sang it, calling it "Song of the Spirit Horses."

Except for singing, I was silent. Sun Moon and I communicated by look and gesture, and as the best of friends do, we understood each other perfect. I was filled with my own music, and that made me feel whole. The music wasn't about Lake Tahoe, it was about me. But Lake Tahoe inspired it, and the walk and the day gave birth to it.

We ate Maggie's sack lunch in lovely quiet. I thought maybe Sun Moon would get impatient with silence, with not being paid attention to, after a while. But she didn't. And in an important way I was paying attention to her. We headed back slow.

As the sun was setting, we sat down on a boulder a quarter mile from the lodge. The snow on the summits to the west burned pink and orange. Out to the east the lake lay still as a lake of perfect dream, mirroring the violet eastern sky.

I looked at Sun Moon. "What am I gonna do?" I asked with a foolish grin. "The world is wide open. I can go anywhere."

"Or stay anywhere," she said.

"Home's not out there."

"No, it's in here." She touched her heart.

We looked at each other, and then at the dramatic peaks, and last at the tranquil lake. "May I tell you something about you?" she asked.

I hesitated. Finally I nodded and looked at her, curious.

"You set out to find your tribe, and you think you failed. But you succeeded. It was not Washo, or Paiute, or Shoshone, no. It was musician. Musicians do not have any one place in particular to live. They don't have a skin color, or only one culture. You do have a language. All musicians speak it, and it was given to you so you can talk to the gods, and listen to what they say back. Sing back."

She took my hand. "That's who you are."

I felt a wave lift inside me, and let my feelings ride it. I held her hand. We looked and listened and finally it was too dark to see. We stood, still holding hands, and walked toward the lodge.

"Guess I'll go to the stage with you tomorrow."

She nodded. Then she added, "Daniel has something to say to you tonight."

"I WANT YOU to be my partner," said Daniel. We were past dinner and dessert to third cups of coffee.

"You're a musician. You've worked in a business. You love it here. You belong here at Lake Tahoe."

I thought maybe I did.

"Invest your five hundred dollars in this wood ranch. We'll go shares. You live here and manage this end. I'll live in Virginia until the business is going strong. After we make a bundle of money, we'll do music."

It's hard to think with trumpets fanfaring in your head.

"It is very good for you," put in Sun Moon. Sir Richard just looked on with a grin.

"I'll let you know tomorrow," says I.

It was one of those moments, the room had a glow, the people had a glow.

I took Sun Moon outside. The night was sharp cold, and we wrapped our coats around our shoulders and our arms around each other's waists. We walked down to the lake to get away from the lanterns of the lodge, to make our sounds the soft lapping of the waves and not the bustle of a busy enterprise.

"You think it's good," I said.

She squeezed me. "Wonderful," she said.

"I'm gonna take it," I said.

"Asie Taylor," she said, "you threw away your old life and went looking for something new. What was it?"

"Home. Or that's what I thought it was."

"And what did you find out?"

"Sometimes a home isn't given to you. Maybe it should be. Maybe we should get that just by being dropped somewhere on this Earth."

"But?"

"I didn't get one. What might have been, I got dislodged from. Can't go back to being an Indian. Never was a white man."

"So?"

"These days, everything changing all the time, you make your own home. Your own family, too." We took a few steps before I added, "Maybe I changed bigger than I knew."

The night was cold. We walked back toward the lodge, holding hands. I could feel her mind right in her hand, turning and turning and then settling itself.

A dozen steps from the porch she turned to face me. I wanted to hold her close, but she stepped back, clasping both my hands. "So. Now." She leaned back against my weight. "I ask you. Asie Taylor, will you make family with me?"

Sometimes I don't know *what's* going on in my head. I stammered, "Y-you're a nun."

"I am a woman."

"Y-you sure?"

She spoke like a person who's clear with words. "I am certain. I think long. You change big. Me too."

"You *sure* sure?"

She looked onto the dark lake. "That girl-woman made life . . . I wanted it. I had it." She touched her belly. "I want it again." She paused. "You, our child. I want to jump into life." She smiled up at me. "You jumped into river."

I looked at her, I put my arms around her, then I pulled back. "The river came for me."

She looked at me solemnly. "Life comes for me."

I kissed her, long.

Then we looked around. The lake was gray, the trees black, the sky star-speckled, the lodge a ghost of light beyond some pines. I thought, *This is mine. It is all mine. If I take it.*

I lowered my lips to the one who was willing to be mine, and kissed her. Pretty quick I was thinking of exploring the privileges of matrimony right there on the spot. But we heard loud rolling and squeaking from within, and a window scraped open. At the same time Sir Richard came onto the porch holding up a lantern.

"What news?" he queried.

"We're going to live here," says I. "We're getting married."

In a jiffy music swooshed up, and my spirits were lifted high by Daniel's piano. It was Mendelssohn's "Wedding March" proclaiming matrimony through the open window. I whispered in Sun Moon's ear, "A song we use to march a marrying couple to the preacher."

Sir Richard's mouth was saying, "Congratulations!" but I couldn't really hear it over the music, or over my own excitement.

"March in! March in!" cried Sir Richard even louder.

We did, and Daniel brought the Mendelssohn to a rousing finish.

Sir Richard pronounced, "Since we are without benefit of clergy here, perhaps I shall take it upon myself to administer the sacrament." He cast his eyes about conspicuously. "I see about me, however, rather a babel of religions. A Tibetan Buddhist, a Mormon . . ."

"Indian," Asie corrected.

"Indian, yet another Indian, a Catholic"—with nods at Maggie and Daniel—"and myself, who am, shall we say, no Christian?" He was in high delight now. "The spirit of the occasion seems to me to call for the form of ceremony that reaches back furthest into my own life, the *Book of Common Prayer* of my childhood. I ask the Divinity to look beyond any waywardness in the words chosen, both advertent and inadvertent, and to see the good intentions in my heart."

He faced us and drew himself up. "Dearly Beloved . . . Here I must depart from the path prescribed." He heaved in a deep breath and heaved it back out. "Perhaps the single great force on this Earth is love," he said. "God loves life, and has manifested us, and all creatures, and the world itself as an expression of love. We stand most utterly in the spirit of the sacred when we love one another.

"Your love for each other honors God, honors existence itself. As you are true to this love, it will bring you infinite blessings.

"Now I am able to recall the proper words. Who giveth this woman to be married to the man?"

Waiting for no answer, he joined our right hands together. "Say after me as followeth. I take thee, Sun Moon, to my wedded wife, to have and to hold from this day forward, for better for worse, for richer for poorer, in sickness and in health, to love and to cherish, till death do us part, according to God's holy ordinance."

I said those words, and meant them.

"Sister, say after me. I, Sun Moon, take thee, Asie, to my wedded husband, to have and to hold from this day forward, for better for worse, for richer for poorer, in sickness and in health, to love, cherish, and to obey, till death do us part."

Sun Moon said those solemn words with an utterly happy look on her face.

He looked squinty at us and smiled big. "Since we have no rings, we'll pass over that part. I pronounce that you are man and wife. In the name of the Father, and of the Son, and of the Holy Ghost, Amen."

Sun Moon squeezed my hand. I lifted her chin, lifted it again when she tried to slip by me, hugged her when she squirmed, disregarded her reddening cheeks, and kissed her.

Sir Richard and Daniel applauded. Then Maggie brought out a big bowl of pink sherbet. Daniel did the honors, filling cups with a dipper.

"A toast!" cried Sir Richard. He lifted his cup, and said warmly, "To your happiness."

The taste was strawberry. It has ever since been my favorite.

Daniel offered a second toast—"To our partnership!"

We drank. Maggie handed out pieces of cake.

"Now an important subject," said Sir Richard, "my wedding gift to you." He paused and looked at us munificently. "It is the five hundred dollars I promised Sun Moon. Perhaps you'll use it to increase your investment in this lodge."

"Good idea," said Daniel, smiling. "Partner."

There were more toasts, and the five of us even danced around the piano at one point, Maggie on Daniel's arm. I don't remember the details of the next few minutes because my mind switched to taking Sun Moon upstairs and marrying her deep and strong. That's what I did.

FINISH-UP

THAT IS THE end of my big wander.

What's left of the story classical musicians would call fancy words, but I'll call it a finish-up.

As a young man I set out, not knowing where or why. I took the first step, and fell into my adventure. It was the most important step I ever made, and the best. You know where it led.

There is more to my life, though, and maybe some things you will want to know about the people in it.

Sun Moon and I stayed at the lodge alone that autumn and winter, a long, snowbound honeymoon. It was grand. Our son Pasang was conceived then, and born the next fall.

In the spring we cut trees and floated them across to the mill, to a handsome profit.

Sir Richard and Daniel went immediately back to Virginia, Sir Richard because he had a little matter back to take care of with Tommy Kirk. He bought discreet items at the chemist's shop and showed Tommy's mistress Lu Pu-wai how to slip them into food. Sir Richard knew his beans. When Tommy died mysteriously a few months later, neither he nor anyone else guessed how or why.

In two years Daniel, Sun Moon, and I were prosperous, even halfway to rich, through our wood-cutting enterprise. But we didn't like sending our Lake Tahoe trees into graves in a mountain for the purpose of gouging out silver. So we sold our wood contracts and put full effort into the music school. In four years it failed and took everything we had. We had a lot of fun going broke, though, and made a lot of good music.

While we were going broke in the music business, Daniel got news his father had died and his mother needed him. He headed back to New Orleans. On the way, in East Texas, he got into a bar fight with a man as made a racialist remark, and took a knife through the lights. We missed him bad. Turned out he had willed us his half of the lodge.

Though it was ours, we always let people think the place belonged to Daniel and was only managed by us. This was partly our tribute to our friend, and mostly a ruse. Americans think it's OK for people of color to manage a hotel, but not own one.

Sun Moon and I turned it into a resort. It was a lot of work, but the transcontinental railroad came in at the right time, not way round the south end of the lake like we thought, but right up the Truckee River past the Rock Child and over the old Indian trail, a poor route for them but good for us. We made a go of the resort, and got half-rich again. The best part is, we are open only five months a year, and we live here all twelve. That gave us time for each other, for walks, for snowshoeing, for music, and for Sun Moon's prayer and meditation.

There are several resort hotels on the lake now, and I believe one day there will be more. That will be good for the white people who come here to breathe the spirit of the alpine air and drink the mountain waters, but it will be hard on the Washo people.

We had some fun with the name of our lodge. It's called Gastonia, and the sign over the drive says in big letters, WELCOME TO GASTONIA.

Sun Moon mostly left the running of the lodge to me, with hired help. She stuck to her own life, raising our son, educating him in the Buddhist and the Western way both, meditating long hours every afternoon, and praying for the liberation of all sentient beings.

Today Pasang Richard Daniel Taylor is a fine young man of twenty-seven years, and will go far. Not in music—he has no ear. His eye for drawing, however, is excellent. We had only one child, we never knew why, but we had a lot of fun trying for more.

The Washo and me became dearest friends. I joined into their religious ways by learning their songs. For years I have sung or drummed at the Pine Nut ceremonies every autumn. Washo religion makes more sense to me than any Mormonism, Brotherhood of Life, Catholicism or any sort of Christianity, or, for that matter, Buddhism. We worship things that are real—the four winds, the waters flowing and still, the sway of the sun, moon, and stars, the powers in the rocks. And we don't tell other people what to do, but respect each man's medicine. The Washo way suits me.

We heard from Sir Richard regularly. He always wrote us what a fine time he was having from Africa, Brazil, Damascus, and Trieste, wherever that is. We lived through every clever tactic which he employed against his many political and literary enemies, mourned his defeats, and celebrated his victories. We never thought he was having any fun, though, and he never did go on any more big explorations. Seemed to us his wife, Isabel, got the better of him.

I did enjoy reading his books, keeping in mind that lots of his life, like his adventures with us, could never be told—they were government secrets. My favorite is *A Thousand and One Nights,* which he sent us all sixteen volumes of. As I am a musician, he was a storyteller.

I had a dream that he would visit us one day. It's an easy trip now—you can sleep in a Pullman car across the U. S. of A.—nothing like how we trudged over the California Trail breathing alkali. I pictured us three utterly different friends, the three playing in conflicting keys, being together for a few days on the shore of the most beautiful lake in the world. It's hard to let dreams end, and mine never did until the mail came last fall. A business friend in San Francisco sent a clip from the newspaper about the death of the famous author Sir Richard Burton (he finally got that knighthood).

That was small, however, beside the letter from Pasang last week about his mother and my beloved wife. She had been going to the doctor in San Francisco for treatment for more than a year. This time she asked Pasang to come with her. I'm sure she didn't have a premonition of her death, because she would have wanted me beside her, and I would have wanted to be there. Pasang going along was lucky, though. He read *The Book of the Dead* to ease the passage of her soul to wherever it is going next. He read for seven days, which is a high honor, and I trust that her way is good.

Our life here was good because we put first things first. Sun Moon concentrated on Pasang and her prayers, and I kept my music ahead of the resort. My family and my music. I did play most nights at the lodge, giving folks what they wanted to hear, songs and dances. I also played Gottschalk, Chopin, Schubert, and other stuff our guests admire but don't really like. And I played my own music. Because once I started listening, it was there in my head. If I turned on my fingers, out it came.

I got lucky, too. The folks at Dr. Bourne's Hygiene Establishment, up at Carnelian Bay, asked me to play my own music at what they called a salon every Sunday afternoon. I have done that steadily for many years. I've been invited to Virginia to play from time to time. Jenny Lind came there to sing, and then stopped here, and we made music together at Dr. Bourne's, just the two of us. These opportunities, they've been more than lots of musicians ever get.

Almost every day now since coming to Tahoe more than twenty-eight years ago, I have walked the countryside and listened. From listening I have got lots of my own pieces, for piano, banjo, harmonica, dulcimer, guitar, everything a musician can play alone. And I've got some music written for woodwinds, brasses, and even stringed instruments. From time to time the bands and orchestras over at Virginia have played my music, which made me proud. I've done everything but publish it. My music has been for me.

Curious thing, though. Last summer a fellow from San Francisco heard me play at the salon and said he would come back with one of those new phonographs and take my music down. Wouldn't that be a hoot?

So that's how it came out, my wander. I went looking for big things, what I heard in the river, and to find out who the Rock Child was, and where I belonged. I came to the truth of that, and it was not outside me. I didn't have to go adventuring to find it. Home is always inside, in the heart. In me, in Sun Moon, in Pasang, and in you.

I am lucky, and deeply grateful, that when I figured out that home was wherever I was, I happened to be at Lake Tahoe. It could have been Deseret, the Rocky Mountains, the Nevada deserts, Virginia City, or anywhere. But my good fortune is that at Lake Tahoe, the most beautiful place in the world, I became willing to plant my feet on the earth and live like a human being.

So my big wander gave me a good life.

Not all of it good, of course. After Sun Moon took sick, it has been harder than I'd care to say. When they told us it was liver cancer, we both knew. We only took a few guests this summer, just old friends, and we spent most of the days sitting in the sun, holding hands. I also kept taking my walks and listening for whatever music the gods would give me. Each evening I played it for her.

No marriage is all easy, no marriage all smooth. But some things I know, and Sun Moon knew them, too. I loved her. She loved me. I have set all this story down in her honor.

Pasang wants to do her honor, too. When he came back from San Francisco on the train, he said he's going to finish what she surrendered—go to Tibet, to Zorgai, to her convent, and to her relatives. He wants to tell them about her life. He also wants to see where he came from, and to learn about that half of his bloodline, just as I did once. He is possessed of a restless spirit and a vast curiosity. He thinks that makes him unlike me.

He's asked me for the money to go halfway around the world. I will give it to him. I set out on a big adventure twenty-eight years ago, and it brought me everything good. Now it's his turn to look. It's the zig in his rabbit path.

I hope he comes back one day. He doesn't know how much a father loves a son.

He has a suggestion about that. If he isn't back in maybe two years, he says, I should sell the lodge and go over to Zorgai and find him. Join him, maybe stay forever. Join him anyhow, and have an adventure. He'll write me an address.

You never know.

I am tempted to say no to him, but that might be no to myself. Last time I threw my life to the winds, those powers carried it to a kind of glory. I bet they would again. I am only fifty years old.

You would be amazed if I went to Tibet?

Me too.

Flabbergaster, huh?

AFTERWORD

This book has some fun with history, in an attempt to speak truths that seem to me larger than facts.

Yes, *The Rock Child* is intended to be both accurate and truthful historically. Richard Burton, Porter Rockwell, Brigham Young, and Samuel Clemens actually lived, and if their deeds here are imagined, my portrayals of their characters are meant seriously. (Yes, I believe that Burton was a wonderful madman and addict, and Rockwell a tortured spirit.) Salt Lake City, the California Trail, Virginia City, and Lake Tahoe are depicted in accordance with the record; so are the life ways of the Mormon people, Comstock miners, and Washoe people in 1862. Burton did travel to Salt Lake City in 1860, and the opinions of Mormons attributed to him here were set down in his book *City of the Saints*.

I hope that Mormon people, long sensitive about depictions of their history and ways by gentiles, see that my pictures of Brigham Young, and the Young household are drawn from empathy and in accordance with the record. When sketching the wives and children of the Lion of the Lord in a way that might cause controversy, I have generally used fictional names. Though the record is less than clear about Porter Rockwell, I believe my portrait is accurate.

Asie and Sun Moon are entirely creations of my imagination and my love. So is Gentleman Dan. Yet their dilemmas are as real as the dark history of racism in America. For decades following 1849, tens of thousands of Chinese women were brought to the western United States, and their years as prostitutes amounted to slavery. Male Chinese were also treated as half-human. Indians and half-blood people living among whites faced just the predicaments that Asie faced, often in much more dire form. In 1862 slavery had corrupted the soul of the country, the Civil War was destroying the corpus, and Southerners like Gentleman Dan, aware, were in terrible straits.

The picture offered here of Tibetan Buddhism and Tibetan culture is as accurate as I can make it, and is written from love of a marvelous people and way of seeing the world. If I have used the Sanskrit form of words *(lingam, yoni, puja)* instead of the Tibetan forms, it is because the Sanskrit is somewhat more familiar in the West.

While the settings and situations here are historical, and some of the characters, the action is imagined. To my knowledge, Captain Burton did not travel to the United States in 1862, though he could have (and given the clandestine nature of his life, he may have). He was a relentless keeper of journals, but they were burned by his wife Isabel after his death, along with his letters and manuscripts; the journal entries here, I believe, are the sort he might have made. If Porter Rockwell chased any fugitives all the way to Lake Tahoe in that year, they were not our trio. I do not know whether any of the Asian women brought against their will to America were nuns, though many were surely Buddhists.

All these inventions are my way of taking a look at my country and my peoples, trying to see into their souls, expressing something of how it feels to me to be a human being, and of engaging in that wondrous form of play known as telling a story.

So. History is the foundation of this book. Its soul is imagination, dream, and love.

Win Blevins
Bozeman, Montana
December 29, 1996